M000169677

DAVID KRONFELD

tales of the
HAVURAH

Back cover drawing: Rebecca Jacobs

© 2020 David Kronfeld All rights reserved. No part of this publication may be reproduced, distributed, or transmitted in any form or by any means, including photocopying, recording, or other electronic or mechanical methods, without the prior written permission of the publisher, except in the case of brief quotations embodied in critical reviews and certain other noncommercial uses permitted by copyright law.

ISBN 978-1-09830-241-2 eBook 978-1-09830-242-9

To all those who have passed,
who continue to pass,
or who will pass in the future
through a certain yellow house.

According to tradition, the passionate desire
between the lovers in *The Song of Songs*
is an allegory for the relationship
between God and the people of Israel.

Rabbi Akiva said, "Of all the books in the Bible,
The Song of Songs is the holy of holies."

Our teachers John, Paul, George and Ringo
further expounded: In the absence of one's beloved,
one can muddle through – and even achieve elevated states! –
with the assistance of close companions.

Contents

INTRODUCTION

Believe me when I tell you that I am a religious man. Believe me when I tell you this.

Of course, like you, I despise the falsely pious, and I scorn all those who unctuously clasp their hands while self-righteously proclaiming the saving power of God's glory, if only we believe in Him. Those who pat themselves on the back for having found truth and peace bring out the cynic in me, and my heart is made sour, like curdling milk, to look on them and hear their nasal, whining voices. They are all wind and lies, lying and wind, and I will have none of them and their company.

And yet, believe me when I tell you that I am a religious man. Believe me when I tell you this. Believe me.

Ah, I see. To do this, you would like me to present a philosophy to you, to arrange in rows all my beliefs, and lay out an orderly system into which everything fits, making it all so nice and neat. No, I won't give you a system. Even if I had a system, some tightly concocted philosophy, I wouldn't reveal it to you, because I sense you only want to know about it in order to disagree with it – so that you might find some flaw in it, some little or even major inconsistency, a point of contention that would allow you to dismiss the whole thing out of hand.

You would like to say, politely perhaps, that all this really isn't for you. You would like to maintain your distance. So, no – I won't give you a system, some little box that contains it all.

The best I can offer is the Solar System, and to assure you that somewhere, *somewhere* within that system, there's room for everything.

I may be full of contradictions, but that doesn't mean that I'm confused. I tell you, I am not confused.

Oh, but really, I'm not always this serious, especially when I'm around people. And I expect some company today, so I probably won't sound as grave as I do now, as soon as this person arrives. And the person I'm expecting is a guest of honor. A great and wonderful guest of honor, to whom I will be overjoyed and elated to extend our hospitality.

There it is – I hear knocking at the door.

Who is it?

It's YOU! There you are, a-knockin' at the door. Well, come in, come in. Far out, you're here! I'm so glad you could make it.

Sure, come in. Come right in to our big old ramshackle, tumble-down, wonderful house. Yes, that's the mezuzah. No, you don't have to kiss it. Here you don't have to do anything you don't want to do or don't believe in. Kiss it, don't kiss it, it's okay. It really doesn't matter, you know.

Well, you're in. Welcome to the Havurah, officially known as Havurat Chaim Community, heart of the Jewish counterculture, whatever that is, or was.

Anyway, when you come into a shul, the custom is to say *"Mah Tovu"* – "How goodly are your tents, O Jacob." Well, just how goodly *are* they? How goodly is this one? Let me show you around, and we'll see.

Hey, listen, don't get nervous – relax. I know, you're already having second thoughts about coming here at all. You think maybe I'm going to try to rope you into performing some little ritual or force a doctrine down your throat. Maybe badger you until you agree to put on tefillin or say a little prayer, just to get me off your back. No, I'm not going to do that. I couldn't stand it myself.

So, don't worry. I won't take advantage of that private place inside you where you keep those tentative, intimate Jewish allegiances. I know what it's like to have that violated, or just exposed to the insensitive light of day. I know how you feel. It's like when on TV they show some hokey little drama about a little old Jewish man, or spring a Jewish wedding into the scene, or show a burial complete with kaddish. It gives you the creeps when you think that the whole damn country's watching this and doesn't really understand. Well, it creeps me out, too. I don't know why. Does it matter why? But it gives me the creeps anyway.

Maybe it's because we've been caricatured to death. We can't do anything without it being a parody of ourselves. Maybe that's why it's so uncomfortable to talk about ourselves, even among ourselves.

Oh sure, it's all right to poke fun, to make a couple of jokes, those same old tired jokes over and over, just to shake off the embarrassment, but nothing that deals with anything . . . what shall we say? . . . closer to the heart? Maybe it's because we no longer have a heart, neither a Jewish one nor any heart at all. Maybe we no longer *want* to have a heart. But don't worry about that – I'm not accusing you. I'm not accusing you and I'm not complimenting you either. Just relax. We're friendly here. And it's just us. So, relax and enjoy yourself.

Good – I'm glad you're staying.

So, come in, come in. Let me show you around.

Nobody's arrived yet, it's still early. Shabbos won't begin for a while, so I can give you a little tour in the meantime. I'll show you the place through my eyes.

Where should I start? Why don't we start right here, where we are, in the entrance hallway.

See this old dresser? Everything gets dumped on this dresser – mail, siddurim, old notices, whatever. Inside these drawers here, you'll find all sorts of random junk. Look, here's a grogger, and a wedding bencher, a couple of yarmulkes, Chanukah candles, sticks of incense, a dog biscuit, old Rosh Hashanah cards, a package of rolling papers . . . It goes on and on.

Each item has its own little story, and when I open the drawers and see them all, each one speaks to me, separately and in its own voice. Some things whisper, others shout, some laugh ridiculously, each telling its own little tale. Some of their stories are funny, some are sad, some are strange, and some, well, some are just meaningless gobbledygook.

And they're all mixed together, all these stories, all these voices, talking at once. And somehow, I can't help but listen, no matter what they're telling me. I listen because I like to listen, I suppose. But I really can't help but listen. That's my nature.

Anyway, let's go on.

This way leads into the living room, with its cast-off easy chairs and old sofas with the stuffing falling out. A comfortable place, if a little dusty. And see this poster on the wall, this day-glo picture of a lady with music coming out of her head? It came from San Francisco, from the old Haight-Ashbury days, before I even got here. And this one facing it, this *shiviti*, with all the mystical names of God going up and down the ladder, this came from a little bookstore somewhere in Jerusalem. I think Mel bought it, but then he left it here when he moved on.

The room's a little messy now but it usually gets cleaned up nice and tidy right before Shabbos. We've got a regular rotating cleanup schedule; it's all very intricately organized. Frankly, I don't know why this room hasn't been cleaned up yet. Hang on a second, I'll be right back – I'm going to go check who was on cleanup duty this week.

I'll tell you, I can't say everybody around here is always so *responsible* when it comes to doing their jobs. Hold on, I'll be right back.

Ah, well, um . . . it seems, uh . . . that it was . . . er . . . *my* week to clean up. I could have *sworn* that was next week. Never mind – give me a hand, won't you, and we'll get this place tidy in no time.

Okay, now this chair goes over there by the window, and that one by the edge of the sofa. You know, we sit around on these chairs during our weekly meetings, and we argue and debate about all sorts of things: who should shovel the snow, whether we should daven *musaf* on Shabbos, how much to budget for cat food, why so-and-so is angry at so-and-so, where we should give tzedakah . . . And everybody has opinions! It's amazing we get along as well as we do. At least, most of the time.

Hold on a second – I have to vacuum the rug. We hauled in this rug from across the street when the dentist was tossing it out. Not a bad find!

HEY, CAN YOU HEAR ME OVER THE NOISE OF THE VACUUM? SEE THIS BIG SPOT HERE? YEAH? THIS WAS A BIG WINE SPILL FROM LAST PURIM. WHAT A MESS! PLACE STUNK LIKE A BREWERY. IT TOOK WEEKS BEFORE IT STARTED SMELLING NORMAL AGAIN.

Ah, there. Okay, that's pretty much it for this room. It looks clean enough, doesn't it? I suppose so. Maybe next week they'll clean it up a little better.

Okay, now come in here and let me show you the dining room. Hold on, I'm going to go and get the broom . . . .

See? This is where we have communal meals. How often? No, not every day, for heaven's sake! We're not a *commune*, or anything as radical as that. We used to have communal meals about once a week, all of us together, and it went on like that for years, but then, slowly, once a week fell to every other week, to once a month . . . but that's jumping ahead. Let's not get into history yet. For now, let's just stick to the basic material reality.

See these two long tables? We got these from an old shul in Chelsea that was closing down to become a Jehovah's Witness meeting house. They're great tables – heavy, thick wood. Go ahead, give 'em a bang. See? You don't find tables like this anymore.

Hold this dustpan for a second, okay? Thanks.

Ah, that looks better. So now, follow me and come in here.

This is the most important room in the house. This is the prayer room, or "the davening room" as we call it. This is where we daven. It's nothing fancy, but it always looks nice – clean and simple.

There's not much in this room, but whatever's here is very important. First, there's the ark, that big box with a macramé cover on the front, which holds the Torah. And up there by the ceiling is our *ner tamid*, an oriental brass candleholder that came straight from the marketplace in the Old City. And here's a *shtender*, another relic from an old shul going out of business. And, of course, we have lots of plants in the windows. After all, this is the counterculture, our happy hippie kingdom, and plants in the window are an absolute necessity.

To you, all this stuff may still just seem like old junk, the haphazard bohemian shlock-chic you'd expect to find in a thousand places all over the country. But to us, this is a very special place.

So come in, sit down, and make yourself comfortable.

Where do we sit? See all these cushions on the floor? We sit on them.

What, no chairs? Right, no chairs. Why? Well, some say it's less formal and more relaxed to sit on the floor. Some say it's more eastern, good for meditation. Some say it makes it easier to squoosh in a lot of people.

That's all true, I suppose. But the real reason we sit on the floor is that it just happened that way. One day, in the early days, someone was passing by an upholstery store that was tossing out dozens of cushions. So he brought them all back here and dumped them on the floor, and so that's what people sat on.

But that was even before my time. As far as I'm concerned, we sit on the floor because we sit on the floor. It's our custom. It's the custom of the Havurah.

Anyway, here's where we do our most important activity. We sit around in sort of a haphazard circle – you'll see it all later – and we daven. We spend a lot of time davening here. We like to experiment with the davening, and just see where it leads. Davening can be so many things – self-expression, emotional release, a path to introspection, connection with your ancestors . . . Maybe even a conversation with You-Know-Who.

Anyway, no two davenings here are exactly alike. Each time, someone different leads the davening and adds or subtracts whatever they want. We've had all kinds of services – with music, poetry, stories, exercise, food, spontaneity, in silence, in anger, with laughter, sitting, standing, even lying down. Sometimes they're great and sometimes they flop. But at least we have the freedom to try whatever we please.

I've spent many hours in this room, in just about every mood imaginable. I've been happy here, and sad, angry, horny, excited, afraid, nutty, miserable, bored.

Not all our visitors like our davening. But if you stay a while, you get used to it. The best part is that when you daven here, in a circle, you're among friends. What's a religious community if it's not full of your friends? You look around and see your friends, and they look back at you. Over the years, these relationships grow deeper and more complex. With about twenty people in the Havurah, that means you have twenty different relationships, all present in the room at once. And since *everybody* has this same world of twenty relationships, that makes four hundred relationships all going on at once, crisscrossing each other like a maze of energy passing back and forth, an invisible network, a crowd of histories and stories all present at one instant of time, all in this little room. It's awesome when you start to think about it. It's as if this room were charged full of some invisible force, and only when you become part of it do you start to see it.

But I'm getting off the subject again. You'll see all that in time, as Shabbos unfolds. So, let's go into the next room and I'll point out some of the sights.

This is our kitchen. It's always a mess. It's a junk heap, a dunghill, the black hole of Calcutta, a *hegdish*, a *balagan*, a pit like the one they threw Joseph into. What can we do? We try and try, but we never seem to be able to keep it organized.

See this table with all these dishes and books and junk piled on top? We bought it from a couple who were moving out to California. They were very nice, too. They gave Esther and me a whole load of stuff for practically nothing. When they found out we were Jewish, the woman said, "Oh, that's nice. I used to be Jewish too, but now we're Bahai." And she motioned to her husband who was standing there, all smiles.

Well, those are the times.

Please, don't look in the refrigerator. Thank you.

All right. Now for the sink. Here we have our sink, with a *milchik* side and a *fleishik* side. And *milchik* and *fleishik* drainers, too. And there's a *milchik* sponge and a *fleishik* sponge. And that's a *schmutzik* sponge in the middle, for questionable items. Our kashrut isn't the most rigid, but at least we make an effort. And that counts for something, doesn't it? Doesn't it?

Oh, shoot – there's a roach. A real one, I mean. Nah, leave it alone. After all, it's a living creature.

What else . . . Am I boring you? No? You *sure*? You're not just saying that to be polite? Oh good, good.

And this! This dish belongs to Krishna Kat, our resident feline. This dish is the most beloved object in the Havurah, if you were just to measure how much love gets directed at this dish. It's all Krishna's love, but he sure loves his dish. He loves it with a pure animal love. I never saw such love before.

So now, let's go upstairs. Through here and up this back staircase. Past the garbage cans and brooms. Smells a little from the garbage. Well, don't worry about that – the odor only reaches halfway up the stairs. The second floor is a whole lot nicer.

See? It's pretty nice up here! Well, in comparison with the kitchen.

In this room, we have our library. We've got a pretty respectable selection of books, although it's a little random. Everything from the Talmud to Allen Ginsberg, from Chumash with Rashi to . . . well, this for example: "Yoga and Meditation Explained," by Mahareeshi Somethingorother, whoever he is.

There used to be an order to the books in here, but over the years they all sort of collapsed together. You never know what you'll find. Makes it interesting to browse!

And here's our bathroom. Just a normal bathroom, a little on the rundown side. The reading material isn't even very good – old *Newsweeks*, a few old copies of *Commentary, Rolling Stone*, a *Village Voice* from way back. Nothing to keep you in here too long. But I have some fond memories here. Once, I had a revelation in here. A minor revelation, but a revelation nonetheless.

One night, I was washing my face and all of a sudden I started to think about water. I got really tuned into water. This little faucet may not seem like a mountain stream or a mighty ocean, but suddenly I began to think, "Water! My God – *Water*! The primal substance of life! The essential building block of our existence!" I just let it run over my hands, fascinated. I was thrilled, even reverent. It was one of those experiences that go beyond words. You never know when something like that's going to hit you. So anyways, I have some fond memories of this bathroom.

Besides that, here are the bedrooms. Most members don't live in the house, but in the surrounding neighborhood. Still, a lot of us have lived in the house at one time or another. That's Linda's room, which used to be Heligman's room. And there's Elisha's room, later to be Carol's room. And that one used to be Esther's room and then Chief lived there for a while. They change a lot, people come in and out.

Nobody seems to stay at the Havurah – or in any one place – for too long, but I kind of like it here. I moved out for a while, too – I'll tell you about that later – but eventually moved back in. I feel comfortable here. I feel at home.

So, let's go up to my room, all the way up to the fourth floor, past these other third-floor bedrooms.

Okay, here we are in the attic, on the fourth floor. Up here, there's nobody's room but mine. Nice room, huh? My own lovely mess, with my big old bed and my stereo and my books and my dead plants.

But come over here, just push these heavy curtains aside, and step right in.

It's dark, right? This is the turret. If you ask me, this is the best place in the house. It's a magical place, and wonderful things always happen in here. It's like that special hiding place we had when we were kids. Listen, we'd better not sit down, or we'll stay here for hours and you'll tell me your whole life's story before we realize that it's time to go downstairs and daven.

The turret's like that – in here, time just seems to stop. So, we better not stay too long.

And look out the window. Down there's our garden, and our grape arbor. But let's go back downstairs. It's getting late and it's going to be Shabbos soon.

What else is there in the house? There's the basement, which I didn't show you. That's our dark, cave-like, underground world, piled up with all sorts of things – old furniture, rusty bicycles, old photographic equipment, tattered siddurim, a strobe light, whatever. You can find anything down there, like treasures in a lost tomb.

Well, that was the house. Does it begin to seem more than just any old creaky house? But that's only the beginning. It's just things. Things with stories attached. There's something much more important, something a lot more complicated and full of stories . . . .

But before we get into that, sit down, right here on the stairs, right here next to me. Wanna smoke a joint? I *just happen* to have one right here in my pocket.

This is special stuff, too – Havurah weed. We grew it in the back-yard, behind the garage. You wouldn't believe the debate it sparked off. Some people were real paranoid, afraid of getting busted and dragged off to jail. Others couldn't care about that and wanted the Havurah to grow its own, as a statement. You know, "We are the counterculture." Well, we couldn't come to an agreement. So finally, a couple of us just went ahead and planted it and didn't tell anyone. No one else knew – or if they did, they didn't let on. But every once in a while, there'd be some leaves clipped off and strangely unaccounted for. So we dubbed that the Dope of Elijah and figured that he came by when we weren't looking, smoked some, and left.

Hey, do you have a match? No? Okay, hold on, I'll go get some. We always keep matches on top of the ark to light the *ner tamid*. I'll be right back . . . .

Okay, here we go. Give it a lick and you do the honors . . . Good stuff, huh? Not bad for homegrown . . . .

You know, Elijah keeps coming by the back of the garage every once in a while, but it doesn't seem like the messiah's going to come so soon. A couple of years ago we thought this stuff would bring the messiah. Or the revolution. Or just a real change for the better. But I don't know. It doesn't seem like too much really changed, although things were pretty interesting for a while . . . Hey, could I have some of that? . . . *Sssssuk* . . . Hmmm. Good stuff. Well, it's still a lot of fun . . . .

Look at all those patterns in the smoke . . . .

Hey, what's that – do you hear it? That noise – suddenly, all that noise! It's getting louder! What is it? It sounds like footsteps! This is no stoned paranoia, those are footsteps! Listen! They're all over – footsteps! Coming down from the third floor, coming up the front steps. Don't you hear it? Sure, you can hear it now – they're coming in from the kitchen, coming out of the second-floor bathroom. The rooms are emptying out – they're coming in from the back door, too! They're coming in from all over, from outside, from upstairs! Even up from the basement! All those footsteps! What's going on?!

The front door's opening! Look! –

It's the *Havurah*! HERE COMES EVERYBODY!

Look! – there's Elisha and Esther and Chief and Heligman; Max and Rebecca coming in from outside, Zack comin' down from the third floor, Leah, and Jerry. And there's Linda comin' out of the bathroom, and Marty and Carol, and look out there, there's Mark comin' out of his car, slamming the door and coming up the walk, and Myra, and Ira, and –

Look! *Here they all are*, all showered and unshaven for the occasion, dressed in their flowered and threadbare best, coming in and sitting down in the davening room, taking places on the cushions, getting ready for Shabbos to begin, getting ready for the most important guest of all, Shabbos ha-Malkah, to glide in out of the sky, sailing across the treetops, coming in over the setting sun, wafting her way in through the front door to camp down with us for the next twenty-four hours or so.

So, who are all these people? They come from all over the Jewish-American roadmap – from radical politics, from ethical culture, orthodox yeshivas, the suburbs and decaying inner cities. They come from Zionist camps, from assimilated homes, from every Jewish trip in America. I can't go into all those stories now. But bit by bit, you'll get acquainted with everybody.

But now it's time for Shabbos and that's the most important matter at hand. So come on into the davening room, let's sit down and see what's going to happen.

Here – take a *siddur*.

Hey, we have to whisper now. This is where things get a little spooky. I wouldn't say solemn – we practically never get solemn around here – but Friday night always seems to have a special quality about it: soft and gentle, a little hazy, no sharp edges or glaring lights. See, the lights are low, the candles are lit, there's a quiet, sensuous atmosphere in the room. Relaxing too, no?

What? You want me to shut up? I'm disturbing you? You want to pay attention to what's going on? Okay, okay, I'll leave you alone . . . .
. . . .
. . . .

Good Shabbos!

Well, those were services. I hoped you enjoyed them.

Ah, no – don't tell me what you thought of them. Not yet, anyway. Your reactions are for you, not for me. You don't have to try to please me or say anything to be polite. Better yet – no judgments at all. Not now anyway. It's still too early for judgments.

But now that services are over, I'm just going to go around and wish everybody a good Shabbos. Why don't you take a few minutes to do the same? Don't worry, they're friendly. Nobody bites. Okay? I'll see you soon.

So, did you meet some of the folks? A nice bunch, no? A little weird, sure, but that makes us interesting.

Oh – you mean you didn't get too far with most of them?

Well, I guess not. First encounters are always difficult. You have to hang around for a while before you understand what's going on here. You can't expect too much all at once. We're only human, you know. It takes time, and you have to start with first things first.

Huh? What do you mean, 'Well, okay, let's start with first things first'?

You mean *me*?

You want to know what brought *me* here? Well, I'd be glad to tell you. After all, I really love to talk about myself once I get started. But the problem is, I can't really tell you with complete certainty exactly how I *did* get here. It's a combination of so many conflicting things – of absolute logical necessity and purely random chance. If I try to make too much sense of it, no doubt I can fashion a story of events, of twists of fate and personal decisions, and yet somehow, deep down, I know that I really wouldn't have captured it. I would inevitably exaggerate some things and downplay others, sacrificing honesty for clarity.

It just happened, that's all. It's the trip life took me on.

But I see you find my reluctance to be tiresome. You would like to hear a story, so I'll try to tell you one, for whatever it's worth. It's worth *something*, I suppose. Exactly how much is my only problem.

So, let's try to look at it simply . . . .

And yet, no matter where I try to start, I see that I have to go back a step and start at the one before that. And then at the one before that, and so on, all the way back – to what? Where does it stop?

But this isn't psychoanalysis or a history lesson, so let's just jump in at the easiest point. Let's start a few years after my bar mitzvah – where most kids' Jewish stories end. But that's where mine begins.

Until I was fourteen, I think I was normal. A normal child, playing baseball and teasing girls. Bright, but no genius – normal Jewish bright, let's say. But by the time I was sixteen, I was crazy as a coot. Really crazy? No, just an adolescent. In other words, a hormonal monstrosity; an endless flow of body grease, sperm and roaring emotions, gushing from a wealth of newly discovered organic faucets. I was some sort of animal and vegetable swamp, raw healthy gook, lively as a lizard, slimy as a snake, sick as a bubonic rat. Like Kafka's universe, my body and mind were randomly changing according to no apparently discernible pattern, at least not to me, with only a slight hint of a remotely malevolent intention possibly guiding the wheel.

At the same time, I was, amazingly, busy being a dutiful student, cramming my head into my textbooks, squeezing out my A's during the day the way I squeezed my pimples at night, late at night, my only personal, private solace after a day of competitive high school nightmare. I don't have to go into that too deeply – you know the game.

But into this unfashioned ectoplasmic state of mind, which I carried around inside a body that seemed to me some sentient, too-intimate machine gone haywire, into this mix fell something else: I happened to stumble onto, to be introduced to, and even occasionally sought out by, some very interesting people.

Some of these people were quite alive, while others were still living only between the covers of books. But in either case, a new world opened up to me, a world of ideas, of beauty, of poetry – in short, the whole romantic bag of beans. At the time, it seemed to be of utmost significance.

Of all the new personalities I encountered, everything seemed to crystallize around one person in particular, Mel Blumenhaus, a young seminary student who taught Hebrew school to keep himself barely above the poverty level.

At first, I thought Mel was one of the weirdest people around. He certainly came across as different: he was a big, imposing figure; even though he was still only in his early twenties, he had a beard in the days when they were still mainly the mark of the artist and the beatnik; there were holes in his shoes, which he didn't seem particularly upset about; and he said strange things with a seriousness which then struck me as silly. Who could care about the stuff he talked about?

But soon enough, I was drawn in. He taught a little of this and a little of that, straining the limitations of a Hebrew school classroom. He taught some Torah, a little mysticism, self-awareness and psychology, midrash, gnosticism, existentialism, Hasidism, history, and literature. He taught about davening and I learned how to daven – not to pray, kneeling with your hands clasped, like some goy – but to daven, like a Jew davens, with all its physical rhythms and peculiar intonations that serve to cram in, hurry along, and occasionally lift up a seemingly endless flow of words. Like at services just a few minutes ago.

Anyway, sometimes Mel and I would go out for a walk, just the two of us. He would talk about whatever came into his mind – about his life, his observations, some of his feelings, and he would ask me about what I felt about things.

Who, before this, had ever cared about what I felt? Sure, people cared if I was happy or unhappy, but only so I could be made happy again and returned to equilibrium, and thereby easily dismissed and forgotten.

But now, suddenly there was drama to my inner life, my own little drama, and I was given eyes to look at it and someone to discuss it with. And a language to articulate it. As I struggled to express it, this drama seemed more and more fascinating and worth exploring.

So, why did Mel do this – this extracurricular activity – for no apparent reason? Was he merely a caring teacher who got involved with his students' growth? No, it was more than that. But Mel was always a complicated person, and I hesitate to pin him down too readily.

If perhaps not charismatic – because "charisma" is such a tricky word – Mel was always, at least, intense, excited, and humorous, too. Though still a young man, he easily commanded attention, which seemed to come naturally and without effort. This itself became a source of struggle for him. While in part he aspired to be a guru of sorts, a Hasidic rebbe for the contemporary scene, at the same time he seemed unsure as to whether this role was being thrust upon him and whether or not he even liked it. He seemed both wary and reluctant to assume the very role he aspired to. He was afraid of its pitfalls as strongly as he was aware of its attractions.

But you can never fully know any man's conflicts and demons, any more than you can know the man himself. Whatever conflicts he struggled with in private, I only glimpsed them fleetingly, at rare moments. In the future, I would have further glimpses, and yet, of course, never a full story.

However, every extraordinary figure must have a community in which to shine, and Mel found no ready community which best lent itself to his own amalgam of ideas and personality. And so, he naturally created one, fostering his personal relationships and selectively culling together a loose constellation of friends, admirers, peers, and disciples.

And while he struggled with his role, giving in to it as well as fighting it, his intellectual excitement and emotional capaciousness created a powerful presence that both drew me to it and reflected its light onto my own life.

But as I said, Mel was only a focal point for all my new interests, as I stumbled into new understandings and perceptions, whether with his guidance, the guidance of others, or on my own. I was drawn further into this Jewish world, which seemed capable of absorbing all the anguish and fascination of my adolescent growth. I wanted to learn all that I could about it; I wanted to know everything. I wanted to grow wise. I was drawn to the remaining spiritual flicker of my heritage which had, for the most part, so recently been reduced to ashes.

Soon, some funny stuff began to happen, and it happened with increasing frequency. What was it? I hate to give it a name, but allow me to try to describe it and recount its most striking occurrence.

One Shabbos, at *motzei Shabbat*, in the early evening, as Shabbos was leaving, I found myself in a small, old synagogue. There were very few people and I had arrived on this particular occasion without much concern for the davening. They had needed an extra to make a minyan, so I had offered my body. It was dark, the night was falling, and the electric lights had not yet been switched on. I stood at the back, in the darkening room, not particularly involved with the service.

I held the book and fumbled through the pages. Sometimes, davening is like that. That's a part of it too. But then, without expecting it, without expecting anything for that matter, something came over me – from inside me, or from somewhere else – and began to obliterate me completely. A powerful charge of emotion swept through me, and I suddenly became ecstatic, totally ecstatic, over nothing at all. By now, there was almost no light in the place, and this ecstasy just roared through me; I was only the smile of the Cheshire cat hanging in the middle of the dark night.

"Throw it away," I said to myself. "Just throw it away."

Throw *what* away? I didn't know. Everything. Everything – just throw it all away. Hang onto nothing, just let yourself go and zoom around in this ecstatic surge, let it go wherever it takes you, follow it, enjoy it, trust it even though you have no idea of what it is, except that it's total and intense.

"Throw it away, just throw it away."

I wandered around at the back of the shul, while no one paid me any attention, nor did I wish to attract any. I had no need for attention, for anything, for anybody. I couldn't explain it; I didn't want to interrupt it. I just soared around on the most exciting rush of ecstatic nothingness I had ever known.

And then, after a while – maybe two minutes, or ten, or half an hour – the service was over, the lights went on, and I was back down on the ground, a strangely satisfied post-drunkenness cushioning my brain.

And so, what was it? A psychotic episode? A hormonal imbalance? The voice of God or the roar of the abyss? I didn't know and I didn't care. All I knew was that I liked it, and I wanted it again.

So I followed it, or at least the world in which it happened. I began to daven regularly, and sure enough it would come again, at times, never with the same intensity or with that same complete abandon, but it came. And I kept looking for it, more and more and more.

At this time, I went up to Boston and entered college, still with my head in the clouds, still following that same shiver of whatever it was. It led me for long walks in the woods, wandering among the trees. It led me onto hilltops with wide vistas that looked down onto tiny New England towns way below. It led me deep into the silent stacks of the library late on Saturday night. And it led me back to shul, to the same pages and the same prayers, again and again.

One Friday night I went to Mel's for Shabbos dinner (for Mel, too, had moved to Boston). Friday night at Mel's was always a special time: he hosted a big dinner with the lights dimmed low, there was always the addition of several other interesting people with interesting ideas, plus the challah, the wine, a few words of Torah, usually the study of a Hasidic text. It was a rich, sensuous atmosphere.

I sat there, as usual, without saying much, listening, and learning more than I could offer in return. I never quite understood why Mel even bothered to invite me to these dinners from time to time, but he did so, and I was glad to accept.

On this night, the conversation turned to matters esoteric, about states of consciousness and altered perceptions. It was a topic very much in vogue in those early LSD days.

From the end of the table, like a voice coming out of a forgotten corner, I started to speak. I don't remember exactly what I said, but I talked about how when you're up there you don't want to come back down, and how in coming down you go through pain and sadness and you don't know what to do with it. I obliquely referred to the midrash of the four rabbis who entered an orchard, in which one went crazy, one dropped dead, one ran off to join a fanatical sect, and how only Rabbi Akiva entered in peace and came out in peace.

I watched Mel while I talked; I spoke with the perfect calm of someone who was well acquainted with what he was saying, watching it register on Mel's face, wondering whether he understood me or not. He looked back at me with a wide, troubled eye, his attention sharply tuned to what I was saying.

Finally, when I was finished, he got up and motioned with his head. "Come on, let's go for a walk," he said.

I grabbed my coat, excited to go for another private, privileged walk with Mel. I expected that we would go out, walk silently around the block, then talk of intimate, mysterious things. I expected perhaps a further initiation into mystical ideas, now that he saw the profound quality of my experience. And so I didn't understand it when he got into his car, told me to get in, and drove us off towards downtown Boston. It was only years later that he told me why he did what he had done: he was afraid I was going cuckoo, flipping out completely, about to turn absolutely bughouse in my ethereal, solitary world, and to make matters worse, he was afraid that he was to blame for it all. He wanted to bring me down, back down to earth.

And so I didn't understand when we drove downtown, into the noise, the traffic, and the weekend crowd. I didn't understand when he took me into a greasy little restaurant, full of people jostling in and out, and ordered some coffee and a sandwich, and asked me if I wanted anything. On Friday night? On Shabbos? This crummy restaurant and this rotten food?

"Is that sandwich kosher?" I asked when it arrived.

"Probably not," he said. "I doubt it."

I didn't understand. I didn't understand. I was trying to make sense of it, trying to fit it into some poetic plan, but it didn't go, it wouldn't fit at all, at all. What was he trying to tell me?

We soon left the restaurant and walked over to the Prudential Center. It stood straight up, a huge steel and concrete tower, right in the heart of the city. What were we doing here?

"Come on, let's go up the escalator," he said.

So we rode up the escalator. And then we rode down the escalator. And then we ran up the down escalator and down the up escalator. We ran up and down, over and over, and I kept trying to understand this nonsensical business, but I didn't understand. When we were tired, we went back to his car and he drove me home.

I didn't see much of Mel after that, but I began to see what he was trying to tell me. There was a world out there, a world of realities and things, and not everything was beautiful or mystical, but these, too, had to be acknowledged and lived with. Slowly at first, and then with greater and greater force, I began to want only a world of concrete realities; I wanted to discover and satisfy my appetites, to be initiated back into this world which I had somehow lost sight of.

Soon, it seemed so clear to me that the highest good was no longer somewhere in the stars or the tops of the trees, but that it hovered about two-and-a-half feet above the ground, and it was the motor, the only motor, which whirled around and made everything go, and that the more it was greased, the more the world would spin.

But when I looked around, with my new eyes switched suddenly to an entirely different channel, I was awkward and retarded, the country bumpkin come to the city. What had I been doing for the last few years while everyone else was running around, picking up their little social skills? The price I had paid now seemed too great for a few moments of something which just slipped through my fingers.

I had been a stupid jerk with my mind in a fog while everyone else, or so it seemed, had been busy finding out the feel, the look, and the musky smell of reality.

I turned on my Jewish experience, turned on it with a vengeance. It had kept me naive, awkward, backward. A fool. Everyone had been patting my back for being such a good little boy, that nice boy who thought about God and things like that, and I was fed up with that image.

No – I was more than fed up. I was angry and horror-struck, furious at the blindness of piety, sick at the creature it had made me become. I had to start from the beginning now, in a world in which everyone else had matured normally, at his or her proper animal pace. I was behind and ashamed of it. I wanted out, I wanted to get out and away from it as far and as fast as I could.

I had to profane everything that I had once held holy. I had to sneer at it, dump on it, laugh in its face. I had to be free of any dominion it had ever had over me.

So, what happened next? What happened was that when I opened my eyes to what was going on around me, the late sixties were in full swing, and America was a crazy, exploding place – drugs were everywhere, sex was the new realm of discovery and exploration, and suddenly people, the world, and all of reality itself were offering up new aspects of themselves, more quickly, violently, and amazingly than any one individual could even dare to keep up with.

The one basic tenet was not to be afraid of it. Banish fear and wonderful things would open up, both inside you and before your eyes. Anyway, that was the tenor of the times, whether it was true or not. And so, when I pushed my courage up enough to step beyond the bounds of what I had already known, I was off, on a mad dash towards some pleasure-filled, unspecified finish line.

What do I remember from it? Travel, dope, a motorcycle, a couple of women who were even crazier than I was. In all, I had good times and bad times, fine flying rides and bummers.

Somehow, though, I couldn't seem to conquer it all, for in truth that was the impossible quest: to be at every scene, to camp out on every mountain, to try every drug, to learn every position, to hitch down every road, to hear every concert. You can imagine – it produced anxieties as well as taking them away. In all, it was a mixed experience, although it was undoubtedly an exciting time to be alive.

And it was a good time during which to break into freedom, a welcoming time to empty out the good-boy garbage can and toss its smelly contents into the river. Certainly, it was not a time for uptight, introverted, God-fearing, sensitive martyr trips. So I fit right into the prevailing mood and ran around in my own private frenzy while it seemed like the whole country was trying to do the same.

So how did I get *here,* at the Havurah? We still haven't gotten to that one yet, have we?

Well, again, it was a combination of several things – chance, circumstances, a little soul-searching, and a particular acid trip I took one Saturday night.

To be honest, I was never much into acid. I respected it way too much for that. I feared its power. I knew it could rip right into the middle of my head and make me see everything that was inside there, but distorted and embellished to monstrous proportions, whose terrifying, implacable, and despotic reality would have an indisputable, inescapable logic. Whatever might happen to be inside there at the moment, whatever worries, or doubts, or unhappiness, or even the simple traits of my own personality, might take on monstrous dimensions and lead me to inner places I was fearful to tread.

So I stayed away from acid – I told myself I would save it for exactly the right occasion, when I had my life completely in order, so that whatever would present itself would be nothing but flowers and clear blue sky.

But life doesn't really work like that, and we never have our lives completely in order. None of us. Because the nature of our lives is always to be working on some problem, getting over some obstacle, stuck against some stony challenge. There's always a thorn in our side, even when our hands are full of roses.

Anyway, enough lecture. What happened was that this evening my friend came by with an extra tab that he wanted to share. So he coaxed me a little.

"This is good stuff," he said. "It's like gentle mescaline – I tried it once. I got it from someone I trust. It's nice stuff. You'll see."

"Oh well, what the hell," I replied. "Let's try it and see what it's like."

Gentle stuff? It was a screaming rollercoaster ride, taking off faster than I could realize how far it was catapulting me. Everything broke down – vision broke down into a series of dazzling, flipping cartoons, sound transformed into color, the floor became a buckling ocean, and for some reason I expected God to call me on the telephone, to give me the word, even as I was crawling around on my hands and knees, babbling nonsense, bumping into furniture.

I wasn't alone, either. I watched with perfect understanding as well as utter incomprehension as my friend put his hand through the window, bit the cheek of a young lady friend who stopped by, and ran from room to room, locking and unlocking imaginary doors.

It seems, during an acid trip, that there is a critical moment that you come upon. You hit a moment when you realize that you can either hold on or let go. Hold onto what? Let what go?

Again – I don't know. But for some reason, this time things were a little too crazy, so I said, "Hold on"– onto something: myself, my name, something that was fundamentally mine to rule over. And so, even as reality was playing its tricks on me, transforming into some of its many faces that it normally hides save for special occasions, I said, "Hold on, you, I still have some say here."

What little say I had was very small indeed, in face of this power stronger than myself. And yet I still demanded that my own small voice, however insignificant, be recognizable in the chaos. And chaos it was. Absolute chaos for seven or eight hours.

I came down shaken, strung out, feeling that I had been thrown against a concrete wall and then peeled off like putty.

But if strange results grew out of this chemical encounter, perhaps the strangest was that when it was all over, for some reason my anger and my spite towards my Jewish background were gone. Flushed out of me, burned away. I had somehow made a sufficient break so that I no longer felt I needed to lash out at what had chained me down. I was free of it. I was free to do whatever I pleased, and that if I wanted to go off the deep end, then that was up to me.

I could take what I wanted and leave what I didn't.

Well, to be truthful, the anger wasn't all gone. Not completely. There was still enough for an irrepressible sense of irony to continue to exert its presence. There was something very important about this irony. It was, whether I liked it or not (but I did like it, I found), now as essential a part of me as anything else. To bring this irony into my Jewish life felt as necessary as bringing my hands or my head.

This didn't mean I was about to make a great return, to play Prodigal Son Come Home and fall down on my knees in front of some old white-haired father on the doorstep of the ancient homestead. No, not at all. If I was no longer angry, I also had no desire to submit myself to a previously followed order of established authority. That would have been so easy, so cheap and trite a solution. Just put the same old blinders on, stick my nose in the same old siddur, and pull the same old cart again.

No, there was nothing to be gained by that. Indeed, I couldn't have done it – once again, I would have bristled if merely tossed back towards the other extreme. But there was something I wanted, something basic to my life which I needed again. I wanted my symbols back. "Give me my symbols back," something inside me shouted.

Yes – from the world-wide spectrum of bones and tattoos, of shark-tooth necklaces and swinging censers, jungle tom-toms and magic flutes, from the realm of warpaint, Eskimo fertility gods, Christmas trees, and little pins bearing a picture of Lenin or the Masonic compass and ball, from the world of gold watches conferred after twenty-five years of service, each day of each year marked by the ritual lunchhour martini, from all that I wanted my own symbols again, to wave about and punctuate the lines and turnings of my life. Mine, they were still mine, no matter how problematic that might be. They were there to speak and comment upon my life, to compound it in all its moods, events or states of consciousness, with a rich and intimate overlay. It was my life, and suddenly it seemed important to me again. And, after all . . . I was still a religious man.

A few days later – I don't remember how many, nor do remember how it occurred – I either ran into Mel or called him or somehow happened to be in the neighborhood that he normally frequented. Once again, I found myself having a private tête-à-tête with Mel, and again it bore that same charged sensation of our earlier conversations of years before.

This time, we were sitting in a pizza parlor.

I told him what had happened to me, what the trip was like, and what I had gone through when I came down.

He picked up a piece of pizza, and from behind it, he smiled, "Sounds like you're ready to join the Havurah," he said.

The Havurah? I had heard some things about it, passed along by word of mouth, nothing to be trusted too much. I knew that it was mostly Mel's brainchild, the product of his own religious and social needs and eccentricities. But I had heard all sorts of different things – that it was an alternative seminary trying to express a new philosophy of Judaism, that it held to everything and nothing, that it was a draft dodge, that it was a Jewish commune, an experiment in lifestyles, that it was a den of drugs and sex and Torah. I heard that it was where all the Jewish intellectuals were meeting and where the stoned-out Jewish freaks were hanging out. So, which and what was it? Mel didn't try to explain too much.

"Don't worry about what you've heard. Just come by and meet the people. See what's going on. It's an interesting place. It has its problems, and it hasn't always lived up to everybody's expectations – especially because everybody expects something different from it. But come around – I think you'll like it there."

He bit down on the end of his slice of pizza, and as the cheese made a long string towards his mouth, I thought of all the questions I wanted to ask him.

"Look," I said, "is this place going to try to give me any answers? Frankly, I don't know if I can handle anybody trying to give me answers at the moment."

He ate his pizza and shook his head. "I don't know if it's going to give you any answers. If it does, don't buy them too much anyhow."

"But then what good is it?" I asked, taking the other side.

"Well," he said, thinking a second. "It may not give you any answers but it's a good place to ask some of the questions."

Ask the questions? From a deep, unsatisfied place inside of me, I suddenly had a terrible need to pose one big question, a question to which, for some reason, I would only trust Mel's answer. Anyone else's would only be an opinion, but Mel's answer would carry greater authority. In some very basic way, he still was my teacher, and I trusted and even believed in what he had to say.

I looked around, my eyes quickly scanning the pizza parlor to make sure that no one would overhear. It suddenly seemed like a weighty and yet strangely embarrassing moment.

"Listen," I said, trying not to sound too naive or dramatic, but still as serious as I could allow myself to be, "so tell me – does God really exist?"

Mel didn't say anything. A strange, almost worried look passed over his face.

"Okay, well, listen," I said again, quickly revising. "Do *you* believe in God?"

He waited a moment. "You don't want much," he said slowly. "You just want my guts, that's all."

What? What does he mean? Again, I didn't understand. I didn't understand. I wasn't going to get an answer. There really wasn't any good answer to give me. But I also realized that it wasn't up to him to give me that answer. And yet at least it was good that I had asked the question, no matter how stupid it suddenly made me feel to have asked.

I looked down, still perplexed, and pulled off a piece of pizza. I looked at it. It was red, yellow, and air bubbles made big bumps in the cheese. I bit into it and chewed slowly, because the pizza was still hot.

In the months that followed, I began, intermittently, to hang around the Havurah, coming occasionally for Shabbat and holidays. It wasn't something I could jump into all of a sudden, coming as I was from my years of reaction and cynicism. But as I came more often, and as I grew to know some of the people, the community attracted me more and more. The thought of living in a community – with all these people bubbling with ideas and eager to live them out – seemed so much richer than what I had been making do with for so long.

I learned more about the Havurah, and about what I had already missed during its brief history, of all the energy and creativity that initially went into the group's founding. There had been energy flowing in all directions, with encounter groups, flashing neon Tetragrammatons on the walls for meditation and decoration, touchy-feely sessions, and classes on a wide range of topics both ancient and modern.

There had been a parade of sometimes brilliant, sometimes eccentric people who had already gone their many separate ways – into the rabbinate or academics, into politics, communes, Zen monasteries, or into business or social work. Things had already begun to calm down a little, the group was settling in, and its style and flavor was jelling into a more cohesive community.

But still the flavor of the sixties lingered, and I was determined to join in before it was too late, before all the excitement was over for good. It was an opportunity, I realized, that probably would not come again.

In the meantime, I had started graduate school as well. But graduate school was . . . well, graduate school, with all its silent frustrations, its overly refined study, its irrelevance and boredom, all those stereotypes that are true, to some extent. I needed something to offset it. It became obvious that the Havurah was the place I had to be.

Ach – but none of this really holds together. I *told* you I really couldn't tell you exactly what brought me here. You see, you've already gotten wrong impressions and distorted ideas. You only have the skeleton of what I've really been trying to make you understand. I can't explain it, and I can't make it all sound right. No matter what I'd say, I wouldn't be happy with the way it came out.

I guess I don't like having to explain myself. My actions are my actions and what I do is what I do. I don't want to explain or give excuses, not even to you.

And that's why I'm here.

But anyway, all that seems like such a long time ago. Enough of these explanations, excuses, reasons, reasons, reasons. Who needs them? But if you like, I'll tell you some stories about what goes on here. Then you can come to your own conclusions, if that's something you really need to do.

So, come on over into the dining room. Shabbos dinner is all prepared, the table's set, and all we have to do is sit down, say kiddush and motzi, and then begin to eat. That's simple enough, no?

So, come on over, in here, sit down, and make yourself comfortable.

Right here next to me. Ready? Okay.

And yes – now vee may perhaps to begin.

SEUDAH RISHONAH

A TALE OF CHICKEN SOUP

Here it is, our first course – vegetable soup, a healthy mixture of every leaf, stalk and root we could find at the co-op.

What? you ask. No chicken soup? What's Friday night dinner without chicken soup, right? Actually, most of us here are vegetarians.

Me, I'm not a vegetarian – personally, I love to eat meat. Yum. Sink your teeth into the flesh of a cow. There's nothing like it. Sometimes I even eat hot dogs, which grosses out almost everybody here. It *is* pretty gross when you think about it. All that ground-up muscle and fat, pickled in nitrates and nitrites, stuffed into an intestinal sleeve. So I try not to think about it. I eat it and I lick my lips.

But about the chicken soup, what can I say? Jews and food have a long and complicated relationship, fraught with all manner of neuroses. Some people even think that Judaism *is* food, and they feel their way through the mysteries of the cosmos with their stomachs, poking their bellies into this and that unknown. For them, food becomes a sort of symbolic goo that

35

they eat their way through in order to arrive back at their childhood memories of family, holidays, mother's love, and even the laws of the Torah.

But symbols have a way of changing, and all that greasy Eastern European glop is now something other than the feast of struggling immigrants. Passed, like sludge, through the bowels of the Catskills, it emerged with a decaying, heavy smell of the foibles of a dyspeptic generation, spiced with the snickerings of self-mockery. "Here, *bubbeleh, tateleh,* have some chicken soup" – a derisive laugh in every spoonful.

Too bad – it's not the soup's fault. And it certainly isn't the fault of the chicken.

But enough of this. I don't wish to make accusations. It's nobody's fault. Instead, let me simply tell you a story while you eat.

Linda came to Boston as a refugee of Brooklyn. All through high school, she was sent to the Yeshiva of Coney Island – *"Di Yeshive d'Coney Island,"* it said, in Hebrew letters chiseled into the face of the building. Her parents sent her there to escape the real and imagined perils of the New York City school system. What with the blacks and Puerto Ricans and the dope-smoking in the bathrooms, her parents wanted her to receive a *decent* education, to learn Torah instead of petty crime along with her secular studies.

After amassing a thorough Jewish education, as well as completing all the required courses to pass the State exams, she went on to Brooklyn College, in the days when everybody went to college and yet had more important things to do than study. There were demonstrations, sit-ins, parties, and concerts to go to. Behind the science quadrangle, during lunch hour, Linda and her friends would light up and get high as weather balloons and float up to the *yeshiva shel ma'alah.* But then they would have to navigate their way back down in the evenings, to go home to a kosher meal, to say *ha-motzi* and *birkat ha-mazon* sitting between father on one hand and mother on the other. It was a schizophrenic existence to be sure, free and fettered at the same time.

It felt like living inside her mother's pressure cooker, like one of her big pot roasts, and so Linda would periodically flip the little valve on top and blow her mind in a cloud of smoke, in order to let out a jet of ascending steam.

When college was over – *zoom*, she was out of Brooklyn, out of New York altogether, arriving in Cambridge where all the hippies ran free. But Linda wasn't just any old hippie, with the typical peace-and-love grin on an open face, with all that yeshiva background sloshing through her brain. Filled with contradictions, she couldn't just cut the moorings of her mind and let it wander where it would. A marvelous sense of irony flourished within her.

Gradually, Linda gravitated towards the Havurah. At first, she came only once in a while, on the occasional Friday night. Then she started coming more often. It was a comfortable place for a Jewish woman to be. Finally, she got hooked. She became a member and even moved into the house.

At the same time, she found an office job at the Harvard Business School, of all places. That was another strange marriage, but she was used to living with worse, and so she skated a tactful path between the two, competently doing her job and then coming home with stories about the crazies in the pinstripes. But she was responsible and so they welcomed her there, despite the fact that she didn't completely fit in with the prevailing karma – if you can say that they have a karma there.

One evening, walking down from my room on my way to the bathroom, I heard, from behind Linda's closed door, one side of a very animated telephone conversation. Normally soft-spoken and non-confrontative, Linda was yelling, shouting, raving into the phone.

"No!" I could hear her shout. "That's not it. It's just not a good time . . . Because I'm busy . . . Whatever I'm doing, that's what . . . That's none of your business . . . To hell with that . . . I'll say whatever I goddam please . . . ."

There was a long pause at this point, and then she continued, less excited. "Listen, I'm not trying to get you upset . . . Well, you're getting me upset too, you know . ." (The tone grew a little wilder again) . . . "You can't treat me like that anymore! . . . No! . . ." (the tone decreased) . . . "All right . . . All right . . . All right . . . ."

I could no longer make out the words. I continued on my way.

As I exited the bathroom a few minutes later, I could no longer hear any noise coming from inside Linda's room. Not even a soft, indistinguishable conversation. Total silence. I knocked on her door.

For a moment, there was no answer. Then: "Who is it?"

"It's me – Solomon," I sang out cheerily.

"Come in," she answered, tonelessly.

I peered around the door, just sticking my head in, before venturing in completely. Linda was sitting on her bed, hunched over, her arms wrapped about herself as if in pain and listening to something deep within her body. She didn't even move her head to look at me; she merely raised her eyebrows to watch as I walked into the room.

"How are you doing?" I asked tentatively.

A wry smile began to appear, crookedly, on her mouth. "My parents are coming," she said. "This weekend."

For the next few days, Linda ran around like mad, straightening her room, shopping, cancelling her other plans. She gracefully understood that the rest of the residents of the house would probably get themselves invited elsewhere for Shabbos dinner, and she was relieved to find out that we would not be around; she wanted neither her parents nor her friends to be on show. She knew it would be awkward enough without having to sit through dinner together.

"Look," she told me. "Just don't do anything to upset them. Don't smoke dope or play your stereo too loud, especially on Shabbos."

"Don't worry," I told her. "I may not be *shomer mitvos*, but I have some tact."

"I know. I just get worried."

"Well, relax," I said.

That Friday afternoon, Linda hurried home from work to be sure to greet them when they arrived. Nervously, she ran up and down the stairs, and paced back and forth in the kitchen while dinner was cooking. She cleaned her room again, and even valiantly tried straightening the Havurah kitchen. A few minutes before candle-lighting time, the doorbell rang.

"Oh shit, here goes."

She hurried down the hall to meet them. I stood in the kitchen, fascinated, watching with humored interest as the scene unfolded.

Linda opened the door and I could see a large woman in a baggy carcoat enter the doorway. She reached out with both hands, grabbed onto either side of Linda's head, and gave her a big kiss on the face.

"Linda! Oh, Linda! It's so good to see you," she exclaimed, as if they were long-lost dear ones reunited after years of separation.

"I was home just last month, Ma," Linda answered, struggling within her grasp.

The large woman, who paid no attention to the remark, was followed by a little round man, dressed in a natty overcoat and shocking plaid pants. He wore a sporty hat with a narrow brim and a little feather stuck into the hatband.

"My babydoll," he exclaimed. "How's my babydoll?" And he leaned over and gave her a kiss on the cheek.

"I'm fine, Dad. I'm fine. Why don't you come in."

"Just one minute, I have some things here on the porch," her mother said, and she turned and brought in two large shopping bags filled to capacity. "I brought you some things you could use," she said, following Linda into the kitchen.

"Mom, Dad, this is Solomon. He's also a member of the Havurah."

"Hi," I said, smiling a big friendly smile, being on my best public-relations behavior. After all, *I* didn't have anything to lose here.

Linda's father extended a stubby hand, and shook mine with a firm, manly grip. "Hello there, young man," he said.

"Oh, how nice," Linda's mother added. "So you're also a member of the *Havooreh*," she said, pronouncing it with a Yiddish accent, as if correcting the pronunciation.

"Yeah, I'm also a Havurah member," I said, re-correcting the word.

"Do you live in the house, too?" she asked.

"Yes, I do." I replied.

"That's nice," she said. But then she turned to Linda as if I were no longer present and said, "I didn't know this was a mixed house."

"Mixed house!" I answered, reasserting my presence. "It's mixed up completely!"

Linda flashed me a warning look, while her mother tried to ignore the remark. Her mother switched the subject in an instant.

"I brought you some things," she said, and began to empty the contents of the shopping bag onto the table. "Here, I brought you some tomatoes – 39 cents a pound, quite a bargain. I'll bet *you* can't get them at that price. How much do you pay for tomatoes?"

"I don't know," Linda answered. "Uh . . . 49 cents a pound, 59 cents a pound, sometimes more."

"See?" her mother said, triumphantly. "And here, look, I brought you some melons. I'll bet they're good ones. I can tell – my method never fails. I always pick a good melon."

She smelled one of the melons, bringing it to her nose, and her eyes brightened in unspoken rapture. She put it down on the table and continued her inventory.

"I brought you some nuts. Better you should eat nuts than junk. You know, I've always believed that. I'm the original health food fanatic, before all that health food stuff came along. That's right. But not your father," she said, waving away the man at her side. "He still eats garbage."

By her girth, you would never have known that she was a health freak.

Finally, after displaying a great assortment of edibles, out from the bottom of the bag came the *pièce de résistance*.

"Here, I also brought you some chicken soup," she said, and she held up a pickle jar containing a clear, yellowish liquid. The label on the jar said, "Saltzman's Pickles," with a large picture of a Jewish star. Inside the Jewish star, there was the picture of a pickle. Below the Jewish star, it said, "Try our Gefilte Fish, too!"

"But Mom," Linda said, trying to contain herself. "You know I'm a vegetarian."

"Since when?" her mother answered indignantly.

"For over a year. You know that. I tell it to you every time I'm home."

"So?" her mother replied, her inflection rising. "So you're a vegetarian. You can still have chicken soup."

"I can have anything I want. I just don't want to eat that stuff."

"What stuff? My chicken soup?"

"Not your chicken soup. Chicken. Meat. I'm a vegetarian."

Not to be put off, her mother quickly softened her approach. "Here, take it anyway. You might want it. You'll see."

With that, the matter was closed.

"Well, I'll see you folks later," I said. "See you at services."

I walked away, went upstairs, and kept myself well sequestered for as long as I could.

When I came downstairs at last, services were about to begin. One by one, people trickled into the prayer room and sat down on the cushions. Linda's parents, trying to do likewise, had a difficult time seating themselves so close to the floor. Linda's mother's dress hiked up over her meaty legs, showing the white stocking fasteners which hooked onto her girdle. Linda's father, rigid in a powder blue leisure suit, struggled to find a comfortable position that would not wrinkle his pants.

Other than that, services went off without any further discomfort.

After services, following the round of Shabbos greetings, hugs, kisses, and everybody's formal introduction to Linda's parents (who greeted everyone with smiles: "How nice," from her mother, and a big handshake from her father), we all abandoned Linda to her parents. Although feeling slightly guilty for not having to share Linda's burden, we all skulked out of the house with a feeling of relief.

At Max and Rebecca's, over dinner, the talk inevitably focused on parents.

"I wouldn't let my parents come to services," I said. "I wouldn't be able to daven at all."

"My parents wouldn't want to come to services," Rebecca added. "I think it frightens them. They don't even understand why I would ever want to do it. Besides, they're jealous of the Havurah. They think I treat it too much like my family, and ignore them because of it."

"I'm glad my parents live so far away," said Mark, who grew up in California. "It's just too difficult for them to visit. It avoids all sorts of problems."

"My parents liked the Havurah when they came," Max interjected. "My father thought it was like his *shtiebl*. He just didn't understand the cushions. Besides that, he thought it was the same."

The next day, services were a disaster. No longer willing to sit on the floor "like the young people," Linda's parents dragged over two big arm-chairs from the living room and stationed them at the back of the prayer room. Sitting there, above our heads, it felt as if we were their little children at play on the floor. We could have been busy with jacks and dollies, and nothing would have seemed different.

Linda's mother smiled strangely, looking at all of us, paying lit-tle attention to the service. Her father, on the other hand, quickly began nodding off. His tallis slipped from his shoulders and he hugged it like a blanket.

Chief was leading the davening, and we tried to lend him support, answering at the proper times, half-heartedly singing when the *niggunim* began, but one by one we drifted out of the room – to look at the bulletin board, to sit on the porch and watch the cars go by, to chat in the kitchen or lose ourselves in the library. No one could bear sitting in the prayer room, which had changed from our own private hunting grounds into a domestic living room prison.

Tiptoeing out of the prayer room and into the kitchen, carefully shutting the door behind me, I found Esther and Rebecca sitting at the table, spreading peanut butter onto crackers and popping them into their mouths. Their spiritual level seemed very low indeed.

"Oh, I feel so terrible for Chief," Rebecca said, licking the peanut butter off the knife.

"So why don't you go out there and help him out?" I answered.

"Why don't you?" she replied.

"I asked you first."

"Here, have a cracker," Esther said. We looked at each other and started to laugh. Suddenly Leah emerged from the back stairway. She had been hiding upstairs.

"*Sssh* – they'll hear you," she whispered.

"Here, have a cracker," I said, and handed her the cracker that Esther had just handed me.

Later that afternoon, returning from a walk, Linda and her parents entered Linda's room and closed the door behind them.

On my way through the hall, once again I heard a noisy conversation emanating from behind the closed door. Unable to resist, I stood and listened.

Linda's mother was speaking in a loud, cranky voice.

"Linda, it's so dirty here. How can you live in such dirt? Last night it was dark, I couldn't see, but today I can see, and this place is a mess. And not just your room. The whole house. It's dusty, there are cat hairs on the furniture – I couldn't stand sitting on that chair with all those cat hairs. Why don't you move into a nice apartment? Something modern. Not these old houses. They're so . . . *ucch*."

"I like it here, that's why. My friends are here."

"So, your friends are here. You can still visit them whenever you like. Anyway, how can you have friends that are such slobs?"

"They're not slobs."

"Linda," her father suddenly added, changing the subject. "What I don't understand is why you have this double mattress here. What do you need a double mattress for – I mean, it takes up so much room."

"Daddy, I like a double bed. Listen – you and Mommy slept in it last night while I slept in the guest room. So that's why I have it – for you. For whenever you come."

"Don't be ridiculous," her mother butted in. "We don't need to stay here. Morty – we should have gone to a motel. I told you we should have stayed at a motel."

"Nah, don't give me that. You come to your daughter's house, you should be able to stay there."

"But it's such a mess. Linda, it's such a mess."

"Linda, you should get rid of the double bed. Get yourself a nice, new firm mattress, it's better for your back – this one is so old anyway – and a single bed wouldn't cost very much, even new. I can get you one if you want – we can ship it up to you."

"No!"

"Why not?"

"Because!"

"Linda," her mother said, "we're not trying to get you upset. But you should live in a nice house. And you should wear nicer clothes."

"Well, you *are* getting me upset. And it's my clothes now, too, huh?"

"Linda, your clothes are fine," her father interjected. "It's this double mattress. You say you got it second hand. How do you know who slept in it? Maybe it has bugs."

"I don't care if King Kong slept in it! It doesn't have bugs."

"How do you know?"

"I can tell!"

"They lay eggs. Maybe they didn't hatch yet. Bug eggs can stay around for a long time before they hatch. Ticks can sit in a tree for eighteen years before they bite you. Did you know that?"

"I don't care about ticks!"

"Well, maybe you should."

"And maybe I shouldn't!" she yelled. It sounded like someone was moving towards the door. I hurried off and down the stairs.

That evening, Linda and her parents were going to dinner and the movies. Linda came downstairs all dressed up, and her parents had also changed. Her father wore a checkered blazer with bright red pants. He sported white shoes, which matched his white belt.

Her mother looked, as before, stuffed into a shapeless dress.

Linda looked tired. Her face was pale, drained of life, and her body seemed limp, all bones with no support. There was an air of submission about her, and she didn't reply or even look up as I wished them a pleasant evening before they walked out the door and into the twilight.

The next day when I woke and looked outside, I saw that we were in the middle of a heavy rainstorm. The sewers couldn't accommodate the sudden downpour and rivers ran in the streets. Thunder boomed and the sky had turned a deep, dark grey. It seemed as if the day had stopped sometime before sunrise. To make matters worse, the radio predicted no let-up until later that night.

Around noon, Linda's mother began to get nervous. There was nothing to do, stuck in the house as we all were, and she grew anxious for the rain to stop. They had to return to Brooklyn that night, and although they did not want to drive in the rain, it would have been worse if they had to drive in the rain after nightfall.

In her anxiety, she took to *noodging* Linda, criticizing her hair, her clothes, telling her to get married. No longer resisting, Linda simply listened to everything her mother said. Her father, meanwhile, sat and read magazines, blocking out the universe.

At last, her mother decided it was time to leave. They would drive slowly, they would stop often. And they would get home before dark.

"Linda, we're going to go now, okay?"

"Okay, Ma."

"This is probably the best time to go."

"You're right. This is probably the best time."

"So, we're going to leave."

"Uh-huh. Okay."

"I'll go get your father. Morty!" she yelled, "let's get ready to go. Pack up your things!"

I was sitting in the library, hearing everything that was going on. I heard Linda's parents gather their belongings, I heard her mother's last advice and her father's last remark about the double bed. Finally, they were packed. Linda accompanied them down the stairs, to the front door.

"Linda, we had a wonderful time. It wasn't so terrible having us here, was it?"

"No, Ma, it was wonderful." Only a slight edge of sarcasm surfaced through her otherwise flat monotone.

"Linda, it was good to see you, even if we don't approve of everything you do."

"That's good, Ma."

"You know we love you."

"Yeah, I know. I love you too." Her voice was almost dead. "Take care of yourself."

"You take care of yourself, too."

"Drive carefully."

"We will. I hate the way your father drives – he makes me so nervous. But we'll take our time."

"Good. Take your time."

Her mother leaned over and, again grabbing Linda's face with both hands, gave her a big kiss. There was silence between them.

Then her father spoke. "Well, goodbye sweetheart," he said. "And you remember what I told you, okay?" He gave her a knowing look.

"Goodbye, Dad, Thanks for coming. I'll see you both soon in Brooklyn."

At this point, I figured I should make an appearance, just to be polite, to wish them a safe trip and to represent the Havurah. I walked out of the library and stuck my head over the stairs.

"Bye-bye. It was nice to meet you. Have a safe trip."

"Bye-bye," her mother called out.

"Goodbye, young man," her father said. "So long."

And just as her parents were leaving, about to run out into the terrible rain, Linda's mother added one more word: "This weather's terrible. Be careful not to catch a cold. Have some of my chicken soup!"

"Sure. Okay. Bye-bye," I answered, relieving Linda of the need to respond. Then they closed the door with a hurried movement and disappeared into the dark and windy storm.

Linda came upstairs and passed me without a word. She closed the door behind her and I heard the latch click shut.

I waited for a few minutes, and no sound came from Linda's room. No movement, no radio switched on, no sound at all. I knocked on her door.

"Yeah?" she said, quietly.

"Can I come in?"

"Yeah."

I opened the door and looked inside. Linda was sitting on her bed, her face to the wall, her back towards me.

"Are you all right?" I asked.

"I'm all right," she answered flatly.

"Pretty rough visit, huh?" I ventured.

"Yup."

"Well, they were nice to the Havurah."

"I know."

"They had a good time."

"I guess."

I could think of nothing more to say. I didn't know whether Linda wanted me to leave, or whether my presence was comforting. I began to feel awkward and was about to go, when Linda suddenly started to talk, still facing the wall.

"It's not all their fault," she said, still listlessly. "I guess they had it rough, too. Probably a lot rougher than me. But I can't stand the way they treat me. They reduce me to being four years old again. I can't even help it

– it just happens. As soon as they come, it's instant regression, and they just slip into all their old routines. 'Do this, do that,'" she said, mimicking them.

Her voice began to sound more animated. "They have all these crazy ideas. They want me to live out some miserable fantasy for them, some boring, inhibited existence that they can't even stand for themselves. I can't take it. They fight with each other; they bicker in the restaurants. They disapprove of everything I do. They don't like my clothes, my room's too dirty. To hell with their fucking neuroses. Screw their goddamn expectations." Her voice was getting louder, livelier, angrier.

"I can't stand their harping and their cloying affection – they want more approval than they offer. Goddamn their depression mentality. Goddamn their material insecurity." Her voice was growing wilder. "To hell with their sexual inhibitions. Screw their lousy relationships. Screw their criticism."

She began yelling now, shouting at the wall. "Fuck their fucking neuroses. Shit on their crazy neuroses. To hell with their mishegass. And fuck their goddamn *chicken soup!*" She was on the verge of veering out of control.

"Just hold on a second!" I said, and I ran out of the room, leaving her in a frenzy of rage. I ran to the phone and called up Max and Rebecca.

"Come immediately," I said, and hung up the phone.

I ran downstairs to the kitchen and grabbed the pickle jar full of chicken soup out of the refrigerator. I knocked on Esther and Jerry's doors and told them to come to my room.

At that moment, Heligman happened to be coming through the door. "Come up to my room, quick," I said, and I then dashed into Linda's room, pulling her up, off the bed, dragging her away. "Come up to my room, quick."

"What? Huh? What the hell are you doing?"

"What's up?" Heligman asked.

"What's going on?" Max called out, coming into the house.

"Up in my room, quick!" I shouted, and I dashed into the library, pulled a volume off one of the shelves, and prompted everybody up into my room.

"Huh? What?"

"What's happening?"

Finally, we formed a whole little quorum: Linda, me, Max, Rebecca, Heligman, Jerry, and Esther. I quickly opened the window as far as it could go, and the rain, still beating down, poured in and splattered my desk. The wind rushed in and blew about the room. I unscrewed the jar of chicken soup and held it high in the air.

"Goddamn their depression mentality," I chanted aloud. "Goddamn their financial insecurity. To hell with their sexual inhibitions. To hell with their lousy relationships. Goddamn their criticism. Goddamn their neuroses. To hell with their expectations. To hell with their chicken soup. And God save them from harm!"

Then I read aloud from the book of Ezekiel:

"The son will not bear the sins of his father, and the father does not bear the sins of his son."

"Aw-mayn," shouted everyone, and I quickly shoved the jar of chicken soup into Linda's hands.

"Here, toss it!" I commanded her.

"Huh?"

"Toss it!"

"What?"

"TOSS IT!"

Then, with a quick flick of her hand, Linda flung the contents of the jar through the open window, into the falling rain. It made a whooshing sound and fanned out into a flat, yellowish sheet of liquid for a split second, and then fell and disappeared into the backyard below.

"Hooray!" I said, and suddenly Linda began to smile. A big grin spread across her face and she started to laugh.

Everyone's face brightened and together we chuckled and smiled.

"Thanks," Linda said at last. And with that, cheerful again, she walked downstairs with the others. I closed the window and sat down at my desk.

I sat at my desk for about half an hour, reading a book that happened to be lying there, until suddenly I felt a change occurring somewhere around me. Something strange seemed to be happening. I looked up and I realized that the rain had stopped, and light was breaking through the clouds. A bright afternoon sunshine was beating off the storm. Then, I noticed it.

I looked out the window, transfixed. I stared for a brief moment, then got up and ran downstairs.

"Linda, come upstairs, quick," I said, and once again I pulled at her and hustled her upstairs into my room.

"What do you want now?" she said, irritated. "What the hell are you doing?"

"Look," I said, pointing.

And there, right in our backyard, closer than any I had ever seen, so close you could practically touch it, was a marvelous rainbow. A vertical stripe of color stood suspended, hanging in the air, with one end lost somewhere above the top of the house and the other end jabbing down into the backyard, its extremity, its pot of gold, rooted above the spot where the chicken soup fell.

"Holy mackerel, look at that," she said.

"It's amazing," I answered.

Together, we stood there, with the window raised, looking into a gorgeous prism of iridescent color, several feet wide, which hovered right in front of our eyes, in the bright sunshine that was breaking through the clouds. After several minutes of wide-eyed splendor, I picked up the pickle jar from my desk and handed it to Linda.

"Here, you forgot this." I said. "It's yours."

"What should I do with it?" she asked.

"I don't know," I answered. "Do anything. Throw it out. Recycle it. Or keep it for soup – for chicken soup. Or for whatever soup you like."

She gave me a funny look and then smiled. She took the jar and went downstairs.

ELISHA

Finished your soup? Okay, I'm going to take the bowls away. No, don't get up. Remember, you're the guest. Just stay seated, and maybe listen to my stories. That's all I ask while you're here.

Okay, here comes the main course. Something you can sink your teeth into more than just plain soup. So, while you're eating, I'll tell you the story of Elisha.

Elisha and I joined the Havurah at the same time. Each of us, separately, was seeking to escape from the dead territory of what had become our personal barren grounds, and we looked longingly as outsiders to join in to something we wanted for ourselves – or rather, we wanted what we thought we perceived.

And for each of us, those perceptions proved not wrong but ill-proportioned, not exactly incorrect and yet not at all what we expected. I was seeking an alternative to the arid land of university academics, into which I had already immersed myself, and Elisha was breaking from the bonds of an orthodox yeshiva. Each of us yearned to join "the counterculture" – or what we perceived to be the counterculture – and to let our spirits go free, like letting loose all the animals from the local zoo for the sheer pleasure of watching them run as nature had intended.

But the first time I met Elisha, I felt no common sense of purpose. I saw him only by his appearance and, I now shamefacedly say, my judgment was harsh.

It was a Shabbos afternoon, at lunch at Mel's house, and from across the table I was introduced to Elisha and I was told that he, too, was considering joining the Havurah. But all I could see was an awkward, overweight, depressingly dressed young man in his mid-twenties, with a plump face and short, oh very short hair. Those were the days, of course, when the long-haired was a cultural hero and unkempt was a fashion of its own, and we followed real, although not strict, codes of appearance. Elisha fit nothing other than that from which I had sought to break away.

"This guy is going to be part of the Havurah that I want to join?" I thought. "This straight-looking dumpy guy is going to be part of my hippie paradise? What's happening here – are they fishing for members? Is everything very different from what I expected?"

I smiled at him and said hello. I paid him no further serious attention.

How was I to know, then, sitting at that table, that inside that excess baggage built up by too much kugel and cholent, behind the stumbling gestures and tentative words, beneath the silly clothes and unsure speech, dwelt a mind and a spirit that humbled mine in comparison? For if his soul were a well, a deep, dark well full of clear and sparkling water, mine in contrast was a shallow, dusty pit of lime, a narrow, empty hollowed-out hole at whose bottom lay a bit of mud and crumbling rock. And were his mind a mill, through which ran a rapid stream, turning a giant wheel that spun a powerful stone, mine in comparison was a little hurdy-gurdy machine, a hand-held organ grinder attached to a monkey who cranked out a tinkling, honky-tonky little tune.

But how was I to know all this, sitting at that table on a Shabbos afternoon? My subsequent realizations have been my retribution.

So, what had brought Elisha to that Shabbos table? What had led him down a road that was not a fork in his path but an altogether perpendicular avenue from the path he had been on?

Before returning to the Northeast, from where he originally grew up, Elisha had been out in the Midwest, in the most orthodox of orthodox yeshivas, the most scholarly of scholarly institutions where the Torah is studied in an unbroken tradition dating from the time of the destruction of the Temple, and whose line of succession snaked its way through Babylonia, across north Africa, into Spain, France, Germany, into Eastern Europe, and finally into little pockets of preservation scattered across the face of the modern world. There, in Or Ha-Torah Rabbinical Academy, he learned *mishnah* and *gemara*, *rishonim* and *acharonim*, *midrash* and *halachah*, prayed three times a day, fasted on fast days, feasted on festivals, wrapped himself in tradition, bound its laws onto his heart and onto his body, and, as was his belief, awakened early each morning to do the service of the Creator.

But in all that, in which every possible thought in the mind of man has its response, its allusion, and its counterthought in a holy book, and in which every waking moment has its mission in the evolution of the cosmos, still, there was a deficit. And so, at night, Elisha attended a local university, where he studied mathematics and psychology, a foray into secular learning that first had to be approved by the head of the yeshiva himself.

And yet, one foot in the door, and how wide the new world grows! It dawned on Elisha that outside his world, beyond its all-encompassing arms, waited a world, as if a different planet altogether, that seemingly could never be brought into the tradition's embrace. They were like skew lines which never meet and, traveling in different directions entirely, exert upon each other almost no influence. The attraction of making that leap onto the other plane, to see what was there, steadily grew inside of him.

"I saw my whole situation clearly one day," he told me later. "It was the day on which Martin Luther King was shot. I was walking home from the university one night, all by myself, and to get from the university to the yeshiva I had to go through a large section of the local black ghetto.

"I had no idea of what had happened. I never listened to the radio or read a newspaper, and so I just took my normal path through the ghetto. It was late, it was dark, and I was the only white person on the streets, dressed in my little black hat and black suit. And nothing happened to me. Nobody said anything. I just walked through the ghetto as if in a magic circle.

"Nothing happened! I was totally oblivious. When I got back to the yeshiva someone told me what was going on in the world, and remarked that to walk through the ghetto then was a sure way to get my head cracked open or a bullet in the back. But it was as if only someone so totally lost in another world could even dare to go there, much less walk right through it, alone at night, that he couldn't be taken seriously. I felt as if I was living in a time warp, a different century altogether, and so was invisible. And frankly, I believe that I *had* been in a different century."

From there, his awareness only grew, until finally the world of the yeshiva seemed ridiculous, a hermetic little island in a vast, alien sea. To Elisha, the sea became the alluring world, the vaster ocean into which he longed to plunge. But, patient and obedient, he could not merely quit, like a high school dropout, and run off with nothing to show for it. So, he decided to graduate, to finish in proper style, receive a rabbinical ordination, and *then* leave.

Patiently and silently, he studied all the necessary passages, the entire prescribed course of learning, in order to be given *smicha*. He worked diligently, evoking only the slightest suspicion among his teachers and fellow students. Some sensed that something was afoot, a few could see the distances growing between him and them, but as best he could, Elisha contained all his doubt, his enthusiasm and his heretical ideas.

At last, the day of his examination came. Humbly, he answered all the questions his teachers put to him. He discussed this text and that answer, and gave each problem its fullest consideration. He passed the exam, the ceremony was carried out, the handshakes were exchanged all around, and the papers were written and signed.

And then he left the yeshiva, and it all came out.

In his wake, the yeshiva was in an uproar. There was a temporary ban on all future ordinations. Friends turned their backs on him, and he was denounced publicly in class and in private conversations. He was considered an apostate, a traitor and a lost soul. It was a minor scandal and the word spread beyond the yeshiva, to other yeshivas in other cities. The threat of the *apikores*, the non-believer, burrowed its way like an invisible worm through Or Ha-Torah Rabbinical Academy, causing reaction and counterreaction to fly back and forth within its walls.

But Elisha was out. He had left all that behind. Before him, a new world opened up, with the colors and frenzy of a psychedelic flame. New sensations, new ideas, new experiences, awaited his innocent soul. Shy and naive, he stumbled through a world whose protocol he did not know, like a third-generation immigrant, and he found himself caught between his desire to learn and his lack of sophistication, which held him back and inhibited him.

But at least he could read, and he read everything he could get his hands on. In his reading, he happened to find out about the Havurah, a mixed-up Jewish counterculture community that both understood the language he already knew yet promised entrance to the world to come.

He visited, he talked to Mel, he met all the people at Havurat Chaim, and he wanted in.

What could have seemed more appealing? The world beckoned to him, and the Havurah was a way to soften the blow concealed in the beckoning hand. The world was full of marvelous excitement, and the Havurah, he felt, promised to help him see it without guilt or shame. The counterculture! Ah, the counterculture, throwing off the burdens of the previous generations – and a Jewish counterculture at that!

And so, when I saw that strange, awkward person sitting across from me at the table, how little I realized the chaotic world he was straining to embrace, and the wide-eyed fascination with which he greeted it.

But in time I learned. I threw away my superficial impressions and what I saw instead, over the ensuing weeks and months, was a voracious mind devour new ideas and sensations with an insatiable appetite. Commonplaces became the cause for wonder: Chinese and Italian restaurants became, to Elisha, exotic dens of illicit yet licit delight. Previously banned magazines piled up beside his bed – *Scientific American, Commentary, The New Republic, Playboy, Penthouse,* underground newspapers, each in its turn. The sex magazines were no doubt the most troubling, and they, too, piled up until, satiated with them, knowing them for all they could offer and realizing what they could not, he finally dumped them in the garbage in one great purging pile. At last it was a real woman that he needed, and the time for that was also approaching.

Movies, too, astounded him. Not having seen them since he was a child, not even on television, the fantasies projected on the modern screen made his mouth gape with wonder, each one exploding into his head like the seeds of new worlds, one after another after another. Beaches and woods seemed equally amazing, no longer merely metaphors in mystical texts but palpable, explorable realities.

As I grew to know Elisha, I took great pleasure in his fascination, cheering him on at each new step. It was not his act of overturning inhibiting beliefs that excited me, but I loved his realization that things he had previously held as evil or empty were, in fact, marvels in themselves, each with its own intricacies and profundity, each one a wonder of creation.

But above all, it was music that captured his soul. His first major expenditure was for a stereo, and when, after several months, the time finally came for Elisha to give in, with trepidation and fear as well as with no small excitement, and make his first foray into the field of the wondrous weed, he did not indulge in the heightened taste of food, or beg to be taken for a ride in the car to watch the world whoosh by in front of his eyes, nor did he run to the movies to watch a colorburst grab his imagination, but it was music he wanted, music that demanded his complete attention.

He sat down and played, over and over, the third movement of Haydn's 96th symphony. After playing it over and over, he actually started to weep.

"It's so perfect and so beautiful," he said, the tears running down his cheek. "It's so clear and joyous. They could make a religion out of this."

After he had listened and wept all he needed, he fell into a deep, restful sleep.

2

But not everything for Elisha was wonder and excitement. One thing held him back and caused him enormous pain. Simply, his parents were sick with grief at what they saw happening. They bit their hands, they could not sleep. What's more, Elisha's parents were no ordinary parents, whom the young can easily shunt aside and whose distress can be ignored as needless worry. Elisha's father was himself a rabbi, and led a small, aging, orthodox congregation in Fall River, a small, blighted mill city an hour's ride from Boston.

Even if he is your father, a rabbi cannot be taken lightly. And so, there in that decaying city, Elisha's parents tore themselves apart at what they had done wrong, at what Elisha had done wrong, at what God had done to them and how He was trying them. And because he was still, after all, a dutiful son, every other Saturday night, after Shabbos, Elisha would go downtown and board a bus to carry him to Fall River for another encounter with sorrow, family distress, and with spoken and silent accusation.

But my story is not about these predictable encounters that took place month after month for over a year. Rather, it is about one Saturday night that wasn't like the others.

Though it was supposed to have been one of those weeks in which he made his regular visit, this was a night of reprieve for Elisha. His family had gone on a trip to New Haven, to attend a weekend conference of New England orthodox rabbis. And so, Elisha was free to go to a party – not a large, wild party, but a small, friendly gathering taking place in the neighborhood. Mark, another Havurah member, had just moved into a new apartment and was having a housewarming celebration.

Elisha and I walked there together. It was a cool evening in the late fall and the trees had already begun to grow brown and bare. I wore a light woolen jacket, but Elisha still wore a long black overcoat, a solemn carry-over from his earlier wardrobe. We didn't say much, and the silence between us was awkward. So I stabbed into it directly, hoping to elicit conversation.

"I'll bet you're glad you don't have to go to Fall River tonight," I offered.

Elisha thought about it for a moment. "Yes. I am," he said.

Was that the whole conversation? I wondered. My heart sank. But after a pause, he continued.

"I'm very glad about it," he said. "It's a great relief. Each time I go, I know exactly what I'm in for, and each time it turns out just as I expect. But I go anyway."

"To make them happy?"

"That's just it – I go to make them happy, but it doesn't make them happy. They just keep looking at me sadly. My mother keeps feeding me and feeding me, and every once in a while my father throws in some comment about sin and morality.

"He gives me *mussar spiels*. Last time I was home, he gave me this long lecture about *shikses*." Without being aware of it, Elisha fell into his father's speech patterns, and repeated their conversation verbatim.

"'Elisha,'" Elisha said, unconsciously imitating his father, "So what is it you want? You want *shikses*? You think that's better than finding some Jewish girl and getting married? I know what you think. You go to the movies, don't you, and you see all those naked women. You look at magazines, and that's all you see. Naked women. It's *znoos*, Elisha, it's degeneracy. You should get married, and you'll find out that that's not all life's about. We're not animals, Elisha. We're not animals."

"So, what did you tell him?" I asked.

"I didn't tell him anything," Elisha answered. "He thinks he understands, but he doesn't understand anything. He sees it only in his terms."

"And that place you live in," Elisha continued, again slipping into his father's speech, "it's an abomination. It calls itself Jewish, but it's not Jewish – it's *apikorsus*. And what do they know there? – they mix up everything all together, they do whatever they like, they throw out this *halachah* and that *halachah*, just if they don't happen to like it. How can they say they follow mitzvahs if the whole idea of *mitzvah*, of something you're commanded to do by God, is something you reject? It's not a mitzvah if *you* decide what you like and what you don't like. It's not up to you. You know that, Elisha, you're a smart boy. You've learned." He paused, and then continued.

"And what else do they do there? I hear stories about that place, Elisha. I hear stories about drugs there, and sex. Don't try any drugs, Elisha – you'll become an addict, it'll kill you. You want to end up in a hospital?"

And then his voice trailed off to a whisper. "I'm ashamed enough, Elisha. You don't think they talk about you? The other rabbis, they know. They've heard. And it makes me ashamed in front of them. They say it's a terrible thing when a man has lost his faith, and it hurts me to hear that said about you, a rabbi's son – a rabbi yourself!"

At this point, Elisha coughed up a laugh. "If he only knew about the Havurah. It's really such a bourgeois place in so many ways. Drugs and sex! He's afraid I'll go to orgies! I only wish there *were* orgies! It's funny how everybody looks in from the outside and figures that's what has to be going on in there. And then when you get inside, you see there are many of the same taboos inside as exist on the outside. But everybody figures that a place that manages to break some barriers is able to do it to all of them. And that's what scares them – the possibility of really destroying taboos. They'd love to do it themselves, but since they can't, they get scared and defensive if anyone else can, even a little." He laughed again. "It's ridiculous."

"That's the great myth of the Havurah Orgy," I said. "Every year they say, 'This is the year for the Havurah orgy,' and of course, every year, it's only a myth."

"And then, you know what he did?" Elisha added, ignoring my comment and returning to his original topic. "He pulled something straight out of his weekly sermon and laid it on me. Last week's *parashah* was the Akedah, so that's what he had on his mind. 'Elisha,' he told me (and here Elisha slipped, again, into his father's voice), 'look at the Akedah compared to the way the goyim see what goes on between a father and a son. I know,

I've read around, I took some college courses, too. I know what I'm talking about. Look at the Greeks. That Oedipus myth, where the son kills his father and then marries his mother. And look at the Christians – they believe the father kills the son. That's not Jewish. What happens to Abraham and Isaac? They go *together*, Elisha, they walk together up the mountain, they share the same vision. So, what are you rebelling against, Elisha?'"

And then, continuing his father's words, but hesitantly, as if he didn't know if he should share this part with me or not, he added in a low voice, "'*Ach*, Elisha – you're killing me.'"

I was silent. Finally, I asked, "So what did you say?"

"Again, I didn't say anything. I felt like saying, 'Oh, yeah? But look what Abraham was leading Isaac *to*!' But I didn't. I didn't say anything. Because I couldn't talk to him in his terms – that would be futile. Every ideology has its own escape valves and its own ways to cover itself. Freudian psychology, Marxist economics, every religion – they all have ways to cover up their own inconsistencies and throw the problem back at the person who doesn't believe, making *him* the villain rather than revealing a flaw in the ideology itself. And so, if I even chose to speak his language, he would have answered in a way in which *I* would be wrong. So, I just said nothing. Nothing at all."

We walked on in silence until we reached Mark's new home. It was an old frame house, slightly rundown, like so many others in the area. We paused at the stairs and then walked inside.

At the top of the stairs we pushed open an unlocked door and Mark rushed over to greet us.

"Hello! Hello!" he bubbled. "Come into my brand-new home. Sit down, make yourselves comfortable."

I could see into the living room where a few ratty chairs and an old sofa ringed the room. There was a smattering of people inside and the lights were low. I was just about to throw my jacket onto whatever surface would hold it when Elisha stopped in the hallway to admire the only piece of furniture that stood there, a small table on which the telephone sat.

"This is a marvelous table," he said aloud.

Mark came over and stood behind him.

"This table is amazing," Elisha said again. "Where did you get it?"

Mark was pleased it was noticed.

"That's an old family piece," he explained. "My great-grandfather made it when he first came to this country; it was part of a whole set, I think, but the rest just disappeared. He was a carpenter and made his furniture by hand. When my grandmother died, she left it to my parents, but they didn't know what to do with it and stuck it in storage. It was just gathering dust, so I took it. I keep the phone on it."

I went over to the table, where it was being admired. In truth, it was a marvel of design.

It bore no human or animal pictures but had a motif of flowers within flowers within flowers. Its intricacy was astounding and yet rough-hewn, almost peasant-like in character. Together we admired it, but Elisha seemed far more taken than I was.

"This is incredible," he said. "Amazing,"

His mind was still so agog with the world, I thought.

"I'm glad you like it," Mark answered.

I went to the living room, poured myself a glass of wine, and plopped down onto the sofa. Elisha, too, entered the room. Hesitantly, he lifted the bottle of wine. "Is it okay if I take some?" he asked Mark.

"Sure. Go right ahead."

Elisha poured himself half a thumb's worth and then sat down on the floor.

What is time on a Saturday night? Something to be spent, to be squandered, to be disposed of with as little pain as possible and a maximum of frivolity. Half an hour passed, an hour, and I was doing fine. The wine helped and the conversation was good. Elisha, too, grew more comfortable. In that dark room we all talked and laughed.

Suddenly, the phone rang.

"Elisha, it's for you."

Elisha went over to the table, where the receiver was lying on its side, like a child asleep. He picked it up and put it to his ear.

I watched him as he stood framed by the doorway, the bright light of the hallway illuminating him from behind and making him stand out starkly against the darkness of the living room. I watched as his face grew blank and impassive. Dully, he stared down, without concentration, at the roseate pattern in the table, as if seeing but not seeing, looking through it and yet not even realizing it was there.

I had no idea of exactly what he heard. But I knew, at that moment, despite the wine I had drunk, from the cold otherness which pulled Elisha totally out of the party's mood, that something powerful was happening to him from the other end of the telephone line.

He pulled a little pad from his pocket and scribbled something on it. Then he looked into the room, located me in the darkness, and beckoned for me to join him.

"Please come with me," he said.

I grabbed my jacket and followed him down the stairs. On the street, he spoke.

"My father just died. Heart attack. I have to go to New Haven." His words were clipped and direct. The darkness swooshed down around us.

Mark came rushing down the stairs after us. "Are you okay? Why are you rushing off? Is everything all right?"

"Yeah, it's okay," Elisha said. "I just have to go. I'll tell you later. Really, I'm sorry."

"That's all right," Mark said. "See you later." He went back upstairs and we heard the door close behind him.

We hurried off, retracing the steps we had taken earlier in the evening, but this time with the sense of urgency that only a death can bring.

"Could you take me to the bus?" Elisha asked.

"Sure," I said. "You want me to drive you instead?"

"To New Haven? No, no. I'll go myself."

"Do you want to borrow my car?"

"No, I'd rather not drive. Just get me to the bus. Call the station, find out when it leaves."

When we reached the Havurah, I called the station while Elisha grabbed a few items. There was one more bus leaving that night. In silence, we sped downtown, just in time for the last departure.

The station was practically deserted, and our footsteps resounded coldly on the stone floor. The overhead fluorescent bulbs cast a harsh light over the rows of empty benches. Elisha bought a ticket and handed it to the bus driver. I watched, saying nothing, as he, too, said nothing, merely nodded to me, and disappeared into the bus. I watched it pull away, and then I returned to the Havurah.

The next time I saw Elisha was late the following afternoon, at the Fall River cemetery. Nothing travels as quickly as the news of death, and there, in the cemetery, all the different avenues of Elisha's father's life were suddenly united. Old people huddled together in little groups, like the many tilting gravestones that dotted the landscape. Family, rigid and stunned, stood around, staring aimlessly. And we, outsiders, Elisha's friends, stood off by ourselves, talking in low whispers, oddly present at the graveside of a man we didn't know, but there for the sake of his son.

Together, we all awaited the hearse which was on its way from New Haven to this mournful ground, bearing the body of Elisha's father, along with the living bodies of Elisha, his mother, and his only brother.

It grew late. At last, we saw the long, black hearse pull up through the cemetery gates, slowly drive up the driveway, and come to a stop. Everybody rushed to meet it.

Elisha got out, the first to do so. The ripped pocket of his shirt hung down and flapped against him, and his face bore the frozen look of terrified surprise, like the snapshot of a man seated in the front car of a rollercoaster about to career crazily down the first great slope. He turned around and helped his mother out of the car.

His mother was not an old woman, but neither was she young. She was small and stocky, and her eyes were red and swollen. Passively, she let herself be helped from the car.

Elisha's brother followed. He was a thin, sallow young man with a slight growth of beard on an already haggard face. The word was whispered through the crowd that he was not well.

And then the back of the hearse opened, and a long, plain, light brown box was slid out. Hands reached to grab it, and suddenly it was jostling its way through the crowd, which parted to make way for its passage. It led the way and the crowd followed behind, letting the coffin direct the path to the waiting grave.

We picked our way through rows of gravestones. As the pit came into view, the obviously waiting hole into which Elisha's father was to be lowered, his mother grew suddenly violent. Undrugged, neither sedated by pill or injection, grief stabbed her afresh as she saw this new addition to the scene, this final destination which would receive her husband's body and claim its undivided hold upon it. Her hands shot out and she clutched the air.

"My beautiful man," she wailed. "My baby, my darling beautiful man." On either side, arms held her back as she struggled forward with her hands like a drowning swimmer. "My beautiful. My love. My baby, my husband," she cried out. She sobbed and howled and then she grew quiet again.

We reached the grave. The casket was lowered in. As the wife of the dead man sobbed and cried, restrained and supported by dozens of hands, a man with a black hat and a long curly black beard began to speak above the crowd, delivering a eulogy in Yiddish.

He spoke on and on, and I understood not a word. When he finished, he stood with his hands clasped in front of him, and he swayed back and forth, his eyes shut tightly, while saying prayers for the dead.

And then he stopped, opened his eyes, and, as is the Jewish custom, picked up a shovel, jammed it underside upwards, deep into the mound of sandy earth by the side of the grave, and tossed a great shovelful onto the coffin in the pit.

Then, as is also the custom, he handed the shovel to the man beside him, who did the same, tossing in his own shovelful. Then Elisha took the shovel and did likewise. It was passed next to the old men of the congregation. Each one, with his feeble arms, barely able to lift the shovel itself, dropped the end of its point into the waiting mound and flung a tiny clump onto the coffin, sending a dusting of earth over the large box. One by one they did this, until each had added his share.

Suddenly a murmur went through the crowd. "Yes – no – should he? Shouldn't he?"

What were they talking about? I recognized the sound of urging and encouragement: "Go ahead, go ahead," like when old men drape a tallis over you and push you up for an aliyah.

I saw Elisha's brother step forward, bend down, grab a fistful of light brown dirt in his pale, white hands, and then, with a jerky, spastic motion, fling it into the grave. He then disappeared back into the crowd.

"Good! Good!" they mumbled.

But then, we looked in, and saw such a tiny pile of earth scarcely covering one side of the coffin. After all that, it still was open to the sky, barely buried. And so, from a motion by the man who had said the prayers, Mel moved forward and also took up the shovel. Another shovel was handed to Heligman. Together, with far greater strength than any who preceded them, they thrust their shovels deep into the waiting pile of dirt, kicked them down until the head was entirely covered, and over and again brought up heaping shovelfuls which they tossed upon the coffin.

Some of the older men looked puzzled. 'Who are these young people?' they asked themselves.

Each shovelful made a thumping sound as it hit the coffin, followed by a little rattling spray of sand. Time after time it continued, wordlessly, as we stood by and watched. And then they passed their shovels to Chief and to Max, who again followed with heaping shovelfuls. They worked at it, over and over, and then passed it on to other members of the Havurah, to Mark, to Leon, to me, to Ira. Soon, all the young men of the Havurah had entirely covered up Elisha's father, while the aged, withering congregants stood by and stared, with a mixture of approval and distrust playing in their weak and watery eyes.

And that is the story of the death of Elisha's father, although the story of Elisha himself does not at all end here.

But I see that you've already finished your dinner. It's time for some singing and then *birkat ha-mazon*.

OF TURBOT AND A TURRET

Aaah.

Now that we've finished Shabbos dinner, are full and satisfied, and there's nothing more we could ask for – or so it seems – and now that we are done with the interminable *birkat ha-mazon*, let me tell you the story of a different dinner I had one Friday night, a couple of years ago.

In the old days, there was magic in the air. Everything went right, everything was an adventure. People were less afraid of doing the right thing, because the straight and narrow was really a broad, expanding highway down which you could roam in all directions, like a child in a field of poppies, without worrying about crossing over into some improper realm, past the mean "No Trespassing" sign of forbidden territory.

That's not to say that everything was up for grabs, but rather that once the restrictions were lifted, we were certain that newer, more human directions would be found, growing from essential truths rather than imposed on us from received conceptions.

Oh, but enough of this. I don't mean to preach, and sometimes I can sound that way.

Back then, those were the days when Esther and I were lovers, or were having an affair, or were enjoying sleeping together as friends, or were "getting it together," or whatever you call it. I don't know what to call it because we ourselves didn't quite know what it was and we weren't pushing too hard for a definition, because, well, we didn't *need* a definition at the time. We were young and we enjoyed each other's company. It was simple – although perhaps not really quite that simple, because nothing ever is – but that was sufficient for a while at least.

It was a Friday night. The lights were low and the house was neat, as happens, miraculously, once a week in that brief period between Friday afternoon and Saturday evening, after which, like the world, due to no one's fault in particular, it returns to its normal state of chaos and confusion. But now it was beautiful, our counterculture hippie house turned into a palace.

And something delicious was cooking in the oven: a wonderful aroma filled the whole downstairs, permeating the air like a friendly incense. Something delicious was cooking in the oven.

Services had just ended. Everybody had gone around and hugged each other, exchanged some words, said "Good Shabbos," a process that sometimes takes as long as the services themselves, sometimes even longer. Certainly it was as much fun, and it was a basic although unofficial Havurah activity. The hugging and chatting were about over, and people were going off, in little groups of two, five, six, or whatever, to enjoy Shabbos dinner in various homes.

As it happened, this week the people living in the Havurah house were on "Guests." To be on Guests meant making sure that any Shabbos guests from out of town had a place to eat and feel welcome. It's a lovely task, to be sure, full of mitzvahs and good deeds that get stored up in the world to come, but tonight, we knew, was going to be a strange night. Elisha, Esther and I, who were the members of the house eating at home that particular Shabbos, were expecting two guests. One was a woman whom Elisha had invited, his own personal guest, a quiet, pretty woman with long black hair whom Elisha, with his new outlook on life, was simply aching to get to know better, and the second, who had called earlier in the week to let us know that he was coming, was Samuel Goodman.

How can I begin to describe Samuel Goodman? If the Havurah is made up of monsters, with one foot in one world and one foot in the other, he was a monster too, but with one foot in one world and two feet in the other. And his two feet were in what he liked to call "the *yeshivishe velt.*" Goodman didn't know whether to make the leap and throw over his academic studies entirely and commit himself to living in a yeshiva, or whether he should become a hippie with a yarmulke. He couldn't figure out whether he was a *ba'al t'shuvah* or a free thinker. He was terrified of women and painfully awkward around them, which of course made it easier to be a *ba'al t'shuvah*. Full of tics and stutters, dressed like his mother's little twelve-year-old in baggy pants, a pot belly bulging at his middle, he didn't cut a dashing figure. But his heart was sweet and good, humble and meek; without a doubt, he caused himself more pain than he caused others.

"Good Shabbos, Samuel. How are you?" I asked.

"*Boruch ha-Shem,*" he said, his head bobbing up and down. "I – I – I don't remember your name, I'm sorry."

"It's Solomon," I said. "We've met a million times before."

"I – I know. I just didn't remember. It slipped my mind."

"That's okay. No big deal. Well, I heard you' re staying for Shabbos."

"Th-that's right. I – I walked all the way from Brookline."

"That's a long walk. You could have taken a bus."

"I – I know, but the b-bus ride might have lasted into Shabbos. I was a l-little late, and I didn't want to be on the b-bus when Shabbos came."

"Well, you could have gotten off the bus before Shabbos and walked from wherever it let you off. It might have been easier."

"I – I know," he said. He looked a little panic-stricken when he realized this possibility, as if he had been caught sinning. "I just d-didn't want to do that."

"Okay. Well, no matter."

Esther walked over to greet the guest. "Good Shabbos, Samuel, how are you?"

"Oh, I'm fine. Good Shabbos, I'm fine," he stammered. Esther's presence upset him, although he tried to be calm. He looked at her very quickly, up and down, and then turned to me.

"Is that dinner? It smells good. Wh-what is it?"

"It's fish," I said. "Doesn't it smell good? It's got mushrooms and cheese and spices. In fact, it should be delicious."

"Oh, fish," he said, half-dreaming. "What kind of fish is it?"

"What kind? Uh, it's turbot."

"Turbot!" he exclaimed, and his eyes filled with fear.

"Yeah, turbot – cheapest fish in the supermarket. Is that okay?"

"Oh my God," he said nervously. "Turbot!"

"What's the matter? You don't like turbot?"

"It's not kosher," he said, with the terror of scandal in his voice.

"What do you mean it's not kosher? Of course it's kosher."

"It's not kosher," he insisted.

"Gee, I always thought it was kosher," I said. "It's like a halibut or a cod or something like that. That would make it kosher, I suppose. How do you know it's not kosher?"

"I a-asked my rebbe. I saw it in the market, too, and I had never heard of it before, so I went and asked my rebbe if it was kosher and he said, 'no.'"

Esther turned to me and said, "Well, we sure have been eating a lot of it lately."

"Yeah, but I still think it's kosher," I answered.

"My rebbe says it isn't."

"Well, let's ask Elisha. He should know. Hey Elisha – come here for a second."

Elisha, who had been talking in great earnest to his black-haired guest, came over. She followed behind.

"Hi Samuel, Good Shabbos. How are you?" Elisha said.

"*Boruch ha-Shem,*" he said, again nodding up and down.

"Elisha," I said, "Samuel said that his rebbe said that turbot isn't kosher. Is that true?"

Elisha just looked blank for a moment. Then he stuck out his lower lip, made a vague gesture with his hand, and said, "I dunno. I thought it was kosher. Why shouldn't it be? Doesn't it have fins and scales?"

"I don't know," I said. "I never saw it except cut up into fillets in the supermarket display case. But I think it's kosher. Maybe it's not."

"What did your rebbe say?" Esther asked. "Did he know what kind of fish it was, or did he just say don't eat it if you don't know what it is?"

"He said not to eat it. He said he didn't think it was kosher."

"He wasn't sure?"

"No. But he said don't eat it."

"Well," I said, "maybe he was just playing it safe."

"Well," Samuel said, shifting from foot to foot, a bit uncomfortable, "I wouldn't want to do what my rebbe told me not to."

"I can understand that," I said. "I certainly wouldn't want you to go against what your rebbe said."

Elisha, always genial, agreed. "Sure, I wouldn't say to go against your rebbe," he said, slowly shaking his head.

"Not me," Esther said, putting her hand to her chest. "I wouldn't want you to go against your rebbe. Not me."

The three of us stood there, shaking our heads slowly, disclaiming all disloyalty to one's rebbe, while Samuel shifted from one foot to the other, and Elisha's black-haired friend stood silently by, her hands behind her back.

"Not me."

"No, sir. Not me."

"I wouldn't, not me."

"Well," said Samuel finally, "wh-what do we do about dinner? We'll have to th-throw it out."

I looked at Esther. She looked at me. We looked at Elisha. He looked back at us.

"We should *throw it out*?" I said. "But then, what's for dinner?"

"But it's not *kosher*," Samuel insisted.

"Hmm . . ." said Elisha.

"Hmmm . . ." said Esther.

"Hmmmm," I said. And Elisha's black-haired friend looked on, in turn looking at each of us, her eyes wide and expecting.

"Well," said Elisha with authority, "I guess we can't eat it."

"But then we'll have to do something else for dinner," I said. Then an idea came to me. "Listen," I said. "We'll have to eat at different houses. Let's ask if we can eat with other people in the Havurah. If we split up, they can make room for us. How about that? Would that be okay with you, Samuel?"

"I guess so," he said. "I – I'm sorry for the inconvenience."

"No inconvenience at all!" I answered. "I'll be right back."

I dashed across the street to Max and Rebecca's. They opened the door – they were on the verge of saying kiddush.

I explained the situation and asked if they had room for one more – Samuel.

"Sure," said Rebecca, always generous. "Send him over."

I ran back across the street. "Samuel," I said, "I've arranged dinner for you with Max and Rebecca. Is that okay?"

"It's okay with me," he replied. "But what will *you* do for dinner? You can't eat the fish – it's, it's *traif.*"

"Well, we'll probably figure out something. Open a can of tuna fish or something like that. We'll scrounge up something."

"Is that okay? Tuna fish for Shabbos dinner?"

"Sure, sure. But Max and Rebecca were all set to say kiddush, so don't keep them waiting."

"Oh my God – I don't want to miss kiddush!"

"No, I guess not."

"Well, bye-bye. Good Shabbos. Have a good dinner." And with that, he scooted out the door and ran across the street.

We watched him go, turned to each other, and laughed. "Well, what do we do now?" I asked.

Indeed, what *do* we do? Could we just lie to Samuel and go ahead and happily eat our turbot, now that it was suspect? Do we throw it out only on the grounds that it *might* be suspect? Does Samuel's rebbe decide for us too?

"Well, I'm not against eating it," Esther said.

"Well, neither am I," said Elisha. "I don't think it's traif. But on the other hand, we can't just lie to Samuel like that."

He turned to his dark-haired friend. "Would you eat it?"

She looked back at him with total innocence. "Sure, I'd eat it."

"I'd eat it too," I said.

"Well," said Elisha, "we all agree that we'd all eat it. So, what do we do with it?"

Esther, forever ready to turn to the devices of modern convenience, had a bright idea. "Let's eat it with plastic forks on paper plates. That way, even if it does turn out to be traif, we won't have traifed anything up."

Elisha looked at her. Then at me. He scratched his cheek. Then, the rabbi spoke. "Well, I guess," he said hesitantly. "But do we just eat it here, in the dining room, like a regular Shabbos dinner, if it's suspect?"

"Listen," I said, "why don't we eat separately. Esther and I will take our portions up to my room, and you two can eat in Elisha's room. That way it's just like our personal decision. How about that?"

Esther, I could tell, liked the idea. Elisha, after scratching his cheek for a minute, liked the idea too. He turned to his friend. "Would that be okay with you?" he asked, again a bit hesitantly.

She smiled a small smile and shrugged her shoulders. "Okay."

"Great! No problem!" I exclaimed.

Then, in an instant, a flurry of activity began. We ran into the kitchen, going to shelves, into drawers, pulling out paper plates, plastic forks and knives, glass *yahrzeit* tumblers which, since they were glass, were unable to attract *traifos* to their non-porous surfaces (according to the rabbanim), getting the challahs and pulling the salad out of the refrigerator.

Everything was ready in no time at all, stacked on trays and ready to be taken upstairs, into the land of no contradictions. All that was left was the fish.

Esther went over to the oven. We all gathered around as she opened the oven door and, with a potholder, slid out the fish. And there it was, two great, big, white fillets of turbot, like two great slabs of leviathan, covered with spices and mushrooms, swimming in a light sauce and giving off a strong, delicious aroma that went right to our readying appetites.

"Mmmm . . ."

"Ummm . . ."

"Yummm . . ."

The level of excitement rose in each of us. We were hungry and filled with anticipation. Quickly, we divided up the fish with our plastic knives, put it onto paper plates, and took the whole thing up to our rooms.

"Have a good dinner," I said to the two of them.

Elisha was a little embarrassed. "Yeah, you too."

"We will," I trilled, as Esther and I hurried up the stairs. We went up to the fourth floor, to my room.

"Let's eat in the turret," I suggested, and Esther quickly agreed.

I pushed back the thick curtain that covered the entrance to the turret. It was cold inside, and pitch black. I brought over my electric heater, plugged it in, turned it on, and within a few seconds a soft, orange glow lit up the bottom of that little room. We could barely see the wooden walls around us and over our heads, and, as they converged towards the peak, they disappeared into the blackness.

We sat down on the cushions on the floor and spread out our feast between us.

"Oh, we forgot some napkins. Wait a minute, I'll be right back." I jumped up, found my way through the opening, and hurried down the stairs.

On my way down to the kitchen, I passed Elisha's room. The two of them were sitting at a tiny table and Elisha was leaning forward, talking again in great earnest, while his dark-haired guest sat staring across at him, silently, her eyes wide and innocent. I hurried on.

I grabbed some napkins and hurried back upstairs. The turret had already begun to warm up, and Esther had neatly arranged our dinner plates on the floor.

"All set," I said, as I sat down.

"Do you want to say kiddush? Or shall I?"

"You say kiddush," Esther said.

I raised the glass of wine and rattled off kiddush by memory, in one great stream of syllables. I ran together all the words, which told of the marvels of creation and rest, and then of that second birth, the passage from slavery into freedom. Had I stopped to think where I was, I would undoubtedly have lost my place and been unable to continue.

Then Esther removed the cloth from on top of the challah, picked up the loaf, said the *motzi*, sprinkled a little salt on it, and broke it in two. She handed me one piece while she pulled the innards out of her half and started to eat it.

"Before we start, there's one more thing," I said.

"What!?" Esther exclaimed, half peeved and half surprised. She was obviously hungry and wanted to begin our dinner. "What else is there?"

"Well," I said, "I *just happen* to have this joint in my pocket."

"Oh, goody!" And she clapped her hands in sudden glee.

I lit the joint and took a deep toke. I handed it to Esther, who also took a deep toke. We began to relax. We each took a deep breath. Another toke, and we were more relaxed. Back and forth, until the joint was smoked down to a tiny little roach and went out.

By then, we were very relaxed. We weren't sitting up anymore but were lying on our sides, resting on our elbows. We began to giggle. But our appetites were still strong and hearty, and we were famished. The munchees grabbed hold of us, and with great enthusiasm we dished out our wonderful wonderful wonderful leviathan, smelling richly and sensuously of frankincense and myrrh, and we heaped up the luscious, colorful delights of the garden, covered with spices and oil, next to our mythic creature of the deep, on our paper plates with our plastic forks.

What a marvelous feast it was! There was wine, and challah, and all types of delicacies. Everything was delicious; our taste buds were sensitive and grateful, pleasure was bursting on our tongues and then sliding down and satisfying a deeper, hidden appetite inside.

We ate and laughed and drank and were happy. We were fascinated with every bite we took. That such wonderful things could be was beyond us. All we could do was eat joyfully and be thankful. The heater glowed and made the turret warmer and warmer, a toasty, cozy warm.

We didn't talk much but our eyes twinkled with delight and satisfaction, as we gobbled up everything, leaf by leaf and morsel by morsel, and drained our cups until the last drops were gone. We licked the rims of our glasses and mopped up our plates.

At last we were finished; there was nothing left to eat, and we were no longer hungry for any sort of food. We felt warm and well fed, and our skin was now being toasted from both inside and out.

And now, we were hungry again: another appetite blossomed within us, stoked by the fire of our new warmth and well-being.

The understanding between us at that moment was one of perfect harmony and we grew tremendously excited by what we knew was to follow next. We pushed our plates aside. Not carelessly yet with great liveliness, piece by piece, layer by layer, we removed our earthly garments. We stretched out on the cushions and the orange glow of the heater illuminated our bodies with a bright and cheerful light.

I won't bore you with the details of what happened next, although I'm sure that the details wouldn't bore you at all. We went this way and that, doing one thing after another, repeating our feast again, with all its savor and fascination that such wondrous things can be. The turret closed around us, holding us safely within it, and its tapering top stretched up into the sky while we lay at the bottom as if in the mouth of a fruitful horn of plenty, in a magical tetrahedron, the inhabitants of a dark and wooded bower that stretched up like the tents of the righteous, way above our heads.

At last we were all done, immobile, wrapped around each other, feeling full and satisfied.

We were silent for a long time, until finally Esther spoke. "Thank God that turbot's traif," she said, with satisfaction.

"But it's *not* traif," I answered her. "It's kosher. That's the *whole point* of it all."

Then, in a voice that betrayed a tiny, tiny bit of peeve and disappointment, she asked me, softly, "That's not the *whole* point of it, is it?"

I paused. I heard the heater's steady hum and felt its warm air blow over me. Deep in the midst of my deep sensation of wellbeing, I gave a little, tiny start.

"No-o," I said slowly, measuring my words. "I suppose it's not the *whole* point." And then I was silent, and I listened to the hum of the heater, droning on into the night.

THE MYSTIC

Yes, those were days of freedom and discovery. They were innocent and semi-innocent days.

And yet, for all their breadth and scope, expanding on a cloud of naive exuberance, they were also caught, as it were, on the point of a thousand intersecting forces, and balanced delicately on that point. Indeed, the balance was more delicate than we realized, and being perched so precariously, they were subject to the slightest atmospheric disturbances. Even the push and pull of our own human nature, reaction and counterreaction, without the need of any external pressure, was enough to keep us from getting lost in them entirely.

So here's a different story, for all it's worth.

The telephone rang. It rang again. And again. I got up to answer it. Why did I always have to answer the phone? Other people were also living in the house, why don't they ever answer it? Some communal spirit, I grumbled. I was annoyed. I picked up the receiver.

"Hello?"

"Hello, is Ira there?" breathed a soft, smooth, female voice.

"Hold on."

I tramped down to Ira's room and knocked on his door. No answer. I turned and was about to leave when a voice from within, a small, low voice, called out, "Yes?"

I opened Ira's door. Ira's room, large and irregular, was dark; it was always dark, except for a small candle burning on his desk. Shadows devoured almost everything, and the candle, scented, sent a delicate fragrance through the room, mingling with the shadows. Corners disappeared into blackness; barely visible were the strange pictures and symbols hung on his walls. Odd, antique pieces of furniture were placed around the room. An oriental carpet covered the floor.

Ira sat at an old wooden writing table by the window which looked out into the black night. A book was open beneath the candlelight. Ira didn't even look up.

"Phone, Ira," I said tersely.

"Who is it?" he asked, in a cool voice.

"I don't know," I answered. "A woman."

"Could you tell her to call back?" he said. "If it's my mother, tell her I'm studying. If it's Consuela, tell her I'm meditating."

"Sure, sure," I said, closing the door. I left him to his shadows.

What did he think I was, his secretary? What made him so special that he could put people off like that, and tell others to do his bidding?

I knew the answer, of course. It was because he thought he was a great mystic. When caught up in his spiritual meditations, he couldn't be bothered; nothing was worth being disturbed for when he was communing with the great Being. Certainly, nothing was as important as that. All activity must be suspended and taken care of by others, during his moments of sublime inspiration.

But what about me? Wasn't I also a hippie holyman? Didn't I also understand all about the great peace-love-soul connection? Maybe not always, but I'd had my moments, my own personal revelations, and I didn't take them lightly. But this condescension, this superrighteousness that he carried around with him as he played out his role of being our elect-in-residence, it was maddening.

I picked up the phone. Somehow I knew that this was not his mother on the other end. "Hello, Ira's busy at the moment. Could you call him back later?"

"Oh, surely," whispered the voice. "Oh, I hope I didn't disturb him. You know, he has such important spiritual business to attend to."

Sure. I know. "Is this Consuela?"

"Yess," she answered, in a sibilant hush.

"Well, he told me to ask you if you could call back later because he's meditating."

"Oh, good – *good*," she said, with extra emphasis on the second 'good.' "He has such fine meditations."

"Yeah. Well . . . I guess you could try him in about half an hour."

"Do you really think he'll be finished by then?" There was a note of anxiety in her voice.

"I really can't say," I replied. I waited, rather impatiently, for her next comment.

"Well, just tell him that Consuela called. *Could* you? Could you do that?"

"Sure. I think I can do that."

"Oh, *thank* you," she said breathily. "Ba-bye."

"Bye." I put down the receiver.

Him and his weirdo friends, I thought, as I walked back to my room and closed the door. What was he doing down there in his dark room behind closed doors, anyway? Was he transmuting his soul into hoops of fire and jumping through them in weightless flight? Was he swinging, like a gymnast, through the cosmic monkey bars? Or was he sitting there, head in hands, pronouncing the unutterable names of God and being accorded strange spiritual powers? Did he have visions of the mystical spheres, did he melt into white light? Or did he just stare out the window and look at the stars? Who knows. He certainly spent enough time in there.

"Ow!" I suddenly yelled aloud, as a splinter from my coarse wooden floor drove itself into my big toe.

"Jesus Christ!" I howled, as I felt the throb of pain. I hobbled over to my bed and sat down. I took off my sock and, holding my foot in my hand, stared at my foot. There, jabbed into the fleshy part of my big toe, was a large splinter. There was even a little blood around it.

"God*damn*," I said, and I hobbled over to my desk and rummaged around in a junk-filled drawer for a pin and a pair of tweezers.

Standing there, on one foot, the other held into the air, I finally dug out what I needed, hopped back to my bed, and sat down.

Probing with the pin, pulling with the tweezers, I managed to butcher my toe in a minor fashion and extract the painful sliver. I held it up, between my thumb and forefinger, and examined it.

At first, I marveled at its size. "This is a freakin' big splinter," I said aloud.

I stared at it in wonder. But the more I looked at it, the more I realized that, as an entity, as a thing in itself, it was not really very big at all. In fact, it was tiny. Barely the length of my fingernail and ever so thin, it was practically nothing, nothing at all.

Scrutinizing it, I suddenly felt a strange sensation and then a peculiar shift of perspective. It was as if I was a huge monster inspecting a tiny, delicate gem. It seemed as if I were sitting very far up, peering all the way down at something very far below. I rolled the splinter between my fingers, felt its consistency, watched it twirl. Then I looked at it again.

Could I, I wondered, see *into* the splinter, through it, beyond it? Could I, if I tried, see it break down into its ever-tinier components, observe the frenzy of its molecules, see the spin of its atoms? Could I see the world-within-worlds contained in this splinter?

Could I see its raw material essence, and how that essence itself came from the primal chunk of life, matter, and energy that, together, composed the universe? If I tried, could I see the divine sparks, exiled into worldly matter, that pervade all material creation? If I made the effort, could I look at this splinter, this sliver from my floor, and perceive the totality and oneness of everything?

I stared. I tried to imagine. My eyebrows knit together in concentration.

But nothing like that came to me. Instead, as my mind began to wander off, memories came to me, pouring up from inside my brain, and I thought of a Friday night dinner that occurred just a few weeks earlier in the Havurah dining room.

The lights had been turned down low, even lower than normal for our regular Friday nights, and I sat at the table with Ira and his friends. Ira's friends came from all over town, a motley group that he had assembled from all the different spiritual trips in Cambridge. I looked around me: There was Ira, Consuela, Robin Raven, Yankele, and Elizabeth. I was there because, after all, it was my home, too, and I needed a place to eat, so I joined them for dinner.

Around the Havurah, Consuela had been nicknamed "The Countess" because she always wore long black dresses that trailed along the floor. Of

Mediterranean origin somewhere, small and bone thin, almost emaciated, she held herself erect. She was proud and dignified, and had dark eyes, dark skin, and a slight accent to her breathy voice.

"For a long time I frequented Sister Scarlet," she had told me, "but now I spend my time at the Four Seas."

"The Four Seas?" I asked.

"Yes," she replied, with perfect poise. "The Cambridge Cosmic Consciousness Center."

Robin Raven, sitting next to her, dressed in blue jeans and a T-shirt, her breasts bouncing around underneath, was endowed with amazing energy and an unusually intense stare. Having herself bounced around from commune to crash pad all across the country, she had picked up a truly catholic range of orientations, an extensive vocabulary of religious jargon, and a prodigious number of vivid experiences – road trips, acid trips, sexual adventures, hard work, fun, poverty – an awesome personal odyssey within just a few short years. Ira had met her at Wednesday night Sufi dancing at a Cambridge church.

Across from her, dreaming to himself, sat Yankele. Yankele was pale, thin, and had a long scraggly beard. There were large circles beneath his eyes. In his younger days, he had been part of a Jewish-hippie-mystical music group that toured the country, playing backup tambourine for a folk-singing rabbi who told Hasidic stories, sent his audiences into frenzies of dancing and singing, talked about peace and brotherhood, and ran around from city to city visiting pockets of his young, starry-eyed followers, and then running off again for his next engagement. Having quit the music group, Yankele was now living in Cambridge, teaching Hebrew school and quietly studying Zohar on the side.

But Elizabeth was always the guest of honor, the crowning jewel in Ira's entourage. Elizabeth was Ira's soulmate; she was his deeply beloved, the locket he clasped to his bosom.

"This," he had said to me, introducing her with a great flourish, with a royal gesture of adoration and amazement, his hand stretched out as if offering a holy vessel, "this is E-*liz*-a-beth." He pronounced each syllable individually, each with its proper intonation and hidden meaning, as if reciting the title of a 17th-century poem.

Elizabeth was a large, fleshy woman, with a hopelessly romantic soul. Not much to look at, her hair pulled back in a prim bun, she nevertheless sent Ira into raptures whenever he beheld her face. She spoke of their destinies, of beauty, of the heart's truth. She studied "The Fine Arts," she said, a capital letter on each word. She painted large landscapes with huge red setting suns and tiny figures walking beneath them along long, twisting, lonely roads.

The motzi was barely whispered, in order not to break the spell of Sabbath peace. A long pause separated every word. A long sigh, with eyes delicately closed, followed the blessing. Afterwards, Consuela quietly slipped into the kitchen and soon emerged holding the main dish.

"This fish is *celestial*," she said rapturously, and she placed the celestial fish on the table in front of us. The salad, which soon followed, was also celestial, composed of celestial tomatoes with celestial lettuce. The bread, baked by Robin and Yankele, was also celestial.

Dinner was eaten mostly in silence. Occasionally, one of them would emit a sigh of pleasure, a soft moan of bliss. The only other communications were the long, soulful looks passed back and forth, deep intimate stares of knowledge and acceptance sent from the eyes of one into the eyes of the other. The stares were followed by weak, loving smiles.

I tried. I really tried. I tried to summon up that part of me which could appreciate all this, which could enter into this beatific spirit that was expanding all around me. But I couldn't. It was too much – too romantic, too naive, too self-consciously perfect, too *something*, and it made me cynical instead. A perverse imp goaded me on and I wanted to shout blasphemies, to sing out dirty songs, to get up, right there on the table, and commit some horrible abominations before their wonder-filled eyes.

But I didn't. Instead, I closed myself off and descended inward, pushing myself into a private world of memories. And what arose in my mind were merely impressions, vague recollections, disconnected pictures, images pulled out of a lost and distant realm, images of the jagged, shining edge of escalator stairs, like metallic teeth, moving below me, going upwards or downwards, moving brightly and menacingly, somewhere in a cool nighttime world.

And behind it all was the sense of another world of memories, a different, almost visceral set of recollections which were just beyond my grasp, and to which I no longer had access.

I sat there, wondering about that world, in order not to get carried away by my need to scream out against it.

The next week Ira again invited his friends for Shabbos dinner, and asked me if I would be joining them.

I lied. I told him I had somewhere else to eat. And so, after services, I got into my car, drove downtown, and ate my Shabbos dinner at Hamburger Roundup, from a bag, in the midst of noise, glare, and piles of paper trash.

Still staring at the splinter, I smiled wryly at the recollection. "I guess I'm not much of a mystic," I said, and I gave the splinter a quick little flick, and it shot out along its trajectory and landed in the wastebasket.

COMMUNAL MEAL: A TABLEAU

Okay, enough of dinner. Let's push away from the table and move over here into the living room. The living room is nice and quiet now, but as I told you earlier, this is where we have our group meetings. It's not quiet then, that's for sure. Group meetings – whew! What a madhouse.

But at least group meetings are preceded by communal meals, which is a good way to take the sting out of them.

As you might imagine, communal meal is nothing like Friday night dinner. It's definitely a weekday experience, with everybody running in and out, excited, tired, caught in the middle of their week. So, let me introduce you to some more of the folks.

Sit down here and make yourself comfortable. Close your eyes and I'll close mine, too, and let me think back to what it was like on a typical evening when I was just beginning to get really comfortable here.

Let's see: a typical evening, nothing extraordinary. Let me paint a picture for you, a tableau, like one of those huge Renaissance paintings of feasts or grand ceremonies, where everything is happening all at once, with one person – me, of course, the narrator – looking straight out at the viewer.

But a painting is nothing like a verbal picture, and so I'll have to bend the rules of storytelling a bit. But don't worry about that. Don't even waste your energy to look for a plot. Just sit back, close your eyes, listen, and watch . . . .

I was upstairs in my room as usual, working away at my own little project, whatever it was, and I began to hear the sound of feet and voices, of people coming into the house. The sound of activity increased as new people entered, bearing bowls or pots of food, or brown bags filled with things they were going to chop, mix, or cook in the Havurah kitchen.

I kept on working, unconcerned about my own particular contribution to the evening's meal, because this evening my only assignment was to wash the dishes afterwards.

But as the noise grew, and as more and more people arrived, something inside me began pulling me away from my work to make me pay attention to what was happening downstairs. At last I heard Esther's voice among it all, and now that old erotic pull was enough to sever my attention completely, forcing me to leave my desk and follow my impulses to go downstairs and see what was happening.

I clumped down the back stairs and into the kitchen.

Rebecca was the first to notice me as I walked in. She was holding a casserole filled with some brown and green vegetarian concoction, covered with a sprinkling of sunflower seeds. Rebecca liked sunflower seeds – she put them in cakes, breads, salads, yogurt, and ate them plain, just for snacks. As I said, she liked sunflower seeds. She thought they were healthful.

"Solomon!" she said brightly. "Hiya!"

"Hi there Rebecca, how're ya doin'? Whatcha got there? Looks good."

"It's an egg-spinach-and-tofu casserole," she said proudly.

"Hey, that sounds good," I complimented her. "What's that, sunflower seeds?"

"Yeah!" she said brightly, as if I had astutely figured out something that was difficult to comprehend. "They're really good in casseroles."

"I'm sure they are," I answered. "But I thought you told me that Max was cooking for tonight. Don't tell me *he* put those sunflower seeds in there."

Max, standing by the table, turned toward us at the mention of his name.

"Hiya, Max," I said. "Hey, you didn't make this. Rebecca did."

"I know," he said glumly. "I tried to make something, but it didn't come out so good." He shrugged.

"Max thinks that if you put anything organic in the blender and then cook it, it's edible," Rebecca cut in.

That didn't sound so unreasonable, so I decided to ask for his recipe. "Well, Max, what did you try to make?"

Max attempted to answer nonchalantly, as if he had simply suffered a culinary misunderstanding. "I tried to put bean curd and melon together," he said.

Yes, that sounded unappetizing, I thought. I was about to accept his answer when Rebecca added a dash of truth to what Max had just served me.

"He tried to make bean curd and cantaloupe *rinds*," she said, trying not to embarrass Max too much. "It was awful."

"Cantaloupe rinds!" I exploded. "Max, that's horrible."

Max defended himself. "Some animals eat it. I figured I'd give it a try."

"Did you eat it yourself?" I asked.

"Only a taste – it was lousy. I threw it out."

"Well, thank goodness for that. It doesn't sound like even sunflower seeds could have fixed it."

"You know, they might have," Rebecca answered, as if giving it some consideration.

I stared at her. Was she kidding me? And then I saw that, yes, thank goodness, she was kidding me. With Rebecca, I never seemed to be able to tell whether she meant it whenever she said something outlandish. Something about her always seemed so naive and innocent, and sometimes I got the impression that she was just a wide-eyed babe in the woods. And on some of those occasions, I was even right about it.

I walked over to Esther, who was standing by the table, busily pulling something out of a paper bag. I wanted to put a hand on her shoulder or around her waist, but I restrained myself in order to watch without disturbing her. I marveled at the thought that she had perhaps actually gone to some trouble in her preparations, and I didn't want to interrupt her concentration. Then I saw it. She pulled out a big can of ready-made spaghetti in tomato sauce.

"Esther!" I said. "I can't believe you're going to give us *that* for communal meal. From a *can!*"

She looked slightly embarrassed, but only slightly.

"Well, it's not the main dish," she answered weakly.

"Yeah, but from a *can*. That stuff's terrible."

"Oh," she said, flustered. "I came home late, I didn't have time."

"But from a can!" I repeated, harping on my one idea. "How could you do that?"

Esther brightened, because she had a good answer for that one. "It's easy," she said.

"Is that an excuse or a reason?"

But she just smiled at me, a cryptic, seductive smile. A very suggestive smile. What could I do in the face of such a smile?

I turned and walked over to the stove, where Elisha was dreamily stirring something in a pot. I looked inside. It was a big mess of macaroni and cheese. I watched as Elisha just kept staring into the pot. Holding the lid with one hand, he continued to give the contents an absent-minded stir.

That's bad, I thought. We've got to get him out of the kitchen. Looking at all that food builds up his appetite. He needs to lose weight and look good for the ladies.

Suddenly, he turned to me, with a wild look on his face. Still holding the spoon in one hand and the pot cover in the other, he stared straight at me, through me, and suddenly spoke.

"*What*," he said forcefully, "is macaroni and cheese?" It was a rhetorical question and he didn't wait for my answer.

"*Is*," he said, flailing the spoon, "macaroni and cheese 'macaroni *with* cheese' or 'cheese with macaroni'? Which is the basic ingredient to which the other is added? Or is macaroni-and-cheese a new substance entirely, neither basically macaroni nor basically cheese? If so, what turns it into macaroni-and-cheese: is it when you have added a certain amount of macaroni to the cheese or a certain amount of cheese to the macaroni – at what point does macaroni *with* cheese become *macaroni-and-cheese*?

"Or," he continued, "is it not the ingredients, but a matter of cooking – at what point in the cooking process do the macaroni and the cheese combine to become macaroni-and-cheese? Is it at a certain temperature, or after a certain time cooking? In other words, at what point can you no longer separate the macaroni out from the cheese – when can you stop the process and reclaim both the macaroni and the cheese as separate entities?

"Or look at it from another viewpoint. Let's say it's *not* macaroni-and-cheese. If you judge by the cooking process, you cook the macaroni first, so then it's macaroni *with* cheese. But if you judge it by nutritional value, maybe it's really cheese with macaroni, provided you've put in sufficient cheese. Or is it taste? Do you taste mostly the macaroni with the cheese, or the cheese with the macaroni? Or does *that* make it macaroni-and-cheese, because macaroni and cheese is a separate taste entirely? Is it ingredients, is it cooking, or is it taste? What determines the identity of food?"

He turned away from me as abruptly as he had turned toward me. The wild look was gone from his face and again he stared into the pot and gave it a lazy stir.

"I'm hungry," he said. "When do we eat?"

At that moment, Heligman exploded into the Havurah, the doors banging behind him, closely followed by a highly animated animal – Caleb, his big, neurotic golden retriever – who kept jumping up and down and running around him in circles, eyeing the pot which Heligman held aloft with both hands.

"Hiya, hiya," he called out, bearing the pot into the kitchen.

Caleb, seeing the pot was now safely delivered, gave up on it and instead bounded up the back stairs into the regions above.

I gave the pot only a quick glance and a sniff. The pot itself was messy, gooey, dripping and spotted with globs of food, but the food it contained, some kind of vegetable stew, was obviously delicious. Although his dish was sloppy and of questionable cleanliness, Heligman was a true gourmet, Colonel Heligman himself, Duncan Hines of the kosher counterculture, spicing everything according to his southern tastes and an out-of-character refined palate.

But I had no time to spend looking at Heligman's contribution. I ran up the stairs to close the door to my room and head off Caleb from getting into any trouble he might uncontrollably launch himself into.

By the time I got there, I was already too late. I found Caleb in the bathroom. He looked up at me and cowered, and I saw that a bubbling froth was already on his lips, and a long viscous line of green slime was trailing from his chin.

He was foaming at the mouth! He was in a rabid slaver! At his feet was my tube of shampoo, chewed and oozing like a dead, bleeding animal.

"Caleb!"

I picked up the tube and Caleb escaped back down to the kitchen. I put the dead, hopelessly punctured tube back on the rim of the bathtub and went downstairs.

"Heligman," I said, trying to be serious, "Caleb just ate my Prell."

Heligman just shook it off. "What do you expect?" he said. "That's his brand."

I saw that I wasn't going to get anywhere in the way of sympathy or recompense, so I turned away and looked over at the table where Leah and Ira were absorbed in putting the final touches on their creations.

Ira was making a beautiful salad, a kaleidoscope of vivid, healthy color, full of lettuce, cucumbers, radishes, peppers, carrots, tomatoes, and bean sprouts. A few more plump, red tomatoes were still sitting on the cutting board, awaiting their turn to be added to the rest. Ira was cutting with great precision.

"That looks really good, Ira," I said, admiring his work.

"Well," he said noncommittally, "I got assigned to make a salad, so I'm making it."

"But it looks like a real good one," I remarked. "It should be delicious."

Ira didn't seem to care. Then he added, "Well, I won't be eating it."

"What!" I said amazed. "You're not going to eat your own salad?"

"No," he said, "I'm following a special diet these days. I have my own food over there," he said, pointing to a bowl.

Aha, I thought. Ira-dreck again.

Recently, Ira had been on an esoteric diet, convinced of its healing and spiritual powers, and so ate a small and unappetizing selection of what appeared to be almost unstomachable pastes and beans. His various foods had been dubbed "Ira-dreck," a term familiar to everyone except to Ira himself.

I looked over at his bowl. It was small, and undoubtedly its contents were all he would eat during the meal. The bowl contained a runny, milky, yellowish-white substance with some lumps in it. It didn't look very appealing. Next to the bowl was a plastic bag containing little black beans or berries of some kind, all dried up and shriveled, looking like goat turds. A few had been dropped into the white glop.

"Oh," I said.

I turned to Leah. She was carefully cutting a cake into several pieces and arranging the pieces neatly on a plate.

"Hi there, Leah," I said, cheerfully.

"Hi Solomon," she answered, with equal friendliness.

"Did you make that cake?" I asked.

"Yes, I did," she said, proud of her achievement.

"It looks great," I said, in all honesty. But then, as an afterthought, I added, "Is that all there is for dessert?"

She looked at me funny. Uh-oh. Did she think I was criticizing her? I sensed a slight shift in her attitude, an uneasiness. I hadn't meant to do it – I was merely thinking out loud – but it slipped out.

"I just meant if there were going to be a couple of different desserts, so we could have them all," I said, eating my words.

"No," she said warily. "I think I was the only one assigned to dessert."

In truth, there wasn't a lot to go around. It was all being very nicely plated on a neat little tray, in a lovely crisscross pattern, but the pieces were small, barely more than a mouthful each, for so many of us. Perhaps Leah had forgotten that she had a smaller appetite than most of the others in the group. Perhaps two people should have been assigned to dessert. But anyhow, dessert was small indeed, although pretty.

"Do you think that's enough?" I asked hesitantly, trying not to sound critical.

Aha. So that was my complaint. "You don't think this is enough?" she said.

"Well," I said, trying not to offend her, "maybe. It just looks a little small. It's very pretty though." But neat and pretty does not a dessert make, I thought.

"We'll see," she said with a pout. I had hurt her unintentionally.

At that moment, Linda came through the back door, putting her car keys into her bag, absorbed in some meditation of her own. When she saw the kitchen full of people, she suddenly stopped dead and expleted: "Crap!"

"What's wrong?" Rebecca asked, concerned.

"Oh, crap!" she said again. "Oh crap crap crap."

"What's the matter?"

"I forgot that tonight was communal meal!" She was exasperated with herself.

"Well, what were you supposed to bring?" I asked.

"I don't even remember," she said, annoyed with herself. "Salad, I think."

"Well, don't worry," Ira interjected. "I'm making enough for everybody. There's no need for two salads tonight."

"Are you sure?" Linda asked, hoping her omission wouldn't leave too big a gap.

"Sure, it's no problem. You've been saved by divine prescience," Ira said.

"Oh, good," she said, relieved. After a brief pause, she continued. "But now I feel bad that I'm not adding anything."

"Don't worry about it," Rebecca told her.

"Yeah, don't worry about it," I said in a slightly teasing tone. Linda and I were used to teasing each other. It was our special routine. "So what if you're irresponsible."

"I am not irresponsible!" she protested. "I am not. Don't tell me I'm irresponsible!"

"Don't listen to Solomon," Rebecca said. "He's only teasing."

"*I am not irresponsible,*" she again insisted, disregarding Rebecca's peacekeeping effort. This was strictly between the two of us.

"Sure you are," I answered. "What did you bring for dinner?"

"I forgot, I told you! Anyway, what did *you* bring, smarty-pants?"

"I'm washing the dishes," I said proudly, as if there were dignity in the least sought-after job of the evening.

"Good!" she said. "You deserve it."

"At least I'm adding something."

Linda just glowered. "Oh, you . . . ."

"Listen," said Rebecca, still trying to make Linda happy. "If you want, you can still buy something at the convenience store around the corner."

"Well . . ." said Linda, "like what?"

"How about ice cream or something like that," Rebecca suggested.

Leah looked at her quickly.

"Oh, I didn't mean anything special by that," Rebecca said, suddenly recovering. "It just came to my mind at random."

"Ice cream?" Linda said, searching for a general opinion to that suggestion.

I nodded enthusiastically when Leah wasn't looking. Linda caught my meaning and smiled. She didn't know exactly what I was referring to, but she knew I would tell her about it afterwards.

"Okay," she said. "I'll be right back."

As Linda started to walk out, Mark bumped into her coming the other way. They shuffled around each other, laughed, and finally made it past each other. Mark greeted everybody, deposited a paper bag on the table, slid two loaves of bread out of it, looked around the room for a minute, and then beckoned for me to join him in the pantry.

I walked into the pantry, suspecting what was to follow.

Mark put his arm around my shoulder and spoke in a low voice, confidentially.

"Solomon," he said, "I need somebody to lead davening on Shabbos morning." Of course. I knew it.

"But I just led Kabbalat Shabbat last week," I countered.

"I know," he said. "You did a good job, too."

"I wasn't looking for compliments. So, you don't have to butter me up."

"Okay. But this is an emergency."

"What do you mean, 'an emergency'? You always say it's an emergency."

He laughed. "You're right. But it's still an emergency."

He took a piece of paper from his shirt pocket and unfolded it. It was full of boxes, some of which were filled in with names, some of which were empty. This was the gabbai's list, supposedly a voluntary list on which people marked down when they would lead services during the following weeks. Somehow the voluntary system never kept the list completely full, and it was the gabbai's job to make sure there was always someone to lead services. Naturally, some occasional arm-twisting was in order, and Mark was an exceptional gabbai.

"Look," he said, scanning the list, "you're signed up for leading a Torah discussion in two weeks. How about if I take you off that Torah discussion and give you shacharit for this Shabbat?"

I mentally weighed it. Leading shacharit was tougher than leading the discussion, at least to my own way of thinking. It needed more preparation. So, it was an unequal trade. I balked a little and Mark understood exactly what I was thinking.

"Listen," he said, "if you do shacharit this Shabbat, not only do I take you off Torah discussion, but I'll leave you alone for a couple of weeks."

"How long?" I asked.

"Oh, I can't say," Mark answered, reserving his professional prerogative.

No, that wasn't good enough. He saw my hesitation and so continued bargaining.

"All right," he said. "If you do shacharit this Shabbat, not only do I take you off Torah discussion and not bother you for a while, but when I do, it won't be for anything major. Maybe just a Friday night service."

"But you usually don't have trouble getting somebody to lead Friday night anyway," I answered.

"I know," he said. "But when I need somebody for a Shabbos morning, I'll trade it off for the person doing Friday night, and give the Friday night davening to you. How's that?"

Would he remember such a deal? I was sure he would. I was silent for a few seconds. Both he and I knew I was going to give in. That was the way things were, and we both knew the game. But still, the deal had to be consummated.

"So, you'll do it?" he said, encouragingly.

"Well, look," I said. "I'll do it if you can't find anybody else. How's that?"

"Okay," he said. "Fair enough. I'll look for somebody else, and if I can't find anybody, you'll do it."

"Yeah, all right," I answered. I knew he wasn't going to look for anybody else, at least not seriously. I had as well as agreed. But I had added that one condition so that both of us would know that this was a matter of gentle coercion, and at least I wanted it acknowledged.

"Okay," he said. "I'll let you know after the meeting if I find anybody else."

"Fine."

The deal was closed.

We both went back into the kitchen. What could I do? Me this week, someone else the next. That was the way it went, and everybody got his or hers in turn.

While I was thinking about this little transaction, already beginning to toss together in my mind different ideas on which to base a Shabbos morning service, I accidentally brushed into Carol, who was walking perpendicularly into my path. Neither of us had been paying much attention and we collided, gently bumping each other.

In her hands were two large pitchers, each filled to the brim with a different liquid – in one, a yellowish liquid that I assumed to be grapefruit juice, and in the other a bright red cranberry juice. The little jolt of our contact made the pitchers slosh dangerously, threatening to spill.

"Watch it!" she erupted angrily.

"What's the matter?" I asked.

"You almost made me spill the drinks all over the floor!"

"Don't worry. It's all right. Nothing spilled," I answered, trying to calm her.

"Yeah, well you almost knocked this right out of my hands!"

"Chill out," I said, trying to sound soothing.

"*You* chill out – stop banging into people."

It was hopeless. I didn't need an argument, and if I continued I knew that Carol would give me one. She thrived on arguments. As far as I was concerned, she was nuts. There was something wrong with her. She was angry, volatile and moody. I avoided her whenever I could. So I decided not to make any further retort.

I walked to the other side of the room.

Suddenly, Chief came in through the front door, a big smile on his face, a plastic bag swinging from his hands. In the bag were half a dozen little green hairy-looking egg-shaped things.

"What the heck is that?" I said.

"Kiwi fruits!" he said triumphantly.

"Kiwi fruits? What did you get them for?"

"What do you mean?" he said, disbelieving. "Look at them – they're far out! They're from Australia or somewhere. I never had them before, and when I saw them in the supermarket, I had to get them. I'll bet most of us haven't eaten them, at least not this year. So we can say a *shehecheyanu* on them."

"They must have been expensive," I surmised.

"Oh, yeah, they were. But so what? What's important is that we can make a *bruchah* on them." Chief opened the bag and went to put the kiwi fruits in a dish. He was very proud of his find and eager to get to eat them.

"When do we start?" he asked. "I thought I was late – but it looks like I'm not."

"Well, you are, but so is everybody else," Esther said.

Soon, all the food was ready and the table was set. Linda came in with the ice cream, and the others had also come in – Jerry, Leon, Myra, Zack and the rest.

"Who's missing?"

"Mel," I answered.

Just then, Mel came in, carrying a huge pot of some sort of stew – beans, potatoes, carrots, turnips, a whole pot of heavy protein and starch, which would be the main dish, the core of the meal, the substance from which we all would eat.

"Hello hello," he boomed, coming into the room.

"Hello hello," we answered him.

"Okay, let's start."

All the food was brought out and piled onto the table, and we all took seats, in no order or hierarchy. After a quick motzi, we dug in and began our hearty eating session, a loud, gregarious, light-hearted dinner, passing pots and platters this way and that, piling our plates full, taking seconds and thirds, with everybody eating everything that everyone else had brought to the meal.

And that's the picture of all of us around the table, talking, laughing, or eating silently, until the meal was over and all the dishes were stacked up in the sink.

After that, we all moved over, right here into this living room, everybody claiming their little nook or corner, to thrash out whatever topics were on the agenda. Because it's a lot of work to keep a community like this together. A lot more work than it seems.

JOZEF, OR THE MUSTACHE

You can open your eyes now. Tableau complete.

So, you believe you're beginning to understand what goes on here? No doubt, you're even beginning to draw some of your own conclusions. Well, don't think you have *too* good an understanding. Because it's really not that simple to understand.

The truth is, reality takes on many forms, and just because you seem to have one of them figured out, there are others, too, going on at the same time, totally out of your grasp, or of which, at best, you can only perceive a vague notion.

But I'm digressing. Getting lost in the *velt arein*. So, let's get back to the stories. Here's one, as good as any, I suppose . . . .

It was already late morning and, as usual, I had only just awakened and come downstairs for my breakfast. As I was puttering in the kitchen, the phone rang and I picked it up.

"Hello?"

"Er, hello . . . Is this Mr. Havurat?" said a voice over the line. He pronounced it "Have-you-rat."

Oh no, another telephone salesman. I can tell right away. No doubt, this guy was just going down the phone book and came upon Havurat Chaim and simply concluded there was a Mr. Chaim Havurat living at this address. A strange name, no doubt. Jewish? Greek? Maybe Slavic? And

what's he doing in *this* neighborhood? But never mind, just give him a call
. . . .

"Well," I said, trying to break it to him gently, "this is Havurat Chaim *Community*."

"Oh," he said, obviously not understanding anything except that he had no idea of what he was up against. There was a pause.

"Well, am I speaking to the man of the house?"

"Well," I said, "I'm *one* of the men of the house. There are lots of men of the house here."

"Well," he said, seeming to feel a bit more sure of himself, hoping to have hit a nerve, "who makes the *decisions*?"

"Ah, the decisions," I said, and in my mind I conjured up a scene of endless business and religious policy meetings in which we debated issues back and forth for hours. "We all make the decisions."

"Then perhaps I'm talking to the *right person*," he said, trying to get the better of me.

"Well," I answered evasively, "not really. We all make the decisions, but we make them *together*."

"Oh," he said, again a bit lost. "Do you think you can decide on something *now*?"

"Oh, no," I answered. "You see, we have meetings every week or two, and then we discuss at length everything that needs decision-making. It's a complicated process. It could take quite a while."

"Oh." There was another pause, which grew longer. I realized I had to help him a little or I'd never get him off the phone.

"Is there something you wanted to say?" I prompted.

"Um . . . er . . . ah, yes," he said, pulling himself together.

He then launched into his little sales pitch, which he knew by rote and was clearly unable to adjust to unseen circumstances. "I represent Allied Home and Construction Company and we've been conducting scientific research in residential neighborhoods like yours, finding out what homeowners feel in these difficult times of ours. We've determined that homeowners demand both high efficiency of their home insulation and yet durable and lovely exteriors that allow for easy care and high resale value. Your neighborhood is of special interest to us, and we're offering easy budget payment plans on new aluminum siding to the families in your area, if you act now to take advantage of our money-saving offer. Our agent will call on you, at hours convenient to your own busy workday, to give you a free, noobligation evaluation of your insulation needs."

Suddenly, he stopped. Had he finished? I guessed so.

"Well," I said slowly, "that's all very nice of you, but there's a whole lot of us here, and so we take care of the property ourselves, you know, doing whatever needs to be done . . . ."

"Ah yes, yes," he said hurriedly, now realizing he would do best to just get out of this conversation. "I understand perfectly. I see your point." He had done his job. Now let him go, for Chrissake. What type of bizarre, un-American place had he called, anyway? Maybe one of those mental clinics. His discomfort, even over the phone, was obvious. "You're right, very good. Well, good-bye."

"Bye-bye," I sang into the phone, as the other end clicked almost immediately.

2

Later that morning, I was still sitting alone in the kitchen, eating my granola and milk, wasting time by reading the newspaper, when the doorbell buzzed. I got up and opened the door.

There in the doorway stood a slightly haggard middle-aged man, wearing a shapeless dark blue overcoat and a battered hat. His face was greyish, although honestly enough he attempted a cheerful disposition. In his right hand he held a bulky vacuum cleaner, and from his left dangled a long, snakelike vacuum cleaner attachment.

"Hello?" I said.

"Hello there, young man," he said. "Is the lady of the house in?"

What's with this "young man" stuff? I thought. "Um, well, no," I answered. "Actually," I said, being honest, "there are *several* ladies of the house here, but . . . er . . . none of them are in right now."

Several ladies of the house? His eyebrows raised. "Are you the only person here at the moment?" he asked.

"Yeah. Just me."

"Oh," he said. "Well, you see, I'm selling vacuum cleaners and I wanted to show you our latest deluxe new model." He tried peering into the house, looking for thick carpets.

"Well," I said, "we don't really need a vacuum cleaner," which was not entirely true.

"What do you mean you don't need a vacuum cleaner? You can *always* use a vacuum cleaner!" he said, trying to sound cheerful.

"Well, you see," I replied, realizing that an explanation would be ridiculous, "whenever we really need a vacuum cleaner, the people across the street lend us theirs."

"Ah," he said, brightening, "but wouldn't you like your *own* vacuum cleaner?"

"Well," I replied, trying to explain but not really, "that sort of *is* our own vacuum cleaner."

"Then why do you keep it with the people across the street?"

"Well, no, you see, its *theirs*, but they sort of live here too."

"What . . . ?"

"Forget it," I said, trying to think of another approach. That one was clearly a mistake. "You see, we really don't need it. We just don't have a lot of rugs or anything like that."

"But you can use it for *all sorts* of things. What are those? Are those cushions in there?"

"Yeah. Anyhow, forget the cushions, man." How would I explain *that* one?

He took a step back. Something was not right. He was clearly not getting through. Turning to look at the plaque outside the door, which said "Havurat Chaim Community" in English, and then a few words in Hebrew and Aramaic, describing us as a holy community, of which he no doubt hadn't the slightest notion, he suddenly dropped his salesman's attitude completely, withered as it already was, and exploded with exasperation.

"What . . . what kind of place *is* this, anyhow?"

You hit the jackpot, mister, I thought to myself. As I stood there, trying to think of an answer to give him, a short, pithy, more or less understandable answer, leaving out the whole idea of counterculture alternative religious community or anything like that, an answer that would satisfy him and not completely compromise myself, one which would not seem too suspicious and could sidestep all the innumerable contradictions and obscurities inherent in the task, he began, instead, to answer all the questions for himself.

"Are you folks students?" he asked, raising his eyebrows, fishing for a starting place.

"Well, uh . . . yeah. I guess so." *Some* of us were students.

"Ah-*ha*," he said, thinking that he began to see the picture. "You all go to Wispy College up there on the hill?"

I hesitated. Mark went to Wispy College, pursuing a master's degree. He was the only one who fit that description, and he didn't live at the house, but that would qualify, I supposed. So why not?

"Well, yeah, *some* of us go to Wispy College."

"Aaah," he said. "You're some kind of dormitory or something, is that it?"

"Well . . ." I answered, "we live here. But I wouldn't just call us a dormitory."

"But you're not a family or something, are you?"

"No-o-o," I said slowly.

"Well, then you're like a dormitory."

"Okay," I said, capitulating. "It's kinda like that."

"Oh," he said, suddenly brightening. "I get it. You're like a dormitory, but a religious dormitory – this is Hebrew writing, isn't it? You folks are Hebrews, aren't you . . . ?"

"Well, we're Jewish . . . ."

"Yeah, Jewish people, that's right, so this is like a Jewish dormitory for you Jewish people when you go to Wispy College up on the hill." It was amazing how glad he was to be able to construct an understandable model for himself, no matter what the reality was.

"Well, okay," I said, "it's something like that." By now, I certainly didn't want to disabuse him, only to make things difficult for him once again.

He was relieved, and his momentary confusion dispersed. Things were just as he had surmised. And then he added just one more comment.

"Well, heck," he said, trying to be friendly. "I understand now. If I was a student living in a dormitory, I wouldn't buy a vacuum cleaner either." And then he winked at me, in perfect complicity. Sure, he understood. It was clear as day. He hoisted up his vacuum cleaner and started off.

"Have a nice day, now," he called out.

"You too," I answered cheerily. I shut the door as he walked down the porch steps, and then I went back to my breakfast.

3

Almost an hour later, I was still procrastinating over the newspaper, reluctant to gather my energy and push into the day's work which awaited me, when Jozef came in, making his daily appearance.

Jozef Zalzfleish was a very strange character, especially to be found around the Havurah.

For years, we had been invaded by a steady, if small, influx of university students who saw us as terrific raw material for their sociology papers. Since we were such an atypical social configuration, we became the subject of numerous five-to-ten-page papers on any number of topics – counterculture organizations, fringe religious groups, the Jewish avant-garde, alternative lifestyles. A few, more serious-minded people, writing master's theses, had come by and spent several sessions with various members, taking notes, asking questions, and taping interviews. Even journalists had occasionally stopped by to chat and take a few pictures, using us as local color for whatever stories they were working on. Israeli television and even a well-known American Jewish writer had stopped by to get the word on us.

We were, it seemed, good fuel for their purposes, whatever they happened to be. And, depending upon our various moods, we either cordially invited them in or, tired of being treated like monkeys and guinea pigs, gave them short shrift and discouraged their further investigations.

In any event, all these researchers had one thing in common: their ability to misperceive. Misconceptions and misinformation about us were always finding their way into the world, and every once in a while, when word of it would get back to us, we would either laugh or be ticked off, sensitive despite ourselves at what the larger world thought of us. Often, we were totally flabbergasted at how anyone could be so thick-headed as to say about us the things they managed to say.

And so, when we received a letter from Germany, from a Bonn University doctoral candidate who wished to live among us for eight months in order to write a dissertation on *Das Junge Judische Kounterkultur in Amerika*, or something like that, we entirely dismissed it out of hand. What nonsense! Ridiculous! At best it would only be a pain in the ass, and at worst – who knew? Some person we had never seen before, from a totally different culture, would simply come and live in our midst for the better part of a year, snoop around and then take back God-knows-what misinformation about us?

No, it was out of the question. We didn't even give it further thought.

Soon, however, another letter arrived, asking why we had neglected to answer the first, and restating its original proposition. And so, an answer was formulated, polite but intended to dampen his desire, saying that we really could not make any decisions of that magnitude about a person whom we did not even know, to permit such a close penetration into our group that worked so hard to foster a delicate environment of comfortable community and interpersonal trust and expression among its members. If we knew the person better, perhaps we would be able to discuss it, but we really could not encourage anyone to come all the way from Germany merely in the hope of our possibly consenting to such an undertaking.

As we discussed the matter in a business meeting, our past awkward and sometimes unpleasant experiences with all the people who had come, and sometimes pushed their way, into our midst, only to cause tension and dissension, easily won out.

A third correspondence from Germany, however, followed these previous two. The writer stated that he would be arriving in Boston at the end of August, planning to stay for eight months and hoped very strongly that the Havurah would not turn him away.

What should we do? we wondered. Some of us were annoyed at this obvious attempt to muscle in, and yet, if he were coming all the way from Germany, we could hardly turn him away without at least meeting him and treating him hospitably.

And so, at last, Jozef Zalzfleish presented himself to the Havurah, and through a combination of stubbornness, friendliness, and playing on our sympathies, we allowed him to write his doctoral dissertation on us, for better or for worse.

To us, Jozef Zalzfleish was a very odd character indeed. He was a young, religious, German Jew whose family had eventually returned to Berlin, via Israel, and who fit almost perfectly the typical "Yekeh" stereotype. He wore a jacket and tie, had short hair, glasses, carried a little briefcase, and was consistently well-mannered. Besides that, he talked through his nose.

He was also intelligent, analytical, far straighter than anyone who had ever stepped inside the Havurah, and despite his intelligence, he thought himself always to be right and so paid for it by being too close-minded for his own good.

In short, he seemed to have stepped out of the 1920's, a type of Jew we thought didn't exist any longer, except, perhaps, in a much older version, somewhere in the stacks at Hebrew University in Jerusalem.

What saved him, however, was his good-naturedness. Even if his own jokes didn't particularly set anyone laughing, he did at least smile, occasionally laugh at himself, and was always a good target for kidding. As a result, no one felt bad about humoring him and treating him with a slight edge of patronizing camaraderie.

We made it perfectly clear that although we respected his intelligence, we could never help seeing him as anything but a weird and funny duck. He would just have to live with that if he wanted to find out anything about us.

As it turned out, he already knew a great deal about us even before he arrived. How he had managed that was quite a feat in itself; while still in Germany, he read much of the literature that was already written about us – all that he could get his hands on – as well as about other similar groups and about whatever generally fell under the heading of the "Jewish Counterculture." He was, of course, filled with a million preconceptions, most of them false or distorted, and so he had come to straighten out his ideas and see, in living color, what he had already devoured so hungrily in black and white.

The only question that we couldn't figure out was how he had developed this obsession with the Jewish counterculture and why he, so straight and scholarly, had such a voracious appetite for learning about us.

So Jozef found a place in Brookline, the Jewish neighborhood across town, and commuted to us every day, as if coming to work at the laboratory, trying to keep his personal world and his working world separate from one another. Like some meticulous social scientist that he was, he took notes on everything, constantly jotting down this or that observation, on whatever he noticed or heard people say.

He also preserved every scrap of paper he found – photocopied texts that we passed out in study sessions, letters sent to us for any number of reasons, and notices tacked up on the bulletin board. He even saved phone messages on the most inconsequential trivia, often fishing them out of the garbage. Scribbled lines on torn scraps of paper, like: "Linda – yer mudda called" or "Zack, your advisor wants to get in touch with you," were carefully collected, straightened out, and preserved. He even kept a smeared napkin that said nothing but "Solomon – call Max" right above a spot of ketchup. He treated us like an archaeologist uncovering precious artifacts, Schliemann at Troy, Yadin at Hazor, even as we went about our daily business, scurrying about right under his nose.

For the most part, Jozef kept all this to himself, slowly collecting data on everything, but his one weakness was his intermittent need to express his theories. He would talk extemporaneously, set off by the most modest of stimuli, about peer group interactions, subgroup tensions, organizational nexuses, a host of jargony singsong served up in a hodge-podge of conclusions sometimes painfully obvious and other times hopelessly erroneous.

Our one consolation was that he had promised that his dissertation would only appear in German, so the chances of it coming back to haunt us were comfortably slim.

Soon after his research began, however, a problem developed. Hoping to keep his own religious practices separate from ours, Jozef had been coming to observe us only during the week, while spending Shabbos in Brookline at an orthodox synagogue, and davening in the manner to which he was accustomed. When this appeared to become a pattern, we wouldn't stand for it. Shabbos was the most important time for the Havurah, when we all got together, joined by the "fringe" community, and shared our most intense communal moments. It was on Shabbos that the Havurah turned into a coordinated whole and the house became a center of lively activity.

Jozef would understand nothing about our most essential aspects if he missed Shabbos.

Still, he was reluctant to come. He didn't want to adopt our style of davening, even for the time of his visit. Davening was a mitzvah, he believed, not some sociological phenomenon to be observed, and he wanted to daven where he felt most comfortable. Nor did he want to turn his davening into merely another aspect of his work.

But we insisted. We were adamant about being seen in our totality if we were to be seen at all. When he protested, we would have none of it. Finally, we threatened him.

"If you don't come on Shabbos, your dissertation won't be worth shit, Jozef, and we'll write a letter to your university telling them that you didn't even do the most important observations necessary to your research."

What could he do? He had pressured us into letting him come and observe, and so now we were paying him back by blackmailing him into doing it correctly. And so he began, at last, to spend Shabbos with us, staying in the guest room and making Shabbos the way *we* made Shabbos.

At first, he was awkward and ill at ease. He came to services dressed in his jacket and tie, and sat upright in a chair at the edge of the circle while everyone else, wearing whatever was most comfortable, sat cross-legged on the floor, singing and bumping into one another, davening.

His initial impressions were critical and defensive. "I don't like davening in a circle," he said. "I don't like my concentration broken by looking at other people and have them looking at me. I don't want to feel conspicuous when I daven; it destroys the private relationship between me and God."

Also, he didn't know our tunes and he objected to all the things we left out. But most of all, we were threatening his objectivity, and he didn't like that one bit.

Slowly, however, over the course of the following weeks, his attitude gently shifted. He eventually got down from his chair and sat in our circle, and occasionally the jacket gave way to a sweater. Jozef was gradually being seduced into our ranks, and we were quick to notice every change in his evolution.

We began to observe his behavior as much as he observed ours. We made mental notes of when he joined in the singing, of when he seemed to be enjoying himself, and how much he allowed himself to daven along with us. We prided ourselves at each step he made.

One day, we observed a new phenomenon about Jozef, and instantly kidded him about it. There, under his nose, despite his clean-shaven face, were definitely the beginnings of a mustache. He was not growing out his beard, nor allowing a bushy head of hair to crop up, but yes, there they were, the first smudges of a mustache.

"Jozef!" we said. "Look at you! A mustache!"

"You're turning into a regular freak!"

"Hey, man, let it all hang out."

"Jozef, you crazy Yekeh, you're gonna go back to Bonn and turn them all into hippies!"

"No," he answered with embarrassment, smiling, "I'll shave it off before I go back to the university."

Well, what more was there to say about Jozef? We slowly grew more comfortable with him and he grew more comfortable with us, although both parties continued to tend towards opposite poles. After all, it was still only a mustache.

Ah, yes – there's only one other thing I must add about Jozef. One Saturday night, after Shabbos, when most of us took off to go to a movie, or to get stoned, or to get stoned and go to a movie, Jozef and a few of the others stayed in the dining room after Havdalah, having decided to spend the evening playing poker. In a few short hours, Jozef had managed to win all the pennies, matchsticks and bottlecaps that could be found anywhere in the Havurah, upstairs or down.

And on this day that I was telling you about, as usual, Jozef walked into the house carrying his little briefcase, closed the door behind him, and headed into the kitchen, where I was still sitting in front of my unwashed breakfast dishes.

"Hello, Solomon," he said, trying to be jovial, although still inescapably formal.

"Hiya, Jozef," I said, genial but not enthusiastic. I really had no desire to deal with him at the moment. He seemed to be just another interruption.

"What are you doing?" he asked.

"What does it look like? I'm reading the paper."

"Which paper is it?" he asked.

"It's the *Globe*," I answered dutifully.

"Today's?" he asked.

"No, it's tomorrow's."

"Wha-at?" he replied, a bit thrown.

"Actually, I said, "It's yesterday's, but don't make a big deal out of it."

"No big deal," he answered, slightly taken aback. "I just wanted to know, that's all."

"Okay," I answered, allowing myself to be a bit friendlier now that I had begun our interaction by putting him off. "Why don't you sit down and join me for a cup of tea?"

"Thank you, I'd love to."

I got up, turned on the kettle, and went into the pantry for the tea. "You want herbal tea or regular?" I called out from the pantry.

"Regular, please."

I came out with a tea bag for Jozef and a box of Zentner's Wild Valley Holiday Herbal Brew. I put the tea bag in one cup and spooned out some Wild Valley Holiday into a tea strainer for myself.

"May I see that box?" he asked.

"Sure," I said, handing it to him. "You ever try it?"

"No, I never did," he said, not too regretfully. He handled the package as if it were a small statue, turning it around, looking at the colorful picture of tall grasses and distant mountains on the front, then reading the little sayings of laid-back, homiletic wisdom on the side.

"Do you drink this often?" he asked.

"Pretty often," I answered.

"Why do you drink it?" he said, in part asking a normal question, and in part full of wonder, musing to himself.

"I like it, that's why," I said. "You want to try some?"

"N-o-o," he said, hesitantly.

"You don't even want to *try* it?" I protested.

"Well, not now, thank you," he said, putting the package down on the table. "Does everybody in the counterculture have to drink this type of thing?"

"Oh, cut the crap, Jozef, and drink your tea," I said.

He took up his cup and sipped it carefully, smiling contentedly. For some reason, he seemed to be very proud of himself.

What a jerk he can be sometimes, I thought.

When he had finished his tea, he carefully put the glass down next to the package of Wild Valley Holiday.

"Solomon," he said, somewhat ingratiatingly, "since it seems you have the time, why don't we do our interview now?"

"Now?" I said, surprised. "I thought you said you'd set appointments for the interviews."

"I did," he said, "but if we do yours now, I'll be ahead of my schedule."

"Now?" I groaned. "Oh, but today I have a lot of work to do. I was just getting ready to do it."

"But if we get it over with now, you won't have to do the interview later on," he reasoned.

"Now?" I repeated. "I don't know, Jozef."

"Listen," he said, "It won't even take two hours. After that, you'll be free."

I wanted to refuse. I had no desire to be interviewed today and answer all of Jozef's dumb questions about the Havurah. But I also didn't have the resolve to say no to him, especially since it would mean I'd have to start my own day's work right away, in earnest, just to prove I wasn't lying. So I gave in.

"Okay, Jozef, let's go do your interview."

We went up to the library, closed the door, and sat down at the table across from each other. Jozef carefully opened his briefcase and pulled out a pad and a pen, and a little cassette tape recorder. He fiddled around with it for a few minutes, pushing buttons, setting the volume, plugging in the microphone and then set it at the edge of the table, so as not to attract too much attention. Finally, he was ready.

"Tell me," he said, "what was your religious background? Tell me about your family and your religious training."

Should I take his questions seriously or not? I thought. Should I be sarcastic, flippant, wise, or analytical? In each case, my answer would have some truth to it, and yet no one tack would give a sufficiently complete reply. How could he possibly see the whole, complete picture? It seemed hopeless and ridiculous. I decided to be offhand and nonchalant.

"Oh, the usual American routine," I said. "I went to Hebrew school, bar mitzvah classes, they sent me to a couple of Jewish summer camps in the mountains."

"What was your family like?" he interrupted.

"My family? My parents were typical first-generation Americans, grew up in Brooklyn, went through the Depression, chucked most of their parents' religious trip but stayed, you know, 'Jewish in their hearts,' as they would call it."

I talked on. How much sense did any of this really make to him?

"Let's turn to the Havurah," he said, trying to sound very professional.

"Yes, let's," I said, mocking him slightly.

"Why did you originally join the Havurah?"

"Why did I join? A lot of reasons." I told him about Mel, about the sixties, about my own spiritual propensities, about the search for community, about the boredom of graduate school, and about random chance. Somehow, I didn't get the sense that he really understood how all these different things coalesced into one inevitable nexus, which was my life. They were just different components to him, united by a single outcome.

He continued to ask questions, about my current life and about the Havurah. How much money did I need to live on? How did I split my time between my graduate studies and the Havurah? Who were my friends in the group? How often did I lead services? What do I want to be? How long did I think I'd stay in the group? Just a lot of factual questions that I answered as quickly as I could. I had answered them, or similar ones, many times in the past, and I found it all rather dull. I was disappointed.

Slowly, the nature of the questions turned. "What do you think are the Havurah's strengths and weaknesses? What are its functions for its members and for the larger community?" Ah, at last he was asking my *opinion* about something. I could finally get the chance to say what I thought was really going on, to make my own voice heard.

I held forth about the unique place of the Havurah in American Judaism, about what I thought were the pitfalls of American Jewish culture and how we were countering them. I extolled the opportunity to inject creativity into the tradition, and then complained about what I thought was a falling-off in the level of creativity within the group.

Jozef listened to it all impassively, quietly drinking in what I told him without showing either agreement or disagreement. His impassivity troubled me, especially when I got the impression that I wasn't particularly enlightening him on the topic.

He pulled a piece of paper from his pad and handed me his pen.

"Could you make a graph of what you think has been the development of the Havurah over the years, and another of how you think the energy level during the year rises and falls?"

"The first one's easy," I said. "Since I joined the Havurah, the energy level of the group, on the whole, has constantly diminished." To show this, I made a diagonal line which slanted downwards across the page. "As for the other," I said, "it's something like this." I described a curve in which the energy started high around the High Holidays, slackened off after Sukkos, ebbed in winter, sparkled a little with Hanukkah, then plummeted in the dark, cold days of February, and resurged with Purim, spring, Passover, the search for new members, and Shavuos retreat. Then in the summer it sort of disappeared for a while.

"Thank you," he said, taking the paper and sticking it in his notes.

"What?" I thought. No comment, no discussion? Does that mean I'm right, or what?

"Now," he said, "who do you think are the most important members of the Havurah."

"The most important, or the most important to *me*?" I asked.

"The ones you think are most important to the group."

"Now, or since I've been here?"

"Now."

"Hmmm . . . ," I thought. "Well, let's see. Uh, Chief, and Heligman, Elisha, maybe Max and Rebecca . . . and me, of course," I said, beaming.

"What about Carol?" he asked.

"Carol? Well, I don't know. I don't get along very well with Carol. I try to ignore her as much as I can."

"But do you think she's important to the group?"

"In what ways?"

"Well, do you think her presence and influence in the group are strong?"

I thought about how Carol's neuroses and fixed ideas had bullied the group at times, and I had tried to discount them, just to counteract her. But it was true, her presence was at least a strong one.

"Yeah, I guess," I agreed. "Okay – throw in Carol, what the heck."

Carol and I always managed to distrust and disagree with each other, and although I tried, more or less, to treat her with civility, I never paid much attention to her. I often didn't show up when she led services, and she either didn't show up or else conspicuously walked out when I was the davener.

"Hey, have you had an interview with Carol yet?" I asked.

"Yes," he answered, letting on nothing, his voice rising slightly, like a receptionist in a corporate executive's office.

"Well, what did she say about *me*?" I asked, suddenly interested.

"I really can't give you that information. These interviews are confidential."

"She can't stand me, right? She thinks I'm a jackass?"

"If you want to know that, why don't you ask her yourself?"

"She'd never tell me straight. Besides, I can't believe anything she says."

"Maybe she'd tell you straight."

Maybe she would. But maybe she wouldn't. What did I know? Hmmm . . . . Yes, what *did* I know, after all? My own world, my own opinions, I knew those pretty well – or so I thought. And the Havurah? How well do I know the Havurah? How well can *any* one person in the Havurah really know the Havurah? And yet, if we inside the Havurah didn't know the Havurah, who *could* know what was going on in the Havurah?

I looked at Jozef, suddenly suspicious. What does he know that I don't know? I thought. And what does he know *about me* that I don't know? For a second, the whole room seemed to tilt, and I suddenly had a wild image of Jozef as some kind of mad scientist, a crazed inventor standing in front of bubbling test tubes, a silent, demonic magician pulling strings, looking down at us from behind a veil of some incomplete and yet totally different perspective, watching with an eye that saw a different order of things, a world constructed along lines with different knowledge and assumptions.

The image faded as soon as it had come. I looked again. No, no. That was silly. He was still just jerky old Jozef, a good egg, a fusty academic, not completely on the ball, and I was, once again, snug in the center of my snug little world.

I looked at his little boyish face and watched him scratch his upper lip, where the nascent mustache was giving him a bit of itchy discomfort despite his pride in it. I smiled as I thought of him deciding not to shave it off.

"Thank you, Solomon," he said, when the interview was over.

"Sure, Jozef," I said, off-handedly. "Any time. Nothing to it."

When he had put his little cassette recorder away, carefully stowed into his briefcase, I went back to my room, closed the door behind me, and sat there for a long while – scratching my beard and thinking, thinking, thinking.

LIFE'S A PARTY, ISN'T IT?

But too much thinking can get you in trouble. It's gotten me into trouble, right here with you – I can see you're getting fidgety already. You want a little romantic interest again, don't you? I can't blame you, really. Certainly, nothing holds one's attention better than that. Nothing at all. So . . . .

My relationship with Esther was going wrong, sour. The fun and excitement had worn off and we had already been together for quite a while merely out of inertia, from the fear of discomfort, and from sexual need. The multi-colored bird of happiness had flown off, leaving us no longer beneath its wings, and the dark night once again opened up around us. Both of us realized that it was over, over. We weren't right for each other. We had to move on.

It would be difficult, but we were forced to confront it. It was a prospect that held profound sadness and yet excitement, too, and gave each of us a slightly desperate edge. It was a mixture of complicated emotions which was not making our lives any simpler.

And so, when Robert Anderman, a friend from graduate school, called up to invite me to a party, I jumped at the chance.

"Sure, wonderful. I wouldn't miss it," I told him. I jotted the information on a piece of paper and stuck it in my mirror.

The evening of the party arrived. Carefully, I combed my hair, ran the comb through my beard, put on a clean flannel shirt, and left the house, the old nervous rush of adrenaline spilling through my veins.

Up the stairs of his funky Cambridge apartment house I went, taking the stairs two at a time. When I reached his door, I stood outside for a moment, hearing from within all the familiar party sounds, the sounds of voices, rock music, shuffling feet. A scene in which to feel right at home, no doubt. I walked inside.

Walking into a group scene like this, I was always initially shocked to realize that I didn't know anybody. Here was a whole apartment full of people talking, or sitting by themselves waiting to be talked to, pouring drinks, smoking, moving randomly from one room to another, and I didn't know anyone I saw.

Wasn't this what I had been so glad to leave behind when I joined the Havurah – that sensation of being the stranger in a crowded room? What a relief it had been to get away from that, and yet how much harder it was to experience it once again.

I looked around; it was a mixed crowd. There were white people and black people, handsome people and homely people, cool people and uncomfortable people, Jews and Gentiles, gay and straight, men and women. The divisions cut across every line. Every line indeed.

"Solomon!" Robert called out, coming down the hall. He, too, was dressed just like I was, in a flannel shirt and blue jeans. Obviously there was a great affinity between us.

"How're ya' doin'? I'm glad you could come!"

"Thanks," I said. "I'm doing fine. Things are sometimes a little rocky, but I'm okay."

"Oh, with Esther, huh? I was going to ask you. I thought maybe you wanted to bring her along?"

"Nope, not me," I said, and I smiled. I didn't bother telling him that she had recently moved out of the Havurah and into her own apartment, for the sake of both of us.

"Well," he said, "I'm sorry to hear, I guess. Should I be?"

"It's okay," I answered. "It was coming. It had to happen."

Now, Robert was actually a fine fellow. I had known him to be, at times, warm, intelligent, and even a sensitive person. I had spoken to him in private moments and knew him to be perceptive and honest. But this was a party, the social arena where we all turn into grotesqueries of ourselves and then engage in valorous combat. And Robert, this time around, was playing host.

"Well, what can you do," he offered. "Those are the breaks. Listen, I understand how you feel. And what you need right now is to meet someone else. It doesn't have to be The Great Love. But the sooner you meet someone else, the better."

"You're right," I said, matter-of-factly. But I also knew that you are always looking for The Great Love. Even when you don't want to find it, when you tell yourself it's not what you need right now, you're still looking for it. Because you're always looking for it.

"So," I said to him, "do you have anyone in mind?"

"I can't say I had anyone *in mind*," he replied. "But who knows what you might run into, just say hello to people. After all, it's a party – every man for himself."

He thought for a moment. Then he drew closer, as if in confidence. As if selling me a hot watch.

131

"Well," he said, "there's someone you might like. Let me introduce you to her."

"What's her name?" I asked.

"It's Lisa."

"Lisa what?" I asked.

"What do you mean, 'Lisa what?'" he said, feigning ignorance. "Her name's Lisa. It's just Lisa." He was playing with me now, fully understanding my question. "It's just Lisa," he repeated. "Lisa. Lisa Lisa."

"Okay," I said to him, as well as to myself. "So, let's go meet Lisa Lisa," and I followed him into the next room.

In the next room, sitting in the corner, two women seemed to be talking seriously about something. One was heavy, and scowling. She wore a tight leotard top and the rolls of her stomach undulated like the waves of a water mattress. She held a cigarette, whose smoke trailed upwards in a straight line before diffusing into a cloud of swirls.

The other young woman was quite pretty. A beauty even, with dark hair and a soft, glowing face. Good enough for a prince or a sheik's harem. Maybe even good enough for me.

"Okay," I thought, which do I get, the lady or the tiger?"

"Janet, Lisa," I'd like you to meet Solomon. He's a friend from grad school."

Janet, Miss Heavy Universe, gave me an unwelcoming glance while offering a tepid hello, and then took a long drag on her cigarette. The other, obviously Lisa, gave me a quick up and down and then smiled, a big, broad, lovely smile, all for me.

"Hi," she said.

I was temporarily stunned. An incredible reversal! I was right *in* there, suddenly the unexpected recipient of all the queen's favors. "Hi," I said, with enthusiasm.

I drew up a chair and so did Robert. The preliminaries were properly exchanged.

"Yeah, I'm a graduate student in English," I said. "Same as Robert. I'm a teaching assistant, too."

"That's interesting," Lisa said. "I used to be an English major, and I almost went to graduate school, too, but I didn't. I figured I had to do something a little more practical. So now I work for the *Globe,* in the Living section. Sometimes I write a few articles, but mostly I'm still copy editing."

"Far out," I said. "It sounds like it has its share of fun."

"Oh, it does, I suppose," she said. "It's a job. I like it. I like having a job."

There was a momentary pause. And then Lisa filled it. "But I really used to love poetry. I was heavily into Renaissance poetry for a while and did my senior thesis on Shakespeare's sonnets. I discussed his use of various metaphors." She smiled, letting me know she was still on my side.

Janet got up and excused herself – only to Lisa – to get something from the kitchen, where she undoubtedly lost herself somewhere between the pretzels and the M&M's.

Lisa and I continued talking, growing warmer towards each other, while Robert watched with an amused interest.

"I guess grad school keeps you pretty busy," Lisa said. "But what do you do when you're not doing that?"

"Oh, I ride my bicycle a lot, I like movies, I go walk in the woods and hang around with my friends, sometimes I smoke a little dope." I rattled off the usual list of acceptable entertainments.

"Solomon spends a lot of time with this group called the Havurah," Robert offered. "How's it doing these days?"

"The Havurah?" Lisa asked, a little distrustfully. "What's that?"

Oh no. Here it comes. I felt like saying, "Forget it, just forget it. Don't even bother with that one." I couldn't begin to explain. Not here, not now, not at a party, not to these people. Should I even make a stab at it, standing on one leg? No – just forget it.

"It's really too complicated to get into now," I said. "I really can't explain."

"Aw, no," Lisa protested. "I'd really like to know." It didn't seem like she *really* wanted to know. It was more as if she wanted to locate herself in relationship to me.

"No, really," I said, "just forget it. You'd get it all wrong. I'd explain it all wrong." I couldn't explain.

"Aw, c'mon," she said, playing friendly again.

"Well," I said, searching for words, falling back onto the semi-official jargon we used for everybody. "Havurah means like a group or a fellow-ship. We're an intentional alternative Jewish community."

"Oh, really?" she asked. "What do you do?"

"Well, we're an intentional group that got together to establish an alternative lifestyle for . . . modern Jewish life," I said, still searching, using my hands now. "We're, like . . . the Jewish counterculture."

"Oh," she said blankly.

I've got to stop this, I thought. Change the topic right now. Get out of this lead balloon.

"So," she repeated, "what do you *do*?"

"What do we do . . . .? We, uh, we have services, sometimes we have communal meals. We have classes. And we generally spend a lot of time together. And we're friends."

"Services?" she said. "Like what?"

Uh-oh. Here goes. We're treading onto the absurdities now. Might as well throw out the stops. She asked for it. You asked for it too. Go ahead. Jump.

"Okay, let's see . . . . Services. We, uh, sit on the floor, on cushions, usually like around the room . . . ." I was using my hands a lot now, struggling, ". . . and we have services which use the traditional Jewish liturgy as a springboard, but we try to be creative with it, add readings, some people sing songs, sometimes different people present different ideas . . . ."

I was trying to get through it as painlessly as possible, with as much information as I could supply in the shortest amount of time. Why did this make me so uncomfortable?

"Wait a minute," she interjected. "You mean you sit around in a circle, and you *pray*, and you *sing songs*, and you *get off on that*?" she said incredulously, and not without a bit of condescension.

That was it. It was over. Finished. All avenues of easy communication severed, all prospects of getting Lisa either into my life or between my sheets utterly exploded.

"Oh, man," I said, "I knew you wouldn't get it if I tried to explain."

At this point, Robert sensed the damage he had done, and in a half-hearted effort tried to atone for the dissension he had sparked. "It's not what you think it is, Lisa," he said. "I even went there a few times. It's a pretty interesting place."

Lisa just dismissed Robert's remarks as irrelevant. Or worse, they added to what was now becoming a definite shift in our stances, with Lisa on one side and me on the other. It also fueled some strange feeling inside her that was building up and deciding whether or not to come out.

"Well," she said, "I'm sure it's very nice. It just doesn't sound like a place for me."

"You can't really say that," I said. "You don't understand what it is."

"Look," she said, with a quickening self-righteous fervor, "you know, I went to Hebrew school. I know what that stuff's about."

"I would never have guessed," I answered.

Should I really throw out the stops now, should I maybe get sarcastic or downright combative, or was I still trying to salvage something here?

". . . and I'll tell you, I learned a whole lot of bullshit. They tried to teach me a real ton of crap."

"Well," I said, still trying to be polite and yet honest, "there's crap and there's not-crap. It depends on what you do with it."

At this point, she didn't want to hear about that. It was as if she now felt that she shared enough with me so that she could turn abusive. We were part of the same family, and within the family you could say anything you wanted.

"For five years I went to Hebrew school," she went on, taking the offensive, "and they tried to make me learn to read these stupid prayers. I couldn't even understand them. And they taught me all these crazy rules about what you should do and what you shouldn't do, and how you should feel guilty if you ate in a Chinese restaurant, and how you had to be a good-ie-goodie all the time. And I had some gross old man for a teacher who used to pinch all the girls on the cheek, and he stunk of garlic and had warts on his face."

Now she was delivering a lecture and purging herself, at me, of some earlier, unredressed violation,

"You know, I had to sit in that stinky little room three days a week after school and be victimized – yes, victimized – by a bunch of religious old nuts who just got in the way of my being with my friends and spending a normal childhood like everybody else. I can't even believe I sat through all that. I look back at it and I'm amazed I didn't just run away or something. I *hated* it," she said vehemently.

"I'm sure you did," I said,

She glowered. Robert was beginning to feel very uncomfortable. He hadn't really meant to bring all *this* on.

"Listen," I said, "I know how screwed up American Judaism can be . . . ."

"You're right. It is," she interrupted.

". . . but there are some things which aren't necessarily screwed up. That's exactly what the Havurah is trying to show."

But there was no talking to her. What was I doing, anyway, suddenly feeling like I had to defend myself, defend my friends, and become Defender of the Faith? I had my own disagreements with the tradition and my own gripes to bitch about. Still, I wanted to defuse her anger and say something that would make me seem at least better than what she had been exposed to.

"Look at it this way. You said you liked poetry. Do you think there's any connection between poetry, um, self-expression, aesthetics – and religious feeling? I don't mean organized religion, I just mean, well, transcendental experience." Oh, forget this, I thought. I heard myself become preachy, and I didn't like it.

"I don't *believe* in transcendental experience," she said. Whether she did or not was irrelevant. Now she wasn't going to give me an inch.

What the hell am I doing here, I wondered, arguing with this gorgeous, supposedly mature woman, who is throwing me all her adolescent anger at being cooped up in Hebrew school? What's the connection? Why do I have to listen to all this?

"Well, look," I said finally, "I can't solve your problems from childhood. I wish I could, but that's not my line of business. I don't proselytize. Besides, I don't disagree with anything you said."

This last comment was taken by Lisa not as a statement of sympathy, but as one of submission. I had lost the debate I had not even been debating.

"I'm glad you see it my way," she said coldly. And then she got up and propelled her lovely body out of the room.

I turned to Robert.

"Sorry," he said with a shrug. "Good luck with the next one, man."

"Thanks anyway," I said. He took this as a sign of release, which he promptly acted upon. He, too, got up and moved on.

I walked over to a group of people who were standing around in a circle, passing a joint around and around, saying nothing, gently swaying with the music, whose loud presence I suddenly became aware of.

The words to *"Baby, You're a Rich Man"* came floating through the air.

I intercepted the joint and took a few drags.

"Hey, man, don't bogey the jay," said a fellow with long flowing hair in a white gauze shirt with flowers embroidered on the front.

"I've got some catching-up to do," I told him.

"Oh, that's cool, man." And he smiled. I passed it on. After a few more rounds of tokes, I left for the kitchen.

In the kitchen, Janet was pouring herself a glass of Coke and plopping ice cubes into it.

"Hi. Could I have some of that?" I said, pointing to the bottle in her hand.

She handed it to me without a sound. She turned her back and walked off, stopping only for a second to dig her hand into the pretzels for a fresh supply.

"Oh, man," I said to myself.

I intercepted a few more joints as they came floating through, and drank a beer after the Coke. I left the kitchen and went back into the living room.

Everything became altered with the dope. The room looked hazier, the noise was louder, the people, individually, looked more unique. "Monsters," I said.

Then I caught sight of Lisa talking to a guy with a tremendous mustache curled at the ends, probably with mustache wax. He seemed to be some sort of self-appointed character, someone to spot in a crowd. As she stood talking to him, she uncannily sensed my eyes on her, because she suddenly turned and looked directly at me, just for an instant. Yet in that instant, I received the full blast of her disapproval, suspicion and horror, as if I were something worse than a dirty old man who wanted to put a hand up her pants in a crowded subway, worse than a skinny little guy with gold teeth stepping out from a darkened doorway to proposition her with filthy photographs. Worse than those, I was someone who wanted to trick her, to put something over on her soul and surreptitiously bend her to my perverted will. Either that, or else I was just some fucked-up weirdo on a crazy God trip. She turned away, and so did I.

Back to the kitchen I went, where Janet was moving along the side of the table, still preying on M&M's and pieces of cake like a happy, sadistic spider. I quickly had a glass of wine, some beer, and I began to feel woozy. I realized, in a strange flash of insight, that for me, the party was over.

I walked back into the living room and looked around. Lisa was gone, vanished. The guy with the mustache was talking to somebody else, a woman wearing beads, lots of beads. Blue, green, purple. I stared at her beads for several seconds, dangling, jingling, hanging about her neck. Suddenly I snapped out of it and walked towards the door.

"Hey, Solomon!" Robert called out, materializing from nowhere. "Are you going? It's still pretty early."

"I know," I mumbled. "I gotta go. Thanks for inviting me."

"Sure. Well, take care. See you."

I walked down the stairs, this time more slowly and carefully than I had taken them on the ascent. I walked outside and the night greeted me, fresh and dark.

Trying to breathe in the night air, I foundered in the direction of the Havurah, my legs still wobbly. I stumbled my way through the long walk across town.

I finally arrived at the Havurah but did not go into the house. Instead, I walked across the street, down the block, around the corner and up some stairs, leaving me standing in front of a doorway not my own.

I was drunk and stoned, and it was one of those privileged moments in which I allowed myself to believe in God, merely in order to have someone to talk to.

"Listen, God," I said. "After tonight, you owe me something. You know that."

But that did not quite help me suppress the other emotion I felt, which I sensed with a clarity as cold and hard as steel. I felt defeated and miserable for what had happened, for where I was now, and for what I was about to do. I lifted my hand and pressed on Esther's doorbell.

KI HEM HAYEYNU

Ki hem hayeynu v'orech yamenu, uvahem nehegeh yawmam va-lailah
"For this is our life and the length of our days, and
we will reflect upon it day and night"

Well, not long after Esther moved out of the house, I decided to move out, too. A change of scenery would do me good, I thought, even if not too radical a change. I took an apartment about half a mile away, not so far that I'd lose touch, but just far enough to see what it was like to live back in the regular world for a while.

You can lose perspective living in the Havurah, I figured, and for some strange reason I thought perhaps that was no good. Unhealthy. I needed a dose of reality again.

So, as I said, I got a little apartment not too far away, a quiet place where I could study in peace, without the constant distraction of being right in the center of Havurah comings and goings.

* * *

Downstairs, they were beating their kids again. Up through the floor came the hoarse cries of children screaming, "No!" and running around the apartment. Exactly in which directions they were running, I couldn't make out, but I could hear the hurried sound of small feet and the chaos of movement and chase.

The dog, perpetually chained to the radiator, started in to yelp without stop, while I could hear Mrs. Dilboy herself, all two-hundred-and-fifty pounds of her, bump into things as she lumbered after her prey, no doubt wielding a broomstick or a newspaper or whatever other piece of junk she happened to pick up from the floor of their garbage-heaped apartment.

I put down my book, because I just couldn't concentrate any more.

I listened for the sounds. And they came, too, more or less as expected. "Whack. Whack. Whack." Even the dog stopped yelping, as the sound of children's screaming transmuted into the sound of crying. I could practically see her down there, standing above them as they sobbed to themselves, her face puffed from excitement but her arms crossed in triumph.

The calmer, more rhythmic sound of sobbing and tears was a good sign. It meant that silence, and the restoration of order, was on its way, like a dying fall. Soon, the noise died down, as it always did, and even the dog knew to be quiet again. The world downstairs no longer existed.

I picked up my book and continued to stare at its print. I stared for at least five minutes, reading words, sentences, more words, until I realized that I hadn't assimilated anything. I didn't remember what I had read, if, indeed, I had really covered ground at all.

What happened to those minutes, where were they? Who was I kidding, trying to convince myself that I was getting anything accomplished?

My room was stuffy, and I realized that it had progressively gotten hotter and stuffier until I was sweating under my arms. I pulled off my old grey sweater and sat there, just in my shirt. Then I massaged my temples in a slow, circular motion and stretched my mouth very wide, trying to dispel the hot fog which had begun to collect in my brain. But, despite my therapeutic maneuvers, there was still a region I could not seem to reach, which seemed like a tightly shut box somewhere behind my eyes and beneath the dome of my skull. It was shut tight, like my stuffy room, and nothing could pry it open.

Rest time. I stared at my desk, for no reason, just to stare. I looked at each item slowly. A can of pencils and pens, a pile of books stacked on their side, papers, more papers, a few pennies and a dime, all found room on my crowded little desk and remained there, perfectly inert. Perfect existence as perfect objects.

Right across from me, on the wall above the desk, on postcards or clippings, a scattering of faces from old masters and museum treasures either stared at me in silent accusation or else continued in their posture of forever looking away. I contemplated one face, the face of a silent-eyed Renoir bather who displayed her bared torso, with its marvelous, marvelous breasts, in an attitude of complete indifference – an indifference not from apathy, but because her simple-minded attention seemed taken up elsewhere.

How many times had I stared at her, watched her, admired her, while she took absolutely no notice of me? How many times had I contemplated her breasts, which changed with every viewing – now large, now smaller, now youthful, now beginning to sag – without her awareness that someone was there?

"Someone, my dear, is there. Please keep that in mind," I said aloud.

But of course, she didn't smile or acknowledge me in any way. It was as if I didn't exist at all.

I continued to sit there, and again the minutes ticked by without being filled by any content whatsoever. They just slipped off that way, even without my having sanctioned their going. It just happened; it was stronger than I was, so I gave in to it, until I suddenly reemerged into consciousness – five minutes later, or ten, or was it even twenty? – and I was vaguely aware of discomfort in my body.

It was an indescribable discomfort, not localized to any particular area, limb, or organ, but was hidden beneath the skin, like a very fine layer of grated glass, slowly shifting and rubbing against itself to produce an unpleasant agitation. Suddenly I was aware of the content of those minutes; some of the images that had flitted through my unfocused brain stuck with me, and I could only smile wryly at myself.

"Has it been that long?" I asked myself. I thought back.

It certainly was that long. "Three weeks now, or is it four?" No, it was not even four, but five weeks, or maybe six or seven – but there are some things I am ashamed even to admit to myself. Dignity must be preserved, after all. The dignity of the human individual is not to be taken lightly.

"Four weeks, then?" I leaned back in my chair and indulged myself, as I indulged myself every day.

"Where is fame?" I asked aloud. "Where are fame and fortune? And where are all the women?" I allowed my questions to sound rhetorical, mostly to prevent myself from actually having to answer them.

"In time," I said, "in time." But time was certainly taking its own sweet time about it.

At the moment, however, there was nothing to do about it. Without even realizing it, I had suddenly gotten out of my seat, left my desk, and was heading into the kitchen.

Going to the kitchen, I would joke to myself, was my religious act of the day. It was like going to God. I would approach, hoping to find something there, something exciting and satisfying, while I also knew I'd find nothing at all.

I was even aware of the disappointment that would follow once I got there. And yet, I was driven to go. I hoped for a surprise, some tantalizing wonder, something to soothe my appetite – but who would have left me this soothing something? After all, I stocked my own shelves. I knew that I would find the same cans of condensed soup, the same peanut butter and powdered milk, the same box of Quaker oatmeal, cans of tuna fish, raw beans, uncooked spaghetti, all staring down at me in a most unappetizing array. Of course, I knew I could buy something special for myself whenever I went shopping, but there, too, everything on the shelves would have that same, unappealing look. Going shopping just meant buying more of the same. By now I bought by habit.

"*Vayehi binsoah ha-aron,*" I sang out, as I swung open the doors of the cupboard, like opening the doors of the *aron kodesh*. "Hello, God," I announced.

I was proud of my analogy. I smirked to myself.

Yet even while I smirked, I felt my appetite wane with disappointment at the lack of anything to pique it into hopeful existence. I looked at my shelves. Well, maybe a spoonful of peanut butter would suffice. A peanut butter offering from the manna in my kitchen.

As I twirled a soupspoon into the thick, light brown paste, I looked out the window, and for the first time that day I became aware of the world outside. What time was it? I looked at the old clock radio perched atop the refrigerator. It said two-thirty.

I thought about it and did a little calculating. I had gotten out of bed at ten, and started working at my desk at about eleven, or maybe it was eleven-thirty. I had actually worked fairly well for part of the day, and so I credited myself with three hours of solid work. Not bad, I figured. Another solid hour or two and I could feel as if I done a good day's work. And since there were so many hours left to the day, it seemed that now I could allow myself to get some fresh air, to take a walk around the neighborhood, pick up the paper or maybe even stop by at the day-old bread store and buy a loaf of day-old bread. One thing I felt I had in common with the working-class people in the neighborhood was that we all shopped at the day-old bread store for our slightly stale staff of life.

I went downstairs, opened the door and walked into a dull, grey afternoon light. The porch was strewn with broken toys belonging to the Dilboy children: a doll without arms, a derailed rocking horse, a toy trumpet with no mouthpiece. I picked my way through them and descended onto the sidewalk.

Across the street, a group of young locals huddled under the lamppost, standing silently and staring into space, doing nothing. They had nothing to do. When they saw me, they sullenly turned their backs, turning inward into their little congregation. One of them spit on the ground. I pulled up my collar and walked on, paying them no further attention.

After a few blocks, I reached the commercial center: a colorless intersection lined with small shops selling discount cosmetics, bargain-basement clothing, and household necessities. A five-and-dime, a doughnut shop, and several bars were also prominent attractions. I headed into the day-old bread store and pushed open the heavy glass door, which made a little bell jingle.

Inside, the store was lined with shelf after shelf stocked with day-old bread. Day-old pumpernickel, day-old rye bread, day-old white bread covered the walls. There were also day-old English muffins and plastic bags full of day-old rolls. An old woman with a shopping bag was surveying the display.

I decided to stock up so I wouldn't have to return for a few days. Scanning the shelves, I pulled out what seemed to be a goodly assortment and I stacked it onto the counter. The store keeper, a small, lame, aging man, hobbled over behind the counter and perched himself at the cash register.

I looked at him carefully as he rang up my purchase. Once I had seen his name under his picture in a local flyer that had been stuck in my mailbox, in which I was told that "The Merchants of Daley Square Welcome You" to their various establishments. I couldn't tell whether this short man with thinning hair and an expressionless face was Jewish or not. Neither his face nor his name, which I recalled was George Miller, could give me enough of a clue. I suspected that he was, as were a few of the other local Edomville merchants. However, even if he were, it would not have been good business to recognize me as a *landsman*. Certainly, I was readily identifiable as Jewish, but my long hair and beard made me too strange, either for him to be comfortable with or else for him to side with, especially with other customers in the store.

Silently, he took my money, looked at me once, then said thank you in a noncommittal way, and put the money into the cash register. I picked up my bag of bread and left the store.

Walking out, the bag of bread in my arms, I decided not to go back to my studies but instead to go pay Max a visit. Today, I knew, he would be home, locked away in his own little world, also studying.

But Max was very different from me. After all, I was no longer a passionate student, and so I did what I had to and avoided the rest, but Max approached his studies differently. He had a wife, scholarly ambition if not devotion, and a shrewd businessman for an uncle (who also employed Max's father) who constantly heckled Max about being a graduate student.

"Max," his uncle would say, "what does a university professor make? Peanuts! Come into the business, you'll make twice as much, no problem."

As a result, all these factors combined to make Max approach his studies with intensified seriousness, a forced idealism, and the deadly earnest of scholarship as a business.

And so, as I detoured towards Max's house, I also knew that my appearance would undoubtedly upset him. Whenever I came during the day, he viewed it as an interruption. It shook his concentration. And although – and precisely because – I loved Max, shaking his concentration was exactly what I wanted to do. I wanted to remind him that in the midst of all this study of the humanities, he was still a human being.

Arriving at his door, I knocked on the glass, making a little "tink-tink-tinking" with my fingers. I waited with a wry trepidation as, after a few seconds, I heard from inside a chair being pushed backwards and scrape along the floor. Then I saw a hand push aside the white window curtain. And then I saw Max.

He looked at me through the window with no visible emotion. The door swung open. "Hi, Solomon," he said flatly, and immediately he returned to his desk.

"Hiya, Max," I said, following him to his desk.

"I'll be with you in a minute," he answered. "I just want to finish something."

I took a seat near his desk, and I watched as he re-immersed himself into his work. He was taking notes on something, and as I calmly sat watching him, I took notice not of what he was reading but of what he was doing. Even though it was well into the afternoon, he was still wearing his pajamas and a big, dull, grey bathrobe. All that showed of his pajamas was from his knees down, a crumpled, light, billowy material that stopped somewhere above his bare ankles.

On his feet were an old pair of slippers. His hair had also not yet been combed that day. Luckily, he had a beard, so he didn't look particularly unshaven. I wondered if he had even washed. It wasn't that he was slovenly, and certainly not because he was lazy, that he kept himself like that all day. Simply, since it was a day of studying, he probably woke up bright and early, along with Rebecca who was off to work by seven-thirty, and after she left the house he just sat down at his desk and started in. Why waste time getting dressed?

At last he put down his pen, but he didn't close his book. Instead, he merely pushed it away, a very small distance. A tiny distance. It was more of a ritual push than an actual one. Then he looked up.

"Well, how are you doing, Solomon? What's new?" he asked, trying to be polite. I knew he meant well, even though it was hard for him.

"Oh, I'm okay. Nothing special. Nothing's up," I said, as I unzipped my jacket and leaned back, making myself comfortable.

This made Max a little nervous – he didn't want me to make myself *too* comfortable. "What are you working on?" I asked.

"This? I have to give a class about political theories on the relationship between government and business. I still have a lot to read, and I really want to do it thoroughly." It was a gentle hint.

"I can imagine," I replied, taking a deep breath.

"And so, what are *you* working on these days," he asked, searching for a topic.

"Me? Ah, some crap. I dunno. Garbage." I picked up a book from his desk and lazily scrutinized it. He waited.

"Well," I continued, "I'm reading through all these sonnet sequences. After a while, they're all the same. They're coming out of my ears. Who cares, anyways?" I could feel my negativity increase his uneasiness one more notch. He cracked his knuckles.

"Your trouble is that you don't know what you want to do in graduate school," he said at last. "You're floundering."

"That's true," I said, matter-of-factly. "I'm lost. I have no concentration anymore. But do you know why?"

"Why?" he asked, tentatively.

"Because it doesn't have any *meaning* for me anymore. So what if I read ten sonnets, or a hundred – or a thousand? All together they don't mean as much as one good sonnet meant when I was an undergraduate. Now, all I do is read them to know *about* them. I don't read them for what they are."

"Well, now you're a professional. It's different."

"It's shitty."

"Well," he agreed, "sometimes it's shitty. But you have to look at it more practically. You have to evaluate it from a cost-benefit perspective. You want to be a professor, right?"

"I don't know; let's say I do." I answered hesitantly. "Well, maybe. Okay."

"So if you do, then you have to accept what it takes to get there, and just do it. It's work, but that's life."

"It's shitty," I muttered again, sulking, finding nothing else to say. There was a brief silence, which I finally broke.

"Listen," I continued, "I can't stand the loneliness of it. I just can't sit all day by myself locked away in a little room. Somehow that doesn't seem like the goal of all this – sitting by yourself, not talking to anybody at all. And I can't only see it in terms of the future. I have to see it in terms of the present. This is my life, man. This is how I spend my day. And it stinks."·

He just looked at me. I was making him nervous.

"It's crazy, Max," I went on, getting excited. "It's absolutely absurd. And worse than that – it's goyish, too. The model is totally goyish. In a yeshiva you don't study alone. You don't sit all day without talking to anybody. In yeshiva they study together, in one big room, or in pairs, working over the same text, and you have someone else to sound your ideas against. But this university business, it comes out of the monastic life. It's a development of the church and the way they studied there, every monk locked in his own little cell, living his ascetic life, communicating with nobody at all, except, of course, if he happened to plug into God – then you don't need anybody else. But that's not Jewish. Max, we're just modern-day monks, that's all."

I looked at Max, sitting there in his bathrobe and slippers.

"Look at you," I said, gesticulating. "You even *look* like a monk, wrapped up in your robe, sitting in your bare feet. All you need is a rope around your waist and you'd look like Saint Francis."

I laughed, and that pushed it a little too far. Max began to take the offensive.

"So, go *join* a yeshiva," he said. "If all you want to do is study something that seems meaningful to you, fine – go study in a yeshiva. You'll certainly learn a lot."

"Yeah," I said, deflated. "Me in a yeshiva, right? The problem with a yeshiva is you've gotta buy the whole thing. Hook, line, and sinker – tallis, tefillin and yarmulke. Ah, shoot, man – I'd go crazy in a yeshiva, too."

"Well, then," he said, "then you have to play the university game. And when you do, you have to look at it like a business. You're selling your brains: you write an article, you speak to professors, you do what you've got to do to get somewhere. You learn to enjoy what you can, and you make a life for yourself." He smiled grimly.

"Doesn't sound so attractive, if you ask me," I answered.

"Well then," he said, pulling his last ace from his sleeve, "the only other alternative is to be like Zack."

I stopped to give it some thought. This one had to be weighed.

Zack had once been a rabbinical student, but, for whatever reasons, he gave it up and went into academics instead. Unofficially, he had become the community's resident scholar, the Havurah's own brilliant academic.

Talented and intelligent, over the years he had amassed a tremendous store of information and knowledge. He had moved into the Havurah house, into Ira's room after Ira left, and filled it with books from floor to ceiling, making the huge, odd-shaped room look like an antiquarian's library or a rambling second-hand bookstore. Books were everywhere. Piles of books were stacked up in corners where there was no longer room on the crowded shelves, and many of the piles had fallen over, scattering books all over the floor.

He knew what was in them, too. We were awed at the scope of his intellectual achievement, and yet we were also frightened at the tenor of his life. For, despite the fact that Zack was several years older than either Max or me, he was still only a graduate student. True, he was further along than either of us, already working on his dissertation, but he had spent years and years on it. And over the years, as he labored over it, it became more than just a dissertation; it took on the intimate properties of his own personal life question. He wrote whole chapters and threw them out; he crossed out huge sections and pared them down to little paragraphs. For weeks and months, he would follow the winding track of one idea, only to discard it at the end of the journey. It was a never-ending process, always prone to further refinement and subtlety.

And he suffered for it. His professors told him just to finish it already, not to worry so much about it, to simply get it done and move on to the next step. But Zack couldn't let it go, even though it grew more obscure with every new development, always more specialized, demanding a smaller and smaller audience, if indeed, there could ever have been any audience other than just Zack himself.

He lost sleep, he even became an insomniac. All night long, when everyone else was asleep, Zack would prowl like a ghost through the corridors of the Havurah, going from the library to the bathroom, from his room into the kitchen and then back into the library, thinking, worrying, contemplating his dissertation. Big bags grew under his eyes, and his face grew paler and greyer.

I frowned. So that was the only alternative. I got up and buttoned my coat. "Okay," I said. "I'll go."

Max, I felt, took no relish in his victory. He knew it was unfair. He felt lousy about it.

"Look," he said, growing softer, "why don't you call me up tonight, sometime after Rebecca comes home, and maybe then we can all go out and do something – we'll go out for ice cream, or something like that."

"Sure," I said, quietly. "I'll call you tonight. I'll see you later."

And with that, I picked up my big bag full of day-old bread, and I left.

NIGHT LIGHTS

As you can see, I eventually moved back into the Havurah. Right back to my room on the fourth floor, with the turret and my dead plants still hanging in the windows. I liked it up there. I was glad I could return. It didn't change my life much, but at least I was back at the Havurah . . .

I awoke in the middle of the night and I couldn't get back to sleep. I lay there for a long time, trying to push myself back down into myself and fall asleep again. Nothing. I rolled over and switched on the light. The clock read 3:25.

What does one do at 3:25 in the morning, unable to sleep? Should I read? I had no desire to read. Exercise? No, not now. Eat? Yes, maybe eat. Perhaps that might satisfy whatever it was that needed attention. I slipped on a pair of underpants and went downstairs.

In the kitchen, I pressed a button and the overhead fluorescent bulb flickered and went on with a tiny buzz. I went over to the refrigerator, pulled at the door, and looked inside.

What did I have to eat? And what did I *want* to eat? The light in the refrigerator illumined a harsh white interior stained with occasional splotches of dried-up liquids, spots of reddish brown like clotted blood, and dark yellow smears. Inside were a few jars and bottles full of unappetizing sauces and soups. A bottle of juice. A dried-up apple, some wilting celery. A potato wrapped in aluminum foil. A lot of animal and vegetable matter in varying stages of decay.

I looked at my shelves. The same stuff. Bread. Peanut butter. Uncooked this and that. I wasn't hungry anyway.

I walked out of the kitchen and into the prayer room.

The prayer room was dark, except for the ner tamid, which cast a strange glow. Illumined by candle, the ner tamid sent out a huge circle of light that covered almost the entire ceiling with a soft, yellow candlelight that seemed to pulsate as the candle flickered. The light moved as if a thing alive, its circle growing larger, smaller, larger, across the ceiling. All else was dark.

I sat down on one of the cushions. What was I going to do – pray, perhaps, or even just open my mouth, to say something, anything? I had nothing to say. There was neither a message I had to deliver nor anyone to whom I had to deliver it. Only the candle flickered, casting its circle of light.

And so I sat there in my underpants, as midnight thoughts crawled through my brain.

I wondered about the room I was sitting in. This room, with its hanging plants and its macramé ark, and its cushions scattered across the floor. It is told that once the Baal Shem Tov could not bring himself to enter an apparently empty shul.

"It's too crowded," he said, "there's no room."

"Too crowded?" his followers asked. "It's empty."

"No," he answered them, "it's full. Full of unascended prayers."

Is this room, too, full of unascended prayers? Is it full of any prayer at all? And yet, what a wondrous amount of things have happened in this room. How many people have come here, how many different stories have gone on in this room over the years, hundreds and hundreds, all of which but a tiny few I'm totally ignorant.

Yes, the years. How many years have I been in this room? Over four years already, almost five. I've seen strangers and friends come and go, people get bored or grow ecstatic, good times happen and pass, crowds gather and disperse. And yet here I am, still sitting here, still sitting on these cushions. Sometimes I feel like the Old Man of the Mountain here, and sometimes just like the dummy who got left behind.

What about all those friends I grew up with, of whom I lost track years ago, who went on to become lawyers, engineers or accountants? Where are they now? Are they all asleep now, somewhere in their little apartments, getting their bodies ready to go to work in the morning? I wonder – am I the only one who can even walk into a place like this at 3:30 in the morning, much less the only one who is doing it now? Am I the only one who would even want to? All those locked-up shuls in suburbia. But am I also the only one with no real job to get to in the morning, no place waiting for me to arrive and perform a skillful little labor? Do I have such a deep and complicated soul that it demands such a luxury – and is this such a luxury after all? To sit in front of the ark and the ner tamid in my shorts in the middle of the night and contemplate my sleepless hours? Is that what it all boils down to – and is this what I've changed my life for? To watch the ner tamid flicker in this crazy way? But would I do it differently if I had the choice again – would I, after all, give up this strange satisfaction of sitting here in exchange for a cushy job whose only choices, on sleepless nights, are the bathroom mirror or the Alka-Seltzer?

I don't know. I don't know, and yet, I think not. Don't ask me why.

I continued to sit there and the ner tamid continued to flicker.

Soon, I supposed, I would grow tired and go back to sleep. Then, suddenly, I heard footsteps. Zack was coming down the stairs.

I stood up, making noise so as not to startle him by abruptly appearing out of the darkness, and I walked into the lighted kitchen.

"Oh, hi Solomon," he said, looking slightly distracted, almost as if being caught in the act of something he'd rather not be discovered doing.

"Hi, Zack," I answered, being friendly.

"I just came down to get a bite to eat. I couldn't sleep," he explained.

"Well, I did the same. Maybe I'll sleep now. Good night, Zack." I headed up the stairs, smiling to myself, leaving the scene in order to give Zack the full privacy of his own midnight snack.

Well, that's enough for now, I suppose. You look ready to fall asleep yourself. So good night to you, too. I hope you sleep well. Don't worry about waking up early -- services don't start here until pretty late in the morning. We call them for 10:30, and even so they usually don't start until almost eleven. We go easy on ourselves here, especially on Shabbos. After all, Shabbos is a day of rest.

Anyway, sleep tight. I hope you enjoyed my stories, and I hope I'm not boring you with all this talk. Stories are important, you know. Somehow, we can't live without them. If someone doesn't tell us stories, we start telling them to ourselves. You'll see. Just close your eyes, let yourself drift off to sleep, and before you know it, you'll dream yourself some stories of your own.

I hope they're pleasant ones.

So, good night now. *Lailah tov.* Good night.

SEUDAH SHNIAH

Good morning! How are you this morning?

Are you still stoned? Yeah? Me too! I'll tell you, this is good dope we grow around here. If you haven't come down yet, I'll bet you'll stay stoned for the rest of the day.

And what a lovely way to pass the time it is. Relax and enjoy yourself. After all, that's what Shabbos is all about.

But it's time for services again, too. Not like last night, with the lights low, with everything mysterious and ethereal; now it's daylight out, clear, bright daylight. Clear, bright, stoned daylight for davening and reading the Torah. So come on into the prayer room again.

Look – people are already arriving. We've just about got a minyan now, so we might as well begin. Here's a siddur, here's a tallis if you want one, and here are two empty cushions, right next to each other, just for you and me . . . .

Good Shabbos again! I hope that services weren't too freaky for you. No? Good, good. We'll make a crazy Jewish hippie out of you yet. You'll see.

Kiddush time! Time for kiddush!

Would you like to make kiddush?

Ah, I see. It's still a little early for that. I understand. I forget that just because I'm comfortable here, not everyone else is. You still need more time. I understand.

So, I'll make kiddush, okay? Here goes:

"The children of Israel shall keep the Sabbath, observing the Sabbath throughout the generations as an everlasting pact. It is a sign between me and the children of Israel forever that in six days the Lord made the heavens and the earth, and on the seventh day he ceased from work and rested.

"And so the Lord blessed the seventh day and made it holy."

Lchaim! Boruch ata adonai, elohenu melech haolam, borai pri hagafen.

Aw-mayn. Drink up!

Aaah, what a breakfast.

But now it's time for lunch! So, help me shlep all this stuff outside, okay? It's too nice a day to eat indoors, so let's eat in the back yard. Here, take this bowl and I'll take that one. Can you carry this too? And this? I've got the dishes and the challah, and so now let's go outside and sit beneath the grape vines.

Here, put it all right here on the grass. Aah, it's lovely here. Our lovely little garden spot, right beneath the grape arbor. Look up at the sky. See the birds?

Well, let's say motzi and dig in.

Yumm, ummm . . . . This is good stuff. Not bad for leftovers. Not bad at all . . . .

Whew – I'm stuffed. I'm just gonna lie down for a minute and . . . . . .

Hey man! You still there? Holy mackerel, I must have fallen asleep. I just nodded right off. Well, what can you do – you're *supposed* to sleep on Shabbos afternoon. What's Shabbos without a good long nap? In fact, I'm so pooped all of a sudden that I'm just gonna stretch out right here and go back to sleep.

Hey, while I take my nap, I have something that maybe you'd like to look at. Something to bore you, perhaps, to send you right off to sleep as well. You see, once I had these dreams of becoming a writer. I thought I'd write a whole bunch of stories about the Havurah. Somehow, I thought it was worth preserving for posterity. Maybe I was a little presumptuous. Anyway, I went and wrote a load of stories, trying to capture some idea about what goes on around here. But somehow, the project just died. It was really too big for me. So I gave up.

But I did manage to write a passel of stories anyway, a mishmash of tales from all the different years I've been here. There's no order to them – there are early stories and late stories, all jumbled together. Like I told you, I'm not so good at organizing.

Anyway, if you'd like to read them, I'll be glad to let you. Normally, I don't do this – it's not like I show them to everybody, expecting to be told I'm a new Sholom Aleichem or anything like that. But you're a nice person and I can tell you're not interested in being too harsh a critic. You just might enjoy them. So, read whatever you like. Like I said – maybe they'll help you fall asleep.

Here they are, in this little old notebook. I just happen to have it with me.

Wake me up in a little while, okay? Man, am I tired . . . .

ROSH HASHANAH

It was to be my first Rosh Hashanah at the Havurah. Only a few days earlier, I had come out of the green woods and mountains, where I had been spending the summer, to set up my new life in our rambling old house.

I was still filled with youthful enthusiasm, and believed I was about to join in and become part of that frenzied wave of creativity, rebellion and madness that was washing over America, tossing up onto its shores strange creatures from its hidden depths, shaping them into new configurations and then leaving the country cleansed, purged and refreshed.

I was eager to be part of such an exciting moment.

In the days that preceded Rosh Hashanah, the last days of Elul, my main objective was to settle into the house, a task that didn't promise to be particularly strenuous.

Down to the basement I went, to see whatever furnishings I could scrounge up. The Havurah basement was full of old furniture, boxes, junk and cast-off possessions of every sort, all of which had been left behind by people who had previously lived in the house or who had merely been passing through and needed a place to store their things, which, no doubt, they would never come back to reclaim.

The old wooden stairs creaked under my feet as I descended, and I pulled a cord that snapped on a dim little overhead bulb.

In the semi-darkness, I peered around to see what I could find. A musty, damp odor pervaded everything, a smell of mildew, of earth, of heating oil, of the old building itself, creating its own individual odor accumulated over the years under previous inhabitants as well as from its present owners. Boxes were heaped up on other boxes, furniture was chaotically tossed around. Table legs stuck obliquely into the air, chairs hid beneath lamps and pots, and empty bookshelves stood like gaping mouths.

At first, I just looked around, taking everything in. Then, with an eye on individual items, I began to inspect particular pieces.

I pulled at a chair leg and extracted a dark brown desk chair. I looked at it critically. A long crack streaked through its seat and a white, moldy fluff grew along one of its legs. I rejected it.

Then I noticed a desk, lying on its side in the corner. It was still clean and in good shape, its writing surface smooth except for a couple of long scratches along its edge. It would do. I decided to take it.

Next, I located another chair, this one in better condition than the first. I removed a box of dishes from its seat and sat down. Did it wobble? Only slightly. It could easily be fixed with a bit of glue and perhaps a screw or two.

A bookshelf stood alongside the wall, filled only with dust. I ran my fingers through the dust, revealing a shiny hardwood streak in the otherwise powdery grey coating. This was obviously a find, a treasure. I would take it, for sure.

One by one, the pieces passed beneath my purview.

As this process continued, my critical eye gave way to a visionary one. I began to think of what other pieces I might need and how I might arrange the furniture in my room. I could put the desk by the window, the bookcase by the door. Or perhaps the bookcase by the window, the desk in the far corner.

Each piece must not only be judged for itself now, but for its place in an entirety which was beginning to emerge, if still only in my mind.

I continued to rummage, enjoying the surprise of chance discovery. I spotted a large, steel, double-sized bedspring pushed up against the wall. I tilted it away from the wall and noticed there was a door behind it, but the door had no handle. It was barely distinguishable as a door, because it looked like just another wooden panel of the basement wall. But with the bedspring removed, the door was discernible, especially by the metal door-knob plate, brown and rusty, that nevertheless lacked a doorknob which so obviously belonged there.

I poked my finger into the hole where the doorknob should have been, and I pulled, but I did not have enough strength in just my one finger to pull it open. The door was shut tight, jammed closed by years of immobility. I shrugged and continued to look for more furniture.

Finally, I had all that I needed: a desk, a desk chair, an easy chair, a big standing floor lamp, a little night table, and a bookcase. All I had to do now was schlep it all upstairs.

I climbed the stairs, into the kitchen, where Ira was sitting at the table eating a lunch of raw cashews and goat's milk. I looked at his plate, decided not to comment, and asked his assistance. Together, we dragged all the furniture up to my room.

Alone, again, up on the dusty fourth floor, I began dragging my new-found furnishings into their places, locating where each piece found its natural setting.

It's funny how a room is like that – no matter what the room is, and what the furniture may be, you always manage to find a way to make it work. True, you have no choice but to make it fit, but inevitably the desk goes right into one corner, the bookcase finds its place up against one of the walls. Although the desk wouldn't fit where the bookcase is, nor would the bookcase fit where the desk goes, it all eventually makes sense. It takes on its own sense. And then you live in it and learn to thread your way amongst it, as it becomes the new scenery of your life.

But it hadn't gotten to that stage yet. I stood and admired my new, old things. Together, they lent the room a certain bohemian charm, a lived-in, cheerful feeling of self-imposed poverty that required no worry or upkeep. I flopped down into the easy chair and looked around, hoping, without imposing too much shape on my fantasies, that this would be a place in which, in the coming year, I would experience friendly conversations, wonderful amorous delights, and spend my solitary hours deeply absorbed in study and meditation.

2

As Rosh Hashanah drew near, the Havurah became an absolute madhouse. People ran around cleaning, shopping, and making food for dinners. But worst of all was the telephone. On the day before the holiday, the telephone would simply not stop ringing.

"Hello . . . . Yes, this is the Havurah . . . Six-thirty tonight, ten o'clock tomorrow morning . . . . You can wear anything you like, whatever's comfortable . . . . No, it doesn't cost anything . . . . Anyone can come . . . We're at 613 University Road, you know where that is? . . . ."

This conversation was repeated dozens of times, all day long. The phone was beginning to drive me crazy; it was a day of tremendous noise.

But finally the day waned, the sun sank in the sky until it was almost behind the houses across the street, and the Havurah began to fill up. From all over Cambridge, Boston, even from the suburbs, people flocked to Edomville and to the Havurah. There were those who came regularly, those who came once in a while, and even those who had never come before.

Of this latter group, some arrived all properly dressed in jackets and ties or fancy dresses, awkwardly trying to bridge the gap between the synagogues they had grown up in but did not wish to return to, and the laid-back style of the Havurah. For the most part, they sat quietly in the back and tried to overcome their confusion as to why they had come in the first place.

But I didn't think about them too much. A little cynicism and some sympathy for their uptightness, perhaps, and a little pride at belonging to the place that could, at least, draw them in, for whatever the reason. But that was the sum total of my concern.

Instead, I looked around at the members of the Havurah, the people with whom I would spend the coming year. I looked forward to adventures I was sure would occur, all the intimacies and personal revelations which were bound to follow. Here, I was sure, was the flower of our generation, the nerve center of the social revolution, the Jewish experimental chamber from which excitement and creativity were already exploding into the charged atmosphere.

I also looked around at the women. I searched all their faces, looking for just that one, the right one, whom I might recognize as the one to pursue and love. But nothing like that came clear to me. Instead, I saw lots of women, all different, and none flashed me that look of instant attraction and recognition, partly, perhaps, due to my own unsureness which colored the way I looked at them, the way they looked back at me, as well as the way I looked away, in turn, from each of them. Nothing was clear.

But still, I was excited. The house grew full and stuffy as bodies were packed together. The sense that something was *happening*, that something was upon us, filled the room.

Mel, leading the services, began with the traditional melody for Rosh Hashanah, which I hadn't heard for an entire year, hadn't even thought of for a year, and as I recognized it, so submerged and yet so clear as it re-emerged to the forefront of my mind, I was momentarily startled. Then, I was flooded with a warm feeling of the holiday, the sudden sensual recollection of Rosh Hashanah: again the cram of bodies, the sense of expectation, the change from summer into autumn, the subliminal presence of the oncoming dusk, the apples and honey that I knew would follow, all converged together in one focal point in my brain.

3

The next day, again there was a crowd, but the sensation was different during the daytime. Services were longer, and the task at hand – davening, rather than the hungry anticipation of a holiday dinner – insured a slower pace.

At one point, Leon, who was leading, began to intersperse his own remarks into the service. He launched into a little *drash* which played upon the words "Rosh Hashanah."

"Shanah," he explained, "comes from the root word of '*shnayim*' or two, because it's something that repeats itself. It's something that goes in a cycle until it comes back to the same point. And yet, from the same root we get the word '*shinui*' which means change, going from one thing to another. *Shanah*, then, means both repetition and change at the same time, the intersection of both of these ideas. And Rosh Hashanah is the very beginning, the head, the focal point for this intersection . . . ."

I had heard this before, and so I paid only slight attention as I continued to look around at the various women in the room.

After the Amidah, during the leader's repetition, while I tried to get my head back into the book, Mel looked over at me, got up, and with a sidelong nod, motioned for me to follow him. It was that same nod he had on occasion given me when I was younger; it was the nod which meant he had some ideas he wanted to share.

I gladly followed him out the door. When I was younger, I was always fascinated by Mel's insights, and I knew that whatever he would say would be interesting. Being called over to hear it had always seemed like a rare and special privilege back then.

I followed Mel into the backyard. For Mel, this was already his fifth year at the Havurah. He had seen it unfold from the beginning, and he also had seen each year return. Mel knew the Havurah well, all its subtle and not-so-subtle dynamics, its potential and its failures, while I was still eager to jump in and find out what I could. I wondered what he had to say, on this of all days.

We stood in the yard. Mel wore his big tallis still draped over his shoulders even outside the house, in the open, although no doubt the goyim were bound to be looking on, wondering at this unusual striped thing that the weirdo hippie Jews were wearing.

"I had this strange feeling sitting in there today," he said to me. "I wondered what it would be like if God walked in from the street to see what we were doing. In ancient China, they believed that their god went from one house of worship to another. He would come in the door, look around, and say, 'Oh, this is how they worship me in this house.' Then he would go on to the next one. So, I wondered, what would God see if he walked into this house? And I figured he'd say, 'Oh, that's nice. Here they sit on the floor, clap, sing, and read a lot of prayers. That's nice.' And then he'd go on his way."

I was crestfallen. I felt that Mel had said exactly the wrong thing, unwittingly deflating all my enthusiasm for having come to the Havurah, to set up my life here, of all places, and join in its endeavor. My heart fell with his words.

I knew he hadn't meant to disillusion me, but something in what he said took all the specialness away. He noticed my disappointment and quickly realized what he had done.

"Well, I'm not saying the Havurah isn't a good place to be," he said, trying to backtrack from the meaning his words might have betrayed. "The Havurah is still a fine place. I don't mean to say you shouldn't be here instead of somewhere else. In fact, the Havurah is still the only place I feel comfortable right now."

But the damage was done, if only slightly. He had told me that this was not the perfect place after all, that other places, other approaches, were also worthwhile. He told me, hidden in his words, that he himself was thinking of moving on to new experiences. But he was sorry for conveying the meaning I took away. He changed the topic.

"Here," he said, summoning me over to the grape arbor. "Smell the grapes – they're almost ripe."

He reached under the leaves, lifted up a large, purple cluster still attached to the vine, and held it as if a full sack of water. I bent my head down toward his cupped hand and smelled the gentle fragrance, which was gathering and growing, even then, in that very moment, as I lowered my nose down into the grapes and breathed their sweet aroma in.

"AND YE SHALL REJOICE IN YOUR HOLIDAYS"

K'shoshana beyn hachochim. Mahn shoshana?
K'nesset Yisroel. (from the Zohar)

The door buzzer rang. It rang and continued to ring, keeping up its loud, irritating buzz as long as whoever it was on the other side insisted on keeping his or her finger on the button. I was all the way up on the fourth floor, and the damn buzzer just wouldn't stop.

"Okay," I shouted, "I hear you. I'm *coming!*"

I hurried down the stairs as quickly as I could, just to stop the insistent noise.

"Okay!" I yelled. "Enough! *Sha* already!" It still rang. "*Coming!*" I hollered.

By the time I reached the bottom of the stairs, I was furious. I felt like an angered Pavlov's dog, with no choice but to respond to an infuriating bell. Whoever this is, they're going to get a piece of my mind, I vowed. The maddening buzzer didn't stop until I opened the door.

As soon as I swung the door open, I immediately had to stifle my anger. I summoned all my composure as I saw the woman who stood there, her hand still near the buzzer.

Before me stood a large, terribly pale woman, with a fat, rippling pink scar along one side of her slightly contorted and highly unattractive face. Her thick black hair was disheveled and knotted; it stuck out from her head in all directions. She stared straight at me with deep, twitching eyes. I understood in an instant – she was crazy.

"Yes?" I asked, waiting to see what would happen.

"Yes," she said, speaking slowly in a monotone. "Yes – I'm Susannah. Shoshanah on holidays. I, uh, called up earlier in the week. I talked to Linda her name was and I asked if I could come spend Sukkos with the Havurah I've heard so much about you and Linda said I could come for the holiday that you make provisions for guests and so I'd like to be here for Sukkos. I've come."

She spoke slowly, with almost a complete lack of inflection. Halfway through her speech, she had begun to rock slowly back and forth.

"Well . . . I . . . uh . . . I guess that if you made arrangements already, then it's fine," I said. "Why don't you come in?"

She stepped into the entryway, holding a shopping bag. Her change of clothes, I imagined.

I looked at her. She was young, but not that young. At least we only get the fairly young crazies, I thought. That's the youth culture for you.

"Why don't you sit down," I offered, motioning to a chair in the living room.

"Is Linda here?" she asked, again in a monotone.

"Uh . . . no, not yet. She'll be here soon, though." I sure hope she comes soon, I thought. Maybe I can find out from Linda what this woman had told her over the phone, who she was, and how long she wanted to stay.

Our guest sat down in the armchair, but her back remained straight. She folded her hands in her lap, like a child in school being good.

Her clothes were dirty and spotted. Then I noticed that she also brought a powerful smell with her, the stink of perspiration and body odor. She smelled as if she hadn't washed for weeks, and soon the entire living room began to reek of her presence.

Oh no, I thought. How the hell are we going to deal with this, too? What is *this* going to be like?

"I want to talk to Linda," she said in a growly voice, as she began nervously rubbing her hands up and back against her thighs. "I want to say thank you for letting me come."

"Well, uh, you don't have to thank her now," I said, myself now also getting a bit nervous but trying to be polite. "You've only just arrived."

"Yes, but she was very kind," she said, still rubbing her thighs, rocking.

"Well, okay," I said, trying to be agreeable. "She should be home soon. She'll talk to you then. You can wait here until then, if you like. Just make yourself comfortable. There are books to read over there, some magazines . . . ."

"I brought my own books," she said, still blankly. "I'm reading Aristotle."

"Oh, well, that's fine," I said. "Pretty heavy reading material, but good as any, I suppose." I wanted to get out of there and leave her until Linda came. What was I supposed to do in this situation?

"I have to get some things done before the holiday," I said. "I'll see you later, okay? Linda should be home soon." I knew that Linda would just be thrilled to be dumped with such a crazy guest. But why was I supposed to play host?

I turned to go back upstairs.

"How are you doing?" she suddenly called out, for the first time with any inflection, trying to keep my attention.

"Oh, I'm doing okay. Pretty busy before the holiday, though. I have to go take a shower, help prepare dinner, get my room in order . . . ."

I quickly rattled off my list of chores, trying to let her know I was busy. I certainly wasn't going to launch into a serious discussion of how I was doing. I wasn't doing *anything* as far as I wanted to discuss it with her. I just wanted to get out of there.

"Linda will be home real soon," I said. And I hurried back upstairs.

Up in my room, I shut the door and stood there, thinking. I felt terrible – I knew I had beat a hasty retreat, but what, in fact, was I supposed to do? No one else, I thought, lives in a house where crazy people are free to enter off the streets, right out of nowhere. So why do I have to feel guilty about not being the perfect host?

Besides, I was afraid of getting hooked in. "We're not a counseling center," I said to myself.

And yet, we were supposed to be a bit of everything: counseling center, synagogue, hub of counter-culture activity, house of learning, social club, the model Jewish community. We did what we could. But after all, in the end, we were only a group of about twenty people, also busy with other concerns, who struggled to run a nutty little community with no help from anyone else except for their overbearing expectations.

From all sides, we were criticized for not fulfilling everyone else's vision of what they thought we should be. And it was the crazy people who were the hardest to please.

We'd had lots of crazy people come by in the past – along with everyone else who came by, looking for God, friendship, their ancestors, lovers, a good time, a freak out, or a place to crash. Of the many visitors, some found what they were looking for, a few stayed to join the group, some realized our limitations, and some went away bitter.

But the crazy ones always let us know how we had failed them. And often it was not at all pleasant.

One fellow, William Ratman, was the most notorious of all the crazies who ever came by. He was a nervous little person, with a thin face and sunken eyes. He stayed for Shabbos, then extended that for a few more days, and then just kept staying on, with no intention to leave, until he had created a crisis in the group. After a month-and-a-half, and much internal Havurah wrangling and debate, it had finally become imperative to tell him to leave.

Ratman couldn't accept that – he couldn't accept that we didn't want him to stay with us forever and always, to be our close friend and intimately share his life with us.

"How can you call yourselves Jewish," he demanded, "if you don't care for every single Jew!"

We offered to contact professional help, but that was only met with anger.

"Look, you're welcome to come to services," we finally told him as we showed him the door, "but we can't put you up." It was sad, but our sadness soon changed as there shortly followed unsigned hate mail, mysterious piles of garbage left on our front porch on random mornings, and harassing phone calls in the middle of the night.

The last I saw of Ratman was as a silent face on a crowded 7th Avenue Express subway train traveling beneath Manhattan's Upper West Side on a cold winter's night. I slipped into the next car before he could notice me.

And then there was Betty Deutsch, a big blubbery girl who would come to services and sit in a corner to weep and bawl to herself. Sometimes her weeping was silent, and sometimes we would have to stop in order to help her calm down. Comfort, however, did not seem to be what she was seeking. After services, she would invariably corral someone and attempt to talk for hours, delivering a rambling monologue, more associative than logical, about how God is our father and loves us like a father loves his children.

Eventually, people avoided speaking to her. Even saying "Good Shabbos" was a dangerous invitation to a long harangue. And yet, for a while, Betty still came to services and sat weeping to herself. As no one would dare talk to her anymore, her attendance grew increasingly sporadic. Eventually, she joined the Children of the Lord, a local fundamentalist Christian fringe group. A year or two later, she returned and left a stack of pamphlets outside the door.

There was also Kenny Beck, who apparently had no permanent home and so gave out the Havurah's address as his. We received unpaid bills from department stores and calls from people to whom he owed money (which we declined to pay). He would sit quietly in the back of the room, staring fixedly at the women. Over the months, he asked out every unattached woman who came by the Havurah and was turned down by each. To him, it didn't matter who they were. If the Havurah would yield him a girlfriend, no doubt he would then get his own apartment and become a responsible human being. Until then, responsibility was our problem. Eventually, when there were no new women to ask out, he disappeared, although we received his unpaid bills for months afterwards.

And then there was Stanley Mankowsky, who came one day in the middle of the summer, saying he needed money. When no one wanted to give him fifty dollars from their own pocket, we suggested asking a charitable institution. At the mention of an institution, he screamed and yelled, threw a siddur through our window, and ran off, out of the house.

So, what would Susannah – or Shoshanah, since the holiday was almost upon us – want from us that we couldn't provide? Did she have some obsessive need through which she viewed the world, a vision she was about to impose on us and demand that we satisfy? I wasn't eager to find out, but I was sure that, soon enough, I'd know.

I went down to the second floor to shower for the holiday, and as I walked out of the bathroom I ran into Linda coming up the stairs.

"Hi, Linda. Did you talk to Shoshanah downstairs?"

"Sssh!" Linda said frantically, putting her finger to her lips. She grabbed my wet hand and pulled me into her room, closing the door behind us.

"Well, I guess you met Shoshanah," I said, laughing at her alarm. "What's the story?"

"She's *cuckoo*, that's the story," Linda said, poking her finger into her head. Linda was getting animated, as she usually did. It was her Brooklyn heritage.

"Obviously she's cuckoo," I said, "But she also said she talked to you earlier in the week."

"Yeah, she called up. She sounded weird, but *everybody* who calls this place sounds weird. How was I to know she was this loony? So I told her she could come for the holiday, because, after all, there *was* room. So now she's here."

"Well, did you talk to her when you came in? She was very anxious to meet you. I'd say she was looking forward to it."

I was teasing Linda, because now she was the one stuck with the Havurah's problem, through no fault of her own. And she was marvelous when flustered.

"Yeah, I talked to her. I can't say we had much of a conversation. She told me she was grateful to be our guest for Sukkos. Then she said something about her grandfather being a great Hasidic rabbi and how she missed the bus getting here and walked from Harvard Square and then she started talking about Sukkos when she was a child – but it was all mixed up. And then she took out this crumpled rose from her shopping bag and said it was a present to the Havurah. So, I said thank you. I stuck it in water and put it on the table. That made her very happy."

"It seems like you're getting along fine," I said.

"Hey, look," Linda expostulated, "I'm not responsible for her. So I talked to her on the phone – big deal! She's the Havurah's guest, not mine," she said, jabbing her index finger into her sternum. "You're just as responsible for her as I am."

"I know," I said. "Don't worry."

"Besides," Linda giggled, pinching her nose, "she stinks. You can't get near her."

"I know that, too," I said. "And that's a real problem. Well, we'll see what happens. Good luck." I left the room and went upstairs to get dressed.

By the time I came back downstairs (taking the back stairway in order to avoid the living room), several Havurah members had already arrived and were finishing their last-minute dinner preparations in the kitchen. As soon as I walked in, they ran up to me, huddled around, and whispered, "Solomon, who is that woman in the living room?"

"That's Shoshanah," I explained. "She's the Havurah's guest for Sukkos. We all have to be very nice to her."

"But she's a little crazy, no?" Rebecca said.

"Yeah," Max answered, "she's got to be. She looks crazy. You can tell."

"Well, did she say anything when you walked in?" I questioned.

"Yeah. She said, 'How are you doing?' as soon as I walked into the house. I said, 'Fine.' Then I came in here."

"Me, too," Myra said, stifling a laugh. "She just said, 'How are you doing?'"

"Well, at least she's friendly," I said. "What's she doing now?"

"I'll go look," Rebecca said, and she opened the kitchen door a crack and peeked through.

"Nothing!" she whispered. "She's just sitting there with a book on her lap and her hands folded."

"Well, she's reading Aristotle," I explained.

"What?" Rebecca asked, puzzled.

"Nothing – forget it," I said. "Hey, listen, Rebecca, you're a social worker. Why don't you go out and talk to her? Have a conversation."

"Oh, no," Rebecca said. "I'm off duty. I don't have to be a social worker all the time. *You* talk to her."

"I did. Well, a little," I said. That was an exaggeration, and I knew it.

"Besides, she really smells," Leah said. "Do you think we can tell her to take a shower? We can wash and dry her clothes in the meantime."

"We can't do that," Mark protested.

"Why not?" I answered. "That's a good idea."

"Because you can't just tell a guest who comes in for the first time that they have to take a shower and wash their clothes."

"We'll say the Havurah's a holy place," I suggested. "You have to make a ritual purification when you come here."

"Oh, bull!" Mark said.

"Well," Leah said, "then why don't we just explain to her that she should show respect for a synagogue and the other people who come to daven. Explain it to her. Be frank."

"That's better," Myra commented. "But you really can't say that the first time you meet her. Maybe the next time she comes."

"Next time?" we said in unison. Visions of William Ratman, Betty Deutsch, and a host of others – or God knows what? – ran through our minds. We looked at each other, not knowing what to think.

"What are we going to do?" Rebecca asked.

"Well," I said, "at least I know what *I'm* going to do, right now."

"What?"

"Incense!" I said. "We're a hippie holy-place. No reason not to have incense. It'll cover up her smell."

"Do we have any?"

"Yeah, I know just where it is."

I went into the pantry, over to the junk drawer, which was full of all sorts of odds and ends – string, two groggers, thumb tacks, an empty pushke (or pishke, depending on where one's grandparents came from), a few yarmulkes, a broken letter opener, rubber bands, a sock – "Who's sock is this?" I said, holding it up – a comb – "Who's comb?" – a few dried-out ball point pens, a tube of rubber cement, old letters that never got delivered – "Hey, here's a letter for Kenny Beck from Filene's Basement" – and there, under all that junk, I pulled out a package of Celestial Heaven Strawberry Incense.

"Celestial Heaven Incense," I said, "made by the Rama Rama people, at least a quarter of whom are Jewish anyway, nice boys and girls escaping their parents, all looking for, well, . . . Celestial Heaven. Support Jewish businesses. 'Buy the Blue and White,' as they say in Israel. Let's go burn some incense."

I left the kitchen and walked into the dining room, where I could see Shoshanah sitting in the living room nearby, and where she could see me.

I knew it would provoke some sort of communication. Carefully, I went around the house, placing incense sticks in the dining room, in the prayer room, and finally, in the living room, lighting them as I went. They began to generate a thick, musty, strawberry odor, a heavy cloud of smoky fragrance to mask the other odor in the room.

"What are you doing?" Shoshanah asked, with a note of interest in her otherwise flat voice.

"I'm lighting incense," I told her. "You know – a little sweet savor for the holiday. Makes the place seem a little exotic. It changes it from an everyday place into something special. They used to burn incense in the Temple, so we do it here, too, sometimes. Especially on Shalosh Regalim." I was amazed at how appropriate and natural my bullshit sounded, even to myself.

"That's nice," she said. "I like incense. I like the smell."

"Yeah," I said with a smile. "It makes things smell nice, doesn't it?"

She didn't answer. She went back to her flat silence.

Did she take that as an insult? She couldn't take *that* as an insult. Or could she? How the hell could I tell what was in her mind, anyway? I continued to smile.

"We'll be having ma'ariv soon," I said. "Right after that, we'll have dinner in the sukkah."

"Good," she replied. "I like to be in a sukkah. She stared off and distractedly started pulling at her hair.

"Good," I answered. "Ma'ariv will start real soon."

I went back into the kitchen, where the others were waiting.

"Did you talk to her?" Rebecca asked.

"Sure," I said. "We had a heavy discussion."

"No, really. What did she say?"

"Nothing," I said. "She seems very nice. Why don't you go talk to her?"

"Maybe later," Rebecca said, hesitantly.

Soon, the rest of the Havurah started to arrive.

"Hey! What's all this incense?" boomed out Heligman as soon as he entered the room.

"*Sssh!*" I said, "Come in here."

There, deep in the kitchen, we explained the situation to the new arrivals. Then, slowly, trying to seem natural, we all sauntered into the prayer room for a quick ma'ariv. The air was now so thick it was difficult to breathe.

"Daven fast," I whispered to Max.

Max davened quickly. The holiday, normally greeted with enthusiasm and relaxation, was quickly hustled in.

When ma'ariv was over, and the holiday at last was upon us, we were ready to go outside and eat dinner in the sukkah.

"Come," I said to Shoshanah. "Let's go eat in the sukkah."

How should I speak to her? I wondered. Like a social director, or a parent to a child, or like a peer?

Stacked in the kitchen were all the dishes, utensils and food to be taken out to the sukkah in the backyard.

"Here, Shoshanah. Why don't you carry this pot of vegetables? Do you think you can carry it? Okay. Easy now. Just follow Leah." Shoshanah took hold of the pot very carefully, as if it was fragile and precious, and proceeded out the door. A stench of body odor mingled with the smell of ratatouille.

"Whew," I said.

Finally, everyone had taken something and gone outside. Only Rebecca and I were still in the kitchen.

"Is that it?" Rebecca asked.

"I guess so. Wait a minute – is there anything left from last week's communal meal?" I wondered.

Last week, right after Yom Kippur, the Havurah had broken its fast together. There had been an abundance of food, as usually happens at the end of a fast, and a lot had been left over.

"You want to eat last week's leftovers?"

"Well . . . let's see what there is," I suggested.

Rebecca opened the Havurah's refrigerator. She pulled out a bowl with the remnants of a soggy salad, its lettuce leaves so wilted and water-logged they looked like old seaweed.

"Uch," she said, "let's throw this out."

"Wait! Don't throw it out!" I countered urgently.

"Why not? Are *you* going to eat it?"

"No," I admitted.

"So then why not throw it out?"

"Because," I said, "it's not *rotten*."

"So, should we wait until it's rotten and *then* throw it out?"

"Well," I said, hating to see it dumped. "Just don't throw it out."

"Okay – have it your way," she answered. She stuck it back into the refrigerator. Then she pulled out a pot of cold rice, its contents all stuck together.

"*Yecch,*" she said, looking inside the pot at the white lump of mush. "We can't eat this. I suppose you want to save this too, right?"

"Well," I replied, a little embarrassed. "Yeah. At least it's better than the salad."

"Oy," she said, and rolled her eyes. She put the pot back into the refrigerator.

Next, she pulled out a container of sour cream. Pulling off the lid, she looked inside, suspiciously. She sniffed at it. "How old is this stuff?" she asked. "This isn't from last week, that's for sure."

She read the label. "Do Not Sell After September 3," it said, stamped across the cover.

"Today's October 8!" she exclaimed. "This is about five weeks old! Let me throw it out," she implored.

"Well," I said, ". . . it's not *bad* yet, is it?"

"I don't think it will kill you, if that's what you mean. But let's toss it out. No? Okay," she said.

I was getting very embarrassed. But how can you just throw out good food like that?

Finally, she pulled out a big glass jar full of a thick, purplish sludge. "What's this?!" she marveled.

"That's borscht," I said. "It's the borscht Jerry made from the beets he grew in the Havurah garden."

"That was over a month ago!" she expostulated.

"I know," I said sheepishly. "What do you think we bought the sour cream for?"

"Oh, no," she said. "Well, we can't eat any of this tonight. Tonight's a holiday. Let's at least be good to ourselves. And whatever you want to do with this stuff, feel free."

She put the jar back in the refrigerator. In a last experiment, she squeezed a piece of challah that was sitting there, wrapped in a plastic bag. It was stale. "Forget it," she said.

Finally, we went outside. The sukkah was large and circular, based in design on a geodesic dome. No doubt, it was the very latest in sukkah-building, revealing the march of progress in even this most traditional of structures. Covered with leafy branches, with large, thick blankets hung as walls, it resembled exactly what it was – a strange wilderness hut.

Inside, awaiting our arrival, the group was tightly seated around our two big tables pushed together. There were two empty seats remaining, right next to Shoshanah, one for Rebecca and one for me. As I sat down, dreading it, I noticed a soft breeze blowing through the sukkah, and that Shoshanah – either by luck or by the quick thinking of one of the other members – had been mercifully placed downwind.

"Right next to the guest of honor," I said, smiling, as I pulled in my seat.

Yes, I thought, the guest of honor. For at that very moment, we began the "*seder ushpizin,*" the ritual of welcoming traditional guests of honor into the sukkah. It is an old custom, especially practiced in Sephardic communities, in which each night a different Biblical personality is welcomed into the sukkah, supposedly bringing with him the other *ushpizin ila'in*, the other exalted guests.

Tonight, the first night, we welcomed the presence of Abraham and Sarah into our sukkah, to sit with us at the table. We recited the Aramaic formula:

"*B'matu minach, Avraham ushpizi 'ilai, d'yetvu 'imi ve'imach kol ushpizi 'llai: Yitzhak, Ya'acov, Yosef, Moshe, Aharon, v'David.*"

"Abraham, my exalted guest, may it please you to have all the exalted guests dwell with us: Isaac, Jacob, Joseph, Moses, Aaron, and David."

"But that's only symbolic," I said to myself. "What we really have here is a crazy person, in the flesh, sitting right next to me and smelling like a gym." I didn't know what to make of it, but then dinner began.

During the meal, Shoshanah said little but displayed a prodigious appetite. She heaped her plate high with everything that came by, and took seconds and thirds of all she could get. Either she was famished, I thought, or she had an absolutely monstrous metabolism. In any case, she was still going strong long after everyone else had finished.

But that didn't matter. No one had to wait for her. Dinner in the sukkah is supposed to be a festive meal, relaxed and leisurely, and eventually people began to sing, while Shoshanah continued eating. Finally, after many songs and *nigunim*, after everyone was quite done, it was time for a bit of Torah, a learned word to complete the meal.

"Elisha, give us a little Torah."

"Yeah, say something."

Elisha, embarrassed at being put on the spot, was nevertheless flattered to be asked to speak. After a half-hearted protest, he rummaged through his mind for something to say. At last he was ready.

"I – I don't have a lot to say," he began. "I don't want to get into the type of discussion I had in yeshiva. But I do want to say something about the nature of the holiday.

"Sukkos," he began, growing more comfortable with speaking, "is unlike any of the other holidays. It doesn't celebrate a specific event, but rather a way of life. As opposed to the exodus from Egypt, which happened at a specific moment, or the giving of the Torah, or Purim or Hanukah, which all celebrate a single happening, Sukkos celebrates something that went on for years, all year long: living in sukkahs.

"But first, we should ask, what is a sukkah? The English translations have all been terrible. Sometimes they're called 'booths,' or else 'tabernacles.' But 'booths' makes me think of a restaurant: either you sit at the counter or you sit in a booth. Or a telephone booth – a glass box. And a tabernacle, if that means anything at all, makes me think of the Mormon Tabernacle Choir, some incredibly huge, baroque, goyish temple in Utah, where a million people sing in one giant building. Neither of those is anything like a sukkah. *This* is a sukkah," he said, motioning around him. "A shack, if even that. A hut. When we wandered in the desert, this is what we lived in.

"So, what Sukkos really celebrates is a way of life, a mode of being. And it's a life that's unstable – it's peripatetic, out in the rain and wind. It's unprotected and unsettled. And so, once a year, we live out this same instability once more. In a way, it's very Jewish. It's like Jewish life throughout history, reduced to its extreme.

"But even while it represents absolute instability, it also reflects stability – somehow you're more aware of being in a shelter when you're in a little hut than when you're in a big house and don't even notice the problem. And so the sukkah gives us back this sense of being aware of the need for shelter.

"To take it even further, we say '*Ufros aleynu sukkat shlomecha*' – Spread over us your 'sukkah' of peace – when we talk about Shabbat and the coming of the messiah. We don't say 'tent of peace' or 'roof of peace,' but 'sukkah of peace,' the sukkah being the very paradigm of shelter. So when we sit in the sukkah, we're celebrating a life of instability, and yet at the same time we're enacting a physical representation of what it will be like when the messiah comes and we can live in absolute tranquility and complete protection, in the 'sukkah of peace.' It's a contradictory mixture of instability and yet complete protection. It's a paradox."

He shrugged, smiled modestly, and was silent. He was done.

"*Yosher koach*," someone called out.

"That was lovely," said others.

I looked over at Shoshanah who, paying no attention whatsoever, was contentedly sipping her tea.

The next day, everyone furtively asked questions about Shoshanah. They watched her movements, whispered about her behind closed doors, and sought out every little bit of information. Even during services, they snuck out to discuss the matter further.

"Where did she sleep?"

"In the guest room."

"Whose sheets did she use?"

"The Havurah's sheets."

"We'll have to wash them right after the holiday. Maybe she even has bugs."

"What's in her shopping bag?"

"Who knows!"

"Where does she live?"

"Somewhere in Boston."

"Did you talk to her?"

"Not much."

"Has she been acting crazy?"

"No. Not yet, anyhow."

"She eats a lot."

"I saw!"

In services, however, Shoshanah was having a wonderful time. She was davening up a storm, belting out songs in a loud, foghorny voice, off key, enraptured. She rocked back and forth with more animation than the most pious *shuckler*. And she seemed totally unaware that all the people sitting near her had retreated to the edges of the room or into another room entirely, driven out by her smell. A stick of incense, constantly burning, could only get so strong.

Before Hallel, the esrog and lulav were passed around.

There is a midrash that explains the four kinds as follows: The esrog is beautiful and has a beautiful smell. The palm branch is beautiful but has no smell. The myrtle has a lovely smell but is not beautiful, and the willow is neither beautiful nor fragrant. And so it is with people. Some have a beautiful appearance but no inner beauty. Some are beautiful inside but not outside. Some are beautiful both inside and out, and some have no beauty at all.

And so, what was Shoshanah? I wondered. Certainly, she had no external beauty, and if her smell was any indication of her internal world, well, let's not even get close! But what was really inside there? I had no knowledge of it; she seemed as opaque as she was unpleasant to smell.

When the lulav and esrog were passed to Shoshanah, a wide-eyed, childish excitement spread over her face. She handled them clumsily but with great awe, and I noticed every eye watching her. No doubt, we were all afraid lest she injure the esrog, break off its point and render it unusable.

This did not seem to bother Shoshanah, who enthusiastically began shaking them as she had seen the others do. But instead of a little shake in this direction, a little shake in that one, up, down, in all the six directions, she started to wave them about frantically, in no pattern at all. The lulav flapped wildly as she whipped it this way and that. Ecstatically, she shook them and shook them, as if trying to shake something out from inside them. Perhaps, I feared, she would work herself into a rage and suddenly spin out of control. We watched with trepidation and held our breath.

And suddenly she stopped. She passed them on to the next person and we breathed easily again.

Hallel began, with singing and excitement. In the hands of a skilled leader, Hallel always worked us up to a high pitch. The tunes were lively and rhythmic, easy to jump into and lose oneself in.

The heavens are the heavens of the Lord
And the earth he gave to mankind
The dead shall not praise God
Nor those who go down into silence
But we will praise God
From now until forever
From now until forever
Hallelujah

Does Shoshanah count in that? I wondered. Is she, indeed, among the living who rule the earth? What is her praise like? I thought about how Shoshanah was only one among so many crazy Jews. Did Jews produce more crazy people than other cultures, or did it only seem that way to us? Because, indeed, we seemed to attract a whole lot of crazy Jews . . . .

But Shoshanah was unaware of my speculations. Again, in her deep, uncontrolled voice, she sang like a person totally lost in her song and completely meshed with her prayers.

Later that afternoon, after services, after lunch, after taking a nap and while the sun was sinking low in the sky, Shoshanah came down to the kitchen while I was sitting there drinking tea. She stood by the table, a bit nervous, swaying slightly. She was getting ready to speak.

"I – I don't want to disturb you," she said. "Especially after lunch. Lunch was delicious. I enjoyed it very much. But I'm still hungry. Do you have anything to eat?"

Do I have anything to eat? She was asking the wrong person. I only had just a mess of junky things on my shelves. I got up and looked inside the refrigerator at my own few items, and then at the Havurah's communal shelves.

"Well," I said, shocked at what I was doing, "there's some borscht and sour cream. We have some left-over rice, a little salad. And here's some challah . . . ."

I pulled out one thing after another, putting them on the table. At each one, she nodded, as if saying, "Yes, that too, I'll eat that . . . ."

I fetched her a plate and utensils. She sat down, very carefully, at one end of the table, and I sat down at the other.

I watched. It was as if I were observing an experiment. My squeamishness at her smell and at her apparent madness had changed instead to a mute fascination.

At the sight of the food, all her attention turned to eating, as if I were no longer in the room. With great energy, she scooped out the ancient sour cream, poured the old borscht over it, and broke the stale challah. She had one bowl, two bowls, three bowls. I watched as she polished off the jar of borscht, dug out the last of the sour cream, ate the soggy salad, mopped up the remaining dressing with the stale bread, and then started in on the cold lump of rice.

At first, I couldn't believe I had actually gone ahead and served her these horrible remains. A wave of guilt mingled with my fascination as I watched her devour everything with such gusto. To her, it was all perfectly fine food, and she ate it with an appetite that was truly amazing.

At last, she sat back, done. As if coming out of a trance, her demeanor changed completely. Once again, she acknowledged my presence and started to talk.

"My grandfather was a rabbi," she said, prompted by nothing in particular. "He was my father's father. But then my father married my mother. She killed my father; she drove him to an early grave. She gave him headaches and a bad heart. I lived with her, but then she ran away. Now she's a waitress in New Jersey. I live with my sister who never gets out of bed. I have to take care of her. If I didn't, she'd starve to death. I worked for the mayor for a while. I was a consultant. But then the budget was cut and I lost my job. So I went to study at Harvard. I studied American History, but I left Harvard and went to MIT. At MIT I study philosophy. My sister studies philosophy, too, but doesn't get out of bed. She sits and listens to the radio. If she gets up at all it's only to water the plants. She says she's going to get a job soon, but she won't. She likes it in bed. But I don 't like it in bed. There's nothing to do."

She stopped. Was she waiting for a reply? How could I reply? How much of what she said was true and how much did she make up? And where was the point in all of it? She's probably just so crazy that I can't believe anything she says, I thought. Why bother?

"Oh," I said.

She just looked at me. Then she smiled. "So how are you doing?" she asked, trying to be friendly.

"Me? Oh, I'm fine. I'm enjoying the holiday." Boy, she's crazy as a loonybird. Where did *that* come from? "Are *you* enjoying the holiday?" I asked, being polite.

"Yes, very much. Your services are very inspiring."

Her voice was flat and dead again, and she said "inspiring" with a peculiarly false ring. Was she putting me on? Who could tell?

"They were a very holy experience," she said. "I remember my grandfather's sukkah. He used to have pomegranates hanging from the ceiling. There were apples, too."

She stopped. She looked at me expectantly, awaiting a reply.

Was I supposed to reply to *that*? What do you say? How the hell was I supposed to have a conversation with a crazy woman?

"I like pomegranates," I said. "They're my favorite fruit."

"They're red," she said. "They have pits inside."

No kidding. "Do you ever eat pomegranates these days?" I asked, searching for something to say.

"Only when I read Aristotle. I always read Aristotle when I eat pomegranates, but I don't always eat pomegranates when I read Aristotle."

"Oh, I see," I said. What the hell was this?

"My mother took our pomegranates away. She said they'd make our clothes dirty."

Aha! So now, have I hit upon a hidden complex, or is she just being crazy? Why try to analyze her?

"Well, they do stain," I answered.

"I certainly wouldn't want them to stain my clothes now," she said. "These are my best ones."

Her best ones? They're a mess, and they haven't been washed in ages.

Suddenly, she got up. "Well, thank you for giving me such a lovely snack. I'll go upstairs now and read." And she turned around and went upstairs.

At that point, Linda came in and closed the door after herself. "Were you talking to her?" she asked, whispering and pointing beyond the door.

"Yeah," I said. "We became good friends."

"What's she like?" Linda asked, fascinated.

"She's crazy," I said, matter-of-factly. "Totally nuts, as far as I could tell."

"So what's she doing here?" Linda asked, with a dramatic shrug.

"She likes Sukkos, it seems. She came for Sukkos."

"Is she going to come back? Did she say anything about that?"

"Nothing at all. Who knows – maybe she'll become a regular."

"Oh no!"

But Shoshanah did not come back, at least not for a while. After the holiday she suddenly vanished, and it wasn't until many months later that she returned again, this time to plague us with the violent, full-force gale winds of her insanity.

PURIM SPIEL

Chag Poo-reem, Chag Poo-reem, Chag gadol hu la-y'hu – What?! *Damn!* Are people coming already? Who are those voices downstairs?

But it was only Linda and her *shaygetz* boyfriend coming in from outside. Finally, today he said he would come to services. Shabbos, holidays, he would never accompany her, but for Purim he relented. It drove Linda crazy. She, whose uncle was the fanciest rabbi in Milwaukee, whose great-grandfather had written a *sefer* you could still buy in little shops in Jerusalem, she always found herself getting involved with a gentile. Nice ones, but goyim all the same.

"What can I do?" she used to say to me plaintively, seemingly drained of resistance. "I only meet *shkotzim*. I don't know why. It's my destiny."

Her destiny? That was debatable. Where else to find eligible Jewish men than around the Havurah? But I wasn't going to argue, because I knew it caused her enough misery. She was torn between two poles that seemed uncompromisingly mutually exclusive and she certainly couldn't bridge the two in any manner that offered much satisfaction.

But tonight was Purim, so to hell with all that! I had other things to worry about. Purim! And there wasn't much time remaining before the crowds, the hordes, the mad crush of all disenfranchised Jewish Boston would descend on the Havurah for the one night of the year when they would let their hair down and all their neuroses out, and turn out in full, unabashed regalia for the best megillah reading and freak-out party any-where that fell, somehow, under what could be called "religious auspices." If the Havurah did anything right, it was Purim; we sounded Purim to its inner depths, found where its holiness lay and pulled it out, extracting that core of sacred experience that dwelled within it, in Purim in particular, its own special and uniquely shining essence.

For us, Purim wasn't just a holiday for children with groggers. It was for *us* – *we* celebrated it, *we* needed it, *we* let it wash over us with its fren-zied tide. It was the closest any Jewish holiday came to a Dionysian purge, a complete mind blitz, and damn but we had a reputation for doing it well.

Our reputation! Yes, it made me nervous just thinking about it. We put it all on the line on Purim, and the quality and depth of our own year-round experience could be judged by the intensity of our Purims.

So I had spent the whole day running around, buying pretzels, potato chips, wine, whisky, as well as scrounging up some serviceable dope, and taping a kaleidoscope of music – over six hours' worth – including rock, jazz, Gregorian chants, Hasidic *nigunim*, songs of the humpback whale, whatever. You can dance to all of it if you get looped enough. In fact, it is amazing how well they all manage to blend into each other. But it takes a little planning, too – you can't just drop people from the Rolling Stones into the fourteenth century. You have to orchestrate it, build up to it, catch the proper turn in the music, and then – *bam!* – then you can do anything. It all washes together and makes perfect sense.

But the play, the *Purim Spiel* – that was the highlight performance of the evening. A little corps of us spent a nervous week creating a ridicu-lous bunch of songs and patter to illuminate and embellish the story. How would it fare this year? That was always the heart-pounding question!

And the darn telephone kept ringing and ringing all day long.

"Hey, will somebody get that!" I shouted, tired of answering it.

Downstairs the front door opened.

People already?

No, it was just the troops, Havurah members starting to come for the pre-party preparations. I went down to see who had arrived.

In walked Rebecca and Esther, each with a huge platter piled high with hamantaschen.

"Hey, look at that – gimme one," my hand already reaching out to grab.

"Don't touch!" said Rebecca. "They're for later."

"Later? Whattaya mean later? Maybe there won't be any later. 'Later' is a concept unheard of on Purim."

"*Later!*" she insisted. I want everyone to have a chance at them. It's not Purim yet, anyway." Then, very proudly, she added, "They're whole wheat hamantaschen. I baked them from scratch."

"Oh really? And those are home-made whole wheat hamantaschen too, I suppose?" I said to Esther, needling her, disbelieving.

"Of course not," she said. "Me? Whole wheat hamantaschen? Don't be ridiculous. I made them from a mix."

"Well, I'll make sure to eat Rebecca's," I teased.

"Go ahead," she said aloofly. "You won't even know what you're missing." She gave me a sly *I-know-something-that-you-don't-know* look.

Ah, of course. How stupid could I be? "Well why didn't you put the dope in the whole wheat ones!" I exclaimed. "That way I could eat what's good for me and get ripped at the same time."

"Well, that's the way it is," she said, feigning hurt emotions. "Life's like that sometimes. You get one or the other."

"Not tonight it isn't," I said. "I'll have both."

The door opened. Oh my God it's a person. They're coming early. Too early. It's making me nervous.

In walked a very nice young man, looking around, a little bewildered.

"Is this . . . ?" he started to say, hesitantly.

"Yes!" I said. "But you're early, so just make yourself at home."

He sat down tentatively in the living room, apparently unaware of what to expect. Well, he looks like he's ready to get his head pried open, I thought to myself.

Another nice young person came in, followed by another.

"Uh-oh," I said.

Then, more troops started to arrive. Chief came in wearing a straitjacket with a tallis over it. Heligman came in with a rubber bear mask, and overalls.

Here goes.

And the phone kept on ringing and wouldn't let up. On a whim, I decided to attack it.

Rrrrinnng. I picked it up.

"Hello. Eight o'clock. Okay?"

"Okay."

I slammed down the receiver and the phone just rang again.

"Hi. Eight o'clock. Okay?"

"Okay."

Slam again.

Rrinng.

"Hi. Eight o'clock. Okay?"

"No, wait—"

"Yeah? We're at 613 University Road. You know how to get here?"

"That's not – "

"Anyone can come. Get here early, 'cause it's already starting to fill up."

"No, that's not what—"

"Okay. Sorry," I said, slowing down. "What's the problem?"

"Well," she started out with a big sigh, "I heard that the Havurah was the place to come *after* the megillah reading but that it's no good to come to the reading itself because it's not a kosher reading. Is that true?"

I was immediately indignant. "Not a kosher reading! Who told you that?!"

"Well," (again the big sigh) "this guy at Harvard Hillel said . . ."

"Harvard Hillel!! Some crazy frummy, huh?"

She was hurt. "Don't say that!"

"Oh. Okay. Terribly sorry." I paused. "So, what do you want to know?"

"Well, is it really a kosher reading? It's important for me to find out."

"Well of course it's a kosher reading," I exploded. "No abridgements, no English translation, straight from the megillah . . . what else could you want?" Then I thought for a minute. I'll push it all the way. Go for broke. It can't be *that*? Or can it? "Well, as far as I'm concerned it's a kosher reading. Some of the chapters *are* read by women. And who knows – maybe one of them has her period. You want me to go ask? I'll check it myself if you want. *Hashgachah pratit.*"

"Really, I didn't mean . . ."

"Okay, I won't go that far. I'll just make a general announcement: 'If there's any woman here who is going to read from the megillah who is having her period, just gave birth, or is undergoing some other sort of horrible bodily emission, you don't have to tell me if you are or not, but just wear gloves while handling the scroll.' Okay? How's that? It's the best I can do to guard against uncleanliness. *Toomah!* Hey – *you're* not unclean, are you? Then you shouldn't sit next to anyone, you know. There's no mechitzah here, so you have to be your own policeman."

There was a silence. Maybe she was taking me seriously?

"Look," she said embarrassedly. "I really didn't mean to get into all this. I didn't even mean it specifically. This guy just *told* me that it wasn't a kosher reading. But then a friend told me there was always a good party afterwards."

"Oh. I see. And you just accepted that. It made sense. Keep the two separate. Any place with a kosher reading just couldn't have a really good party afterwards. Uh-huh. Would you like that, keep them separate, the holy from the profane?"

"Don't get upset at *me*. I'm just repeating what someone said. If it's really a kosher reading, I'd come."

"Well, okay," I said. "Take it from me. It's a kosher reading. No problem. As long as the women don't put the megillah in their underpants, you're safe."

"*That* was gross," she said petulantly. "Now I don't know whether I should come. That was really gross."

"Okay. I'm sorry. So I'm gross. Look, it's getting really busy here. Use your judgment. We'd love to have you. See you at eight. G'bye."

I put down the receiver. So I was gross. You can't always be proper. The holy is in the profane, etcetera. Jacob Frank and all that. Maybe I upset her? Aw, it's good to freak her out. She was probably a semi-frummy trying to make the break. Maybe I helped a little.

I was awakened from my messianic reverie by the next call of urgency.

"Solomon!" Esther was shouting. "Solomon, come quick!"

I went over to see what was happening.

"Solomon – the toilet's broken!"

The toilet's broken! Oh *shit*. Instant visions of 200 drunk revelers unable to use the bathroom, with the toilet overflowing, clogging up with unspeakable things, turning yellow and dark inside, spilling onto the floor, stinking. A mess. Oh no! I ran over to see.

Instant relief.

"No, it's not broken. It's just a little screwed up sometimes. That's normal. You have to open the tank, jiggle this little jobby here, push that down, and – *voila!*" I flushed it and the water in the bowl swirled downward and disappeared. I felt proud of myself. So competent.

But there was no time to rest on my laurels. More people were arriving and the time was flying fast. My adrenaline was cranking up and beginning to zip through me. I had to get the Havurah together to practice our skit one last time before its big debut.

I turned to go upstairs, but there was Jozef, dressed, as usual, in his suit jacket and white shirt. But at least today he wore no tie – slowly, he was loosening up, and I enjoyed watching his transition from his strait-laced German world into ours, however slightly. He was a good guy underneath all those proper manners, I thought, which were a craziness of his own special kind.

"I'm looking forward to tonight," he said, with a slightly nervous grin. "I've heard so much about Purim here and how important it is to the group. I'm sure I'll learn a whole lot that I didn't know before."

"I'm sure you will, Jozef," I said. "If you're lucky, you'll learn a *whole* lot. But excuse me, because I'm really busy at the moment."

I ran upstairs and bumped into Elisha. "Hey Solomon," he said, "where's the megillah?"

"Where's the megillah?" I shrugged. "I don't know. Leon has it. Leon always has it – it's his."

"Leon's in California, remember?"

"Oh my god, that's right! He went to California last week and won't be back for a month. The megillah's somewhere in his apartment!"

Instant panic again. My heart sank to the bottom of my stomach and turned putrid. I ran up the stairs.

"Chief!" I screamed. "Where's the megillah?!"

"Leon has it."

"He's in California!"

"Oh no!"

Heligman ripped off his bear's mask and stared in disbelief. That was enough to send terror into my vitals. I ran back down the stairs and out the door, bumping into some strange people just coming up the steps.

"Is this . . . ?"

"Yes!" I screamed, and ran down the block, wearing nothing but my T-shirt and jeans.

Outside, the night was cold and clear. Stars twinkled up above in the clear, dark sky and mounds of snow still covered the ground. The street was quiet as I pounded down the block, my heart now filled with the exploding sense of a mighty mission.

Man, if we don't have a megillah, we're screwed. What are our alternatives? Read it from a *book*? I could just see the Kosher Reading lady going into a manic slobber. She'd have my head, no doubt about it.

I reached Leon's apartment and went around the back. Luckily, I knew about this secret way to get inside the back door. All you had to do was push the lock a little to the right, heave the door up . . . Sort of like the toilet.

I hope nobody sees me doing this. If any of the local hoodlums see this, boy, he'll be cleaned out in ten minutes. And if a cop sees me, what do I tell him? That I'm just breaking in to take his megillah but that it's okay because today is Purim and we need it for religious purposes? (Okay, Joe, lock him up, and throw that communist propaganda thing into the wastebasket . . . .)

Just a little tug here, a little force there . . . . The door opened up and banged against something solid. I pushed on something heavy, maybe some furniture, that scraped across the floor, making a horrible noise. Who knows what I was doing to his floor? Well, no stopping now. I pushed until I was in.

It was dark. I felt my way around and reached a light. Click, and there was light.

Now, where would I keep a megillah if I were Leon? In the spice box? Behind the TV? At the bottom of the closet inside one of my galoshes?

Dummy, don't get carried away with the ridiculous. Not now. Use your head.

Yes. My head. I almost forgot about that one, didn't I? I went into the bedroom. Look for a logical place, 'cause you don't have all night.

Right. I went over to the dresser and pulled open the top drawer. Shirts. Lots of shirts. I rummaged through the shirts and there was no megillah among the shirts. Next drawer. Sweaters. Flip flip flip flop. Nope, no megillah in the sweaters.

Next drawer. The next drawer was full of junk – tchotchkes, cuff links, a hairbrush, contraceptives. Hmmmm. Very interesting. What brand does he use? And I wonder why he puts all this in the *third* drawer?

No time, dummy! Keep going. Don't ask questions.

Fourth drawer. Underpants. A jockstrap. Socks. A megillah. *A megillah!* The megillah! I gave a little shout of triumph, did a little dance all alone in the room, and then ran around turning off lights, pushing the whatever-it-was back against the door, and then I ran out the front door, slamming it behind me, and back out into the cold night. I reached the Havurah and now there was already a crowd of people streaming into the place.

Who *are* all these people? I wondered. How come they never come any other time, anyhow?

But again, there was no time for questions. The place was filling up fast and we still had to practice the skit before services started.

Upstairs, the Havurah was already more or less assembled. A shout of joy greeted the appearance of the megillah. It was a good omen, yes. Things were going right.

But still, we had to practice. I wanted to make sure we had it all down. To put it mildly, I was nervous, and all this excitement wasn't having a calming effect on me.

Suddenly, my sharpened senses perceived that a joint was being passed around, and that while I was gone, my fellow Havurahniks had already started on their night's journey. I was taken aback, shocked.

What?! My actors are getting stoned!? Before the play!? How can they *do* that?! They have to put on the greatest dramatic performance of their lives, and they're getting *stoned?!*

"Hey, what are you doing, smoking dope before the performance? You won't remember your lines! You'll flub up the show! Jesus, we spent all this time writing a skit, and now you're taking it as a *joke*?"

"Here," Marty said, "have some of this." He handed me the joint, with a knowing smile.

"Well, okay," I relented. Heck, after all . . . .

I took a big toke. I held onto the joint for a moment as other fingers were already reaching out to pluck it away from me. But I figured that I deserved an extra toke, after having shepherded this stupid skit into reality, which was about to become a parody of itself in the hands of some stoned and giggly Havurah members who didn't seem to understand how *serious* this Purim play was. How it fit into traditions dating back to the middle ages. How it combined the scriptures with modern life like an epic cross-cultural masterpiece. And all the time and effort and downright *genius* that went into it.

So I took another long hit off the joint, and by the time someone finally snatched it away, I didn't really care. The dope worked fast. It took my head about five stories up in an elevator, and I suddenly realized that I was going to have a very good time.

I relaxed.

Ah yes – Purim. I had forgotten. I had forgotten the inevitable magic that always took the holiday away with it. What was done was already done, and there were no more rehearsals to run through or worries to worry about. Everything had already been set in motion, along with all the other forces far beyond our poor powers to add or subtract; it was now set to unfold, like a spring in readiness about to *sproing* into the unknown yet cyclically repeating path of time and experience. I suddenly realized that the holiday had already begun. The odyssey was already under way.

And our dumb skit? That was only a tiny part of it all, a skeletal form given to harness but a minor morsel of the energy that was already there, brought in and generated by the hordes of people now arriving. I began to lose my sense of attachment to it already. What I had worked and worried over was only ego, personal ego, and I understood that *that* was going to slip away before the night was over.

Ah yes – here comes Purim!

By now, the house was a blaze of lights. Crowds were flooding in. Every room was lit, as familiar and unfamiliar faces came running upstairs, downstairs, crushing together in all the available space, anticipating whatever it was to sweep them away. Excitement was everywhere; electricity filled the air. The crowd was hyperactive, rowdy, turned on. They wanted it, and so it was time to give it to them.

"And we're gonna do it!" I suddenly shouted aloud.

The others looked at me, surprised by my outburst. They couldn't figure out what the heck just floated through my mind.

"Look," Mark said, putting his hand on my shoulder in a calming gesture, "if you really want to have a rehearsal, I guess we can run through it one more time."

"Rehearsal?" I looked at him blankly for a moment. I had already forgotten about that. "To hell with rehearsal!" I said with passion. "From now on, it's anything goes. I'm going up to get dressed."

I ran upstairs, leaving them to fate and to Purim.

In a frenzy, I looked around my room. What to wear? I poked my head into my closet. Nothing unusual. Just the same old stuff. Jeans, old shirts . . . garbage! Hmmm. I pulled out my one tie and tied it around my neck, right on top of my T-shirt. Vintage Fred Mertz.

"Yes, that looks good," I said into the mirror. But I needed more. Nothing outlandish, but more. Something to top it off.

To top it off! Yes! A hat! I needed a hat! I looked around and saw the lampshade, a wide, cone-shaped lampshade, like a Chinaman's hat, sitting atop my lamp. I pulled it off and stuck it on my head. Beautiful. A lampshade! What could be more perfect? But there was a problem: There was a big hole in the top of the lampshade. It fit on my head all right, but about this hole . . . . After all, it wasn't *really* a hat, it was still just a lampshade. Even I knew that.

A yarmulke. It needs a yarmulke. So I pulled out a yarmulke and put it on top, covering up the hole, fitting perfectly. It was obvious: whenever you wear a lampshade on your head, you also need a yarmulke on top of it. Or underneath if it doesn't fit on top. But on top is better. Be *proud* of your yarmulke. *Halachah k'beit Havurah.*

Well, that's enough of a costume, I suppose. Very impressionistic. Just the hint of a costume. A symbolic costume. But a costume none the less.

I charged back down the stairs. What time is it? Oh my God it's already ten to eight. I ran all the way downstairs, heading for the kitchen.

A noisy sea of people was in the house now, a veritable sea, an undifferentiated mass of primordial human matter filling all the open space, seeking its own level, spilling and sloshing into the corners, puddles of people on the stairs and in the hallways. I waded through them, trying to keep from going under. Creatures of the deep, like seahorses or phosphorescent-eyed fish, stared up at the floating lampshade. Whatsamatter, you never saw someone dressed up before? I waded on, slogged my way into the kitchen.

The tables were piled high with *shalach mones* – edibles, brought from everywhere, offerings, ritual sacrifices to the Purim deity of bacchanalia, humble gifts to Yudkayvovkay himself under one of his many guises, which we would consume in his and our own behalf.

Linda was standing with a pile of hamantaschen, trying to find room for them on the table.

"Hey, how's Charlie taking to Purim so far?" I asked.

"He's really freaked out by all this," she said.

"Well, aren't *you*?" I asked again.

"Well, uh . . . yeah," she smiled crookedly.

"So – good! He's getting into it."

From the kitchen, I started up the back stairway to get to the second floor. A rubber bear's face was coming down towards me, followed by Esther who had changed into a gold sequined evening gown with her hair done in little pigtails, amplified by the most garish make-up I could imagine, a black wheel around each eye, with long spoke-like lashes pointing in every direction.

"Oh man, Esther, you look great for the part. How did you ever think that up?"

"What do you mean?" she said. "This is the way I used to look in high school."

"Oh," I said. I didn't know where to go from there, so I turned to Heligman. "Hey Heligman, who's leading services? We really ought to start soon."

"I am," said the bear. "Don't worry. I have it all under control." He gave a shrill giggle.

"Good, good." I let them pass and continued on into the library.

The library had suddenly been turned into a stoned and monstrous parody of a beauty salon. People were doing this and that to themselves and to each other, crazy-combing their hair, painting their faces, trying on all sorts of clothes. Max, with a completely out-of-character flair for the meticulous, was artfully parting his hair down the middle, a cross between Alfalfa and the Phantom of the Opera, splotching it down with hair tonic, his bald spot be damned!

"Look," I said, "we better go down and take our places or we'll never get a place to sit." Then, in one last burst of anxiety, I added "— and don't forget your scripts!" That was the least I could expect.

I didn't wait for any replies. I ran back down the stairs.

I could barely get through the sea this time. How could the sea grow any more full? Waves, like the tide, were undulating this way and that. I dove my way through, having to breaststroke my path through the crowd of standees, and finally I side-stroked and then skin-dived into the center of the davening room, where a little space had been set aside for the members of the Havurah. These were our reserved seats – the only time during the year that we resorted to such blatantly self-serving tactics.

I surveyed the crush. They had come armed with an arsenal of groggers, pots and pans, whistles, bottles, anything to make a deafening noise to drown out that accursed name. They were laughing, talking, but all were waiting expectantly for the spectacle to begin. It was a bomb of energy waiting to explode.

But the crowd didn't want services. They hadn't come to *pray*, but to hear the megillah. Yet this was a service nonetheless, and so the bear banged several times on the *shtender* set in the middle of the room and called for quiet.

"*Sha!*" he cried, like some beastly, hirsute rebbe. And there was quiet. We were ready.

He began the service in a way that sharply sliced into a dormant, well-buried part of me and split my head completely open: He launched into the traditional High Holidays melody, the one that opens the evening service on Rosh Hashanah. The incongruity was almost terrifying – it awakened all my *yomim noraim* associations, reached into the most solemn sanctum of my cosmogony of time, and exposed it to the cockeyed world of Purim. It was hilarious; it was frightening. The holiest of days, suddenly turned into a monstrous reincarnation of itself, reappearing totally out of place. Or was it? Was it *really* out of place? After all, Yom Kippur is also called Yom Ha-kippurim, which, according to one Hasidic interpretation, means "a day like Purim."

This added a new sensation to what was already underway, as if a transparency overlaid atop everything else, lending new colors without changing the image.

Heligman raced through it quickly. Few people had books; few were following along. This was no time to *daven*, but to go nuts. Only a small coterie bothered to say the *amidah*, as the rest of the crowd stood there, waiting for the devoted few to finish. At last the service was over, but it had already made its point. Those who understood, understood.

And then the noise began again, with the expectancy that something momentous was about to unload. What was the megillah reading going to be like this year? What inanity was it to be coupled with in order to turn it into something more than just a story? What common experience from our contemporary culture had we summoned up in order to translate the traditional biblical tale into a modern and more ridiculous idiom?

I switched on a tape recorder and a whizz of violins revved up an introduction, and then a full orchestra boomed out through the speakers across the room, launching into an unmistakable melody that resided deep in the subconscious of everybody present. An overture announcing

"Somewhere Over the Rainbow" let everybody know exactly where their heads were going to be this evening.

The Wizard of Oz! Laughter and delight bubbled up and spilled over the crowd, as this reality, too, pried open another buried yet potent place in their psyches, wherein were housed a resonant world of pregnant associations and ringing memories.

The Havurah stood up, scripts in hand. Okay – time to act like idiots. A one an' a two an' a one-two-three:

> *Weeeeee're off to read the Megillah*
> *And not the Megillah of Ruth*
> *We're not gonna read the Song of Song of Song of Song of Songs*
> *We're not gonna read the Eicha scroll*
> *We won't read Ecclesiastes at all*
> *Because because because because because*
> *If you want to read those there are books in the hall*
> *(dee doodle dee doodle dee doo)*
>
> *We're off to read the Megillah*
> *The story of Esther the Queen*
> *Of Mordechai who was a nice guy*
> *And Haman the rat who was mean*
> *Of Vashti the Queen who was kicked from the hall*
> *For not answering Ahaseurus' call*
> *What gall what gall what gall what gall what gall*
> *What gall to ask her to dance with them all*
> *(dee doodle dee doodle dee doo)*
>
> *We're off to read the Megillah*
> *And you better stay till the end*
> *We know it's a little crowded in here*

So just sit on top of a friend
We'll read a few chapters, maybe all ten
And if you like 'em we'll read 'em again
And again and again and again and again and again
So let's start it right now and then say Amen

Amen.

And when our introductory caterwaul was over, throwing everyone in the room back into their childhoods, then our kosherest of kosher readings began, as Leah read from the scroll in its traditional melody. Once again we heard about the 127 provinces from Hodu unto Kush, which drunk old Ahaseurus, who had an eye for pretty ladies, waved his mighty scepter over. And again he called for Vashti and again she refused to come. And so, once again she vanished from the royal graces, as well as from the scene entirely, leaving a vacuum in the royal chambers for some sweet young lovely to come, from out of nowhere, from virgin anonymity, and try to fill.

Esther took the limelight now, in her pigtails and her frightening eyes.

In my play-pretend, Esther was my star. I had written this song with her in mind, giving her a big, juicy part. She was Liv Ullman to my Ingmar Bergman, Sarah Bernhardt to my Sardou. A week before Purim, Sherry, one of our new members, who had eyes on the starring role, the momentary chance to show off, came to me to complain, petulant and annoyed at this seeming injustice within our egalitarian community. "Does Esther always have to be Esther?" she pouted.

Does Esther always have to be Esther! It was obvious, clear as the limpid air. It was a tautology, dammit. "Yes, Esther is Esther," I said, and, playing at director, walked away in an artistic huff.

And now Esther stood up there, and despite the costume, or perhaps because of it, exuded a sensuality that cut me to the bone. We had ended our relationship a year before, cut our emotional ties and cauterized the wound, but she still switched on that erotic hot plate beneath my skin, and I ached in anticipation of her voice. Oh, to have her again for a night.

The audience was excited, receptive, and Esther – exercising her theatrical talents whenever she had the opportunity – stood up there like a cockamamie siren, holding the audience in her hand, and waited for the moment to sing out her portrayal of Esther the Innocent, the healthy good-girl come from the backwoods provinces, from the pain of a shattered family and the deep protective love of her guardian Uncle Mordechai, suddenly dropped into a new environment which was more than she could comprehend.

"Where . . . where am I?" she said in feigned confusion, dazed and bewildered, looking around at the audience, at the air, innocent and naive. "Why . . . why, I must be somewhere *over the mechitzah!*" And then she sang:

Somewhere over the mechitzah
Jews have fun
Sitting together on cushions
Yum bum bum bum bum bum
Somewhere over the mechitzah
There's a place
Where beneath the beards and the bibles
Grins a happy Jewish face

Someday I'll put my kipah on
And find my paranoia's gone
Behind me
I've even tried a Krishna trip
Buddha, EST and chocolate chip

To find me!
But somewhere over the mechitzah
Shul is swell
They daven because they like to
Not 'cause they're avoiding hell

Some place inside that yellow house
Is Krishna Kat and Mickey Mouse
And Moses
They daven so respectfully
They take their shoes off and you see
Their toes-es!
Somewhere over the mechitzah
Jews feel high
I'd like to feel that way with them
Ya ba ba bai bai bai

Ah, Judy Garland, America's favorite tragic young innocent. The audience was getting into it now, laughing and willing to accept any incongruous craziness thrown its way. It was a good beginning; things were going well.

Now Chief stood there and held the megillah in hands which stuck out from beneath his straitjacket and started reading the next chapter. He told of the feast, the choosing of the new queen, and among other things, of Mordechai exhorting Esther to remember her faith but not to mention it as she went in to impress the king.

When the chapter ended, suddenly a dozen Moshekins, Havurah members with squeaky voices, stood up and squeaked out at Esther, who stood goggle-eyed in their midst: "Follow the halachah! Follow the halachah! Follow the halachah!"

Follow the halachah
Follow the halachah
Follow follow follow follow
Follow the halachah
If ever a code, a code there was
The shulchan aruch is one because
Because because because because because
Because of the wonderful things it does
So! Follow the halachah
Follow the halachah . . .

And then all the little Moshekins kindly told her, in their best pedantic manner, all the things she was to remember if she was, indeed, to follow the halachah:

Well, if you go to a restaurant
You can't eat any pork
And if the day is Saturday
You can't do any work

> *You can't knit a nightie with wool and linen*
> *For shatnes, you know, is a great sin-in*
> *You'll be in more trouble than you've ever been in-in*
> *So check all the gatkes that you've been sleepin' in-in*

And follow the halachah . . .

When you get up in the morning
You've gotta put on your straps
You wrap them seven times around
As if you're doing laps.

If a siddur falls in front of you
You know the proper thing to do
You kiss it and it kisses you
'Cause it's a siddur and you're a Jew

So, follow the halachah . . .

And if you have a baby
You must circumcise your son
That way he won't be cut off from the Jews
Though it may cut down on his fun

And if it's a girl you're out of luck
And halachah is really stuck
She's got all the legal rights of a duck . . .
And we can't find anything else to rhyme with "uck."

Why? 'Cause we follow the halachah . . .

We were getting nuttier and nuttier. And each of us was grabbing our brief moment in the sun, instant glory, the thrill of being a pop star to an audience going wild with glee. It drove the adrenaline to new heights and pushed our blood to pump faster and harder. It was the white light, life only in the present, which knew no future or past but only the thrill of the instant, winging along so quickly and happily that there was no chance even to stop and realize it was flying by.

On and on the reading went, each chapter followed by its twisted Ozian counterpart, a cultural soup boiled up in one big pot and flavored with anything found in the closet. The crowd waited, restless, its groggers poised on itchy trigger fingers, ready to go off at the first mention of the villain's name; when it hit, the crowd went up in a fury, until that and every succeeding Haman was drowned out and obliterated, razzed away in a roar of noise and energy that poured forth from a crowd swept along on Purim fever, which built up, needed an outlet, and then regained its energy with each new wave of idiocy that we dumped on its head.

The room grew hotter. Windows were opened and still it was steaming inside. But no one paid attention to how cramped and crowded they were. All of that fell away and was washed beneath the tide of the moment.

We took to ad-libbing, and the congregation answered in kind. Everything seemed funny now, whether indeed we had meant it to be or not. The slightest humor set off waves of laughter, because the crowd's willingness to laugh grew greater and greater, surpassing all normal boundaries.

On and on it went, until at last the villain was hanging from a tree, the wicked witch with her horrible warts and sinister cackle melted away under her black and evil clothing, only to leave a pile of rags and a rousing, elated cheer from all the little Moshekins rescued from catastrophe.

Esther, Uncle Mordechai, Auntie Em, The Wizard, the Tinman and the Scarecrow, Ahasuerus, Toto, Parshandata, the Lion, and all the good people of Shushan and Moshekinland joined together to sing their joy:

Ding dong, Haman's dead
Squeezed a rope around his head
Ding dong, flamin' Haman's dead

Hi ho the derry-o
Zeresh was the next to go
Ding dong, flamin' Haman's dead

Ding dong and hip horray
Another Jewish holiday
Ding dong, flamin' Haman's dead

Ding dong let's all be merry
Then write it up for Commentary
Ding dong, flamin' Haman's dead

And so the reading came to an official close, and we were happy and spent, our tongues hanging out of our mouths. Another year's mishegass down the drain in a blaze of silly glory. Everyone was invited to stay for the party that started immediately.

I pushed my way into the kitchen to help bring out goodies and get the party rolling. In an instant, Jozef approached, his little pad in one hand, shaking my hand with the other and congratulating me and the Havurah on our "presentation of a lovely and very interesting Purim spiel." His little eyes shone, something was clicking and working furiously in his racing brain, as if he had been tossed a million small coins which all were making little *bing-bing* noises as they fell through their assigned slots in the hopper and tallied up some flashing, mechanical score, soon to let the big, theoretical tractor trucks rumble their way through.

"You know," he said in his high voice, tweedling his index finger at me, "this will be *critical* to my dissertation. It demonstrated the Havurah's position in the dialectic between the dominant culture and the subculture, but equally important was the tension between the subculture and the counterculture which commented upon it and upon the larger culture as well. Very interesting," he said again, the words all coming out of his nose.

"Good for you, Jozef," I said, humoring him. "You're getting it. But you ain't seen nothin' yet. Here, have one of these." I reached for one of Esther's hamantaschen and encouraged him to eat it. "Be happy, it's Adar."

He mumbled a quick prayer before biting into it. Don't forget to say *t'filas haderech*, I thought to myself. And I took out several more and stuck them into the pockets of his suit jacket. "Have a couple, man, they're real good. Made special for the occasion."

"Mmmm, they *are* good," he agreed.

"Enjoy them," I wished him, in all good friendliness and honesty. And then I turned my back and he disappeared into the crowd.

Esther came over. "Esther! You were wonderful!" I exclaimed, and I ventured to give her a risky kiss on the cheek.

"Gee," she said, blushing, eating it up. "I'm glad you think so."

"You were great," I repeated.

But there were more important things now than to hand out individual accolades or bask in personal glory. The important thing was to get the party under way, to keep it going and keep Purim going. "Here, help me with this stuff."

"Hey – not *my* hamantaschen," she said. "They're just for the Havurah."

"Not all of them," I said mysteriously.

"Whattaya mean 'Not all of them'?"

"I decided to give Jozef a taste."

"To Jozef! Oh, no. Well, maybe one won't do anything to him, he's so straight."

"I gave him more than that. Maybe three or four."

"No!"

"Yes," I admitted sheepishly.

"Oh, my God. I better find him and claw some back."

Then Chief came over. "Chief! *Shkoyach, shkoyach*," I said, shaking his hand. "Let's get this stuff out."

We pushed our way back into the other rooms, which were still crammed with people. As we brought out the goodies, a million hands grabbed, "gibme gibme", gobbling them up before we could even put them down.

"Hungry crowd," I said.

"A good sign," he answered.

More and more of the stuff was finding its way out to the crowd and into their stomachs. It was time to start up the music, to get them dancing and jumping around before they got sluggish with food.

I ran into Charles, standing in the corner, looking a bit lost. "Hiya Charles, how's it goin'?" I asked cheerfully.

"Is it always like this?" he asked, a bit overwhelmed.

I was tempted to tell him that all Jewish holidays were like this, that this was little more than a fast day compared to others, but I stopped myself and decided to be straight with him.

"Only Purim," I said. "Only Purim."

Which means you've got to squeeze it dry and get every last drop out of it that you possibly can, I thought to myself. I plunged down into the basement, to search for something.

In the basement, on a little shelf beneath the stairs, was exactly what I was looking for. I brought it upstairs. I switched the tape on and then began to set up my little surprise.

"What's that?" someone asked.

"It's a strobe light," someone else answered.

"A strobe light? Boy, those things are passé. They went out years ago."

"I know," I said. "We're traditional here."

I switched it on, turned out the light, and the strobe started up its jerky, flickering illumination, making the entire room flash on, off, on, off, chopping all fluid motion into a staccato series of stop-action images thumb-flipped quickly before the eyes. It encouraged bodily motion, for the sheer joy of seeing your own hands, feet, and the bodies of others appear in such a strange, herky-jerky way.

Good, good, I thought, as people quickly picked up on the impulse and started to move.

The strobe had another effect, too. It started a small exodus of all those who realized that a serious scene was about to unfold and that if they didn't have the energy to participate, now was a good time to head for the exits.

The crowd thinned out, leaving the crush a bit depleted, now only crowded rather than unbearable.

"Time to get some other things going."

I grabbed Chief, Mark, Max, and a bunch of others. Up to the turret we go. A good way to start the evening. A few others caught the drift and quickly followed.

The turret now became the center of operations for all unofficial savory sacrifices. We sat in a circle on the floor, passing joints in every direction. Around and around and around it goes, where it stops it goes up your nose. *Ooh la.* Purim was invading my head completely, chasing out the last remains of organization or responsibility.

"Let it go, let it go, God bless it." Everything was out of my hands now, out of the Havurah's hands, out of any particular guidance other than providential. I sucked in some more of the funny stuff. The taste that refreshes. Ah, yes.

In the dim light, faces grew big, small. Music was coming from somewhere though I couldn't tell where. I started talking to someone, or perhaps someone was talking to me, I couldn't tell who, as time started in on a new dance step, slowing down, or maybe it was speeding up, free from the normal pace of chronometrics. It would need an Einstein to figure out how it was going now.

Einstein. Relativity, yes. Relativity. Relate. Relationships. Religion. Reluctance. *Relax.* Yes – relax. Don't worry about all those things now. Just take a walk around the house and see what's going on.

I picked myself up, stumbled through the curtains and out into the world again. First, through my room. Stop and look around. My room. My room, with all my things gathered over the years, stuck up on the walls, put in drawers and shelves. Chairs which tell stories, my bed: stories again; my clothes – also stories; my books – stories on top of stories. My life – oh, don't get caught up in that stuff *now*. There's a *party* going on!

Pull away and down the stairs I go. A woman is standing there, a slightly too desperate karma exuding from around her. Don't bump into that one, it looks hungry but not too edible. At least not yet.

"Hiya," she says a little too forcefully.

"Hello," I answer. Who is this person?

"The play was wonderful. It was very funny." Buttering me up. She wants to gobble.

"Play? Oh, that. Thanks. It was lots of fun." Be sociable now. This is a straight conversation.

"I like your hat," she says coyly.

"I like yours, too."

"But I'm not wearing a hat!" she protests.

"Well, neither am I, to tell you the truth."

"I can *see that*. But then why are you wearing it on your head if you don't *consider* it a hat." A realist, this one.

"Well, I'm *considering* it. I'm a very considerate person."

"*Are* you?" she says, probing, serious now.

"I don't know. Are you?" Always deflect the question. Man, look where these straight conversations get you.

"I asked you first."

"I asked you second."

She is non-plussed. Oh, if she only could have given me a good answer to that one. This Purim I'd rather be played with than hunted.

Giving it a stab, I add, "Did the reading satisfy you?"

"The reading? It was okay. Why?" Puzzled.

"Oh, nothing, nothing. Just a little experiment, that's all. Listen, don't leave the party yet. The night is young." She gives me a puzzled look again, but then I turn away.

And there is Heligman the bear now talking to Jozef. The bear still looks like an old, hairy Hasidic rebbe, and Josef is trying to impress some obvious theory upon him. A weird encounter. The *hasidim* and the *misnagdim*, *tete-à-tete* and upside down.

"Hello Jozef, how are you feeling?"

"Fine," he answers. No effect yet, I surmise.

"Good," I answer, patting him on the back. "Catch you later."

Into the library. Hmmm . . . what's going on in here?

Lots of people in the library, milling around, talking. This one looking distractedly through some books, there a group slung on the sofa, laughing, very much at home. I never even saw them before! Well, oh well . . .

"Solomon!" and a light tap on the shoulder.

Turn around and there is Rebecca, eating one of her whole-wheat hamantaschen it appears, and very content, just gliding easily in the comfortable, cottony air. No sharp edges on her, none at all. Good old Rebecca. Her eyes sparkle.

"*Glook!*" I open my mouth wide with a big noise. She doesn't know what to make of it at first and then she understands. She plays airplane with the hamantaschen, *rrrrrmmmmm rrrrrmmmmm* around and around in front of my mouth and then, the plane coming in for a landing, *nnnn-yoww* into the hatch. Big bite, make sure to nip her thumb in the process.

"Ow!" she cries. A lovely ow.

"Yum. Delish."

"Solomon, are you stoned?" she says suspiciously.

"No!" I protest.

"I'll bet," she answers, somewhat skeptically.

"Rebecca, my dear," I say, putting my arm around her shoulder, "I guess there are some things it's better you shouldn't know."

"You're a dummy," she says, and gives me a shove.

I follow the trajectory of the shove, letting it propel me along whatever abstract vector in space a theoretical physicist might choose to describe. Out of the hallway, over to the stairway. The stairs open up and offer themselves so I go down them. Back, down into the sea, getting shallower but still a sea, and over into the dining room, the dark, underwater chthonic realm where dancers are squirming around to the music like eels, electric eels fitfully lit up by the blinking strobe.

Look around between the blinks. Who's down here anyway? There's Chief, dancing with Leah. That's nice. Neither dances too well, but that is certainly not the point. That they're dancing, that's fine. And there's Linda and Charles. Whattayou know. He seems to have loosened up a bit, but still is dancing very self-consciously. Hasn't let himself go yet. He's doing all the steps like they're supposed to be done. Well, he's trying his best to be comfortable here, no doubt.

Oh my God, there's Robin Raven, dropped in from the clear blue sky. Haven't seen her in ages. Dancing by herself, doing her own trip, oblivious to all other realities. Ah, she knows how to use her body. And oh no there's Kenny Beck, nervous crazy man in fine normal form tonight, just standing in the corner, hiding behind a drink which he is swiggling around in his hand, the liquid making little round sloshes in his glass, while his attention is riveted on Robin Raven's body, boggle-eyed, watching the boogier's bobbling boobs. Wouldn't want to be in *his* head, no sir.

But too much of this binary opposition! What do they think this is, a discotheque? It's Purim, dammit, let's break this nonsense a little wider open.

Go over and take Chief's hand and Robin Raven's and in a flash the boogie-ing is over and we are tuning into each other and doing some weird threesome strobe-light sun-worship dance. It only takes a minute for others to catch on and the little two's all facing each other have suddenly melted away and the gyrations have melted too into some sort of sinewy wriggle, a more primal ooze, like trilobites or worms slithering in the air. No forms anymore, at least nothing predictable, which is fine because suddenly it is sitar-music time and the boogie-ing would have had a crisis of some sort or another trying to deal with it, so why not this, which now goes on and on for some unchartered, stretched-out taffy-like segment of time.

On and on and on and the dancing incorporates everyone who passes by, even Kenny Beck has joined it now.

Suddenly Jozef comes flying and lurching into the room, a big wonderful grin on his face. His suit jacket is off, his shirttails are falling out of his trousers, and his little pad, his tiny little scribble pad that goes with him everywhere, is flap-flapping from his pocket like an unhinged window shutter in the high wind.

He sees me and bounces over. "It must have been that glass of wine I had," he confides, amazed, completely certain that I somehow know exactly what he is referring to.

"I guess so, Jozef," I say, and I pull him in. He blends in with the rest.

But then I tire for a moment, drop out, and by chance find myself in the kitchen, eating some hamantaschen or other, and all of a sudden the phone rings. I lunge for it and grab it off the wall.

"Happy Purim!" I yell into the receiver.

"Happy Purim to you, Solomon," says Mel from the other end. His voice is cheerful and calm.

"Mel! Mel! Hey, where are you, man?"

"I'm in Purim, where else should I be?"

"I don't know – you tell me!"

"Well, I'm in Purim. Purim is a fine place to be. I'm also in Chicago at the moment, but mostly I'm in Purim. How are things at the Havurah?"

"Uh, I think it's a good one, man."

"Good, good. Well, listen – keep your shirt on and the party alive; I'll bet you're managing just fine. And let me say hello to some of the other folks, too."

"Okay. Bye, man . . . . Hey, it's Mel," I say, turning to Elisha, who takes the phone from my hands and also receives a private word, a little message all for himself, and then Elisha also finds someone else to pass the phone along to.

The rest of the night went on and on, as I traveled upstairs, downstairs, into the library, into the bathroom, out of the bathroom, into the turret, back into the dancing, meeting this one and that one along the way, having conversations and falling out of them, bumping into people, having minor epiphanies, laughing, and going on again, all of us stray souls floating through a friendly, happy night.

As the hours went on, slowly the Havurah emptied out, as people went home in groups of two, three, five, or alone, in whatever combinations of friendship or intimacy their luck had bestowed upon them. At last, only the diehards remained, a smattering of Havurah members and non-Havurah folk who just kept the activities going, on and on, as if they had no beginning and no end. At last, somehow, I found myself in the prayer room, lying on a cushion, entirely exhausted.

As I lay there, I noticed that, slowly, others, also exhausted, were gravitating towards the prayer room as well. Esther, Chief and Leah, Linda and Charles, Heligman, Diann, Elisha, and even Jozef, one by one flopped down onto the cushions, sprawled out with fatigue. Even the uptight woman from earlier in the evening, who, to my surprise, had not gone home yet and who now seemed at last to have unwound, came into the prayer room and propped herself against the wall.

The music in the dining room had run out, the strobe had flickered its last and had finally been turned off, and we just remained like that in the half-light, the spent aftermath, slowly breathing, in and out.

I don't know how it began or who started it, if indeed it originated from any one individual point at all. All I knew was that after a while, after we had been lying there, we were soon all piled together in one big jumble, like kittens in a litter or hamsters in a nest. We began hugging each other, hugging and nuzzling into one another as if we had always been together that way, as if it were the most natural and common thing in the world for us to do.

Oh, certainly there were boundaries there. Each of us knew that the Havurah would never be able to handle an orgy, an actual bump and grind. That was still a myth, and always would remain one. And so, we led it to another plane, all of us just hugging and hugging, gathering from each other a deep physical comfort rather than the high-strung pleasure of erotic stimulation, all hanging onto each other with the last of our fading energies, until even those, too, had reached their final and ultimate limit.

At last I had no more strength even for this, and I dropped out, setting myself loose, and I lay back, flat on my back, looking up at the ceiling. I watched the *ner tamid* continue to dance its pulsating flicker, while I myself no longer even had the energy to move. All that could still move were the thoughts in my head, which continued to careen about and crash into one another, until even this crashing stopped, and my mental restlessness ceased and grew calm.

We know so well, I thought. We know so well all the dichotomies: Jewish and Goyish, smart and stupid, justice and mercy, good and evil, and especially *mitzvah* and *averah*, should and shouldn't, do this and don't do that. We spend all our time thinking about them, worrying about them. We never forget, we never lose sight of all those things, no matter how blotto we allow ourselves to get. But at least on Purim we get a reprieve, not from the reality of those differences, but from the tension between them, from those terrible tugs-of-war that twist us into little knots and then pull, tighter and tighter, each end straining for an opposite pole.

But now at least we can stop and step back, look from a different angle, from somewhere outside the lines, and see it all, losing its conflicting energies of push and pull. Good, evil, evil, good. One existed to force the other into birth, the other existing to emerge from the confrontation, both part of an organic whole, a necessary blossoming-forth of events that all led inexorably to this day.

Mordechai, Haman, Haman, Mordechai. It's so clear who was who. And yet – who were they, anyway? Were they so opposed that they didn't realize they were all part of one big story? And what blank, eternal realm do they now inhabit, if anywhere, other than in our memories of them, in which they are all so bound up with one another, a yin and yang of one big duality rolled up into itself?

There, my thoughts stopped. And then, somewhere behind my forehead, a great white flower sprung up and exploded inside my head, and its white, white lotus petals reached out and wrapped themselves around my mind like the white, white tallis enshrouding the hazan on Yom Kippur when he kneels down and brings his forehead to the floor, and the tallis flows all around him and ripples out onto the surrounding bimah, and the ripples flowed out and outward and I followed their rippling as it expanded and became a great white sea, and I rode that sea out until it ended in the dark region where water and sky meet on the horizon, and I drifted off into a deep, deep, heavy sleep, and I lay there, stoned-out dead, for the rest of that interminable night.

PASSOVER IN THE PARK

(allegro, molto vivace crescendo;
poi meno mosso)

Just a little more, don't stop now, we're almost there, just over this little stream, take this little wooden bridge – Caleb, dummy, don't go in the water you'll get all wet, oh, hell – here we go, look at Caleb in the water, now just through this little gate right here, big old wrought iron gate, sign says, "Public Garden," here we are, one, two and we're IN! Hooray! Whoo-ee! *Whoopee-do!* We have arrived!

"Hey Esther, lookit all these blossoms – pink and white, all these little green leaves, hey look over there, they're purple, look at that crazy purple stuff growing on that tree –"

"— and yellow over there, look, there's yellow –"

"Caleb you beast, stop shaking water on me! Heligman, this is a wild animal you have here. Come on, Caleb, let's go run up that hill there – "

"woof woof"

"Woof woof yourself. Come on –"

Run. And Caleb runs too. Chugging over the grass, up the hill, stomp stomp get to the top, here we are, pant pant pant. Caleb panting too sticking his long pink tongue out of his mouth heh-aheh-aheh. Here come Esther and Heligman, Elisha bringing up the rear, not used to running, a little on the plump side, too much kugel but he'll get over that soon enough. Fall down in the grass, spreadeagle arms legs stuck out, whew that was a run.

228

Look at Heligman, standing up on the top of this grassy hill now, stretching his hands way up in the sky, what's he gonna do? He's singing! in his basso profundo, some old spiritual his mammy taught him no doubt –

Rock-a my soul in de bosom o' Abraham

Rock-a my soul in de bosom o' Abraham

"Hey what's all this stuff about bosoms you're singing?"

And Esther starts in to do a little jig to Heligman's song, dancing around, pirouetting on the bosoms, snapping her fingers, clapping her hands.

Elisha going with the music, a little push in this direction, then a little push in that direction, his eyes closed. Suddenly the singing stops.

"Hey, I'm going to climb this tree! Solomon, get up off the ground, climb this tree with me."

And Heligman starts in to climb this big old tree with branches sticking out almost like a ladder for his feet. *Alleyyy-ooop*, and he's up on the first branch, the rest being easy from there. I follow, looking up at his tuchas as he is right over my head a couple of branches higher. Up we go, the branches getting smaller, and we are high off the ground, if you fall you break your head. High enough.

"Hey you two, come on up this tree, it's easy." A skeptical look from Esther, a skeptical plus apprehensive look from Elisha. "Come on." So Esther grabs hold of the bottom branch and wraps her legs around the trunk. "Blaaargh" she cries in tangled terror. "You can do it!" A few great contortions, her legs working furiously, and she is, yes she made it, up onto the bottom branch! Hooray! Carefully, she steps up the easy staircase of branches and she is up the tree also.

Elisha looking up, a weird perspective, all foreshortened as we look down on him from above. "Come on you can do it." Elisha being goaded on by three now, and the fourth goad, from inside, finally prods him to jump and grab the bottom branch. "Yaaaah" he yells and he is up onto the bottom branch, amazed at his capabilities. His own strength freaks him right out. He pulls himself up onto it, hugging onto it, realizing that he is, *hotdamn!* in a tree. Up he comes, coming closer, his face traveling up to meet us, here he is, all*right!*

And then there we all are, up a tree, and suddenly Caleb starts barking and jumping at the tree woof woof, too bad, too bad, he is just a wild beast and can't make it up the tree. "Sorry, Caleb, you stay down there. You keep watch. Ward off cops and robbers. We have some powerful business to attend to."

"Huh?"

"Wha...?"

"What do you mean?"

But no words need explain as I pull from my pocket a little plastic sandwich bag with a patented seal that locks the freshness in, and in this bag are lots of little green leaves, which remind us of spring. "We've come about as high as our hands and feet are gonna take us, so now we must lift our *spirits,* elevate our *minds* . . ." And I pull out a little flat cardboard package with the Zig Zag man on the flap.

"Why didn't you just roll some before we left?" Esther says.

"I didn't have *time.* We just came here so quick I didn't have time to roll *nothin'.* I just grabbed my stash and my little golden roach clip and brought it along with me," I say, pulling a paper out from behind the Zig Zag man.

"Let me see that for a minute," Elisha asks, taking the package of papers. "Hey, we can't smoke this stuff," he says, amazed, astounded, crushed.

"Why not?"

"This is rice paper. It says so right here. Rice is *humetz*."

"Oh man! Listen, we're not gonna *eat* it. We're only gonna *smoke* it."

"It doesn't matter – you can't even *own* it. You've gotta sell it to the goyim, or burn it."

"Well, so let's burn it right now. First, though, let's put a little of this funny stuff *inside* of it, just to facilitate combustion . . ."

"You've got to burn it *before* the holiday."

"Man, if I burned it all before the holiday, I wouldn't be able to walk for a week!"

"I didn't mean that."

"Well, listen," says Heligman, not wanting to lose this marvelous opportunity just because we cannot figure a way around it. "The Sephardim eat rice on Passover. They don't think it's *humetz*."

"That's right," I say, hope springing up like a palm tree in the desert, "the Sephardim eat rice on Passover."

"Well, in that case we must be ecumenical about this. Share in the heritage of our brothers of the eastern tribes . . ."

So I roll this great big fat joint for all of us, twist the ends, give it a lick, and prepare to do the honors.

"Friends," says Elisha, clasping his hands in front of him, "we are now about to partake of the great Sephardic tradition of Roasting the Paschal Joint. But no one is to be caught still smoking after midnight, because the park closes at eight."

Aw-mayn. And scritch goes the match and swoosh we are on our way. Around and around it goes, perfectly protected by a million little green leaves which shield us from all our foes who might give us the evil eye.

Smoke it all in, that's right, breathe deeply and let all that sacred incense fill up your lungs. Deep breaths – *and away we go!*

Zoom, and we are on our way, quickly gaining altitude. Up, up we go, into the sky, clear up out of our heads and into the blue, this is Cape Canaveral reporting to brain center, what a blastoff! Keep going, man, don't stop now. Whoosh, and we are flying over the park, free of our bodies, free of gravity, reaching the abyss that suspends itself over outer space. We have broken through the barrier and we are on our way. Yes, we are higher than this tree, higher than that little kite up there in the sky, higher than those big white fleecy plump and juicy clouds that are now taking on a million shapes and changing their faces a hundred times, as we look down upon them from above, through the windows of the spaceship of our minds.

Our minds. Our mind. My mind. Your mind. Yes, your mind. What goes through your mind when you are stoned? Everything goes through your mind. Nothing goes through your mind. That is, everything *goes* through your mind but nothing goes *through* your mind. Your mind goes through your mind. Yet your mind doesn't go anywhere – it's just there. Your mind is in your mind, where it belongs. And whatever is in your mind, is on your mind, goes through your mind, and stays there.

At last my fingers stumble into my pocket and pull out a little gold roach clip with the head of an animal. This is where all joints come to an inevitable end. I squeeze the long neck and the animal's mouth opens up and I put the little smoked-down butt-end inside between his jagged little teeth. I put my mouth next to this little monster's metal jaw and suck in one last long drag of paschal sacrifice before the remaining embers go from red to black and wave farewell forever. All gone. Just lean right back against your favorite branch and watch your brain leak out of your ear.

"Hey man, this is good dope . . ."

Yeah. We just sit there, real mellow now, the rush is over, all relaxed. Time goes by. Time keeps going – a minute, an hour, a day, a month, a year, ten years, twenty, thirty, forty . . . Time stops. What is time? And what are we, just cruising along in the upper stratosphere, away from clocks and calendars? We are stoned, just floating stones. Blotto, we just float freely now, freefloating, relaxed. We are gone with the wind.

Then we are very relaxed.

"Uh-oh," says Elisha. "I gotta go pee."

"Me too," I say.

"I could get into that," remarks Heligman. "But that means we gotta get down."

Yes, down we now have to get, back down to earth, our bodies calling us back, physical reality once more exerting its magnetic force upon our floating souls.

Look down at the ground. "Man, that is *far away*. That is going to be difficult."

Slowly this time, one by one, we make our way back down to that bottom branch. Hold onto it, lower yourself down, easy does it, that's right, just hang there for a second, ah, now let go

THUD

Bump, goes the spacecraft. Landed.

Now, where to pee? How about that clump of trees over there? All hidden, nobody to see us. "Let's go there."

Into the trees I go, stand facing a tree. Look at the tree trunk, watch an ant crawl up the tree trunk, fascinating! while my bladder relaxes and I sigh with relief. After me, in goes Heligman. After Heligman . . .

"Hey, I can't go in there," says Elisha. "What if someone sees me? What if I get arrested? I can see it now: '*Rabbi's Son Arrested for Perversion in Public Garden.*' It would knock him over."

"Oh, man, that's ridiculous, just go ahead."

Finally, all trepidation, in goes Elisha, a criminal's fear sneaking through his bones. We see his back.

"CLICK"

"Huh? What happened?!"

"Esther, where'd you get that camera?"

"From my pocket."

"Oh no – evidence!" moans Elisha, unable to move, unable to run, unable to protest in any way, still riveted to the spot while the floodgates are open. "How could you do that to me? What if someone sees the pictures?"

"We'll take a dozen glossies," I say.

"Elisha, you'll *love* it," Esther says. "Someday you'll look back on it, and you'll remember that once you were a stoned-out freak, peeing against a tree, right outside in a public park. It'll be precious."

"I'll bet," he says, skeptically.

Out comes Elisha, a strange mixture of guilt and giggles.

"Your turn, Esther," he says.

"I don't gotta go," she says, coyly. But then, in goes Caleb, sniffs a minute, picks up his leg, and follows the rest of us.

"Let's go lie down over there," says Esther.

And so we all go lie down beneath a bush, our heads together while our legs stick out like the spokes of a wheel. Everything is still light, still floating but less so, lying there, looking up at the sky which just a few minutes ago we were floating through like dandelion seeds. Blue, blue, and big fat clouds.

"Man, it's sure good to get out of the house," says Heligman. "First with the cleaning, then with the seders, all that rush-rush. Diann and I were really getting on each other's nerves. I had to escape for a while."

"Oh, it was good for me, too," says Elisha. "Seder with my folks was rough, with their being all upset about the way I live my life. They don't seem to realize that it's *my life*, and I can do with it what I please."

And then Esther reaches up a hand, unseen to anyone else, and tickles my ear. "Spring really turns me on," she says.

We just continued to lie there, our bodies growing heavier, our backs pressing down into the fertile earth, looking up, watching the sky, beneath a lilac tree on which the flowers still were yet to bloom.

A DAY IN MAY

It was a beautiful day but I hadn't known it was a beautiful day because I had spent the whole day indoors, typing. I hated to type, but I had to do it, so I did it. While I was typing, I turned on the radio. Too noisy, too noisy. I couldn't concentrate on my typing, so I shut the radio off. After a few hours, as it grew later into the afternoon, I decided I had typed enough. "I'll leave it for later, do only a few pages a day from now on, and get some other work done instead." I picked up a book and a ripped flannel shirt, just in case it was cold, and I went outside.

Outside it wasn't cold, and I took a chair from the porch and put it under a tree in the backyard. The trees above me were in their early spring bloom, and a soft green light bounced off the little leaves. The flower buds were pink. I sat there reading and suddenly Krishna jumped up next to me, onto the edge of the chair. I hadn't seen him coming, was startled, and when I started, Krishna got scared in return and jumped off the chair. Warily, he sat down a few paces away.

Suddenly, along the fence, crawling in the still-naked grape vines that twisted in and out of the metal chinks, came a scruffy-looking squirrel. I watched the squirrel scamper along the vines and towards a strange-look-ing, dry, flat object caught in the vines. It looked like a flattened mushroom or a colorless piece of desiccated orange peel. The squirrel approached the object, picked it up quickly and put it to his mouth.

Then I realized what the object was. It was a piece of pita, all dried out. How it got caught there, I had no idea. Maybe when the dogs broke into our trash some stale pita fell out, and maybe this pita was picked up by an animal or the wind and ended up being caught in the grape vines. But who knows? Maybe someone had put it there for the birds. Anyway, the squirrel began to take a few tiny bites on the pita, chewing in a tiny chewing motion. He ate gingerly, and the noise made a little *rasp rasp chick chick* as he nibbled and chewed. Suddenly I remembered that today was Yom Ha-atzmaut. How could I have forgotten?

The squirrel kept eating the pita, holding the piece of pita in both hands in front of his face. It looked too large for him. In fact, it looked like I look when I try to eat a falafel. But the squirrel was making a much better job of it, eating rhythmically, chick chick rasp rasp, while I eat falafel very sloppily, first from this end, then from the other, trying to keep from eating all the salad first and then being left with the dry falafel balls on the bottom, trying to keep the falafel balls from falling out through a tear in the pita, trying to keep the tahina from dribbling all over my arm.

I stared at the squirrel as he stood there, upright and alert, eating his pita as if it were the most natural thing in the world for him to do, and I held my breath. I just watched him. So did Krishna. Suddenly, for no apparent reason, the squirrel got very nervous. He stopped eating. He looked at me and he looked at Krishna, who were both looking at him. Then he took the pita in his teeth and scrambled along the fence towards a branch. He hopped up and jumped along the branch, holding the pita, flying from branch to branch, grabbing onto swaying twigs and up the branch of another tree. He ran all the way up the tree, far above our heads now, and I could no longer see him. He was gone. Silence. Then I heard it, chick chick rasp rasp, up above my head somewhere. I looked and couldn't find where it was coming from. Then the noise stopped, and it didn't start again.

I went back to my reading. I stopped. I put the flannel shirt on the ground next to me and tried to go back to reading. Krishna sneaked a little closer to my chair and sat down. I turned the page. I reached out and petted Krishna, scratching his neck under the chin. A bird flew along the fence and Krishna looked at it. The bird flew away. A neighbor from next door started to hang out her laundry from the second-floor balcony. It was shirts and pants. There were also two towels and a few socks. Then she went in.

Suddenly, one of the legs on my chair cracked, and the chair lurched backwards and I fell off balance. I got up and looked at it, and I saw that the wood had completely snapped. I picked up the chair and leaned it against a wooden pole in the yard. I sat back down and started to read again. It wasn't too comfortable that way because the chair wobbled. I closed my book, picked up my shirt, and walked inside.

Inside, a man was fixing the stove. He nodded at me. I walked upstairs to my room. I opened the window. I put my shirt in the closet and laid the book on my desk. Then I lay down on my bed, looking up at the ceiling. The ceiling was blank. I just stared at the ceiling. And as I stared, fixing my eyes on no point in particular, memories swooped down upon me like a phantom bat, and swallowed me up completely.

SHAVUOS RETREAT

Zacharti lach chesed n'urayich
Ahavat k'lulotayich
Lechtech acharai bamidbar
B'eretz lo zeruah
Jeremiah 2:2

Every day, early in the morning, Chief came in to change the lamp in the *ner tamid* before running off to work as director of the South Shore Mental Health Clinic and Drop-In Center, where he supervised the activities of over 150 retarded, chronically crazy, or mildly dysfunctional and neurotic clients, as well as a ragged staff of starry-eyed social workers and the relatives of local political hacks. Everyone else in the Havurah was glad to let him worry about making sure the lamp was always lit, but for Chief, it was a privilege, a quiet moment of private offering and a personal daily ritual.

Nobody was quite sure why the name Chief stuck to him so well, or exactly what it referred to. Was it because he was director of the mental health clinic, or because he was, like his clients, also a bit askew, an Indian chief in modern guise? No matter, it was only a name used around the Havurah.

Chief was also the oldest member of the Havurah, only by a few years, but they were critical years, because, basically, Chief wasn't really part of the "hippie" generation, whatever that meant. Rather, his deepest sympathies lay elsewhere; the models he secretly yearned to follow when he was young were the beatniks. It was Ginsberg and Kerouac – not Ginsberg and Leary – who danced his wildest dreams.

But of course, back then he had been too young, and now he was too responsible, to toss it all in and join in the dance. Instead, he would occasionally sneak off to some protected corner where he could allow his fantasies to run their course, and only afterwards would he force himself back – back to his job, back to his life.

Today, however, was slightly different. He walked quickly into the Havurah, the door slamming behind him as he looked around, anxious and hurried.

"Hey there, Chief!" I said. "What's up?"

"Hi Shloimie, how's your ass?" he said quickly. "Did you see Linda? She was supposed to leave a note for that friend of hers to come in while we were gone and light the candle in the *ner tamid*. I want to make sure she didn't forget. Somehow, I'm not too confident."

Of course, since I myself never look after the *ner tamid* and just assume that it was always there, I forget about such problems. But Chief didn't, and today the Havurah was going on retreat, leaving the city for a three-day jaunt, taking off *en masse* to a rented hideaway in the country, to spend Shavuos in the clean air and wild beauty of nature – wild compared to our city standards – and both to celebrate the holiday and be alone together, just the Havurah, in order to do whatever it was that the Havurah had to do. And of course, during that three-day period, the *ner tamid*, which needed a new candle every twenty-four hours, would have to be tended by someone else.

"No, I haven't seen her," I said. "Maybe she's upstairs. Maybe she's downstairs. Maybe she's in the back. Maybe she's not at home."

"Okay, okay," Chief said, not particularly interested in my mishegass at the moment. "I've got to get in touch with her. And can you help me load some of this stuff into my car?"

In the dining room, stacked on the tables, were many of the necessities we were taking with us – bags of food, *chumashim*, pots and pans, and an odd assortment of musical instruments including tambourines, whistles, maracas, and triangles that we had picked up for a bargain at a local pawn shop. Most important, there in the middle of the table was the Torah scroll, wrapped up, as some of us called it, in the Holy Shmateh, one of those purple velvety cloths with gold braiding and tassels at the corners, which we had received from some old synagogue in a previously Jewish neighborhood that had gone out of existence as all its congregants moved to the suburbs.

"Help me with the pots and pans and the Torah," Chief said. "That's what we have room for in the car."

Chief and I had agreed to go together in his car, and I was sure we had room for more. And since we were leaving early, I figured it was best if we took as much as possible.

"Don't you think we could take some of the *siddurim*, too?" I offered. "We have plenty of room. The Torah and the pots and pans won't quite fill up the back seat. There's still room in the trunk, and maybe even in front."

"No," Chief said nonchalantly, "we have another passenger, so there won't be any extra room." He busied himself with the pots and pans, poking around in the cardboard carton.

"Oh yeah?" I asked. "Who else is coming?"

Again, Chief tried to sound offhand. "I told Leah she could come with us." With that, he scooped up one of the cardboard cartons and, accompanied by the noise of pots and pans banging around against each other, he headed for the door.

Leah! So Chief offered Leah a ride! What did *that* mean? No doubt, it contained some hidden meaning, yet to reveal itself. But it would. On retreats, undisturbed by normal city life, everything that goes on in the Havurah becomes clear. That's the *purpose* of retreats.

But back to Chief and Leah. The two of them held the dubious distinction of being involved in the Havurah's most confused and confusing relationship. Off again, on again, they had been driving each other crazy for the past few years, making each other happy and miserable according to no regular pattern. Their relationship had first become a public fact more than three years before, also at Shavuos retreat. Everyone began to notice that Chief and Leah had been paying an unusual amount of attention to each other, and then, after two days of being in the woods, undisturbed by civilization, as it were, they were suddenly seen strolling arm-in-arm beneath the trees. Eyebrows raised and whispers flew back and forth along the lines of gossip which run, like a maze of telephone wires, behind the backs of every Havurah member. But soon it was accepted and incorporated, a new dynamic in the group, to be dealt with along with everything else.

Yet as an intimate relationship, as the private encounter between one man and one woman, things did not progress so smoothly. There were *problems*. Chief was too wild in spirit for Leah. She loved the fact that he was so responsible, that he was Director of the clinic, that he was intelligent, kind, and knowledgeable about Judaism. But if he was so knowledgeable and responsible, why did he insist on holding onto all those other ridiculous trappings – the embarrassing Indian prints of naked goddesses locked in erotic embrace with fiery pagan gods tacked up over his bed, or the unexplainable late-night binges of listening to his ancient collection of homemade tapes on which some old bum played the saxophone and read little one-line poems? Or his insistence on wearing his ragged old sweat-shirt with the sleeves cut off when he could certainly afford some decent casualwear for a quiet evening at his apartment?

His complaints, on the other hand, were no less real. "She's so straight," he would lament to me. "In this crazy hippie culture, with all these liberated, mellow women supposedly running all over the place, how come I get involved with a straight girl who wants to be just like Mommy and Daddy told her to be?"

He always had plenty of anecdotes to tell me, annoying little examples of her behavior.

"You know what she did last night?" he once complained. "She came into my house and asked for a glass of water. So what if I gave her a glass I had just drunk from, and if there was still a little orange juice on the bottom? She got mad, she told me I was slobby, and then started railing about how I never wash my dishes and just leave them in the sink for days – and then she *threw the water out!* 'It's just orange juice,' I told her. 'And I was the only person who drank from the glass. If you're willing to kiss me, you can drink from a glass I had orange juice from.' But she just got ticked off and told me I offended her sensibilities. She gets annoyed at me a lot."

"To hell with that," I told him. "Forget it – dump her. There are plenty of other women. And they won't give you such a hard time. They'll love you for who you are, instead of fighting it all the time. What right does she have to put you in a little box, anyway?"

And so, periodically, he would dump her. With great weeping and wailing, with angry words and hurt feelings, and especially with making each other feel marvelously guilty, they would split up, once more, forever.

But then he would lament again. "It's not easy to start all over with someone else. Where else am I going to find a woman like Leah who understands my weird Jewish trip? I'm not a *frummy*, and on the other hand I don't just buy Israeli bonds. Not too many women can deal with more than that. And I'm getting old. I can't go running around with the little girls out of college. Besides, I think Leah's real pretty. I'm attracted to her – what can I do?"

And so, after weeks, months, or only a few days of separation, they would be back together again. For each of them, if only they could eradicate a small part of the other's personality – only the flaws, of course – they would be deliriously happy with what remained. Except for these unwanted extras, they would be a perfect couple, a match for all time.

For the last several months, however, their relation had seemed severed for good. For far longer than ever before, they managed to stay apart. They avoided each other's presence, came by the Havurah at different times, and even went out with other people. It seemed they had finally forged separate existences. The rupture was complete.

So now, what was this cryptic clue that Leah was coming with us in the car? Was Chief getting interested again and trying to patch things up? Or had something already started, still brewing quietly, known only to them, rekindled during surreptitious meetings at each other's apartment? Was this the new beginning of another public revelation? Or was it, after all, only a helpful gesture to a former friend after the fury of their mutually unhappy involvement had, so they might have believed, subsided for good?

And was I now, in fact, the extra passenger, or was she? Or was it purposely planned this way, so that all of us would arrive as a friendly threesome, rather than Chief and Leah showing up as an awkwardly unexplainable couple? In time, I surmised, I would find out.

I picked up the Torah, wrapped in the Holy Shmateh, and went out to the car.

"Here comes de guest of honor," I said. Chief opened the back door of his old Dodge and I slid her in. "Hey Chief, do you want me to sit in the back seat with the Torah and the pots and pans, or should Leah?" I asked innocently enough, probing.

"I think we can all fit in the front," he replied, without the slightest inflection. Then he went inside.

Inside, he was dashing all over, trying to get in touch with Linda to straighten out the business with the *ner tamid*, while he packed some last-minute cartons. He finally located her still at work and he turned on the speakerphone so he could pack his cartons at the same time.

"Hello, Harvard Business School Placement Office."

"Hello, Linda?"

"Uh, yes."

"Linda, this is Chief."

"Oh, hi Chief."

"Linda, did you get in touch with that friend of yours about the *ner tamid*?"

"Oh yeah, she said she could do it, no problem."

"Did you tell her that you have to light the candle from a fire that's already burning? So she'll have to use the candle that's there before it goes out. After all, it's going to be a holiday, so she can't light the fire with a match, because you can't start a new fire on a holiday."

"That's right! I forgot to mention it. I'll have to call her and tell her. Thanks, Chief. Bye."

"See you soon."

-2-

Later that afternoon, Chief and I picked up Leah at the subway stop. Small, slim, with long dark hair, she was still dressed in her work clothes, a neat and pretty dress that fit tightly to her body.

"Hi, Solomon. Hi, Larry," she said to both of us equally, looking into the window. I wondered if she was the only one around the Havurah who called Chief by his real name. I skootched over and she got into the front seat.

"Oh, this is going to be *fun*," she said. "I was so glad to get out of work today. I had to ask my boss for permission to take off for the holiday. At first, he gave me a hard time and didn't want me to go. So I tried to convince him that I'd put in all this overtime, and had gotten all my work done anyway. But he still didn't want to let me go. He just wanted to give me a hard time. Finally, he saw me talking to *his* boss and he thought I was trying to go over his head, so he let me go. I didn't realize it was going to be so unpleasant."

"Well, forget it," Chief told her. "Just relax. We're going to the country."

"I only hope that he isn't upset about it when I come back." she said, biting her lip.

"Oh, forget *that*," I told her. "You have the right. It's your life."

"Well, I know . . ." she said hesitantly.

"Look, if he gives you any trouble, give him trouble back," I told her. "And if he's still a bastard, quit, and then tell him to go jump in the lake."

"Don't be silly." she said to me. "*That's* totally ridiculous."

"Why?" I said, indignant that the clear simplicity of my idea was not appreciated.

"Because it is," she answered.

I said nothing more about it as we zoomed off towards the highway and then northwards to the New Hampshire woods.

-3-

The ride itself was uneventful. We stopped here for gas, there to rearrange the pots and pans which were banging around and making a terrible racket, and once more, only briefly, when Leah and I were thirsty. The whole time I kept trying to catch little clues about the state of affairs between Chief and Leah, but they were few and unclear. Leah kept taking little peeks across me at Chief, but he just kept his eye on the road, staring forward.

At last we arrived, after a long, bumpy stretch of winding dirt roads, and pulled up at a big old house in the woods. It was ancient and irregular, and at night, no doubt, it would look like a haunted mansion, but in the daytime, set among the trees in their beautiful late-spring greenery, it was a lovely rustic sight. From the cars parked in front, we knew exactly who had already arrived.

Inside, we were greeted by a coterie of cheerful, excited friends. On retreats, in that first encounter with the country, everyone experiences a marvelous lift, and the grumpiness and low-level hassles that invade our normal lives suddenly disappear, at least for a while, and everyone is uncommonly bright and ebullient.

"Hi there," called out Rebecca as we walked in. She was in the kitchen, already slicing vegetables for dinner.

"Hiya," said Elisha, who was looking over Rebecca's shoulder and munching on a carrot.

"Look who's here," said Max, who was somewhat awkwardly standing around doing nothing, swinging his arms.

Even Caleb came bounding out of nowhere and leaped upon us, his paws already muddy and wet.

"Down, Caleb," I said, although of course he paid no attention.

"Hello hello! Hello hello, we're here."

"Well," Rebecca said, "go upstairs and choose where you're going to stay, and then come down and help me with dinner."

Go upstairs and choose a place to stay? Easier said than done. I glanced over at Chief, who looked at me then looked at Leah. Leah was eyeing Chief nervously, obviously flustered. I picked up my things and walked upstairs, as Chief and Leah held a secret little conference.

Upstairs there were several rooms, some large, some small. The large ones were filled with several beds, the smaller ones had four beds, two beds, or double beds. Generally, we left the smaller rooms for the couples, and the larger rooms, the "barracks," were for the single people. However, space was always tight and it was hard to assure privacy for all. Being officially unattached at the time, I found a large room and tossed my knapsack onto an empty bed next to one strewn with what I recognized as Elisha's city clothes. I noticed as Chief and Leah came up the stairs, poked their heads into this room and that, finally chose a smaller room with four beds in it, and threw down their stuff in opposite corners. Now what the heck did *that* mean?

"Hey Shloimie," Chief called out, as he entered my room a few minutes later with a towel slung over his shoulders. His white, skinny legs poked out from a pair of shorts and twisted a gnarled path down to the floor.

"What's up?" I said.

"You want to go do mikveh?" he asked.

"Mikveh? Where?"

"Right here in the pond. It's a great place to do mikveh. The water's real clean."

"Far out! Let's go!"

We went downstairs, passing the kitchen where Rebecca was still cutting vegetables.

"Are you going to help me?" she asked.

"We can't, "I told her, "we're going to do mikveh. Want to come?" I was teasing her, because I knew she'd say no.

"No-o," she said, realizing I was teasing her. "You go do mikveh without me."

I turned to Max and Elisha. "Hey – you want to do mikveh?"

"Sure," Max said, "I'll go get a towel."

"No thanks," Elisha said. He was just about to reach for one of Rebecca's chopped vegetables, stopped himself mid-action, and put his hands back in his pockets. "No – I, I don't think so."

At that point, Leah came into the room. "Larry, where are you going?" she asked.

"We're gonna go do mikveh," he said, brightening.

"Oh," she said coldly. Then she turned to Rebecca and, to deflate our enthusiasm but not too unkindly, said, "They just want to go skinny dipping."

"I know," Rebecca said, playfully. "They're terrible."

"How can you *say* that!" Chief protested. "Mikveh isn't just *skinny dipping*. You have to *purify* yourself for the holiday. For Shavuos! *Z'man matan toratenu* – the receiving of the Torah!"

"Yeah," I chimed in, lending moral support. "You've got to *cleanse* yourself. Get rid of all that *shmutz* you've accumulated. Immerse yourself and wash your sins away." I grew dramatic. "You have to make holy ablution and purge yourself of daily living. You have to make a symbolic purification to allow yourself to enter a symbolic world."

"Yeah," Chief said, shaking his head emphatically.

"You guys just want to go skinny dipping," Leah repeated.

At that moment, Heligman came down the stairs with Esther.

"Hey, we're going to do mikveh," I called out. "You want to join us?"

"Yeah!" Heligman said, instantly enthusiastic.

"I don't know," Esther answered, hesitant but interested. "I'm embarrassed."

"Don't be embarrassed," I told her. "There's nothing to be embarrassed about."

She looked at me skeptically, not quite buying it. "Well," she said, "I'll come along and then I'll decide."

"No siree," I answered. "You either do it, or you stay here." Then I added, "You just want to *peek*."

"Me!" Esther answered in mock horror, as if falsely accused. "I don't even care about such things. I don't even want to *know* from such things. I only look at faces anyway." Then she added, "Okay, let's go."

"Yay!" I answered. "Let's go jump in the water with no clothes on!"

The five of us, accompanied by Caleb, who came bounding along after us, walked down a dirt path to the pond. The sun was growing red, sinking in the sky over an unbroken line of green trees which ringed the water. A fresh, leafy scent filled the clear, late-afternoon air. It was perfectly quiet, except for whatever sounds we made.

We dropped our towels on the ground and slowly began to take off our clothes. We started with our shoes, deliberately untying the laces, then off came our socks, then our shirts, and finally, as everyone was sneaking quick looks around, the men mostly glancing over at Esther, while Esther threw a quick look at the rest of us, we pulled down our pants and stepped out of them.

And then there we were, five naked Jews and one dog standing on the edge of a pond in the woods of New Hampshire. We breathed in the fresh, cool air.

"*Boruch atah adonai, elohenu melech ha-olam, asher kidshanu b'mitzvotav v'tzivanu al ha-tvilah*," Chief called aloud, the sound bouncing off the water and echoing among the trees.

"*Aw-mayn!*" we answered, and then ran into the water, splashing and then jumping in so that we were completely submerged. Caleb saw all the excitement and jumped in after us.

"Whooa," Heligman called out as he surfaced. "It's co-o-old."

"It's goo-ood," Chief said, sputtering.

"I'm freezing," Esther called out.

Max swam straight out, as if swimming laps, to the other side of the pond and then back again. The rest of us paddled around, stretching, swimming, gabbing as we floated, up to our necks. The water was cold but refreshing, and we stayed in until we could take it no longer.

Finally, we emerged from the pond. Standing there, dripping, we dried ourselves, but the initial flutter of self-consciousness was gone, even for Esther. Easily, we rubbed ourselves dry, looking around at the woods, at ourselves, talking, glad to be out there, together, in the beautiful country.

"Oh, that was so good," Chief said.

"I'm all goose bumps," Esther pouted, rubbing her legs dry.

We dressed and headed back to the house, feeling strong and healthy. Inside, Rebecca and Leah, still chopping vegetables, greeted us.

"Did you have a nice swim?" Rebecca asked.

"Oh, it was *wonderful*," Chief answered, almost swooning with delight, "The water was so cold and clean."

"You did mikveh?" Leah asked, a bit skeptical.

"Sure," I said. "And when we got out, we had a quick orgy in the woods."

Leah stiffened almost imperceptibly, but she didn't answer.

Chief looked at me quickly. He didn't know whether to get angry at me or burst out laughing.

- 4 -

Within a few hours, everyone had finally arrived. The house was full of activity now, with people running around, preparing dinner, changing into holiday clothing, unpacking, talking, or whatever. The rooms had mostly filled up, although the two empty beds in the room chosen by Chief and Leah remained empty. Somehow, they had been passed up.

I sat on the edge of my bed while Elisha, next to me, was lying on his back reading the *East-West Journal*.

"Hey, look at this," he said. He leaned over and shoved the paper under my nose, pointing to a picture. It showed a yogi in a most incredible posture. His body was twisted in conflicting contortions: His arms snaked around his back, his head went in an opposite direction, and his feet were tangled beneath him in what appeared to be a hopelessly inextricable knot. And on his face was a beatific smile.

"Can you imagine being twisted up like that?" Elisha marveled.

"Sure," I said. "But smiling at the same time – that's the hard part."

At that moment, Heligman came knocking on the door. "*Ma'ariv,*" he called out, "*ma'ariv, yediot, ma'ariv,* time for *ma'ariv.*" He disappeared into the next room, still calling aloud his message.

We went downstairs for the evening services. All of a sudden, people started pulling the cushions off the couches and tossing them on the floor in a circle, recreating the setup in the Havurah prayer room.

"What are you doing?" I said. "We don't have to sit on the floor. There's nothing that says that that's Havurah policy. We can do whatever we want here."

"We don't *have* to do it," Max said, "but it happens anyhow. You can't help it. The Temple was a recreation of Sinai, the synagogue is a recreation of the Temple. The Havurah is our recreation of the synagogue, and this is our recreation of the Havurah. It's an unbroken line of descent, straight from Sinai. And tonight being Shavuos – how can you argue?"

"Well," I said, enjoying his logic but not his conclusion, "it seems to me that sitting on cushions on the floor here instead of sitting on the couch doesn't make me feel a whole lot closer to Sinai." But I gave in and grabbed one of the cushions from off a big old easy chair and flopped it onto the floor. "Peer pressure," I muttered, "that's what it is."

Heligman started in with the service: "*Borchu et Adonai hamvorach*"

"*Boruch Adonai hamvorach l'olam vaed*," we answered.

And then I started in to reading the first paragraph, zipping through it like an old-timer. But you never know where it will take you when you start to daven. Sometimes it takes me nowhere at all, and I can't even bear to read the words. Other times I just zoom right through them, jumbling all the syllables together and just enjoying the flow of sound. Sometimes I pay attention to the words and follow what they have to say. And sometimes, something jumps out of the page and pulls me in, an idea or a metaphor, and I lose myself in a train of thought that spins out, away from the page and into my own private world. This evening, I didn't even get beyond the second sentence before I was already gone.

"Who rolls the light from in front of the darkness, and the darkness from in front of the light." Ceaseless rolling, never ending, like rolling a huge stone around and around. God as Sisyphus – to mix cultural metaphors – rolling night up the hill and rolling daylight down the hill. The hill? The hill is Mt. Sinai – you struggle to get to the top of the mountain, and then when you get there you roll right back down. But what happens at the top, that moment of standing at the top of the mountain? You freak out. You do a little dance. You yell and scream, "I'm at the top!" – then the whole thing rolls right back down and you chase after it. Moses and the ten commandments. Got up to the top of the mountain, freaked out, came down, threw the tablets at the Golden Calf, went back up the hill. How many times does this go on? Moses twice. Finally, he went back up the mountain – a different mountain – and died there. Me? Who knows. Having all my ups and downs, highs and lows. Peak experience and then doubt that the peak experience ever happened. I keep going in circles – or cycles. And the Havurah, it keeps going in cycles too. I've been in the Havurah for years now and I keep coming back to Shavuos retreat, thinking, "Next year, where am I going to be next year?" And then I'm right back here, gone through the cycle again. And the Havurah? Next year? We ask that question every Shavuos, projecting about the year to come and looking back over the year that just happened, before summer arrives. A harvest of first fruits. Sometimes it looks like a good year, sometimes not so good. Last Shavuos – that was interesting. We invited Stan and Bev to come to the retreat, on a whim. Freaked them out so bad they joined the Havurah straightaway, right out of suburbia, and moved to our neighborhood. But now's another year, same problems again, looking for new members as old ones get ready to leave. And all the other problems, too, which repeat themselves. The Havurah's like Sisyphus, too, you think you've gotten somewhere and then all of a sudden everything changes and then you've got to hustle to get it working again. I'm tired of it. But Shavuos is fun – Shavuos is fresh air and green trees. Shavuos is the period of rest between up-the-hill and down-the-hill. Rest? Not only rest. Shavuos is time spent on top of the mountain.

Then, before I knew it, *ma'ariv* was over. I wandered outside, looking up at the sky turning dark. Rachel, a new member – a "rookie" as we called them, a species that was becoming more and more rare – also came outside. Together we just looked up at the stars. There were only a few.

"What happens after dinner?" she asked. A simple question of procedure.

"After dinner? Nothing much. Relax. Take a nap if you want. Because at midnight we all get up and study 'til dawn. At midnight, on Shavuos, according to tradition, the sky opens up. And you're supposed to stay up all night studying Torah. So that's what we do. But we don't start until midnight. Until then – Free Time."

We were quiet. We wandered around under the darkening sky, looking up, wondering if the sky ever really opened.

"Dinner! Time for dinner!" Rebecca called out through the window.

"Chopped vegetables," I said to Rachel, as if whispering a secret. "Lots of chopped vegetables."

- 5 -

Dinner was a typical Havurah meal. Big pots full of food. Pass this pass that, around and around, thank you chatter chatter globble shlurp um yum. Birkat ha-mazon and then clear away the dishes. I left the table, deposited my dish in the sink, and started out of the dining room.

On my way up the stairs, I ran into Esther. "Are you going to take a nap?" she asked me.

"I don't know. I'm not really tired. How about you?"

"I'm not really tired either."

"Why don't we go for a walk?"

"Okay."

As we walked out the door and into the clearing in front of the house, we both knew that this was no simple walk. For us, it was almost a ritual, which we repeated at random intervals, ever since our relationship had broken up for good, more than two – going on three – years ago. It was a time to show a friendly interest in each other's lives, touch a few old bases, let each other know that we were still on good terms, reminisce a bit, and exchange some gossip, bringing us back to the present. We enjoyed doing it, but it always ran its little risks and had its subtle innuendos.

"So how are you doing, Sol," she asked, as we started walking along the road.

"I'm doing okay. Pretty good, I suppose."

"That's good. Are you still seeing Adrienne?" she ventured. Adrienne was a woman who had been coming around the Havurah, fairly regularly for a while, and eventually we started seeing each other in other locations as well.

"Yeah, I still see Adrienne. It has its ups and downs, though. Sometimes good, sometimes less so. But it's not really going anywhere. And you – are you still seeing Henry?"

"Uh-huh," she said simply. Esther had met Henry through a cousin who lived in Stamford. On alternating weekends, she would travel down to Stamford to see him. Sometimes, he came to Boston. As a result, Esther was around the Havurah less and less, especially for Shabbos.

"Yeah, I still see him. The traveling is hard, though. It's hard to have a long-distance relationship."

"I suppose it is," I said. "It's certainly harder than living in the same house," I added. She let that one pass. We walked on a little more.

"It's weird still being around the Havurah," she said. "It's been a long time now."

"Yeah," I said. "What is it – five years now, for both of us? A lot of people have come and gone. A few people still hang on, though. The old diehard hippies."

"Yeah," she said, "like Chief, Max and Rebecca, Heligman . . ."

"And us," I said.

She laughed at that. She never really considered herself much of a hippie, and she knew it.

"Talking about Chief," she said, "you came in the car with Chief and Leah, didn't you? What's with them – are they on again, or what?"

"Who knows," I said with a shrug. "They're always off and on. I wouldn't be surprised if things were starting up again. They're acting awfully secretive. Something's up."

"Do you remember when it all started with them? It was right here on Shavuos retreat. Remember, it was such a surprise when all of a sudden we saw them together? Nobody had suspected a thing, and then – *boom!*"

"Right," I said. "That was a strange retreat, remember?"

"Mm-hmm," she said, smiling. "That was when we were already on the outs. That was a *terrible* retreat for us. It was miserable. I was so glad Chief and Leah started their thing then, because at least it got the group to stop talking about *us*."

"Oh, I didn't care about that. Somehow, I never think that anybody talks about me behind my back. Only about other people."

"That shows how much *you* know," she offered.

"Well, who cares anyway? But that retreat was certainly a downer for us. That was also the retreat when Heligman fell in the water with all his clothes on, and Chief came late because his car broke down and he had the Torah in the back seat. Remember?"

"Oh, that was hilarious," Esther said, getting excited. "He didn't know whether to leave the Torah at the gas station so as not to carry it on Shabbos."

"That's right," I said, suddenly remembering the details. "It was a big debate. He called up and asked our opinion. We decided it was better to carry the Torah in the car on Shabbos than to leave it in a garage. Remember how Max wanted to drive out there and pick up the Torah? But it would have been too late anyway by the time he got there and back."

"That's right. Hey, that wasn't such a terrible retreat after all," she said.

"Not for everybody," I corrected.

"Yeah, I suppose so," she said. After a pause, she added,

"Well, I'm glad we're still friends, even if our relationship never worked out."

"Me, too," I said. "So we weren't destined for each other. It's worked out okay."

"Yes, it has," she said. We walked on a little more.

"What do you think about the new members?" she asked.

"I don't know. Some seem pretty interesting. I like Rachel and Jack. I think they'll be good for the group. But there isn't a big crop these days."

"There sure isn't. What's going to happen to the Havurah?"

"Who knows," I said. "Who knows?"

Finally, we headed back. It was late. We stopped in front of the house, where Rachel and I had been looking up at the few, scattered early-evening stars just a little while before. Now the sky was full of stars, brilliant and numerous. The house, strange and angular, stood out in shadowy silhouette against the dark trees and black sky, its lights burning inside. It seemed a looming monolith in the midst of the wild, dark night.

"Let's go in," Esther said. "It's getting cold."

"Yes, let's go in," I answered.

- 6 -

At midnight, the *tikkun* – the midnight study – began. We sat around the table in one great circle, ringed with 24-hour *yahrzeit* lamps, which provided illumination – as well as a flame, just in case we needed to light something. After all, you can't start a new fire on a holiday, so how else can you light a joint without breaking the rules?

Zack began the session by passing out xeroxed copies of a sixteenth-century kabbalistic text. It was a poetic commentary on the *tikkun* itself. Word by word, we went over it, following its argument. Mt. Sinai, it explained, was not just the event of receiving the Torah, but it was a marriage ceremony, the marriage between God and Israel. God, the groom, marries Israel, the bride, and the wedding contract he gives her is the Torah, a contract which existed from all eternity and which will exist until all eternity. We, who study the Torah on the night of Shavuos, taking part in the "tikkun," the "fixing up," or "making perfect," are like those who adorn and beautify the bride before her wedding, putting silver earrings on her ears, combing her hair, decking her out in jewels and finery, making her ready for her dazzling moment. Sinai is the place of convocation, and the people are both its witnesses and celebrants. On and on, its analogy and metaphors expanded and digressed, painting a vivid tableau of the marriage between God and his people, a perfect marriage to last for all time, re-celebrated each year on the festival of the Torah.

A few of us adjourned for a moment, for a private session in which joints were passed back and forth, which allowed our fantasies to enhance the metaphor and expand upon the text.

When that was done, we put the xeroxed copies aside and played another fantasy game. This one, led by Myra, was a personal vision session, in which everyone was to offer his or her own individual thoughts.

"Well," Myra said, introducing it, "I wanted this to be sort of a free-for-all. There's a midrash that says there were 600,000 people at Sinai and each one had a different experience. So, I thought we'd try that here – to let everyone discuss his or her own interpretation of Sinai."

"What is Sinai to me, in twenty-five words or less," I said. "Something like that?"

"Well, I thought that maybe we could be a little more serious than that," Myra said coolly.

"Sorry," I said. Why was I always teasing people so much?

"That sounds like *fun!*" Heligman exploded.

"So why don't you start," Myra suggested.

Heligman thought about it with a long pause. To get it all into one scene, to say what you *really* believed happened at Sinai, that was no easy matter. In fact, it was almost impossible. As soon as you want to express one idea, you feel you can't really say *that*, and should say something else instead. And then maybe something else instead of that.

Everybody watched Heligman as he thought, wondering what would finally surface. Suddenly, we saw a big, broad smile break out on Heligman's face, as he obviously got in touch with something that he felt was somehow, in some way, at the core of the experience.

"I think," he said smiling, "that Sinai was the most dramatic, exciting moment that ever happened. Picture this: thousands of people standing at the bottom of the mountain, all trembling, not knowing what the hell is going to happen, and then suddenly, booming, thundering out of the sky, you hear, 'I AM THE LORD!' It's the conflagration in *Gone with The Wind*. It's Cecil B. DeMille and a cast of thousands, quivering and screaming in fear and ecstasy. Thunder and lightning! Trumpets and windstorm! The whole world shakes, the ground rocks, the sky opens up, Moses stands on the top of the mountain with his hands outstretched, he receives the Torah, and everybody shrieks and howls." He stopped. "How's that?" he asked, beaming.

"Well, do you *believe* it?" Myra asked.

"Sure. Why not?" Heligman answered enthusiastically. "Can you think of anything better?"

He had a point. *Why not?* And he wasn't being entirely facetious. But better, he sparked our imagination and got us to think of Sinai as we imagined it ourselves, in our own terms.

Max, the political scientist, spoke up. "Sinai is the beginning of government. When the people left Egypt, they were just a motley bunch of slaves. They weren't a nation yet, just the raw material of a nation. A nation needs government, which orders its behavior so it can function as a unit. So, when they stood at Sinai they had some kind of experience – who knows what – which imposed government upon them. Maybe Moses went up the mountain so he could come back down and say, 'Now I've got it' – the word, like the constitution, which imposes form onto a people. They accepted his constitution in order to become a nation. And it's a scary thing to accept a constitution, because you never quite know where it will lead you. It may seem fine in theory, but in practice it always presents new problems, which test it out. That leads to things like the Supreme Court, which must weigh the arguments around new eventualities against the intention of the original theory. Sometimes its interpretations are hard to accept . . ."

I saw that Max was about to get carried away with his theorizing. But this was not supposed to be a lecture, so at his first pause I interjected my own opinion.

"To me," I said, "Sinai is the great transcendental experience in the midst of everyday chaos. It takes place in the wilderness – not the desert, but the wilderness, a wild, disorderly place. And in that wilderness, everybody was just wandering around, in no apparent direction, getting nowhere. It's a little like my life, but let's not get into that. Anyway, all of a sudden, *zap-o*, something just reorders everything. For a moment, you see it all from a new perspective, you get a great rush of excitement, you feel you've had some privileged experience, a breakthrough, you've learned some truth. You think you understand something absolute. Maybe God. And then, suddenly, it's over. You wonder if you even really had it. You go back to wandering in the desert. But it's changed you. You know you had something, although you begin to wonder what it really was, after all. That's not so clear. But you know you had *something* -- and you liked it. You want to get it again. So you look for it again, and even when you can't find it, you remember you had it, you carry that memory with you into your next stage. The amazing thing about Sinai is that it happened to the whole people, all at once. It wasn't just about one individual, but everybody together. It's like the sixties, when everybody was freaking out at once. But there, in light of what's happened since, the analogy seems to end."

At that point, Elisha interrupted. "In relation to that, there's a debate in the midrash about what they really heard at Sinai. One opinion says that Moses got the whole business on Mt. Sinai, the oral law as well as the written law. Another opinion says that only the Ten Commandments were revealed at Sinai. Another midrash says that only the first commandment was heard – 'I am the Lord.' And another says that only the first *word* of the first commandment – *Anochi*, "I" – was heard. And finally, another midrash says that they only heard the first *letter* of the first word – the aleph, which is silent."

That made everyone else silent too. But it wasn't enough of an answer for me. I wanted Elisha to commit himself further.

"So, which of those do *you* believe?" I asked him.

"Well," he said hesitantly, "I don't know. I used to think that the first was true. Then I thought that only the last could be true. Now I don't know anymore. I think I believe in all of them, at different times." He just shook his head, as if lost, with nothing else to say.

Suddenly, breaking the mood, Leah spoke up, taking a new tack. "Well, if we're talking of midrash, I'd like to mention the midrash of *na'aseh v'nishmah*. It says that when God offered the Ten Commandments to Israel, they said, 'We will do and we will listen.' First, they were willing to *do*; then after that, they wanted to find out what they *had* to do. Their acceptance preceded finding out what the commandments were all about. So, for me, Sinai was the acceptance of responsibility. It's only when you have a responsible attitude that you can be a responsible nation." Then she added, "The same goes for people."

She shot a look over at Chief. He caught it, almost as a challenge, and immediately was ready to parry. He leaned back in his chair and took a deep breath.

"About six years ago," he said slowly, "a friend and I were hiking in the Canadian Rockies. We'd been hiking for days. Then we got to this one mountain that was supposed to be particularly beautiful at its peak. So we decided to take the path that led to the top of the mountain. It took hours. Finally we got there, and it was incredible. There was a mist hanging over everything, and a long stretch of white snow on the ground, even though it was summer. Between the cloud and the snow, you lost all sense of normal perspective. It looked like things were close, but when you started walking towards them, you realized they actually were much farther away. And above all, it was beautiful. Everything was white, with blue in the distance, against the brown of the mountain. The air was amazingly clear, clearer than I had ever experienced; the whole scene was breathtaking. And it played with your perceptions. Then, I understood what Sinai must have been like. There was no abstract concept coming out of it – it was just an incredibly beautiful physical reality. What *was*, was beautiful. The real world itself was mind-blowing, and the only thing it said was, 'Here I am' – 'I'm beautiful. Enjoy me. Accept me for what I am.' When you just learn to appreciate what *is*, that's all you need. And at Sinai, everybody saw the mountain, just the mountain standing there, and they understood this. And it freaked them out."

He looked back at Leah, who didn't seem to appreciate his private insight. She looked away as people turned to look at her.

The night wore on. Linda spoke, and then Rebecca started to offer her opinion, but at that point my head grew heavy and my eyelids drooped. I was suddenly too sleepy to stay awake any longer. I put my head down on the table in front of me – just for a second, I told myself – and when I opened my eyes, everyone else was gone.

I looked around. Outside, in the brightening dawn, they were all standing there, about to hear the reading of the Torah. I had slept for hours, and now, upon awakening, the *tikkun* was over, *shacharit* was over, and the Torah was about to be read.

I fought the desire to let my head fall back upon the table and give myself up again to blissful slumber. I stumbled upwards; in my drowsy stupor, I tried to persuade my legs to move forward. It seemed like a tremendous effort, and I yawned and felt like sitting back down. But how could I miss the Torah reading, the Ten Commandments? I forced myself up, out the door, into the day.

The sun was coming up, and I had to squint and shade my eyes. A mist was rising off the pond, a chill was in the air. I looked at the others, whose eyes were bleary, bloodshot. Their faces were tired and drawn, pale and white in the morning light. Their mouths hung open in fatigue and their hair was scraggly and unkempt, evidence of their all-night vigil. Wrapped in sweaters, blankets and jackets to ward off the morning chill, they made a motley, exhausted group. But they all paid attention as Chief stood over the Torah and read out the section on the Ten Commandments.

What a strange scene it was, listening to Chief read out of the Torah on a little table that had been dragged into the clearing in front of the house. What was this bearded, aging semi-non-conformist in a tallis doing, reading from the Torah in the middle of the New Hampshire woods at the break of day? And what were we if not some crazy sect, a lost tribe, out there, away from civilization? But there was no time to think about such things. We listened, hearing every word, and when it was done, we all ran upstairs, to our beds, and fell asleep, each to dream his or her own private dream, until awakening much later that afternoon.

- 7 -

Later that day, the group's members awoke whenever they awoke, and went downstairs for breakfast – or lunch – whenever their bodies told them to arise. By the time I opened my eyes again, it was already mid-afternoon, and, looking around the house, apparently everybody else had been up for a while. As I went into the hall, towards the bathroom, I peeked into Chief and Leah's room, the door to which was wide open. The room was empty, but I noticed that their two beds had, finally, been pushed very close together.

I washed, dressed, and went downstairs. Outside, various Havurah members strolled around, threw frisbees, went swimming, sat under the trees and talked. General recovery from the night's ordeal. While I poured myself some Cheerios and milk, Esther walked by.

"Good morning," I said.

"Did you just get up?" she asked, amazed. "Everyone else has been up for hours."

"So I'm lazy," I said. "What else is happening?"

"Nothing," she said, "although it seems that Chief and Leah are getting something worked out."

"How do you know?"

"Well, they were just seen walking into the woods by themselves, *holding hands*. In front of everybody."

"Holding hands! In front of everybody! My goodness, that's heavy stuff," I said, spooning my cereal.

"Don't make fun," Esther said.

"I'm not making fun. I wish them success and happiness. Really," I replied.

Later on, I caught Chief alone in his room. "Hey, Chief," I said, "it looks like you and Leah are getting it together again."

"Yeah, well," he said, "you know how it is." He pulled on his mustache.

"Same old stuff?"

"Same old stuff. We went for this walk in the woods earlier, right? She thought that maybe that was a good time to drop the bomb. She told me I have to decide to get serious, or else she was going to leave me for good. She didn't say I had to marry her or anything, but just that I had to be *serious*. Be a serious person. She said I should be responsible about our relationship."

"Oh yeah? So, what happened?"

"Nothing," he said. "I said 'maybe.' I told her not to give me an ultimatum. I said we have to let the relationship take its natural course."

"And what did she say to that?"

"What could she say?" he said. "She didn't say anything."

But then he quickly changed the subject to something else that was on his mind. "I wonder if Linda's friend changed the candle in the *ner tamid*," he said, looking away, somewhere beyond me, over my shoulder, into the air.

TISHA B'AV AT FENWAY PARK

It had been a warm, beautiful summer afternoon, and now the afternoon was beginning to grow late, although several hours of daylight still
remained. What I had done with the day I no longer remember – after all,
it was summer, and the days of summer flow by like a running stream, with
nothing to call them back and nothing to mark their motion by. And we
are like people who sit by the edge of that stream, staring into the water, our
minds drifting contentedly, thinking of nothing in particular.

But this summer, there was something different happening in
Boston, something that even I, with my previously complete indifference
to such things, could not avoid. The Boston Red Sox, the frustration of all
New England's sports fans, were finally, for a rare change, playing marvelously well. The entire town was aware of it, and suddenly it became a
topic of conversation even among the overeducated and the apathetic. It
could be overheard in snatches on the subways, it was making its appearance in store windows and on billboards. They were headed for a pennant,
everyone agreed, and local hearts opened up to embrace this strange new
passion. Baseball fever swept the region like an invading army swooping
down from the north, and the Red Sox were the home team, the local army
of our tiny city-state, out to defend the honor and the heart's blood of all
the good Boston people.

Yet what the hell was baseball? I thought. A senseless, unproductive, enclosed system of mock battles and mock heroes. There were more important things to care about that demanded our energies. What was happening to America? The counterculture was dying – long live the counterculture! – and people were leaving their communes and political rallies, their experiments in personal growth and alternative living situations, to sit in a stadium and watch a bunch of grown men converge on one small spot, to bang a ball and chase it around a tiny, insignificant plot of ground. Was this where all our new and noble quests were ending up? Was this what now consumed our hearts and minds?

But cultures are contagious, and I, too, found myself inexplicably drawn in, wary yet strangely fascinated by this new phenomenon which was quickly blossoming, boiling up like a pot and spilling over into the surrounding atmosphere.

You must know what stands in front of you, I thought, and so it was time to make the personal journey and see for myself just what was happening there, going on in the heart of the city.

I certainly didn't want to go there alone. A baseball game is not a private encounter, like a movie, where you can sit by yourself when the lights go out, alone with the picture, watching scenes materialize before your eyes from out of nowhere and hear voices in the dark. Rather, it's a group outing, a shared communal experience. So I went to Max and Rebecca's house to see if I could interest them in such a silly thing.

Tink tink tink, I knocked on their door window. In a few seconds I saw a hand pull aside the curtain and then I saw Rebecca, with her dark eyes, peering out at me from behind the lace. When she recognized me, her eyes lit up and she smiled.

"Solomon, come in," she said, opening the door.

I walked in. "Hi," I said. "Listen, I have a proposition."

"Oh, no," she said, half-teasing. She never quite trusted my ideas.

"I don't know if you'll like it, and if you don't that's okay."

"All right – what is it?"

"Well, would you and Max like to go to a baseball game tonight?"

I quickly realized that I had to sell it a little more or the idea would fall flat. So I continued, without her reply. "The Red Sox are playing, they're doing incredibly well. They're winning like crazy. And I haven't been to a baseball game since I was a kid. And tomorrow they go on a long road trip. So I figured that now was a good time to go. And besides, I bet you'll love it, sitting out there under the open sky, watching the sun set, then the stars come out . . ."

"Today?" she asked, quizzically.

"Yeah, today. Why not?"

"Well," she said simply, "today's Tisha b'Av."

It hit me like a stone wall. "Holy mackerel," I said, "how could I have forgotten? I can't believe it just slipped my mind like that."

How, indeed, had it happened? Last night, hadn't I sat on the floor in the Havurah with about twenty-five or thirty others, with even the cushions stacked up in the corner, the lights out and candles burning all around the room? Just last night I had been listening to Lamentations and singing songs of mourning. Just last night I had thought about the destruction of the Temple and the pain of exile – only to forget it completely by the next morning and go about my business. How could I forget like that? Maybe it was the fault of summer, when all the days seem alike. Or maybe the further into *galut* you go, the more you forget that you're in *galut*. Or maybe I was simply stupid and insensitive. Whatever the reason, I was astonished at myself.

"I can't believe I just forgot like that," I apologized.

"That's okay," Rebecca said. "Maybe we can go anyway, if Max thinks it's all right. Tisha b'Av is almost over, anyhow. There's just a few hours left." Then, a little sheepishly, she added, "Frankly, I wouldn't mind going. But let's see what Max says."

She turned and retreated into the next room. As she opened the door, I saw Max sitting on the hassock at the foot of his easy chair, rather than in the easy chair itself, his knees drawn up almost to his face. He was reading a book and seemed lost in thought. He didn't seem to notice when Rebecca walked in.

"Max!" she said, and he finally looked up, a little peeved at being disturbed. He closed his book on his finger so as not to lose the place.

"Max, Solomon's here and he wants to know whether we'd like to go to the baseball game."

"Today?" he said.

He threw me a stern, almost disapproving look, through the doorway. I felt stupid standing there, with Max undoubtedly thinking that I was the only person he knew with such little respect and sensitivity that I could possibly even suggest going to a baseball game on Tisha b'Av. If I hadn't at all known it was Tisha b'Av, that would be one thing. But to have been aware of it and *then* still ask, that was another matter. At last, he decided to acknowledge my presence.

"Hello, Solomon," he said, almost absentmindedly.

"Hi, Max," I answered.

He still looked a bit angry, partly annoyed and partly disgusted. But he sat there, thinking, for what seemed a long time. Then, I realized that he was seriously considering it. And I realized, too, that his annoyance was not merely at my own insensitivity, but at his own desire. He, too, wanted to go to the baseball game, and he was more annoyed at me for tempting him, for sowing that thorny seed into his otherwise barren field of activity, and suggesting the troubling possibility of doing something that seemed clearly out of place, than for offending his otherwise pure intentions. He was angry at himself for being so interested. The issue was straining his resolve. Finally, he looked up at Rebecca and spoke.

"Okay, I'll go," he said. "But I still won't eat."

So Max was still fasting! I, in my blissful ignorance, had broken my fast as soon as I woke up, and so hadn't had to face the issue of whether I was going to fast or not.

"I broke my fast at lunch," Rebecca admitted. "I only fast into the afternoon anyway. There's a tradition like that."

But Max was still fasting. So, while Max returned to his reading for a few last minutes, Rebecca and I made peanut butter and jelly sandwiches and several hard-boiled eggs which we loaded into a large paper bag, along with an assortment of carrots, apples, raisins, and oranges, enough for our own dinners and a late dinner for Max to break his fast upon. And with that, we set out.

The subway was full of people, all bound for different destinations. Tired men were returning late from work, young couples were dressed up and going out. Women sitting with shopping bags between their knees were jostled up and down with the motion of the cars, their packages bouncing in their laps. Here and there, however, scattered throughout the crowd, were a confrerie of others, each with a small sign – a man wearing a baseball hat, a small boy with a glove, groups of young men holding windbreakers or brown paper bags full of sandwiches, or couples holding items emblazoned with little emblems of one sort or another, or passengers just with a certain look of anticipation on their faces – all recognizable as bound for a common destination. Every now and again, someone pulled a little envelope from his pocket and checked inside, making sure he still had his tickets.

As the train traveled on, the recognizable group grew, eventually outnumbering the others. Soon the train was full of people bound for Fenway Park, all hanging onto the straps and holding poles, and when the train stopped at Kenmore Square it disgorged almost its entire load; everyone funneled through the doorway and into the station.

In the station, there were only people clearly bound for the baseball game. We – and they – all traveled in one direction, along the same ramp, up the same staircase. And there, on the sidewalk, we could see lines of others, converging and streaming forward, coming from across the street, from around the corner, from blocks away, all heading in the same direction and making their way as if in one long procession.

As we walked, hawkers of all sorts offered their many wares to our diverse appetites:

"Hot dogs, get your hot dogs here, hot dogs!"

"Buttons, baseball buttons – all your favorite players!"

"Peanuts, fresh peanuts!"

"Baseball caps, baseball caps, pennants, all the teams!"

"Pizza! Cold soda here. Pizza!"

"Souvenirs! Get your souvenirs!"

We walked past all of them, especially Max, who refused to look at any of the food vendors, feeling somehow that we were on a pilgrimage that differed from the others, if only slightly. And then we reached the slope, where you have to walk up a hill and over the highway to get to the stadium. We trudged up the hill, Rebecca carrying the bag of food, and I suddenly noticed that Max, for some reason, still carried his book. Only I carried nothing.

Up the slope we went, and at the top, directly over the highway on which cars beneath us went whizzing by, we could catch our first glimpse of the stadium. From where we were, we could just see the tops of its wall, and its huge nightlights standing up like towers all around it. *That* was the place we were headed. We grew excited as we approached the stadium and quickened our pace to get there as fast as we could.

There are several gates that lead to the stadium. There's Gate A and Gate B, Gates C, D, and E, there are special gates for the maintenance workers, special gates for the press, and special gates for the players.

"Which gate do we go to?" asked Rebecca.

"Over there, I guess," Max answered. "Gate C – the bleachers. For the paupers like us, the rowdy rabble. The teeming masses. The common folk."

We approached Gate C to buy our tickets. A little man with a big wart on his nose sat in a tiny booth behind a gridded window, like a man trapped in a cage. He was selling tickets. He looked at us sideways, as if to test us.

"How many?" he asked.

"Three," we answered.

We gave him our money and he gave us three tickets. We then handed our tickets to another man, whose left eye was covered with a bandage, who guarded the entranceway. As we did so, two other guards came out of nowhere and checked our bag for any prohibited or illegal substances – guns, firecrackers, dope, liquor. Max opened his book to them, a gesture they didn't seem to understand. And then we were free to enter the stadium.

Inside, people were hurrying in every which way. Some thought the best seats would be in this direction, others thought in that direction. The single procession of people had now shattered into a thousand individual fragments.

"Scorecard, get your scorecard!" shouted a vendor wearing a red apron. I went up to him and plunked my money down.

"You can't tell the players without a scorecard," I said.

"Who are we playing anyway?" asked Rebecca.

"The Tigers," I said. Then we walked up a ramp and into the bleachers.

At the end of the ramp, the playing field suddenly came into view. Green, green, everything was a beautiful green: the grass was a vivid green, the stadium itself was painted green, and so were the bleacher seats. Imposed upon this green was a marvelous mottled rainbow, a pointillism of every color, comprised of the varied clothing of thousands of fans, looking like exotic flowers on a peaceful background. And there, on the playing field, running up and down, roaming all over, batting balls, throwing and catching, were the Tigers, trying to look skillful and mean.

"Where should we sit?" Rebecca asked. "Over there?" she pointed. "Or over there? Or how about there?"

"Maybe there," Max said, pointing to a row of empty seats.

"Okay, let's try those."

We sidled our way past a group of seated fans. "Excuse me, excuse me," we said, as they pulled in their feet, and we sat down.

"Do you like these seats?"

"I don't know." We evaluated the view.

"How about down there?" I pointed.

"Okay, let's try down there."

Back across the knees and shoes, like going through a row of turnstiles, down the stairs, and again into another row. "Sorry, excuse us, thank you. Sorry."

We sat down. The view was fine. A clear panorama of the field stretched out in front of us, with no obstruction. The infield was a bit far away, but after all, what could we expect from the bleachers?

Rebecca looked across the outfield, into left field, where instead of seats the outfield came to an abrupt end against a tall green barrier.

"Look at that left field wall," she marveled. "It's so high!"

"It's famous," I told her. "It has two nicknames. Sometimes it's called 'The Green Monster' and sometimes it's simply called 'The Wall.'"

"The Wall?" she asked.

"Yeah," I said. "The Wall."

At that moment, the seats right next to us began to fill up. Three women in their late twenties, each wearing heavy makeup, tight pants and blouses with low necklines, sat down beside us. One of them, not particularly pretty, had long black hair and very large breasts. Her friend had a bad complexion and was chewing gum very loudly. The third, with a lovely face that was marred only by her exaggerated makeup, had long red nails and hair that was bleached in streaks.

"Hey Mary Ann," twanged out the one with a bad complexion, "Ya gonna get some be-ya?" Her voice was high and nasal.

"Later," said Mary Ann, with the big breasts. "Not now." Then she added, "Tricia – gimme a cigarette."

Tricia, on the end, pulled a golden cigarette case from her purse and handed a cigarette to Mary Ann.

"T'anks," said Mary Ann.

Then the nasal voice twanged again. "Gimme one too, will ya. I gave you gum . . . ."

"Cheezus, Laura, whattaya think I am, Sanna Claus? Okay here." And she handed a cigarette to the other as well.

Then, coming down the aisle just as we had done, saying excuse me excuse me, came a large black man and his large black wife. He was a big man, and he wore soiled working clothes and big oily boots. His wife, wearing a roomy shift that covered her like a bell, followed behind. Her hair was already turning grey, and she wore it in little curls. We nodded at them silently as they squeezed by us and sat down on the other side of Rebecca. The man mopped his brow with a crumpled tissue, pulled out a bag of peanuts, and started eating.

By now, the Tigers were gone, back in the dugout, and the field was empty. Suddenly, a great shout arose from thousands of throats, as the Red Sox, the home team, dressed in white, ran onto the field. Like shining knights they assumed their positions, each one surrounded by a great sea of green.

A distorted voice over the PA system emanated seemingly from nowhere. "We will all rise for the national anthem," it instructed. Then, with the sound of trumpets and drums, *The Star Spangled Banner* blasted out as we all stood there in silence, with a modicum of awe and respect, the whole stadium hushed, as the flag flapped in the breeze high above us.

"*. . . and the home of the brave.*"

"Play Ball!" With that, everybody screamed and yelled, hooted and stomped, clapped their hands and shouted meaninglessly, as we took our seats and the spectacle began.

On the mound for the Red Sox was their big veteran righthander. Originally brought over from Cuba, he could barely speak English but he served up such a marvelous concoction of fast balls, curves, knuckleballs and changeups that he had become quite a star in the Boston pantheon and reaped great profit from living in this foreign land.

His first pitch was a fastball down the middle for a strike, and the whole stadium, always taking the first pitch for an omen, shouted triumphantly, feeling its power. One, two, three, and the Tigers went down in order.

The Red Sox came to the plate with great cheering and fanfare. The leadoff batter, the wiry shortstop, banged a single through the left side of the infield. Then a young rookie, this year's boy wonder, stepped up to the plate and hit a line drive into the gap in the outfield. The whole stadium rose to its feet to watch the ball bounce between the two racing Tigers, and howled its glee as the batter slid into second base, advancing the other runner to third. The next batter, a young black man with powerful arms, lifted a high fly ball to center field, and when the centerfielder caught it, the man on third tagged up and ran home.

"Hooray!" we yelled, and we shook our fists above our heads. And then the old rock of the team, the captain and seasoned star, came to the plate. He stood there with perfect confidence as we cheered and clapped. He swung on the first pitch, blasting a single over the first baseman's head, as the rookie on base turned on the speed and scored the second run.

The stadium was instantly a madhouse, and the cheering didn't die for several minutes. Frisbees and garbage flew in the air. We had quickly gone ahead, and we – *we*, the fans – felt strong and powerful. We were great! But then a quick ground ball resulted in a double play, and the first inning was abruptly over.

Next to me, the woman with the long black hair and big boobs began to chat with a man sitting in front of her. He, too, had dark hair, and he sported a thin mustache.

"How did you like that?" she asked him.

"Beautiful, beautiful," he said, "We're gonna win. We can't lose. Hey, I'm gonna go for some beer now. Ya want some?"

"Oh sure," she said. "I'd love some."

As the man disappeared to get some beer, Laura turned to Mary Ann and asked with great interest, "Where do you know him from?"

"I don't," she answered. "I just said hello."

The Tigers came to bat again, but this time they proved more fierce an opponent. The first batter also banged a sharp single through the left side of the infield, just as the Red Sox had done in the previous inning.

"Boo!" screamed the fans.

Rebecca turned to Max, a little disturbed. "I don't understand," she said. "This guy did just what the Red Sox did, and instead of cheering, they boo him. He did the same thing – isn't that good?"

Patiently, Max explained it to her, in his simplest terms. "You have to understand baseball," he told her. "It's a symbolic confrontation between Good and Evil. The Red Sox are Pure Good and the Tigers are Absolute Evil. Whatever the Red Sox do to get ahead is good, but whatever the Tigers do is bad. That's the basic condition. And so, no action that is essentially evil can ever be good, even if its appearances are good. Essence determines existence. It's a simple world, with no contradictions and no ambiguities. And we, the fans, as people of faith, can only praise good and decry evil. There can only be saints or sinners.

"Moreover," he continued, "If the Red Sox win, that proves our saintliness. But if they lose, we're sinners. And the test of our faith is our steadfastness. But you *have* to root for the Red Sox – there's really no choice – it's the only avenue open to us. Even if their actual playing is beyond our control. What do you think there are all these seats for – we're not just watching, we're part of the whole thing." He shrugged. "But it's a random system. On the road, the Red Sox wear grey instead of white, and then *they're* the representation of evil."

The black man sitting next to Rebecca just sat there, listening to Max, an unsure look on his face. When I looked at him, he turned his head back to his program.

"But what if I feel *sorry* for the Tigers," Rebecca argued.

"That's the simple beauty of it," Max said. "You're not supposed to feel sorry for them. Exult in their downfall. The righteous can rejoice in their righteousness, even with their boot on the chest of their enemy."

"Is that what *you* feel, Max?" Rebecca asked him, as if treading onto private ground.

"Me?" Max said. "No. Yeah. Well, sure, sometimes. I don't know. I'm just explaining the game to you."

"Oh," Rebecca said.

All the while I sat there, keeping score.

At that moment, the man with the mustache came back with the beer. "What did I miss?" he asked.

"Man on first," Mary Ann said. "Hey – thanks," she added, as she reached for the beer.

The next Tiger was standing at the plate, already two balls and a strike against him. He crouched, shaking the bat, ready to jump at the pitch. The pitch was delivered. "Crack!" went the bat as the ball was smashed down the left field line. The batter ran to first and the other runner slid safely into third in a cloud of dust.

"Booo!" yelled the fans again.

Mary Ann, Laura and Tricia, however, busily drinking, chewing and smoking, did not open their mouths or use their voices at all. Instead, together, as if each one was following the same unseen cue, they raised a right hand in the air, made the "thumbs down" sign and shook their thumbs downward. Then the inning continued. By the time it was over, the Tigers had tied the score at 2-2, and the balance of power was reestablished.

Rebecca and I chose that moment to eat our dinners. "Go ahead, go ahead," Max said sullenly, so we did. I started eating a peanut butter and jelly sandwich, while Rebecca chomped on a carrot. It was still barely light out, and so Max could do nothing but sit there while his stomach growled, watching us and also watching, patiently, as the sun slowly sank behind the stadium walls. It was a bright orange sun now, like the oranges that he knew were in the bottom of Rebecca's paper bag.

Little progress was made in the game during the next inning or so. A man left on first, a lot of ground balls, all adding up to nothing on either side. Mary Ann, however, was making marvelous progress with her new acquaintance.

"Hey, you're Italian?" she said leaning over. "Me too, I'm Italian too. What part of Italy are ya from?"

"My mother's from Naples," he said. "But my grandfather on my father's side was from Rome."

"From Rome! Mine, too," said Mary Ann, getting excited. "My grandfather also was from Rome."

"Well whattaya know," said the man, smiling and watching her lean over.

"Yeah, whatta ya know!" answered Mary Ann.

In the top of the fifth, the Tigers got a walk. Not much to worry about – just a walk. A little nothing of an occurrence; it happens all the time. But then the runner stole second and the threat of a run now seemed possible. The next batter followed with a cheap little bunt, a tiny nothing that bounced right in front of the plate, but it worked perfectly, and the man on second easily scampered to third.

The next batter stood in the batter's box, shaking his bat. The pitcher shook off one sign after another. He seemed rattled by the runner on third. The count ran to 3 and 0, and the pitcher's concentration was obviously disturbed. On the next pitch, he threw low, too low, and the ball hit the dirt and bounced away from the catcher, rolling all the way to the stands. The runner on third tore home as fast as he could and easily scored on the error.

The crowd let out a groan. A run had scored, and even though it was a cheap little run, a stinky, sneaky nothing of a run that barely happened, it nevertheless was a run. It felt like a huge burden and the crowd groaned beneath it. And although the next batters were summarily dealt with, the Tigers were ahead now, and the thousands of fans were suddenly laden with an oppressive weight, burdened by a load they had not expected or prepared for.

The black man stood up from his seat and turned to his wife. "Honey, I'll be right back," he said slowly. "I'm going to the men's room." And, shaking his head sadly, he made his way by us and up the aisle.

It was growing dark now, though no stars had yet begun to shine. Suddenly, people all around us started looking at their watches and then looking up at the sky.

"What's everybody doing?" Rebecca asked.

"I don't know," Max answered.

"Me neither," I said. "Maybe they're checking for the exact end of the fast."

"Maybe!" said Rebecca hopefully.

"Fat chance," Max replied.

But at that moment all attention was focused back on the field. The Boston catcher, a powerful man, had just stepped into the batter's box. The Tiger pitcher let go of a blazing pitch and the batter smacked it with great conviction. The ball traveled straight and true, into dead center field and over the outfielders' heads. It bounced off the fence and back onto the field, and the Tiger outfielders had a hard time chasing it down. By the time they did, the batter was already standing on third base, smiling. The crowd stood and cheered. Their hopes were building.

"Look Max, look!" Rebecca pointed upwards with excitement. "There's a star!" And sure enough, there was the first star.

The next batter hit a quick ground ball to the shortstop. The shortstop looked menacingly towards third, keeping the runner from breaking towards home, and then threw on to get the runner at first. One out. The next batter struck out. Two outs. The crowd began to get nervous, and people clenched their fists and held their breath.

"Look Max, there's a second star!" shouted Rebecca. And there, in another part of the sky, was the second star.

"Do you see another?" Max said eagerly,

"No, I can't," Rebecca said.

"There isn't any yet," I said. "But soon – soon!" And while I was still looking up, the man who'd been sitting next to Rebecca returned from the men's room, and, saying excuse me excuse me, squeezed by us and returned to his seat. His wife looked at him with expectation and he merely nodded, as if all was better now.

And then, the Red Sox second baseman, a small, scrappy player who looked like a leprechaun, stood up at the plate. All hopes rode on him, all eyes were riveted to his bat. The pitcher took his time, staring in and staring in, straining his eyes at the catcher's glove, as if the ball might go faster the harder he stared. Finally he was ready, and he threw. The batter swung. The ball hit off the very end of his bat, and, looping in a tiny arc, dropped into shallow right field for a hit.

The crowd went wild as the runner from third crossed the plate. "Tie score! Tie score!" All even again. Tabula rasa, the balance restored.

Then suddenly a new commotion arose in the stands. Dozens of people looked at their watches, and dozens more stood pointing to a spot in the sky.

"There it is, there it is!"

"What?"

"There!"

"Where?"

"*There!*"

And there, on the purple night sky, a small light was traveling across the deepening darkness.

"What is it?" I wondered aloud.

"What is it?" Rebecca asked a man behind us.

"That's the Apollo-Soyuz spacecraft. It was supposed to come over us right now," he said, pointing to his watch, "and there it is."

And there it was, the strange satellite born of that unholy alliance between the two most powerful nations in the world, enemies who totally distrusted each other yet went ahead with a joint spaceshot for a combination of reasons, at once both selfish and well-meaning. What indeed would ever come out of it?

"Is that good enough for the third star?" Max asked.

"Sure," I said. "Why not? Might as well. Besides, when else will you get the chance to break your fast with a spaceship?"

He thought it over for a second. Then he gave in. It was allowable. "Okay, I accept," he said.

"So, what would you like, Max?" Rebecca offered. "Ask for anything at all."

"I want an orange," he answered without hesitation, "and a hard-boiled egg."

"Do you want an apple and some raisins?" she asked him.

"No. Not now. Maybe later."

The fast day was now over. And while Max began to strip the peels away from his orange and his egg, tossing them under his seat, the night swiftly grew darker, and quickly, several other stars began to shine. The Red Sox rally ended and the inning was over. The sky grew increasingly dark, and more and more stars were twinkling, little shining points in the night. By now, Mary Ann had moved down a row to sit by her new male friend, and her two former companions were eyeing her carefully, picking up on every move she made.

Imperceptibly at first, but then growing stronger and stronger, a sweet, familiar smell began to waft over us from somewhere above our heads. I looked at Max and he looked back at me. He smiled – he was obviously beginning to feel better after breaking his fast – and together we turned around to see where the smell was coming from.

And there, about five rows back, was a group of about six or seven freaks with long hair and scruffy beards, latter day Hasidim, furtively passing a tremendous joint back and forth among themselves. Max and I turned back around with a grin and again paid our attention to the playing field, where the remainder of the now-tie ballgame was getting under way.

But nighttime is different from the day, and things that appear so obviously clear in daylight take on new meanings and proportions when cloaked in darkness. Even our attitudes change along with our perceptions, and imagination comes in to fill out and amplify what our night blindness has taken away. The world itself follows different rules during the night, and different animals come out to roam the earth. There are beasts of the day and beasts of the night, and each one lays claim to its own sovereignty.

And so, under a black sky, the baseball game itself began to look different. What had seemed before so clearly a battle between Good and Evil, a clash between opposing forces, lost its distinct sharpness. Even the proportions changed, altered by the fathomless firmament suspended above us. Suddenly, it appeared that we no longer were the faithful followers, rooting in sympathetic harmony for one side's domination over the other. At night, our own powers diminish and we become aware of our mysterious dependencies. And so, although we were still fastened to the game, almost as if its victims, bound to the vagaries of its movements, we were now watching the strange workings of an organic entity, like watching the interchanging shift in clouds, with each one bearing on the next, which held over us the threat of storm or calm. Ten men stood on the baseball field – nine of one side, one of another, but together they combined to form one single body, working like gears towards a common goal, whose outcome was still unknown. The game continued.

New patterns began to dawn on me. "Hey Max," I said, "look at the field. You see – there's so much room in the outfield, but everything in the infield is so close together. It's almost like an explosion, where the further out you get, the farther apart the particles are."

"Hey, yeah," he said. "Everything from home plate outwards gets farther apart, like a mushroom effect." He grew to theorizing. "It's like the atmosphere, or the world – things closer to earth are packed together, but as you go upwards, the distances between things get greater. It's also like an atom bomb."

I looked at the three outfielders, each one alone in a sea of grass, and at the seven players grouped more closely in the infield, with the catcher and the batter so close they could reach out and touch each other. And then I realized what it reminded me of.

"Look Max – it's like in the kabbala. There are ten emanations. The three outer emanations are way out and far apart, lost in the highest realms. Then the seven lower emanations are closer, in a tighter relationship."

"Far out!" he answered, picking up on the idea. "That's right – there's Keter, Chochmah, and Binah, like Center, Right, and Left. And then you go down to two on one side – first base and second base –"

"Chesed and Netzach!" I said.

"— and two on the left –"

"Din and Hod. And the pitcher –"

"— that's Tiferet, which is perfect for the pitcher. The pitcher unifies the whole team, everything concentrates on him, he's the star performer, and then he delivers the pitch to the plate –"

"— and that's the union between Tiferet and Malkhut, which is the catcher –"

"Right! But it first has to go through Yesod to get to Malkhut –"

"— and Yesod is the batter, shaking his phallic bat which joins Tiferet and Malkhut into one relationship."

"Far out!"

We saw the game with new eyes now, and we grinned from ear to ear. Everything was different. Tiferet stood up there in the middle, on the mound, and threw towards the plate. Malkhut stretched out its glove to receive the ball. Yesod swung. It was a sharp ground ball to Din, who scooped it up and threw it on to Chesed for an out.

"Yay!" we shouted.

"What are you getting so excited for?" Rebecca asked.

"Oh, it's beautiful," I told her and went back to watching the game.

The next batter stepped into Yesod, and Malkhut flashed a few signs and made a perfect target with his glove, waiting to receive. Tiferet nodded, and sent a fastball right by Yesod, which thumped into Malkhut's glove.

"All right!" I said. "Strike one!"

Then Tiferet threw two more, just like the first. Three quick pitches and Malkhut received them all, right down the middle. Two outs.

I looked over at Mary Ann, who was now sitting on her new friend's lap. She was laughing and giggling, while he played his fingers up and down her spine.

The next batter stood up at the plate, and on the first pitch he hit a high fly ball and everyone watched to see where it would land. Keter moved into position, pounded his glove, and made the catch. I was jubilant! Three outs.

The game continued this way, and soon I was cheering everything. Pop flies to Netzach, line drives to Binah. Everything was fraught with significance. What did it matter which team was up?

"I don't know about you," Rebecca told me. "You're acting strange."

One inning moved into the next, and the night grew later and later. The sky was full of stars. But after a while, even this new game began to weary me. What was all this Tiferet and Malkhut, this Keter, Chochmah, Binah and all that? Where was it going? So what if there was a ground ball to Netzach, or a close play at Hod? What, after all, did it accomplish? No runs had scored, and I was growing tired. I wanted to go home. I wanted to be in my home, to be safe in my bed, to be delivered from this heavenly struggle. The fans grew restless. The black woman pulled some knitting from her pocketbook, and Mary Ann's new friend went for another beer. Quickly, Mary Ann ran to confer with her friends.

"He says he wants me to come home with him for a drink," she said.

"Oh yeah?" Laura said with great interest, her eyes excited.

But Tricia's attitude was quite different. "Really?" she said skeptically and with a chilly display of reserve. "And what do you think?"

"Me? Well, I don't know. I hardly even know him."

"That's right," Tricia said. "But you've sure been flirting a lot."

"Me?" said Mary Ann with incredulity. "You think I've been flirting?"

"I'd say so," Tricia answered coolly, taking a big drag on her cigarette and then blowing out a cloud of smoke.

At that moment, Laura leaned over and spoke to me. "Hey, could I see your program for a second," she said in her nasal voice.

"Sure, "I answered, handing it to her.

She looked at it a moment and then suddenly seemed startled. "Hey – you haven't kept score since the fifth inning. It's already the ninth!"

"Well," I said to her, smiling, shrugging my shoulders, "somehow it didn't seem necessary."

"Yeah," she answered, "I know exactly what you mean – it's been a long game."

A long game indeed. We were now growing weary, weary to the soul, but still we couldn't leave the game until it was over. We had to stay until the end. We simply had to. There was really no choice.

"How much longer will it last?" Rebecca asked Max.

"Who knows?" Max answered. "If nothing happens in the ninth, it could go on forever."

"Oy," said Rebecca, a little scared. "Forever!"

So we sat there and we waited. Finally, the Red Sox got up in the bottom of the ninth with the score still tied, 3-3. Suddenly the stadium grew tense, and the fans started to clap in a rhythmic fashion. We were impatient, we wanted to win, we wanted the game to end. Stomp, stomp, stomp, the noise grew. Mary Ann's friend, back with his beer, was hollering. The black man beside Rebecca looked intensely at the field now, and the three of us sat there, on the hard seats, straining forward.

Tiferet again peered in to Malkhut. Each player stood suspended in his position, poised and ready. He set; he threw. And suddenly there was a tremendous sound, as the ball leapt from the bat. Everybody rose to their feet, Mary Ann shrieked, the black man hollered, the man with the watch pumped his fist into the air, the freaks with the dope shouted wildly, as the ball, a perfect spinning sphere, traveled in a long, graceful, elliptical arc, like the earth traveling in outer space, and it suddenly disappeared over The Wall, into the blackness beyond the stadium.

"Ayn Sof! Ayn Sof!" Max and I screamed in ecstasy, while thousands and tens of thousands of voices around us shouted hallelujah.

"We won! We won! We won!"

We were happy, and we were free to go now. It was like we were dreaming, and we laughed and sang. And suddenly the crowd surged forward, up the aisles, up the ramps, and headed for the stairs. I turned and looked backwards to where everything was already quickly emptying out, and I watched as candy wrappers blew across the playing field like loose pages from old, tattered books, and saw beneath the grandstand seats popcorn and peanut shells lying in scattered heaps, like the rubble fallen from ancient ruins.

"Time to go home," I said.

YOM KIPPUR

Uch! It was miserable out. I shook myself off as I walked in the back door, coming from my car which I parked in the driveway behind the house. I had spent the evening walking around downtown; I had needed to be out and spend some time thinking, but the miserable weather had cut my walk short. It was unseasonably cold, and the wind and rain had been battering at our little section of the world all day and night. Even my thoughts had been dreary while I had been walking in this storm.

The house was cold. It was too early in the year to turn on the furnace, and I shivered as I stepped out of my dripping raincoat and began taking off my shoes, which had already soaked through.

"Who is that?" called out an unsure, nervous voice from the floor above.

"It's me, Carol – Solomon," I answered. I wondered why she bothered to ask. She never did that before. And she sounded rather unusual. But before I could think much further or continue to get out of my cold, wet shoes, there suddenly came a long, loud buzzing from the front door buzzer.

"Don't open that door!" Carol yelled from upstairs.

Instantly, the person at the door began pounding on the glass. What was this racket? I started up to see who was at the door, but Carol's voice again cut me short.

"Solomon, come upstairs, quick!"

I hurried upstairs. Questions flashed through my mind. Who was out there? A robber trying to get in? A rapist? Why was Carol so frightened?

Carol was upstairs, herself wet and shivering, wearing only a bathrobe that was obviously damp. She had evidently come out of the shower, the bathroom still looked steamy, but she was standing in the hallway, her hands wrapped around herself, as if either trying to warm herself or to hold onto something. Her teeth were chattering.

"It's Shoshanah," she said.

Oh no, not Shoshanah, not again. My heart sank. Lately, Shoshanah had returned, and had begun to harry us with an angry, accusative madness. Whatever had happened to her since that earlier Sukkot was completely unknown, except that something had shifted within her and a more frenzied, harrowed demeanor had emerged from inside. A few days after Tisha b'Av, late at night, Shoshanah had suddenly shown up at our door, for the first time in a very long time, claiming to have no place to stay and needing shelter.

What were we to do? It was late, there was no place for her to go, so we took her in. We told her that she could only stay the night and that we couldn't accommodate her for longer than that. We were not a crash pad, we told her. The Havurah was a private house.

She seemed to accept that at first, but the next day she showed no signs of leaving. Instead, she stayed all day, sitting in the library, most of the time with the door tightly shut, only to emerge every few hours, demanding to be fed.

At first, we were surprised by her strange insistence. What could she understand? Indeed, what *did* she understand? Exactly how insane was she, and what would she do if crossed? Would she get violent?

That day, she was fed, given her usual fare of whatever was in the refrigerator, but instead of accepting it with gratitude, she denounced everything we offered and everything we owned. She called our food a blood libation (although she ate it) and declared that our plates were covered with sin. She yelled at Jerry when he came in from working in the garden because he had his shirt off.

"Cover your nakedness!" she hollered at him. "Don't advertise!"

That evening, we all conferred, and together we walked into the library. Shoshanah was sitting on the couch, doing nothing. We told her that she could not stay any longer but that we would help her find a place if she needed one. She answered that she would leave the next day and that she had a place to go if only she could spend one more night at the Havurah.

One more night? We looked at each other. One more night she could stay in the library, but in the morning she would have to leave.

Although we had done everything we could to make her understand that she could not stay on any longer, the next night she returned and was let in by Rebecca who had just happened to be at the house, doing laundry. Several times during the next few weeks the same thing would occur: Shoshanah would show up sometime late in the night, when it was too late to turn her out without feeling terribly guilty about it, and by some manner, either by inveigling her way into the house by playing on someone's sympathies, or else by catching an auspicious moment to gain entry from someone who had not been notified to keep her out, she would find her way into the house and again station herself in the library. And on one occasion, when the door was inadvertently left unlocked, she again found access into the house.

This had to stop. We did not wish to be harsh on her, to add to her homelessness and force her onto the streets, but we could not provide her with a permanent home. Nor could we cure her. What could we do? We were totally unequipped to handle such a problem. Together, as a group, we approached her again and told her that she could not stay any longer. We tried to explain, although we did not know if it did any good, that we would try to help her find a place at an adult shelter in the city.

As soon as we mentioned an adult shelter, she began to grow agitated. Her face twitched and she started to cite random Biblical passages. "Isaiah 28!" she said. "Psalm 92! This is a Jewish place and it must be charitable!"

In the morning she was gone but returned again that evening. This time, we would not let her in. She rang the doorbell, and rang again, but through the glass we told her that she could not come in. We told her that if she wanted we would place some phone calls to shelters throughout the city, but we would not let her stay at the Havurah another night. However, at the mention of an adult shelter, she turned, slammed the outer screen door, and ran off.

The next morning, as I gathered in the mail, I found a crumpled note stuck into the mailbox. Scrawled in a shaky, childish handwriting, with a chaotic design to the words, the note was entitled, "Bible Homework," with a column of references and verses listed beneath it.

"Read 8th Commandment. Read 9th Commandment. Isaiah 32. 'Thou shalt not turn away the stranger.' 'The house of the Lord is become a house of corruption.'"

It was a mishmash of citations and references which did not match. Along with these were her own comments. "All Jewish organizations are corrupt." "You live in sin." "Do not reveal your nakedness." And then, beneath it all, ludicrously, in capital letters, were printed the words: NO HANKY PANKY.

After this, Shoshanah did not return again, and it seemed she was gone. We had spurned her, betrayed her, and, evil that we were, she had finally left us, angrily, to rot in our own damnation.

But now she was back, on the last night before Yom Kippur. It was already almost midnight, and the weather was too miserable even for a dog or a wild beast to be caught outside, all alone, in the darkness, with no place to go.

"How long has she been here?" I asked Carol, who was still shivering in her bathrobe.

"About half an hour."

Half an hour! For half an hour she had been standing out there, pounding on the door, ringing the buzzer, rattling the doorknob, demanding to be let in.

"She got me out of the shower."

"What have you been doing since then?" I asked. "Have you just let her keep ringing the buzzer like that?"

"No, of course not. I talked to her and told her to wait outside while I made some phone calls. I called as many social agencies as I could."

"And what happened?"

"Nothing. Most were closed and the others were no help at all." She paused, and then looked sharply at me. "Solomon, I didn't want to let her in while I was here by myself. She's crazier than ever."

At that moment, the buzzing and pounding began again. And then, in a loud voice, demanding and yet filled with anxiety, riding up at the last syllable, she called through the door, "Solo*mon*! Solo*mon*!"

For some reason she had remembered my name, and the sound cut into me like a chainsaw. In her voice I could hear her pain and her madness and her frenzied desire to get inside the house. And the form this piercing sound took were the syllables of my own name.

"Solo*mon*!" she called out. "Solo*mon*!"

I cringed, as if touched by electricity or the clammy hand of horror. Carol held onto herself, tighter, closing her eyes, as the sound ripped into her as well.

"I've got to go down and talk to her," I said.

I walked downstairs and approached the door, and I pushed the curtain away from the glass.

There was Shoshanah, her deathly pale face – ugly, round, and puffy, with her angry red scar along her cheek. Her hair was wet and matted by the rain, its points sticking into her eyes. She showed little change of expression when she saw me, except that I sensed in her reaction a slight feeling of relief and yet added urgency as I appeared, not because of who I was but that I offered, one more time, someone else to whom she might plead her case, perhaps this time with success.

"Solomon," she said, still speaking with an inflection that contained no life yet held a frenzied forcefulness behind it. "Solomon. Open up. I need a place to stay tonight." She put her hand on the doorknob, expecting instantly to be admitted.

"Wait a second, Shoshanah," I said. "Where did you stay last night?"

She looked at me, stunned at my inquiry. Then she replied. "Last night I stayed at Open Hearth. But they stole everything I had there. Everything. They took my clothes, they took my money, they stole all my books."

She began to recite a litany of grievances. "They stole my manuscripts there, and all my poetry, and they replaced my manuscripts with forged copies. They wanted to make a prostitute of me. They wanted me to go out on the streets and be a prostitute. They wanted me to take drugs, and they wanted me to sell drugs – they wanted me to become a drug pusher and I refused. They wanted me to starve to death, they wouldn't even let me use their kitchen to cook my own food."

"Wait a second, Shoshanah," I said calmly, trying to calm her down. "I can't believe they really did all this to you."

"They wanted me to be a prostitute!" she repeated. "Mr. Sullivan who's in charge of the place, he said I should go out on the streets, he was kicking me out. And he said, 'Go be a prostitute.' So I had to leave and I've been out all night, and now I'm soaked, I'm completely wet, my shoes are wet, I'm cold, my feet are freezing, my hands are freezing, I haven't eaten anything, I have no money because they stole all my money, so I came to Havurat Chaim because it's a Jewish place and it has to take me in. Isaiah 32. Psalm 48."

She raised a Bible that she was holding in her hand and kissed it. "I want a place to come in and meditate and read my Bible. I'll just sit in the kitchen and be quiet and read my Bible."

I tried to maintain a hard exterior, but I began to soften. It was so miserable outside that she certainly had to be wet and cold. That much was probably true. But I still did not want to give in, because it would only reinforce her constantly returning to the Havurah instead of finding proper help. But did she know about proper help? Every time we offered assistance she had gotten terribly upset. Undoubtedly, she had plenty of experience with these places and wanted nothing more to do with them. She only wanted to get into the Havurah, using her Jewishness as her claim upon us.

"Are you going to let me in?" she said, insisting more than asking.

"Wait a second, Shoshanah. Before we let you in, I have to tell you that if you expect hospitality from others, you can't expect to go around yelling at people and criticizing everybody. Why do you expect hospitality from people you argue with and always disapprove of?"

At first, she didn't want to answer. After a pause, she only repeated, "Are you going to let me in?"

I wanted to let her in, to end her suffering and to end mine at seeing her suffer. But I could not simply let her in, especially after we had told her that she could not stay again, without making her understand *something* of what we were trying to tell her. If I let her in, I knew she would only grow angry again. In fact, I could see her anger building from on the other side of the door, and I was afraid she might even break the glass, force her way in, and get violent once inside the house.

"Shoshanah, you can't come in. You must not feel that you have a right to disrupt other people's homes. And this is not a public place. This is a private house. We don't have room for people to crash here whenever they need a place to stay."

"I'll stay in the library again."

"The library is full. Shoshanah, listen to me. You can't expect hospitality if you refuse to be a proper guest."

"I've had guests in my own home," she said finally. "And it's the right of any Jew to criticize other Jews who aren't living according to *halachah*. Linda even told me that your plates weren't really kosher. It's my right as a Jew to make you go back on the right path."

"No, Shoshanah, it's not your right," I said, staring at her.

"Are you going to let me in?" was all she answered.

"Shoshanah, you said you used to have a house. What happened to it?"

"My house? My landlady kicked me out. She stole my welfare check and said I never got one. This is the third time she stole my check. I know how it works – she steals my welfare check and tells me to get another one issued. And then she splits the check she stole with the guy at the welfare office. So, I wouldn't ask for a new check. I know how it works. I used to be a bookkeeper. And the whole welfare office is behind it, and I accuse the entire welfare office, and the city of Boston, and the city of Cambridge, they're all guilty. And I complained to the mayor and my complaint is on his desk, and he's guilty, with the city of Boston and everyone in the city of Boston, and everybody in Cambridge and everybody in Massachusetts. The whole state of Massachusetts is guilty, as well as the State of New Jersey and everybody in it. And Open Hearth is guilty, and so is Shelter Place, because they have me blacklisted. I'm blacklisted from all those places, they kicked me out, they tried to make me a prostitute. And my mother is guilty because my mother told the president to have my welfare checks stopped, and so the president is guilty, too. And he's the third president in a row who's guilty, and so the entire people of the United States are guilty." She paused. "Are you going to let me in?"

"Wait a second, Shoshanah," I said, trying to reason with her. "I can't believe that everybody in the United States is trying to harm you. Listen, I'm going to make some phone calls and I'll be right back."

I went upstairs. Carol was already on the phone, trying to locate a place for Shoshanah to spend the night. The first place she called was Open Hearth.

"Hello, we have a woman here who needs a place to stay for a night. She's in her early thirties, she's a little nutty but not violent . . . Yes, she has black hair, a scar . . . Yes, Susannah Weiss . . . Aha. . . Uh-huh . . . ." There was a long pause. "Thank you." She put the receiver down.

"They say that Shoshanah has been there longer than their limit and they refuse to take her back because she argued with everybody and yelled at them and made herself a general nuisance. They also said she was getting violent and hit one of their workers. They won't take her back."

The next place we called was Shelter Place. After the same introduction, Carol listened and then put down the phone.

"She's been there, too, and was also kicked out. The woman at the desk said that their bulletin board has only one notice on it: 'Do Not Admit Susannah Weiss.' So, what are we going to do? Should we take her in?"

At that moment, the yelling and banging began again.

"Solomon! Solomon!" she hollered. Both of us stopped and grit our teeth.

"Hold on a minute," I called out. "I'm on the phone."

"I don't know," I said to Carol. "I hate to see her suffer like this. I'm inclined to let her in for the night. But then she also wants to stay for Yom Kippur, which means tomorrow night too, and we simply can't have that. She'll be here for two days and two nights altogether, and then she'd never leave."

The door buzzed loudly again as she held her finger on the buzzer. "And she's obviously incredibly paranoid."

"I know," Carol answered. "She thinks everyone is after her. I hate to do it, either way. They won't take her in anywhere. I don't know what to do. She's also getting more violent."

"So*lomon!* Sol*omon!*" she howled, beating the glass. I paid no attention.

"I don't know either. Part of me says we should let her in, give her a hot shower, a glass of tea, wash her clothes, be kind to her, and tell her to behave herself. And part of me doesn't think that this is at all the place for her."

"I'll make one more phone call," Carol offered.

"Where to?"

"New Jericho House. They're also an adult shelter. I think she once said she stayed there too."

At New Jericho House the woman who answered the phone was different from the others. More of a social worker, less of a functionary, her attitude seemed more concerned and knowledgeable. Yes, they had put Susannah Weiss up for a while, but they wouldn't take her in anymore. She had broken things, she had started fights. They had tried to get her into psychiatric care but Shoshanah wouldn't listen.

There was one place that was always open, the woman told us, and would take her in for the night. They had 24-hour open facilities – it was the Adult Psychiatric Center at Pilgrim City Hospital. Susannah knows about it yet so far won't go there. But if she had no other choice, if other people would stop letting her stay for a day here and a day there, maybe she would go to the hospital. She wouldn't be committed or put away, they would only talk to her, and they were better equipped for her. It was a good hospital and would treat her well, and they could even help her there. In fact, it was the only place that could really offer her actual help rather than merely pitying her. What we should do was tell Susannah to go to the hospital, and if she was desperate enough, she would go.

The woman from New Jericho House continued and said that we really shouldn't worry about Susannah too much because she was very streetwise and could take care of herself. In addition, she had a mother in New Jersey who apparently was very concerned about her and was willing to help, but Susannah wouldn't have anything to do with her, either.

We thanked the woman, hung up, and stood there deliberating, while Shoshanah continued to buzz and bang on the door in a way that made thinking almost impossible.

"We're going to have to turn her away," Carol said.

"I guess so," I answered, hating to do it.

"She's scared and alone," Carol said, still holding onto herself, somehow very attuned to Shoshanah's feelings. "She's terrified and thinks everyone is out to get her. But we can't let her in."

"I know. Okay, let's go."

Together, we went downstairs and pushed away the curtain. Shoshanah was standing there, her face pressed against the glass.

"Are you going to let me in?" she said. "Let me in."

"No, Shoshanah, we're not going to let you in, but listen to why." Carol spoke slowly and deliberately. "This is not the proper place for you. We aren't equipped to provide a place for you. But there is a place that is, and they will take you in."

Shoshanah did not want to hear about it. She interrupted Carol and said, "I need a place for Yom Kippur. I'll just sit in the kitchen and read my Bible. What have I done wrong? I'm a 34-year-old virgin. What harm is there in that? Let me just sit in the kitchen like I used to do . . ." and she faltered here a moment ". . . at my grandmother's house. I beg of you, let me in."

She was desperate and her eyes were wide. It looked as if she was about to cry. It was killing us.

"Shoshanah," I said, "you're welcome to come and daven with us, but you can't stay here tonight."

"*You* want me to be a prostitute too! Now Havurat Chaim is guilty!" She kissed her Bible again. It was her last refuge and her last defense.

"No, Shoshanah," Carol said forcefully. "Nobody is telling you to be a prostitute. But you have to go to Pilgrim City Hospital APC. I hear you've been told about it already. If you want, we'll get you a cab and pay for it. But the APC is a better place than this for you to stay tonight."

"No! I won't go!" she shouted.

"Shoshanah," Carol said, enunciating each word carefully, "you can't stay here. We'll help you get to the APC. But if you try to stay here, we'll have to call the police."

That was the final separation. At the mention of the police, it was as if a huge boulder had suddenly dropped from our shoulders, falling between us and Shoshanah. It was painful and a relief at the same time.

"No!" Shoshanah yelled, and in one motion she slammed the screen door with all her might and hurried down the steps into the wet, dark night.

The next evening, Yom Kippur began. The Day of Judgment, the Day of Atonement, the great and awesome day that comes only once a year.

But this year I couldn't get into it. For some reason, I wasn't open to it at all. That night and the next day I sat in the back of the Havurah, flipping through the *mahzor*, counting the pages, participating only intermittently, bored. None of the davening could grab my attention.

I looked around at all the people – the regular crowd, the occasional visitors, the newcomers whom I had never seen before, now all squeezing together into the Havurah on this one day of all the days of the year. I didn't quite know what I was looking for; I didn't really understand what I was doing there.

The day dragged on slowly, but only in rare flashes, in brief moments, did my boredom melt away. And these were the fleeting moments in which, up from the inner recesses of my mind, surfaced Shoshanah's desperate, insistent voice, calling, "Solo*mon! Solomon!*"

In those moments, I thought of the face of that crazy, paranoid madwoman, and I also thought of how I had kept the door closed tightly against her, shutting her out completely.

SEUDAH SHLISHIT

Hello again. Did you have a nice nap?

What?! You say you didn't get to sleep – you actually stayed up to *read* all those stories? *All* of them? Don't be silly; you didn't have to read all that, just to please me.

You *didn't* do it just to please me? You mean you *liked* them?

Well . . . I'm flattered. What can I say? I'm glad you enjoyed yourself. But I'm sorry you missed your nap.

But come inside now. It's getting chilly. The afternoon is growing late and it's time for *mincha-ma'ariv*.

On Shabbos afternoon, late in the afternoon, as the sun is slowly sinking in the sky, you can begin to feel the passing of time. Shabbos is supposed to be *ta'am gan eden* – a taste of Eden. But in fact, that's all it really is: a taste. Just a taste. A taste of timelessness, a taste of peaceful pleasure. But that sense of timelessness doesn't last, and you can already feel Shabbos beginning to slip away, the taste fading on your tongue even as the sun slips away, falling over the horizon.

And then, as you realize that this peaceful time is leaving, you can't help but think about a time when it won't go away. You think about redemption, the end of exile, and messianic days. And so you add a special prayer

304

to *mincha* and say, "*Uvah letzion goel*" – may a redeemer come to Zion. But who is this redeemer supposed to be, anyway? Where is he going to come from, and how is he going to set about his task?

How, indeed?

So, for a change – just for a change – why don't you listen to a story I'd like to share?

TRIP TO ISRAEL

I stared through the dusty windows of the Egged bus as it bumped and hurtled its way down the road. My window wouldn't open, it was stuck, and so I sat without the benefit of a breeze and watched through the glass as the fields and orchards jigglingly flew past. I saw orange groves, empty of their fruit in the hot summer, and banana groves with their stumpy little banana trees that produced such funny, short bananas. I saw the parched earth, the baking fields, the green plants, and the eucalyptus trees, all flicker past as I traveled from the north down to the kibbutz by the Mediterranean where Max and Rebecca were spending the summer.

It was the summer after the Yom Kippur war and, as after every war or major crisis in Israel, there is a terrible need to go back, to touch base again, to make sure that the country was still there and to see what new changes the events had brought. So Heligman found a job leading a tour of high school students on their first visit to the land, Esther came for a few weeks as a tourist, Mark had gone to work on a kibbutz in the Negev, I had gone to work on a kibbutz in the Galilee, and Max and Rebecca went to a kibbutz on the Mediterranean, on the road that runs between Haifa and Tel Aviv. We were scattered all over the country.

I hadn't seen anyone from the Havurah for over a month, while I did little more than pick pears, eat, sleep, and swim in the afternoons. Slowly, I began to feel my body gain in strength and power. I had grown tan, too, and was proud that my physique, previously so pale and soft, had improved so remarkably in such a short time.

And yet, although I regarded my own development so keenly, I passed practically unnoticed by the people around me, both the kibbutzniks themselves and the other volunteers. They all seemed far more interested in the *blondiniot* from Denmark and Sweden than in just some Jew from America. So I left the kibbutz and decided to pay Max and Rebecca a visit.

The bus dropped me off at a Keren Kayemet sign at the side of the road, which pointed towards the kibbutz where Max and Rebecca were staying. I took up my pack and started down the road which led through the kibbutz's fields before it reached the residential area. On either side of me grew a different type of vegetation. To my left, a cotton field opened up, its short plants forming a low hedge that covered the ground, allowing a long vista that gradually rose up a slight incline and then disappeared into the horizon. To my right grew a jungle of banana trees, like a dense thicket. I plodded my way between them, my pack heavy on my shoulders.

When I reached the center of the kibbutz, which consisted of many low buildings, all very modern and square, arranged in rows this way and that, I began to look for Max and Rebecca. How should I go about it? I stopped one kibbutznik and asked if he knew them. They were volunteers, I told him.

The volunteers, they're down there, he pointed, and then walked on.

I went to the little bunks where the volunteers stayed and asked if anyone knew Max and Rebecca. In the first bunk, a few people, younger than myself, just shook their heads or shrugged their shoulders. Who? Max and who? They didn't know them. I walked to the next bunk and received equally unprofitable answers. Finally, at the last bunk, a young woman, also American, pointed to a group of buildings and told me that's where the married couples stayed.

I ambled over to the buildings she had pointed out and knocked on all the doors, one at a time, going down the row of cabins. No one was in. At last, someone walking by asked me who I was looking for. Max and Rebecca, I said. Who? I described them. Oh. Well, maybe they were that couple who lived in that little room down there at the end of that building. But he couldn't be sure. I should go there and see.

I stood before the door of the little whitewashed cabin, and knocked. I heard a chair move inside and then the door opened.

"Solomon!"

"Rebecca!"

Rebecca jumped up, clapped her hands, and gave me a big hug. "Oh, Solomon, it's so good to see you. And you look so good," she said, stepping back to survey my newly enhanced form.

I looked back at her, eager to repay the compliment, but she was pale and thin, even more than I had remembered. So I said nothing about it. "Oh, it's so good to see you, too," I said. "Hey, where's Max?"

"He'll be here soon. He gets out of the chicken coop in about fifteen minutes. Come sit and talk until he gets here."

We took two little metal chairs and sat in the shade of the bunk. I told Rebecca all about the kibbutz I had been on. I told her about the land up there, about the Hulah valley, about the work I did there and the other volunteers. I also told her about two Belgian women who came from a seminary somewhere in Brussels, who had come to Israel because they wanted to learn more about "the Judaismus," as they called it. Working on a non-religious kibbutz didn't seem to me to be a very productive way to learn about "the Judaismus," I had told them.

"Ah!" they had said, "do *you* know about the Judaismus? Could you teach us something about it?"

I had answered that I did, in fact, know *something,* but I really didn't feel that I was the best person to teach them. I suggested a few other places they might try. But after that, they began to tell the kibbutzniks that there was someone religious among the volunteers. Of course, the kibbutzniks were astounded that there was a "religious" person on the kibbutz. Who could it be? they wondered.

"That's the crazy thing," I said to Rebecca. "Among religious people, I'm considered not at all religious. Among non-religious people, I am. Or at least I'm seen that way."

"Yes, but you like it that way, don't you?" she said.

"Like it? I don't know. I guess so. That's what I am, that's all. And you've gotta like yourself. What else can I be, anyway?"

Then Rebecca told me about her and Max's experience on the kibbutz. Max was enjoying playing kibbutznik, getting involved in the physical reality of kibbutz life.

"And what about you?" I asked.

"I like it too," she said, a bit weakly. "It's hard for me, that's all."

Soon, Max came along, chicken feathers in his hair, chicken shit on his shoes.

"Solomon! How are you?" he exclaimed, glad to see me. He shook my hand in his strangely formal manner, as if wishing me a happy holiday or welcoming me to his business. It was a strange quirk of his. "Listen, do you want to go swimming?" he asked.

"Sure," I answered. "Hey Rebecca, want to come swimming with us?" I asked.

"No," she answered slowly. "The sun's too strong for me on the beach. I get burnt really easily."

"But it's already late, the sun's not strong anymore," I countered, trying to coax her into joining our little expedition.

"I really can't," she said, shaking her head with a hint of sadness. "But you and Max go and enjoy yourselves."

Max and I changed into our bathing suits, took some towels, and set off for the beach. As we walked, he pointed out the different places of interest on the kibbutz: the dining hall, the basketball court, the children's recreation room, and the new houses going up. And there, he pointed, was the library, where he liked to go and read the newspaper. He explained this particular kibbutz's economy, and how it augmented its agricultural production with a small plastics factory that manufactured faucet nozzles, wastebaskets and plastic silverware.

"Why especially faucet nozzles, wastebaskets and plastic silverware?" I asked.

"Who knows? Why not? I guess that's what they like to make," he answered.

He went on to tell me of some of the more colorful people they had met. He told me about one old man he played chess with a few times who had been there since the twenties, and of a young couple who urged Max and Rebecca to stay on the kibbutz, which was always looking for possible new members.

"What do they look for in new members?" I asked.

"Oh," he said, "responsibility, hard work, compatibility, ideological agreement . . ."

"Well, I guess it's like the Havurah, but without the hard work or the responsibility."

Inevitably, our conversation turned to the Havurah, as it always did. When even just two Havurah members got together, there was always this other, larger presence that surrounded them. Every encounter between two Havurah members, no matter where they were, was, in some sense, a Havurah meeting, and every activity they did together became a Havurah activity as well. My talk with Rebecca was also a Havurah talk, my postcard from Heligman was a Havurah correspondence.

And so, now, in some strange way, part of the Havurah, like a wandering spirit, some uprooted, peripatetic embodiment of itself, was presently walking down a bumpy dirt path on a kibbutz in Israel, heading for the shore of the sea. I thought of the Shekhinah, following the Jews through exile, a spiritual presence that accompanied them wherever they went. And yet, here it felt so easy and natural. The sun was bright, the air was warm, birds flitted in and out of the scrubby bushes around us. But at the same time, it felt so incongruous, too. What was the Havurah doing here? Reality seemed slightly out of joint.

"Rebecca has this fantasy that the whole Havurah should move to Israel," Max said.

"That's understandable," I said. "But could you imagine us here? No one would be able to figure out what the hell to make of us. And how could we do it – live on a kibbutz? Then we'd end up making faucet nozzles, too. Or maybe plastic pareve roach clips. Anyway, we have enough trouble taking care of one old yellow house. Could you imagine us having to take care of anything as real as a whole small town, plus its business?"

"Well, that's just it. We'd change. We'd adapt to fit the task at hand. That's what the kibbutzniks did."

"I know, I know," I said. Unlike Max, something about that prospect made me very uneasy, even frightened. And I wasn't quite sure of exactly what it was.

At last we reached the beach. There were just a few other people there and a set of old gymnastic bars for exercise. I went over to it and jumped up to grab its rusty metal bars. Still feeling the excitement of my newly awakened muscles, I did a couple of pull-ups and a laboriously enacted stunt, while Max looked on with admiration.

"Hey, you're getting good," he said.

We went to put our towels and shirts on the sand near the water, and while we did this, one of the older kibbutzniks, a man who appeared to be in his early fifties, got up and went over to the bars. Easily, he lifted himself up, twirled himself around, arched his back and moved up over the bars, did a little flip, and gracefully landed on his feet. He was well aware that we were watching him. Then he came over and headed in our direction.

"Do you speak Hebrew?" he asked us in Hebrew.

"Yes," we answered him.

And then he began his speech. Very courteously, he did not try to engage us in ideological debate, or to overpower our argument with his. He merely stated his case.

"You have to come to live in Israel," he said. "How many Jews are there in the world – twelve, fourteen million?"

"Something like that," Max answered, and I echoed in agreement. "Yeah, that sounds about right."

"So, look," he said. "In Israel there are three million, In Russia three million, in America how many – five, six million?"

"Yeah, something like that, we said again, making vague gestures with our hands.

"But American Judaism has no future. Look at all the intermarriage. People don't care about being Jewish – in two generations there won't be any more Jews in America. Your grandchildren won't be Jewish. And in Russia, they are disappearing. They cannot live there much longer, either. And so, in twenty years, there will only be five, six million Jews in the world, at most. So you have to come to Israel. It's the only place that you can be Jewish. It's the only place that Jews can survive as Jews." He looked at us matter-of-factly, as if it were a truth so obvious that there was no need to argue about it.

Max and I hemmed and hawed a little, making excuses. Could we say he was wrong? Could we say he was right? Neither of us was looking to get into a debate.

"You have to come to Israel, it's as simple as that," he said again. And then he looked at us, each one in the eyes, said he was glad to meet us, shook our hands, and walked away.

"Well," I said to Max, "everybody's got their answer as to how to solve the problem." Of course.

"Everybody builds his life on his own premises," Max said. "And you can't refute it. Who knows, maybe he's right."

Maybe he was right. Maybe he was wrong. We had heard his argument before, along with every other of the myriad arguments on how the future of the Jewish people would unfold. Each one had its aspect of truth, and each one built upon that truth. I certainly had no desire to prevent anyone from doing something that was positive just because it wasn't right for me. But I didn't have to buy it either, no matter how much I might agree with its ultimate goals. At least, that's what I told myself.

"Well, let's go swimming," I said. We left the sand and waded into the water.

The water was warm and easy to get used to. There was none of that painful shudder that accompanies immersion in New England, for this was the warm Mediterranean, and so we just slipped right in. In no time at all we swam out to water that reached up to our necks.

We swam around, paddled, talked, and finally went for a long swim, going far along the beach and then back again. When we had returned to the point where we entered, I saw on the shore two of the members of the kibbutz, a young man and his wife, holding their little child at the very edge of the water. The woman had a wonderful figure, a lovely, supple body. She had dark hair and was laughing. The man had a well-tuned, solid physique, and together they bounced the child up and down. They were obviously both strong and comfortable in their bodies, and they used them well. They were beautiful. With the child between them, they seemed to be the very picture of health.

I tread water for a while, just watching them, from a place that was sufficiently far out in the surf that it wouldn't seem as if I were staring.

"You ready to go in?" Max finally called to me.

"No, I think I'll stay out here a little longer," I said.

-2-

After our swim, we went back to join Rebecca, and together we discussed plans for the next few days. Both of them had acquired a few free days and so could take the next two days off. We decided to go together to Jerusalem.

The next morning, out on the road by the Keren Kayemet sign, Max, Rebecca, and I caught a bus en route to Tel Aviv. We boarded, paid our fare, and headed for the back of the bus where we could all sit together, three across. We had the entire last row to ourselves: It was as if the last row was reserved for the Havurah, and as if the Havurah were going for a ride, a secret, mystery ride – although we were the mystery. No one else on the bus had any idea of who we were or of what kept us together. It was our own little special kinship, of which only we were aware.

314

Once again, the fields, the orchards, and the eucalyptus trees flew by.

At last we arrived at the Tel Aviv bus station.

If there is any place in Israel that resembles a hellhole, it is the Tel Aviv bus station. A large, chaotic, open area, ringed by a million little shops and stalls, it was crowded with people, cars, taxis, all pushing in every direction, trying to squeeze out their own little bit of space, trying to get where they wanted, trying to earn a couple of Israeli pounds. It was hot, crowded, noisy, and smelly. The buses sent up thick, black, gassy fumes that stung the eyes and assaulted the lungs. All around the station, hawkers screamed out "baigeleh, baigeleh, baigeleh, casata casata," while shwarmas of suspicious hygiene turned on their spits, roasting, smoking, tempting the hurrying, harried traveler.

The sun baked and beat down upon everybody: the passengers, the vendors, the women with shopping bags, poor old Yemenite men sitting behind piles of newspapers, and miserable beggars squatting against the concrete wall with a cup or a crooked claw outstretched, imploring. The snarled traffic beeped and honked, adding more jangling noises to the already unpleasant ensemble of smells, sounds, and sights that assailed the senses and wearied the spirit. In the midst of all of this were row after row of bus after bus, a confusing, maddening maze of queues, signs, stanchions, all directing the crowds to go this way or that.

"Man, we gotta get out of this place," I said.

"Soon as we can," Max replied, "but first I gotta pee."

"Me too," I answered, "though I hate to do it here."

We left Rebecca standing by the door, and Max and I went over to the men's toilets. We entered a large, crowded room that smelled particularly uninviting. We stood next to each other, jostled by soldiers, Hasidim, old Sephardic men with long curls, and burly bus drivers. Standing in a puddle of urine that splashed over the edge of the stone trough and onto the floor, we all displayed evidence of the same mitzvah, the same experience, that same original sign in the flesh which kept us all together, one family, one people.

This is a hell of a place to have a communal experience, I thought. I shook myself off and zipped up my zipper as soon as I could.

"Hey, Max, come on, let's get to Jerusalem already," I said impatiently.

"Don't worry," he said, "the bus isn't ready to leave yet, and we already have our tickets. We'll get there. Be patient."

"Well, I just want to get out of here, that's all," I answered.

"Okay. Well, we'll be there soon."

The ride to Jerusalem is always a magical ride, a ride more than just the struggle of the bus and the conquering of distance. It is a ride of elevation from one consciousness to another, from one perspective to another, from profane to holy, as if already entering onto sacred ground, even as the bus travels along the highway that is cut into the spare and rocky light brown earth.

Uphill and then down again, the bus labored in low gear, whining and chugging, as the distant hills shifted, playing a geometric hide and seek, now displaying a new piece of the approaching landscape, now covering it up again, only to reveal it once more, larger, broader, as the next hill is ascended.

At last the buildings came into view, the edge of the city which sinuously crawls out onto the contoured hills.

We had all been there before, Max, Rebecca, and I. In fact, we had even lived there for quite a while, each of us having spent several months at the university. It was there, indeed, during that earlier visit, that Max and

Rebecca had first met, and for them Jerusalem was the city of romance, like Paris or Venice are supposed to be. Each of us knew the city well – its landmarks, its holy places, its neighborhoods. We knew its shops and streets, its markets and its people. And yet, we each still felt an unmistakable excitement as we grew nearer to the city, a sense of anticipation that seemed never to grow tarnished or cold.

Max and Rebecca became, in degrees, more and more affectionate, until they were holding hands and snuggling close to one another. I, in turn, felt my memory open up. I reached into it and suddenly, so easily, impressions and sensations came flooding back to me, impressions that had been forgotten or set aside. I remembered my first arrival in Jerusalem, and that sense, when I was younger, that I was free there, really free, far from my home and my parents. I remembered the color of the houses, the air, the smell. I remembered the friends I'd had there, the girls I had known, the grocer across the street. The alleyway, the apartment, the front door, my clothes, our dishes, the tiles on the floor . . . .

The bus pulled up onto the corner of Sderot Herzl, made a left turn, circled around the back of the bus terminal, came through, stopped, and disgorged its passengers.

Rebecca was beaming by the time we stepped off the bus. Her dark eyes were wide and sparkling, though her skin was still pale and white. The wonderful experience of being back in Jerusalem offered a thousand excitements, ten thousand possibilities. "Where do we want to go first?" she asked, more jubilant than indecisive.

"Let's go down to the Old City," I suggested.

"Sure," Max said. "Let's walk there."

"Fine with me," I replied.

We walked down Jaffa Road, past the new buildings, through a narrow neck of the road crammed with dark little machine shops filled with the smell of wood and glue, and then out again into the broader, busy space in front of the open market in Mahane Yehudah. We stopped and bought a kilo of apricots, and continued down the road. We passed the rows of little shops, the street vendors, and came to the busy intersection of Jaffa and King George. There, we stopped for ice cream. We continued on, through the center of the new city, past the post office, and then a little further, until at last we could see the walls, the old, amazing walls that enclosed and protected the city's ancient heart.

A new anticipation sprung up inside us as we saw the walls again. Each stage in our walk drew us closer to something that always radiated vitality. Each step was another barrier removed, each step meant a little less distance to travel, until we reached the very gate itself. Through the Jaffa Gate we walked, entering even further into the concentrated core of the concentric worlds of Jerusalem.

A thousand impressions, a million sensations burst into our eyes, our ears, and our noses. The same stores were there, but always new and exotic; the same stone steps but always a joy to hurry down. On either side hung a thick, almost living montage of brass lanterns, dangling, jingling, hanging from the walls, of long Arab dresses, embroidered bags, trinkets, beads, bangles, signs, and wonders. We passed through, soaking it in, all the strangeness and dazzle of a thousand things that call to you, trying to catch your eye. But we continued on, aware that something was carrying us forward, making us unwilling to stop and dawdle, eager to fulfill some visceral urge that kept us constantly moving ahead.

Our rhythm accelerated, and now we were aware that we were hurrying, rushing, not wanting to stop or linger for a single item. Past all the stalls we rushed, weaving our way through the two-way crowd, following the path that we had long ago memorized, past this turn and down that alleyway. We knew we had to get to the Wall, that that was now our foremost destination. It was there we had to go before anything else could be done.

Down that alleyway, turn to the right, down those steps, and there it was. The Wall. We walked onto the broad plaza that led up to it, which ended up against the ancient stone.

Rebecca had to go one way, Max and I went another. We walked down to the large and imposing outer edge of the ancient Temple.

There is always a sense of elation at seeing the Wall, always a feeling of surprise and gratification. And yet, once you approach it, there really is no burst of drama, and it is foolish to expect any, for that will only let you down. The Wall is silent; there are no trumpets or flashes of light blazing out from it. It is silent, and it stands there, a warm, unforbidding color, large, impressive, steeped with history and prayer, but silent, always silent.

I walked over to it and put out my hand to touch it. Contact. All I had needed was contact. I expected neither revelation nor inspiration, nor did I fancy that an unknown emotion would surge up from hidden depths inside me and blot out reality or transform me into a spirit or a sage. Contact. I ran my hand along the rough edges of the stone.

Separately and together, Max, Rebecca, and I just stood there transmitting our silent thoughts against the ancient stone, a stone older and more profound than anything we could express with speech or reasonably understand.

We spent the rest of the afternoon wandering through the Old City, buying this, tasting that, following pathways here and there, and following no particular path, heeding no particular itinerary. The afternoon grew late and we had spent all the energy we had earlier started out with.

But still there was one thing I wanted to do, one place I wanted to go, although for a long while I couldn't put my finger on just what it was. I acted on an impulse, a vague sentiment I didn't quite understand.

"Let's take the bus up to the Mount of Olives," I suggested.

It seemed a reasonable thing to do, so we boarded the bus that left from the Damascus Gate, went down into the valley, and then traveled up and ended on the top of the Mount of Olives. We got off and looked around.

The ancient Jewish cemetery is up there on the Mount of Olives, as well as the Intercontinental Hotel. It is from there, too, that you can obtain that famous view, the all-inclusive overview of the city that can be seen on postcards and in all the picture books. I wanted to see that view and just look at it for a while.

Three members of the Havurah stood alone on the Mount of Olives and looked across the valley onto the fabled city spread out before them. It was a beautiful vision, all gold and silver, set among the beige, flesh-colored rocks. My heart strained forward, as if towards the object of its desire. It was the dream of a hundred generations. And there, across the gulf, it lay before me like a sleeping lover, like a jewel at my feet, like a sparkling crown upon a velvet pillow for me to take and set upon my head.

And so, I thought, why don't I stay down there? Why don't I decide to remain there and help rebuild the city up from its ruins? Why don't I just come and be part of her? Why not? I had no business that held me back, no family depending upon me, no overwhelming obligations calling me back home.

Max and Rebecca had their arms about each other.

"We should move the Havurah to Jerusalem," Rebecca said dreamily. "We could sell the house and buy an apartment here, and we could all live near it. Wouldn't that be wonderful?"

Yes, it might be wonderful, I thought. I continued to look at the city before me.

A sandy, hot wind blew up from behind me, from the direction of the Judean desert, and blew some sand across my neck. And then, an usual emotion swept across me, a discomforting realization. It was my own too-precious identity that kept me away – not my identity, but the fear of losing it, the fear of giving up some basic thing I knew I was, and, for better or worse, I shuddered to see obliterated. It was something I somehow could not bear to throw away, and which I knew that staying there would demand to be jettisoned.

And what was that basic thing, so cherished that I could not part with it, so precious that I could not give it up and lose myself into Jerusalem? It was my strange other companion, the offspring of my cultural split, the philosophical bedfellow who shared my nest with me: in short, it was my cynicism, my doubt, my irony which I could not allow to live with me if I resolved to live in that ancient home: my doubt and the smug need always to allow myself to express it, even as I sang my hallelujahs.

No, I thought, I have not set something other than Jerusalem above my chiefest joy. My chiefest joy it still remains. But what I set above it – no, not above it, but across from it, against it – is neither joy nor certitude, a faithless faith, an empty word, a vacuum, a gnawing nothing. And yet, I must admit I do try hard enough to scratch an empty laugh from it, to squeeze out a cold comfort from the grim, unjoyous knowledge of the limp unassailability of my position.

I hunched over as the hot wind again blew up from the desert, blew through the cemetery, and threw its handfuls of sand at my back.

WEDDING MARCH

Time. Human time. We're caught in time and all we can do is make our peace with it and sing in spite of it. We get older, perhaps wiser, we grow and we decay, all at once. The times change around us and inside of us as well.

The Havurah, too, is caught in time, going through its motions and changes. But let's not dwell too much on that. Shabbos afternoon is still Shabbos, and now it's time for *shalesh shudes*, the third and final feast of the day.

Yet in truth, *shalesh shudes* can hardly be called a feast. After eating all day, this is no time for another heavy meal. So instead, we'll have a simple meal, and a slightly sad one at that, to accompany the end of our day of rest and our gradual return to human time.

But hold on a second, I'll go bring out the food. I'll be back in a jiffy.

Ah, here we are: some yogurt, a little salad, some challah, a bit of fruit, and a special bottle of wine. We're all set. Now we can begin.

To accompany our meal, I have a few more stories, if you don't object. After all, what is a meal without a good story or two? Or maybe three . . .

Me, I'm not ready to get married. Sometimes, I have a glimpse into what makes it a necessity, an ineluctable inevitability, like an emotional whirlpool that sucks us in with a powerful downward spiraling force, from which there is no escaping as its waters churn and circle around us, always bringing us closer to that inner locus. We can only throw up our hands and abdicate all resistance as we become trapped in its turbulent, swooping rush, and watch, horrified, fascinated, relieved, as it pulls us in, our legs, our chest, and even our head eventually going under. Whatever causes it to happen – whether it is society's self-serving demands, our own psychological weakness or strength, or some impersonal, biological rhythm that pounds out its drum-like beat and catches each one of us in our own particular step in time, eventually forcing or seducing us to march along – whatever it is, it happens. Even to all us crazy hippies, who tried out this and that living arrangement, toying with our open relationships and many-sided loves, with our supposed freedom to leap and crash from one pad to the next, and simply, with our refusal to worry about it, it happens in the end, whether with benefit of clergy or not.

But as I said: me, I'm not ready to get married. That much I know, and the clarity of that knowledge keeps me, at least, from doing something I would regret after the hoopla of lacy gowns, tuxedos, and a marvelous eating binge will have faded away and left me, along with whoever else it would be, sitting across from me, a confused grin on our faces, with nothing but a gaudy album of gilt-edged photos and lots of china and kitchenware. No, I'm not ready, not yet. I have many places to visit before I am.

But my friend Heligman and his friend Diann, I suppose they were ready. Even though Heligman fought it, denied it, tried to run away from it, and did his best to interrupt the inevitable flow of events, it caught him and it pulled him in.

But let's not rush the story. The afternoon sun is beginning to sink, and I have a long tale to accompany its slow descent.

Heligman, Diann and Caleb all lived together in cohabitational bliss in their low-rent hippie crash pad. They slept on a big mattress on the floor, covered – on the few occasions that the bed was made – with an Indian bedspread, all elephants and mandalas. Other possessions were few and cheap: a deep, swampy, second-hand couch; a floor lamp with a naked bulb that, like a drooping flower, hung from its socket on a dangling wire; some battered old chairs whose stuffing grew up through their cushions; and a bridge table in the kitchen for both simple breakfasts and elegant dining.

Their only possessions of value were their stereo, placed high on an empty trunk where Caleb couldn't get to it, and Heligman's books, his dozens of books, shelf after shelf of traditional Jewish texts: *Mishnah Torah, Mikraot Gedolot, Midrash Rabbah,* even a complete set of Abarbanel commentaries, all with their golden Hebrew lettering stamped across their spines, along with a smattering of everything else in an educated young couple's library. Various posters, acquired serendipitously and without much effort, were pinned haphazardly onto the walls.

The rest of the decor was furnished by Caleb, and was strewn all over the floor. Chewed bones, chewed shoes dragged in from outside, chewed newspapers pulled out of the garbage bin, were found in every corner. Once in a while, Caleb would chew up something serious – one of Diann's shoes or a book that he managed to find on the floor – and for that, he knew he would be punished. In fact, on the occasions when he did some particularly mischievous chewing, Heligman would come home to find the tell-tale remnants all over the floor and Caleb cowering in the corner, waiting guiltily, terrified, like a repentant kleptomaniac who couldn't help but steal.

But Heligman was no disciplinarian. "Bad dog, bad dog!" he would yell at Caleb, and then bash Caleb over the head with a pillow a couple of times. But then he'd toss the pillow away, feeling sorry for Caleb, and just shrug his shoulders and smile. It was all such a game; how could he get upset over it?

Life went on like that, easily, without tremendous consequence, for a year, for two years, even into a third. There were no commitments, no long-range plans. How could there be? They had enough problems, and to make plans would demand a serious evaluation of their situation. Life was too enjoyable without delving into all that. They were young, they liked each other, they were sufficiently compatible, and that was all that really mattered.

Among their problems, though, Diann couldn't always put up with all of Heligman's Jewish activity. "Jewish, Jewish, Jewish," she would say, "I'm tired of all this Jewish. It's fine in its place, but all the time?"

And so, some Friday nights she would just go off with her old college friends and leave Heligman to celebrate Shabbos alone or with the Havurah.

For his part, Heligman would say, "She's so insecure, sometimes it drives me nuts. She worries about our relationship, she worries about her looks, she worries about the police coming in and finding a fleck of dope somewhere under the mattress and then arresting us and throwing us in jail forever. I can't take all that insecurity. To hell with it."

And so, problems just slid by. They weren't really major problems anyway – they didn't get in the way of their having a fine time, most of the time.

But slowly, something was building. A malaise. A discontent with the status quo. Heligman decided that he had to go back to graduate school. Diann was looking for a better job. And most of all, the lease was running out, the rent would be going up, and they knew they would have to move out. So, they had to decide whether it was going to be separately or together.

They decided it would be separately. In fact, they decided that maybe it was time for a change. Time to try new things. Maybe they should go out with other people. Reevaluate the whole state of affairs.

Periodically, whenever the relationship encountered a crisis, Heligman would come by and pay me a late-night visit. It wasn't my advice he wanted, but merely a sympathetic ear. He needed to discharge some of his boundless energy, which grew only more extreme in anxious situations, and our old friendship, which reached back to before the days when he had known Diann, allowed him to confide in me without feeling he was compromising her. And so, I would sit at my desk, lean back, and I would listen and watch as Heligman ran around the room, a one-man cyclone, picking up and fidgeting with one item after another, touching this, testing that, all the while spinning out his story. On this occasion, he came to tell me about their impending separation.

He sat down on my bed. "Diann and I are moving out next week, you know," he said. He got up and started to pace. "She found an apartment over in Back Bay, near B.U." He stopped. There was a pile of books lying on my desk, and he began to leaf through the top book, very rapidly, distractedly. "So, I have to figure out where I'm going to live. I have a couple of choices, but the big problem is Caleb. Some of the places don't really want dogs, and if they ever got to know Caleb they'd probably ask me to leave. He'd chew up everything. I don't know, *I* love him," he grinned.

The grin quickly faded. "Anyway, it's a problem, finding a place that's close to the Havurah. Maybe it would be better to move far away for a while, you know, even if that means being far from the Havurah. I was thinking about moving out to the country, just to see what it's like. I could commute. I need the space, and it would be great for Caleb. He could run around in the woods; he wouldn't have to be cooped up all day and then go crazy and eat up somebody's sneakers. He needs freedom. So do I. Hell, after three years with Diann, I really need a change. I think a change would be good for her, too. She needs a break from me as much as I need a rest from her. She needs to build up her confidence, and maybe meeting new people would help."

While he was saying this, he was quickly flipping through the pile of books on my desk and had already tossed the "used" ones into a disorganized semi-circle.

Well, I'll straighten it up afterwards, I figured.

"I don't think Diann's too happy about it, though," he continued. "She says she agrees, and she says she'd also appreciate a change, but I don't think she really means it. Actually, I know she doesn't. She's miserable about it. Come to think of it, it was mostly my decision." He stopped abruptly. He walked across the room to the window and started opening and closing the blinds, pulling the chords up and down. "I don't know. She *says* she thinks it's a good idea."

"Well," I said, "you can't worry too much about her in this case. How do *you* feel?"

"I think I need a change," he said a bit reluctantly.

"Well, if you think you do, then you do. If it's an idea in your head, then you're probably thinking about it pretty seriously – because whenever anybody says it might be a good idea to spend time apart, then it's probably time to split." I wanted to support him in his decision. I understood his need for freedom and felt he could use some friendly encouragement.

"Of course, of course," he said. Then he changed the subject, as well as his position in the room, and began to examine a poster on my wall, using his hands. "My folks were here last week, you know. They came all the way in from Atlanta."

To me, the fact that Heligman hailed from Atlanta was always a source of wonderment. I would have taken him for a New Yorker if I hadn't known otherwise. But Atlanta always came out in strange ways.

"They took Diann and me out to dinner, I don't know why. Then afterwards, my father pulled me aside – only for only a second – and said, as solemnly as only he knows how, 'Walter, she's a jewel. A *jewel.*'"

I could picture his father pulling him aside and whispering his pointed comment into Heligman's ear. The senior Heligman was not of Russian or Polish stock, like so many of our parents, but rather was a Yekeh, from an old German background, and so, instead of bombarding his off-spring with an emotional torrent, he pronounced instead only a few incisive remarks which, to the well-attuned ear, carried from behind their impeccable facade as much weight as an endless string of pleas and entreaties.

". . . And then," Heligman continued, looking around, not knowing what to fidget with next, "then they offered to pay for a shrink."

"A shrink!" I said, "You think you need a shrink?!"

"Well," he said cryptically, slowing down a bit, "Maybe . . ."

Within the week, Heligman moved out to the country, about half an hour's drive from Cambridge, and Diann moved into Back Bay. Of their possessions, only their books, stereo and clothing needed special care. All the rest was just dumped into boxes in the Havurah basement or left for the next inhabitants.

Out in the country, from the standpoint of an outside observer, Heligman's life took on the proportions of a furious fantasy. He ignored Diann and took full advantage of his new freedom. And, since he wasn't being particularly picky, he found that women were readily available. One relationship followed another. One night, several months after his move, he paid me another late-night visit while I was up in my room, studying.

"Hey Solomon, how *are* you?" he said, entering in seemingly good cheer.

"Fine, fine. What's up?" I answered.

"Just came to talk," he said. "To say hello."

"Well, how's life out in the sticks?" I asked.

"Oh, it's beautiful out there. It's really pretty now, and it sure seems a lot easier just to be myself out there."

"How's Caleb doing?"

"Caleb? He's fine. He loves it – running around in the woods, chasing squirrels. And I don't have to worry all the time about his getting hit by cars." Heligman shrugged and laughed. "He still eats up shoes, though, and anything else he gets hold of. The other day he chewed up the mail."

"Well, I guess that's Caleb."

There was a pause. Heligman looked around, his eyes scanning every available object in the room. At last he picked up a clothes hanger and started twirling it rapidly around his finger. I cringed lest it take flight and wing across the room. But I said nothing. Then, while he twirled, he spoke.

"Has Diann been coming around the Havurah much lately?" he asked.

"Well," I said, "Yeah. She comes pretty often these days. More than she ever used to, that's for sure."

"How does she look?"

"She looks okay," I said. "Normal."

"No, I mean how do you think she feels?"

"How does she feel? I don't know." Then I considered it. "Well, I guess she's kind of unhappy. She tries to be cheerful, but I suppose she's pretty miserable. She doesn't talk about you, though. You're a taboo subject."

"I can imagine," he said, thinking to himself. He stopped twirling.

"But *you* seem to be doing okay," I said, a bit lecherously, hoping to prompt him into a livelier discussion.

"Oh, yeah," he said, trying to sound offhand. "I'm doing fine."

"Oh, come on – it must be a little more interesting than that," I said.

"Well," he answered, smiling, "yeah. It's been fun."

I was hoping he'd offer a few spicy stories, or at least some interesting tidbits, out of a sense of male camaraderie. He knew I'd love to listen.

"Well, yeah," he said, warming to the topic. "It was quite a rush for a while. First I met Nancy, and that was lots of fun. She's more into the Jewish stuff than Diann, so I was able to do that part of my life more easily. But I got tired of her because we didn't really have that much else to say to each other. And then there was Melanie, who is prettier than Diann, but she was all fucked up. She was too young. She was still in college. She was working out her older-man fantasies with me. So, I said enough of that. And then there was Marcia, who was a lot less anxious than Diann, and that was a nice change, you know . . . "

"It sounds like they're all still being compared to Diann," I interrupted.

He was taken aback, but then he relented. "Well . . . uh . . . after all those years, I guess so. She's still in my head a lot, you know."

"Do you still see her?" I asked.

"Well," he said, as he then started banging the hanger against his shoe, "that's what I really want to talk about."

Hmmm, I thought. I knew there was something underneath all this. I also figured that was the end of any hope of hearing exciting tales of erotic escapades with mysterious females in the deep woods of the Massachusetts countryside. Instead, I assumed an almost professional attitude, that of the good listener.

"You know, I call Diann up every once in a while, just to ask her how she's doing."

"Oh?" I said, prompting him, my inflection rising.

"Yeah. Well, if you ask me, she's not doing so well, even though she tells me she's doing fine. I get worried about her."

"Well, sure you worry about her," I said. "That's all right. It's very nice of you. But don't overdo it."

"But the thing is, she makes me feel so lousy. She's not going out with anyone. She just sits in that miserable little apartment with the roaches and the crazy neighbors and she doesn't go anywhere. She tells me she's perfectly happy doing what she's doing. She says she's not *interested* in going out with anyone."

"Oh, great," I said. "It's obvious. She's miserable and she wants to make you feel guilty about it. To hell with that." It made me annoyed. "You're not responsible for her actions. She's free to do whatever she wants – and so are you."

"Yeah – but I still feel lousy about it."

"Great. That's very noble of you. Listen, you have to do what's right for you, and you can't hold yourself back just because of her. Look man, your life goes on and it's clear to me that you're doing something about it, but she refuses to admit it."

I saw that I was bolstering his resolve a little – but just a little. There still was doubt in his eyes. He wasn't sure. He continued to explore it further.

"She gave me this big spiel about how I didn't take her seriously," he said, "and about how I never was serious about anything. Hell, I *lived* with her for three years. How can she *say* I didn't take her seriously? What does she want – that I cut off my thumbs? It didn't work, so it didn't work.

That doesn't mean I didn't take her seriously. I did. And now it's over. Things end."

"Damn straight," I said, bucking him up. "Listen, it sounds to me like you're doing the right thing, and that she's acting screwed up. As far as I can see, you're growing, you're living in the present, and she's just being self-destructive. Besides – what does your shrink think about all this?"

Heligman got up and went over to the window. He looked out and then began pulling on the blinds, riding them up and then letting them drop.

"Aw, screw the shrink. What the hell does *he* know?"

Several weeks later, again late at night, I was alone in the house. Well after midnight, it was one of the few times that the Havurah laundry machine was not busy, so I was down in the basement, pulling one load out of the dryer and transferring another into the washer.

The house was quiet. It was one of those calm moments that fill up the hours between nightfall and dawn, during which there is no sense of the motion of time. Everything, for hours before and for hours afterwards, is black and silent, unaffected by the hurrying sun. Only the moon was sailing silently through the sky. I was alone and peaceful in this motionless bubble of time.

Suddenly the Havurah door was thrown open and a gallop of footsteps pounded across the ceiling above my head.

"Hey, Solomon!" Heligman's voice called out, splitting the calm. "You down there?"

"Yeah. Come on down."

Heligman bounded down the stairs, which creaked and bounced under his fleshy frame. "What you doin' down there?"

Heligman appeared in the laundry room. I was instantly struck by his appearance: He was wearing a big old felt fedora, a beautiful wide-brimmed black hat belonging to another era, and a pinstripe vest on top of his normally dingy and colorless shirt. Of everyone in the Havurah, only Heligman had this genuine flair for comic sartorial splendor, creating an offbeat elegance from one or two odd articles of clothing to enliven the normal uniform of Cambridge grunge.

"A laundry," I said. "Hey, where did you get that hat?"

"Like it?" he said, preening, beaming at the effect he created. He did a little do-si-do around the laundry room so that I could see it all.

"It's great. Where did you get it?"

"Where else? At the Goodwill store! I found it in the bin there for thirty-nine cents. It was a wreck. So, I took it to this fancy hat store downtown and got it cleaned and blocked."

"And how much did *that* cost?" I asked.

"Oh, forget it – it was a fortune. Hey – like the vest, like the vest?" he added, hooking his thumbs into the sleeve holes, crowing, making sure I'd see it all.

"I love it," I said. "Goodwill too?"

"Goodwill! Of course."

"It's far out," I laughed. "What're you all dressed up for?"

"I ain't dressed up," he said, emphasizing his southern accent, falling into the role of gentleman dandy, drawing on that other, incongruous side of his upbringing. "This is jes' mah clo'es, tha's all."

"Oh. Well, it sure doesn't look like *my* clothes," I said, pulling a shapeless twist of limp wet *shmatehs* out of the washing machine.

"Sho' nuff," he remarked.

"Here, help me with this," I said, and I piled the load of dry laundry into his arms and then finished stuffing my wet load into the dryer. "Let's go up to my room."

We walked up the stairs and I switched on the light.

"Just dump it all onto the bed," I said as we entered my room.

Heligman dumped the load of dry laundry onto my bed and then immediately sat down next to it and began to fold it.

"You don't have to fold it," I said automatically, without thinking. "I just stuff it all into the drawers anyway."

Instantly, I realized my mistake. Better to have him fold than to sit there nervously as he went through everything in the room, threatening to break, smudge, topple or disorganize anything that was movable.

"Well, if you want to you can just keep folding," I said hastily. "I appreciate it."

Heligman paid no attention. He simply kept folding without stop.

"What's up?" I asked, as I watched him neatly arrange a pair of underpants.

"Oh, not much," he answered. He proceeded to recount a smorgasbord of unspectacular little events while he quickly went through the pile of laundry.

At last, I demanded a straight answer to the meatier problem that was obviously there. "Hey, are you going out with anybody new these days, or something?"

"No – nobody new," he said, smirking. "I got sick of it."

"So, what has you roaming around here this late at night?"

He pursed his lips before he began to speak. "Well, I'll tell you," he said sheepishly. "I don't know if I did the right thing or not, but the other night I went over to visit Diann. You know, just dropped in. 'Hi! I'm in the neighborhood!' That kind of thing. And, well, you know – we ended up in bed."

"Yes, I know how that happens," I said. I thought back to that drawn-out period of breaking apart from Esther, which suffered one setback after another, when we never could seem to make a clean separation. It was a painful time, when the attraction was still undiminished, or even heightened, despite the unhappy circumstances surrounding it.

"You've always got to go back for a last one, or a last few, or one for the good old days, or something like that. Sure, that's always going to happen. It's a pisser though, because it never quite frees up your head. And each time it just makes matters worse."

"Well, that's just it," he said. "It wasn't such a bad time. It was fun. We had a blast." He stopped. "We still get along so well – that's the crazy thing."

"Oh," I said.

I suddenly got the awkward feeling that maybe I didn't quite understand what was really going on between them. Maybe it wasn't like my relationship with Esther after all, and that something was going on of which I was completely unaware. It was a strange feeling, like the moment of conception or the first growth of a cancer cell. Something dawned on me, although it was still too small to locate. It was a disconcerting feeling that I could not yet pin down.

At that moment, Heligman finished folding the laundry.

"Here, it's done," he said. Then the quest began for something else to occupy him. I winced as I watched him, as if he were a hunter searching for his prey. What would he attack and destroy this time?

He picked up a pencil from my desk and reached into my wastebasket for a scrap of paper. "You mind if I write on this?" he asked.

"Not at all," I said, glad he had chosen something harmless and unbreakable. "Be my guest."

He smoothed out the paper and drew a large box, very square, carefully aligned. Then he started to draw lines from one end to the other, carefully subdividing the box into long rectangles. Then he drew lines perpendicular to these, creating many little squares within the larger one. Then he began to subdivide the squares. He was quite absorbed in his precision doodling, unaware that I was watching with such keen interest.

"Hey, man – your shrink's really doing a job on you, or something," I offered.

He roused himself from his intense concentration. "What?" he said, looking around, somewhat dazed, as if he had been interrupted in the act of something very private. "What?"

The next time I saw Heligman was about three weeks later. He had completely dropped out of sight in the interim, and vague rumors circulated about a renewed yet still clandestine liaison between him and Diann. Then one night, again late at night, as I was sitting at my desk, lost in some graduate school drudgery, I heard his unmistakable, heavy yet energetic footstep bouncing up the stairs.

Heligman burst into view.

He looked terrible. He was again – or still – wearing his hat and vest, but now they were an absolute mess. The vest was wrinkled and hung open limply against his chest. The hat, that beautiful fedora, was beat up and smudged with dust. Deep brown circles beneath his eyes stood out darkly against his drawn, pale face. His face itself looked like a yellow watercolor that someone had rinsed under a faucet. He looked like he had gone through hell and done battle with the devil.

He sagged and flopped down onto my bed. He just lay there for a minute, inert, saying nothing, like a corpse. He had no energy even to say hello. Finally, he breathed deeply and sat up.

"Solomon, I did it," he said with an effort. "I made the decision. The big, scary, radical decision."

Radical decision? I thought. Far out! He's going out to California and live on the beach! He's going to make *aliyah* and join the Israeli army! He was moving up to Vermont to become a carpenter! "What?!"

"I'm getting married."

"Married!" I said, viscerally shocked. "To whom?"

He looked at me with disbelief. In an instant, I understood.

"To *Diann*," he said.

Of course. I was an idiot. Who else would it be? A confused emotion slowly suffused itself throughout my body, spreading like butter in a hot pan. I was stunned, I was sad. Something sank within me and I felt, in some silly, selfish way, that I was being abandoned, although not by a lover or a friend, but rather as if confronted with a convert, someone who had thrown off one belief to embrace another. I couldn't understand his decision. Hadn't he told me of all their problems and the strained times they had had together? Wasn't he still going to look for something better?

"Well, that's great," I said weakly, trying to say the proper thing. Somehow, I felt he was making a horrible mistake.

He looked directly at me. In part, he was trying to tell me something, trying to enlighten me with information I had previously never known. And in part, he was offering an excuse, justifying his decision both to me and to himself. But mostly, he was trying to state the matter in all its simplicity.

"I love her," he said, looking at me. "I love her. I'm in love with her. Hell, it took me long enough to figure out."

His washed-out watercolor face was like a dawn on the horizon, rising over my bed of rumpled sheets and blankets.

And then I understood that he had worked it out, that she had worked it out, and that together they had worked it out, and that things were going to be okay.

-2-·

The day of the wedding was bright, clear and cold. Brilliant white snow covered the lawns and yards, while shining icicles hung from the roofs and window ledges, and big piles of black, sooty snow stood in heaps along the sides of the roads.

For Heligman and Diann, this was to be their memorable wedding day, but for the rest of the Havurah it was more like a field trip or a holiday outing, a great excursion into the wild world. The Havurah house itself was too small to accommodate an entire wedding celebration, replete with family, friends, neighbors, and all the other guests in a wedding entourage. Nor did we have room for all the dancing, eating, music, coatrooms, and powder rooms that play such a vital part of any wedding party. After all, we merely owned a small house with a couple of rooms, big enough for services, perhaps even big enough for a Purim and Rosh Hashanah crush, but never big enough for a wedding.

And so, it was off to suburbia we headed, down to the heart of the bedroom communities, to the land of well-stocked linen closets and deep pile rugs, to Hart's Rock, Connecticut, where Diann grew up, and to the synagogue she attended as a wide-eyed little girl and later as a clever but often brooding and uncertain teenager, dreaming of boys and aching to escape from the house.

In unity there is joy as well as strength, which turned the Havurah into a raucous caravan of foreign invaders bombing down the Connecticut turnpike, beeping messages from lane to lane, waving and shouting to each other at the toll booths, and even at one point descending like the hairy Mongol hordes onto a roadside Howard Johnson for a pre-wedding ice cream and bathroom stop.

At last we arrived, *en masse*, fearlessly, in the midst of this strange yet so uncomfortably familiar environment. One by one, our cars pulled into the temple parking lot, alongside so many others that had already arrived. Judging from the number of cars – cars that I didn't recognize – I realized this was going to be an enormous gathering. Of course: this was a *wedding,* and where else can there assemble, in one place and at one time, all the people important to one's life? We were only one small connection to Heligman and Diann's many life's connections, and there was no way that I, or anyone else in the Havurah, could claim that same vantage point that Heligman and Diann had. Together, they would know all the people there, while we would be only one small set of those many individual points on the fabric of their lives.

We piled out of the cars, carrying our suits, ties, shirts or dresses, on hangers and in plastic bags from the cleaners. After all, a wedding demands a certain uniform, and so we all brought ours along to change into when we got there.

So . . .

Quick, into the men's room, down with the jeans, on with the pants, the nice shirt, my one and only tie, button up my vest, slip into my only suit jacket, comb the hair, look into the mirror, give a debonair smile – (ho-ho, you crazy hippie in a suit) – and emerge! into the carpeted ballroom for maybe just a canapé or two.

"Well hello, Solomon," someone called out.

I turned around. Mel! He was here, too! He came over, smiling, and shook my hand.

"This must be the end of the world," he said. "I never thought I'd see you in a three-piece suit. What happened, did you get a job in a bank?"

"Aw, man, this is my special-occasion suit. The only time I ever get to wear it is at weddings. But each time I wear it, the average price per wearing goes down dramatically. That's why I like to come to weddings – it's economical."

"Sounds like a pretty low-consciousness reason to come to a wedding," he said softly, mocking me with gentle sarcasm.

Oooh – rebuffed by the rebbe. And then I thought, *Hmmm,* I wonder what's on his mind these days.

"Anyway," he said, "look at this crowd. It's quite a gathering."

I looked around and, indeed, it was a mighty assembly. All of Heligman and Diann's friends were there, as well as a few Havurah members who had since moved on, current members and people from the fringes, and scores of transplanted Cambridge types mingling among the aunts and uncles, a whole community in itself, with its own particular, almost integral history, gathered in one place.

There were even some people I was quite surprised to see. In particular, there were a number of women I had known and certainly never expected to have to confront at a wedding. Over in one corner, I noticed Valerie and Karen being introduced to each other by a mutual acquaintance. Karen was an old friend and former girlfriend of Heligman's, and Valerie was a college friend of Diann's. Very strange indeed. For, unbeknownst to either of them, each also had a different mutual friend, a mutual experience as it were, nothing to boast about or get nostalgic over, I reasoned, but nevertheless, both of them had, at one period in my life, after my relationship with Esther had irrevocably ended, found their ways into my own bedroom for a short while. What a strange period that was, bumping in slow motion from one woman to another, not getting terribly attached to any of them. No, nothing to wax nostalgic over, although it did make me stop and pause. It was an odd feeling. I wondered if they would ever become well-enough acquainted to discover the connection. Probably not. They'd never know. I winced to think of what they might say to each other, and then shook it off and passed instead to indulge in a roué's inward smirk at my own bit of private knowledge. Oh, just forget it, man, I told myself, dismiss it from your mind.

"I'll take one of those if I may," I said, as a tray of little gefilte fish balls went floating past. I quickly popped a fish ball into my mouth, and I was left holding a useless toothpick with green cellophane ribbons on the end. Now what do I do with this? I wondered.

But then Chief and Leah came walking along, arm in arm, looking very much the couple, pleased with and solicitous of each other's presence. From the time I had known Chief, he had always been talking about this suit he possessed but which he never had an occasion to wear. And so now, here he was, wearing it, and it was obvious that he'd had it for quite a while. It had skinny lapels, the pants were straight and cuffed, and he wore a thin little tie and a button-down white shirt to go with it, all of which had been perfectly in style about fifteen years earlier. It was a bit ludicrous, but he was happy with it. And so what else mattered?

Next to him, Leah wore a long flowery dress and looked lovely. She seemed well aware of the slight ridiculousness of Chief's outfit, as well as of his obliviousness to it. I had to admit that she bore the whole thing well.

"Hey Chief – lookit you, all snazzed up!" I remarked.

"Yeah! You like my suit? I've had this suit for years and I never get a chance to wear it. Finally, today I got a chance."

Leah gave me a knowing, what-can-you-do glance. She was in a good mood and I was glad about it. I figured that she liked weddings. They put her in a happy frame of mind.

"You look lovely," I said to Leah, trying to be both sincere and friendly.

"Thank you," she said, blushing just a smidgeon, embarrassed but enjoying the compliment. She especially enjoyed being complimented when Chief could hear.

Soon, more people came over, and a whole group began to form. We all stood around, marveling at each other, heckling each other, giving each other little digs about how establishment we all appeared. On the whole, we were rather uncomfortable to be dressed so fancy in front of each other. It seemed worse than being naked.

Then, Esther suddenly appeared from nowhere, looking wonderful and sophisticated, wearing an obviously expensive dress. She had probably been hiding it in her closet and eagerly awaited her chance to wear it, just as Chief had been harboring his silly old suit. No matter how hard Esther tried to be a hippie, she never fully let go of all the old trappings she grew up with. Nevertheless, it was a pleasure to look at her; she knew she looked good and enjoyed it immensely.

"Hey Esther," Chief said, "with a dress like that, we're going to have to raise your Havurah dues."

She laughed. "Frankly," she replied, "I was thinking about suggesting some black-tie communal dinners."

Mel, who had been looking on silently at all this, interjected a comment. "It seems the Havurah has sure gone through some changes since I left," he said.

"Aw, man," I said, shrugging my shoulders and turning my palms upward, "the sixties – they're gone."

But then, escaping from their rehearsals and private photo sessions, Diann and Heligman appeared and approached our little cluster. Our conversation abruptly stopped as all eyes turned towards them.

The bride was attired in a lovely, scratchy polyester gown that didn't quite drag on the floor, sporting a floral design around the midriff. Previously, I had never remarked upon her midriff, especially as a discrete, integral entity. Nevertheless, there it was. The groom, in turn, looking devilish in a dark blue suit with a white carnation pinned to its lapel, played with his jacket buttons and looked around with a mild sense of anxiety and confusion. His beard was neatly trimmed, and, for a change, his hair was combed. Indeed, they were a charming couple.

"Heligman! Diann!"

We hastened to admire them. I especially noticed Diann. To my surprise, she looked wonderful. Lovely. Attractive. Good ol' "I'll-just-sit-in-the-dark" Diann, never at ease in situations of self-advertisement, had suddenly taken on a different bloom, an inner light, and she was now, in her own way, charming and even seductive. I was amazed at the transformation.

"I'll tell you," Heligman confided, "I really wanted to wear tails, just so I could wear a top hat. Imagine! Wouldn't a top hat be far out? But my father said, 'Walter, thiss iss a solemn occasion.' How did he know I just wanted to wear the hat?"

At that very moment, the senior Heligman made an appearance. But he wasn't coming to make a polite social introduction; rather, he came to gather the bride and groom, for it was soon time to get the ceremony underway and their disappearance was holding up the proceedings.

He bowed politely and apologized for the intrusion, but then turned his attention away as he hustled the soon-to-weds to wherever they were supposed to be.

"Walter. Diann. Come, come," he said, beckoning them hastily, waving them in with his hand. "We have to start on time, you know. And now is the time."

Heligman and Diann put up no resistance. They fell in behind the senior Mr. Heligman and allowed his punctiliousness to carry them along. Heligman turned to face us for an instant, flashing a mock-nervous smile, showing all his teeth tightly clenched together in pseudo-fear, just to add a touch of comic relief. Then Diann also turned and gave us a wave, as if she were off for a long journey. And then they were gone, whisked away.

"Well, if this is starting soon, maybe we should go and get good seats," Chief suggested. We agreed and began to make our way into the sanctuary.

At weddings, the Havurah always sat together in a large block, as a single, identifiable unit. We were like the cheering section, the peanut gallery, and it was towards us that the bride and groom knew they mustn't look, lest they break out in giggles or be tempted to send little individualized facial signals. We sat down, nudging each other, whispering, and passed little soundless messages back and forth.

We didn't mean to be disruptive, but we felt this was a group activity that belonged to us in particular, a decidedly Havurah event, and our actions, whether conscious or not, were designed to make that fact apparent, at least to ourselves if to no one else.

Soon the rest of the seats filled as the other guests found their way into that plush and formal hall. To the unattuned eye, we were rendered indistinguishable from the rest of the crowd. But we knew.

When the sanctuary was filled and hushed, and the ceremony about to begin, members of the wedding entourage took their places by the *chuppah*, along with the rabbis. In Havurah circles, one thing never lacking was a selection of rabbis, many of whom had played a personal part in each of our lives. For this wedding, Mel, Elisha and Diann's hometown rabbi were dividing the duties among them.

It was both strange and not strange to see Mel and Elisha standing under the *chuppah*, waiting for the ceremony to start. Surely, we did not think of them as "rabbis" in quite the same manner that most American Jews regard their rabbis. To us, they were just our friends, who happened to be rabbis at the same time. Only Diann's hometown rabbi provided that officious note of pomp and aloofness which people imagine to be the proper bearing for their local spiritual leader.

At last, the wedding was ready to begin. From an unseen source, an organ announced familiar wedding chords, heralding members of the processional who advanced in pairs, marching slowly and stiffly down the aisle, and took their places underneath the *chuppah*. In turn, each accompanied by family members, Heligman and then Diann – the star in shining white, the belle of the ball, the lady of the lake and indisputable target of all our attention – also ceremoniously proceeded down the aisle. We gawked and sat on edge, trying to catch their eyes as they passed. But they were concentrating on something other than their mischievous friends sitting alongside their path. Heligman, in contrast to his usual habit, assumed a demeanor of propriety that doubtless eased his father's mind to no small degree.

Once beneath the chuppah, the congregation silent now, the family and closest friends stood gravely on stage for their public appearance, before hundreds of eyes, three officiating rabbis, God, and all their generations forward and back. The cantor began to sing, the sound seemingly emanating through the top of his head, and welcomed everyone to take part in the event:

"Mi adir al hakol, mi baruch al hakol . . ."

Why was this all so solemn? I wondered. Why couldn't Heligman and Diann have asserted themselves and had a nice *informal* wedding, something relaxed and jolly, without this pompous rigmarole for their parents? To me it seemed they were selling out, even though they had explained to me earlier the mind-numbing complexity involved in trying to please everyone, including their parents, who were, after all, footing the bill. Still, I didn't think *that* should be allowed to have anything to do with it.

When the cantor was done with the opening greetings, Elisha was the first to speak. What he said was simple and sincere. He spoke about having known both Heligman and Diann as friends during the past few years and the pleasure it gave him to assist at their wedding. He spoke of shared incidents he remembered and the laudable qualities he knew in each of them. He then tied this to an idea contained in the *sheva brachot*, the seven blessings at the heart of the wedding ceremony which are repeated again at the end of the festive meal.

"At the end of the next-to-last *brachah*," he said, "it says, *'m'semeach hatan v'callah'* – who causes the bride and the groom to rejoice. In the last *brachah*, it says, *'m'semeach hatan im ha-callah,'* – who causes the groom to rejoice *with* the bride. In the first instance, they rejoice separately, as two separate beings. In the second case, they rejoice together, as one unit. This is what a marriage must be like: First, the bride and the groom are separate individuals, and they must enter into a marriage as complete and mature beings, already whole in themselves. Then, and only then, can they join together as a couple. When their subsequent rejoicing as a couple takes place, it incorporates their wholeness as individuals."

He continued on, mentioning particulars from their individual lives which now had bearing on one another. All these events, qualities and connections now blended into something else as well, without losing their original qualities in the transition; they reflected upon and amplified each other, creating from the union of two people a complex, crisscrossing world of phenomena that endlessly reverberated against each other.

Elisha then was handed a set of gold rings from Heligman's brother and, pronouncing each word or phrase slowly, said them so that Heligman could repeat with care:

"Haray"

"Haray," Heligman responded.

"Aht"

"Aht"

"M'kudeshet li"

"M'kudeshet li"

"B'tabaat zu"

"B'tabaat zu"

"K'dat Moshe"

"K'dat Moshe"

"V'Yisroel"

"V'Yisroel"

Amen. And Heligman slid the ring onto Diann's finger. Elisha then turned to Diann and said, as she repeated:

"Dodi li"

"Dodi li"

"Va'ani lo"

"Va'ani lo"

And she put a ring onto Heligman's finger. They looked at each other, they sighed, and the congregation shuffled its feet beneath their seats.

Then Mel began to speak. But unlike Elisha, Mel did not talk about the world of individual particularities. Rather, he reached out to a level beyond that, where all these individual specifics became united under one larger overview.

"Walter and Diann," he said, as they tried to keep their attention focused on what was going on, "it happens that your wedding is taking place in the week when we read in the Torah *parshat Yithro*. In *parshat Yithro*, there is a simple sentence, which seems very ordinary at first, and which people often gloss over, thinking that they understand it. It says, *"Vayihad Yithro al kol hatovah asher asah Adonai l'Yisrael"* – *"And Jethro was pleased about all the good that God had done for Israel."*

"But the question is then asked, why does it say that Jethro is pleased about *all* the good that God had done? Why doesn't it just say that Jethro was happy for 'the good' that God had done? What do we learn from that additional word "all"? Rebbe Nachman answers like this: Why does it say *all* the good? It's like at a wedding. At a wedding, there are some people who are happy because they like to be at weddings. Some of them like the food at a wedding. Others like the music at a wedding and enjoy listening to the musicians play. Some people are happy because they like to dance, so they enjoy the wedding because of the dancing. Others are happy about the couple itself – they're glad that this one is marrying that one, and that that one is marrying this one. And then there are people at a wedding who aren't happy at all. Maybe they're jealous – maybe so-and-so is jealous because he would like a bride like that for himself. But then there are people who are happy about the whole thing: about the eating, the music, the dancing, the couple, and even about the person who is standing there in the corner being jealous. They're happy about it all, the entire thing. And that's what it means when it says that Jethro was happy about all the good that God had done to Israel."

He went on, expanding on his original point, digressing, poeticizing a bit, creating a vision in which this particular wedding was no longer just a single event in space and time in the lives of two particular people, but how it was larger than that and also smaller than that, too, fitting into a scheme of things that dwarfed it in comparison.

When he had finished, he read out the marriage contract, first in Aramaic, then in English, so that both the couple and everyone else could understand exactly what they were in for.

Then Diann's hometown rabbi began to speak, and I saw immediately that he was set to launch into his standard wedding speech, a long, moralistic, somewhat hokey monologue that could only get away with its clichés because of the sentimental nature of the moment.

"Walter and Diann," he began, clasping his hands for emphasis, "as we stand here in front of God and in front of the community of Israel, about to join two hearts into one . . ."

But I'm not good at listening to long speeches, especially wedding speeches, and soon my mind began to wander. I looked around at all the others staring intently towards the couple under the *chuppah*, each one with his or her expression – there were thoughtful faces, blank faces, smiling faces, tears. Everyone was involved, everyone was part of the scene.

Yes, I thought, everyone has a role in a wedding – the witnesses are just as essential as the couple and the rabbi. Everyone is there for a reason. And everyone at a wedding is involved in his or her own little drama, inevitably seeing their own life reflected in the main drama up at the front.

The older married couples are no doubt sitting there and flashing back to their own wedding day, the spinster aunts squirming a bit uncomfortably, the old bachelors justifying their lives to themselves, the children confused and excited by the pomp and spectacle.

And me, where did I fit into all of this? Which role did I play? I looked over at Esther sitting a few rows ahead and wondered, "What if?" What if we had gotten it together? And why not? Why didn't we? What if – but time had moved along and slowly drawn the curtain down between us, pushing all that into the past. And we had let it, that was for sure. Certainly, I had let it; I had allowed that curtain to fall. I had needed something else, and so had she. But what was it that I had needed? I looked over and saw Valerie sitting a few rows over, and Karen sitting in front of her. And there was Sandra, too, who had had that funny laugh, sitting not far off. Had I needed all that? Had I *really* needed that? In some ways, yes, I had. For whatever it was worth, I had needed that, too.

It was strange sitting there with those four women, each of us looking out onto the same spectacle, all of us having played some part in something similar, preparatory in a sense, but which hadn't led anywhere directly.

Oh Lord, I thought, we need so many different things these days, just in order to get married. We need this and that, trying to fulfill some expectation that we ourselves don't even know if it is possible to meet. Wouldn't it all be a lot simpler if they still just fixed us up at our bar mitzvahs and told us to multiply like rabbits? Yes, a lot simpler, but simplicity was no longer in vogue. The process was now so much more complex. And we expect so much more.

When a young man is in a room with another woman he had once made love to, he is always conscious of her presence and of their earlier encounter, even if she is an outdated love affair, ended and exiled from memory. For in truth, it is never forgotten, never. He will always remember her and their experience together. And here I was, in a room with not one, but four, each different, each a separate world of memories and sensations squirreled away into its own corner of my brain. How strange to see them converse with one another, smile at one another, share their own experiences of each other, totally exclusive of me. It was amazing, it was fascinating.

Slowly, it dawned on me that I was not alone in my creeping recognition of our interrelations. I looked around and took a quick account. Yes, there were other people here who had had relationships that I knew of, relationships that ended and had given way to new relationships. There were women I had known who were also involved with other men present. And there were people present who had relationships with others I had never remotely desired, and yet these same people also shared links with me through other relationships. I then tried to imagine all the relationships that I did not even know about – all the clandestine trysts, the short-lived secret passions, the failed attempts at connection, the quietly guarded liaisons. For who knew of some of my encounters? Not everyone, that was for sure. And neither did I know of theirs. Slowly, this enormous sense of interrelatedness, on the most primal of levels, grew increasingly within me, until an overwhelming sense of being part of something whose dimensions I could not even begin to grasp took hold of me. It was not frightening; it was simply mind-boggling. And everyone else, no doubt, at least somewhere along in this late afternoon, would, I was sure, suddenly realize this same thing, and apprehend this truth as surely as the truth of their own faces in the mirror. We were caught in a network far greater than any of us could map out, something that none of us individually could piece together in its entirety. We were all interrelated, and we were each conscious of only a small piece of the grand design.

I sat back and tried to comprehend this most amazing convocation. We were our own small town, a native village, an extended family, an endlessly labyrinthine soap opera, a printed circuit of interconnectedness, a computer motherboard, a living, throbbing crisscross of train tracks, an overblown map of the New York City subway with all its exchanges and transfer points, a spider web of emotional entanglement, a great bog, a great swampy bog where all oozing life commingled beneath the water's quiet surface. We were a million microorganisms beneath the ocular lens, all bumping together and swimming in a thousand directions while plunked on a tiny slide of brittle glass.

And out of all this ooze and interchange, up from the morass of our erotic give-and-take, which, in some undercover totality, was electrifying and uniting the entire room, up from it all emerged Heligman and Diann, the newly married couple, emerging publicly, front and center, to say, "Here we are," forging this link in front of all of you, forging it with precedence over all other links, past or present, present or absent, this bond is the golden bond, this shining bond stands out above all others, taking its moment in the sun, before heaven and earth, to harden like cement, like some jet-age building block, to break only under the greatest of stress and abuse, meant to be permanent, meant to last forever before it falls back into the rest of the ooze, to disappear from the limelight and to exist, afterwards, merely as a fragment of that great body of interchange, but wedded now only to itself, these two terminals welded only to each other, ionically bonded substances now.

I thought of all the problems they had had, and the threat of breakup that had hovered over them for so long. But now they were a success, a monument placed in the public thoroughfare, a minor miracle, the successful collision of randomly moving bodies, who, in the tug-of-war of conflicting forces that pushed them away from each other and pulled them together, managed to have enough – enough what? Strength? Weakness? Love? Understanding? Mutual attraction? Luck? What actually was it that now brought two people sufficiently together to enable them to attempt such a momentous joint undertaking? I stopped and paused. What actually was it, and what was so permanent about it?

Indeed, permanence was no longer guaranteed. Guaranteed? At best it was only a fifty-fifty chance. But somehow, I believed in this one, I felt good about it and had faith that the two of them had sufficiently gotten their heads in order to realize that they could make it together, and had finally gone ahead with neither hesitation nor regret.

And so there they were, standing up beneath the *chuppah*, the wedding canopy, that stylized little representation of a house, their skeletal and as-of-yet unformed home, an enclosed space in which they would, in some sense, always remain, within its four walls and under its roof, no matter where they may go and what adventures they may seek. Put in a box, they are – a box, a bower, a hut, a shack, a little terrace looking onto the world, a cell, a palace, a hotel room, a phone booth, a suburban split-level house, a basement apartment, a ship's cabin, a sukkah, a storefront, an elevator, a tent, an eruv, a shoe box, a hat box, a safe deposit box, a wallet, a mailing list, a tax form, a family album.

I continued to watch, still not listening to the rabbi's words, paying attention instead to the random associations traveling through my brain. It was fun like that, watching them without listening, as if watching a movie whose sound had been turned off and replaced instead by an alternate commentary. It also put a distance between myself and what was happening in front of me, the whole thing moving as if in a weightless atmosphere, like watching astronauts floating inside their capsule. I watched the rabbi holding the glass aloft and singing, I watched Diann and Heligman's faces as soundless words were pronounced around them.

I was suddenly startled and awakened by a shattering of glass.

"*Mazal tov!*" called out a hundred voices.

"*Mazal tov, mazal tov,*" they repeated.

The bride and groom kissed, and the room was once again a noisy, lively place. Again, I felt myself inside the scene that was unravelling before me.

"*Mazal tov!*" I called out, when I realized what had happened.

It was done – they were married. The solemn tension was broken, and Heligman and Diann strode up the aisle, smiling, beaming in all directions, followed by the rest of the family, all of whom seemed very proud and full of self-congratulation.

We followed in behind and made our way out. I noticed as Heligman and Diann quickly ducked into a little room and shut the door behind them.

That was, in fact, I realized, what they were supposed to do – according to the *halachah* this was the time when the bride and groom would first be alone together, in order to properly consummate the marriage. It was only a symbolic isolation, the essence of the tradition having been shunted aside for convenience and social grace.

But you could never tell with Heligman and Diann.

"Hey Chief," I said, assuming a bawdy tone, "what do you think they're doing in there?"

"Nothing they haven't done already," he said. "And probably a whole lot less."

Soon, the couple returned, and we went to stand in line to congratulate them and their family. Heligman and Diann stood there, exhausted, but obviously very proud of themselves.

"Hey, congratulations," I said to the groom, grinning and shaking his hand.

"Thanks," he said, smiling. "You know, my only regret is that we had to leave Caleb at home."

Just as well, I thought, as I moved on to the next. I'm glad I don't have to contend with him.

"Congratulations to you," I said to Diann, bending over and giving her a kiss on the cheek.

"Thanks," she answered. She was glowing and happy and I was glad to see it. It was her day, all right.

"You look a little worn out by it all," I added.

"Well, you know Walter," she commented.

I moved over and congratulated the parents of the couple, who smiled politely, shook my hand, and asked me my name.

It was time for dinner. At least in this area Diann and Heligman had gotten their own way, in some small manner bucking the tradition. Dinner was vegetarian, in consideration of all their friends who would otherwise have sat there, eating nothing, their stomachs growling, an awful way to spend a wedding.

Vegetarian? the other guests queried, rearing back in horror at the thought. No prime ribs? No chicken? No London broil? *Vegetarian?*

At first, the sight of all those grains and vegetables made the older people pale, thinking they were too sophisticated for all this rabbit food devoured by the younger generation. But soon, with the way they began to eat, vegetarian seemed to have done perfectly well indeed.

However, I quickly found that despite the abundance and savory nature of the dinner, I had very little time to sit down and pig out. There was too much to do, too many other adventures to embark upon.

Shortly after the first course was served, Max appeared, walking in from outside, a big grin on his face. He looked around in slow distraction, as if seeing it all for the first time. I guessed that he was searching for Rebecca, too stoned to find her in the crowd.

"Max," I said, chiding him, "how could you have done that by yourself?"

"What?" he said, innocently at first, but that gave way in an instant. "Sorry," he grinned, not expecting to have been found out so easily. But Max was hopelessly obvious when he was stoned, despite the fact that he always tried to slide by unnoticed. He handed me the keys to his car. "It's under the driver's seat."

"And matches?" I asked.

"In the glove compartment." He went off, in a happy fog, still looking for Rebecca.

"Hey Chief," I said, turning around, "wanna go out and . . ." I put my fingers to my lips and mimed a furtive toke.

"Yeah!" he said, jumping up. Beside him, Leah started to make a slight motion as if to hold him back. But Chief didn't notice it, or at least didn't display any apparent notice. A look of disappointment flit across her face, and then she was still.

"You wanna come too, Leah?" I offered, trying to be friendly but knowing in advance that my offer would be declined.

"No thanks," she said quietly, containing herself.

As we walked off towards the exit, very determined, Hannah Kreindel came over and gave us a wink.

"May I join you?" she asked with a sly grin, guessing where we were headed.

"Sure, come on," I said.

Hannah Kreindel had been around the Havurah in its early days, the old crazy days of its turbulent inception. She was older than most of the others and so had occupied a privileged role of unofficial adviser and observer rather than simply as a member. Slightly more than half a generation ahead of us, in her late thirties already, she now lived out in the suburbs with her husband and two children. Although she came in regularly to visit, over the years her attachment grew less and less. She had known the older members well, and her ideological sympathies were still with us, but she found that life's other demands began to press more heavily upon her.

Out in suburbia, everyone knew her as Mrs. Kreindel, the principal of the local Hebrew school. A small, compact woman, she was regarded as competent, practical – an able educator and administrator. Her Hebrew school, as well as a Hebrew school could be, ran surprisingly well. It was known as one of the more successful ones in the area. Little did the people in the temple know, however, that this charming little woman, who patted the children on their head as they walked along the halls, who ordered textbooks, supervised classes, made out the payroll, and conferred with parents, had once been, and still was – though more surreptitiously now – a freak-and-a-half, a zany lady of the highest degree, a suburban bohemian with a mind awash with mystical stories and a wonderful sense of the absurd. How she managed out there in the suburbs, I could never quite figure out.

"It's a real pisser sometimes," she once said to me. "But you've got to find a place for your kids to grow up. You just have to hope it doesn't kill you in the process."

"By the time I reach your age," I had answered, "I sure hope they invent an alternative, that's all."

The three of us reached Max's car and piled in, Hannah sitting behind the wheel. I stuck my hands under the seat, found the little baggie and pulled it out. I rolled a joint with the fixings inside. Then I had to look for the matches.

I opened the glove compartment.

The glove compartment of Max and Rebecca's car was astonishingly crammed full of junk. The matches were sitting right by the opening, but I lingered a minute, fascinated by the assortment of objects that were there. I began to rummage through them, just to see the full array. There was a flashlight, a few pencils, a sock, a sanitary napkin, a spoon, a paperback copy of Marx's early essays, a pipe, a yarmulke, a half-squeezed tube of hand cream, some green stamps, a broken necklace chain, a few maps, a blue button, all in that tiny little space.

"Hey, look at this," I said, as I pulled out a pair of Rebecca's under-pants. "I didn't know that Max and Rebecca still had any of the old teenager in them." Then I considered. "In fact, they probably don't. God knows how this got here."

"Hey Shloimie, put the panties back and get on with business," Chief said, heckling me.

"Okay, okay," I answered, giving in.

I lit the joint and took a deep toke, then I passed it on to Hannah. She took a drag while quiveringly closing her right eye at the same time, to shield it from the upward trailing smoke. It made her look like a tough lady out of some 1940's B-movie.

"*Takeh,*" she said, "you know, I'm glad they've finally gotten married. I think they're good for each other."

"I hope so," I offered. "I know that sometimes her anxieties get in the way of their just enjoying life and having fun."

Hannah considered my comment for a moment and grew philo-sophical "Well," she said, "when both your parents escaped from Germany by the skin of their teeth, sometimes that experience rubs off on the kids."

Oh. There was a long silence. That was a downer. But then, to bring the mood back up to where it had been, Hannah continued, "In those circumstances, I'd say she turned out rather mellow, all things considered."

Okay. Agreed.

"But she might not be so mellow if she found out we were smoking dope outside the shul at her wedding," Chief observed.

"She doesn't have to know everything that's going on at her wedding," Hannah said with a grin. "In fact, she'll never even know more than just a fraction of it."

This reminded Chief of a similar event a few years earlier. "Hey Shloimie – remember Max and Rebecca's wedding, behind the trees?"

"Sure," I said, smiling at the recollection. Years before, around the time when Max and Rebecca had just joined the Havurah, they invited everyone to their wedding. Right before the ceremony, Chief, Heligman, and I had sneaked off behind a group of trees and lit up outside the synagogue's kitchen.

"Just don't take Max with you," had been Rebecca's only comment.

"That was a long time ago already," I said. "That was a fine time."

A long time ago, yes, I thought. And look what happened in those years. I pressed the button and the glove compartment flopped open again. Again, I surveyed the jumbled contents of the little compartment. The broken necklace, the underpants, the little blue button. What were their stories, how did they get there? A whole world of little intimacies had grown up during that time, each one nailing down their relationship, each one soldering Max and Rebecca more and more strongly together.

Chief handed me the joint. "Here, take this. And get your mind off Rebecca's underpants."

"Listen," I protested, "don't get me wrong. I'm not into Rebecca's underpants as Rebecca's underpants. I'm not even into them as underpants in general. I'm just into them as . . . well . . . cultural artifacts."

"My eye," he said, slamming the little door shut.

And so we continued to sit there, the joint going back and forth, until the windows fogged up and no one could see in or out. When the joint was done, Hannah giggled, made a crazy face, and then quickly regained her composure.

"Time to go back in now," she said, like a teacher reasoning to a class-room of little children. I shoved the dope back under the driver's seat, and we all left the car and found our way back to the shul.

Between the courses, the music and dancing had already begun, kicking off a headlong whirlwind of exuberant motion: a running, jump-ing, bounding round of dance after dance, circles and circles within circles, converging and expanding circles, lines snaking around the hall, all the old and traditional dances, large enough for all to join, to plug in or withdraw at any spot.

But I was never much of a dancer. Instead, I repeatedly let myself be pulled off somewhere, to talk with this one, to go out and smoke some more with that one, to chat, gossip, comment, intellectualize, talk Havurah politics, and flirt with just about everyone I could. The whole thing was a whizz of excitement.

"What a wonderful party," I thought to myself. "I think maybe I'm getting to like weddings."

At one point in all this, I found myself suddenly talking to one of Diann's college friends, a very pretty, light-haired, obviously not-Jewish woman whom I somehow had caught sight of several times that after-noon, and who had also, I could tell, been noticing me. We had made that meaningful, almost magnetic eye contact from across varying distances, unable to refrain from doing so as we wandered in our different directions, and now at last we found ourselves facing one another, talking and listening to each other, somehow very interested in what the other had to say.

Linda stood behind Diann's friend's back and looked on, watching the progress of our little tête-a-tête, an amused grin on her face. And then, unbeknownst to Diann's friend, she shot me a pointed look and mockingly waggled her finger at me: No no no.

Suddenly, a familiar tune started up, and I jumped up and even pulled Diann's friend to join in the dance. They had started in to *"Kaitzad M'rakdim"* – "How do we dance before the bride?" If ever a dance was an outrageous, ridiculous, mystical dance, this was it. The bride and groom sat down in front of everybody, the music took off, and so did the dancers.

Each in turn and in time with the music, groups of dancers came forward and performed before the seated couple, came forward and retreated in rapid succession. They jumped up and down, flashed their skirts or kicked their legs, pirouetted, did the *kazatske*, do-si-doed, made like a helicopter, cakewalked, flapped their arms, saluted each other, did cartwheels, wheel-barrows, mock bullfights, hopped, skipped, strutted, sauntered like Mae West, pounded their chests like Tarzan, deedle-deedled like Tevye, jigged like Pinky Lee, polkaed, made London Bridge, spun around with their backs together and arms locked, got dizzy, fell down, laughed, got up, sang, bumped into each other, kept on going, kept on clapping. Every possible movement that came into our minds, a rhythmic review of all human activity, spun itself out in front of the seated couple. And it was all for the delight of the bride, the Bride, the Cosmic Bride, the *Shekhinah*, the feminine life force, the fertile field, the goddess of the moon, Diana, Diann, all rolled into one. Before her, all life was unfolding, parading, dancing by, paying homage, in all its myriad forms: energetic, grotesque, humorous, agile, lovely, seductive, amazing, silly, dizzying, unexpected, all that the imagination could invent. She watched and laughed, she oohed, she shook her head at our inanity, she, the Bride, from her privileged perch, from her honorary seat, our beloved lady of the hour.

On and on it went. Who remembers what steps I did, together with Chief, with Elisha, with Linda, with Diann 's friend, with a whole group of five and six all together? By then I was stoned quite out of my mind and totally carried away by the dance.

And did she understand it all? Did it even make sense to her? No matter, we did it, we did it until we could do it no more, until our minds were empty of further variation and our muscles and breath were all played out.

At last the music ceased. We stopped to catch our wind, the circle broke up, Diann and Heligman, de-mythified now, got up and walked off to pursue other wedding-day duties. A slow dance started up, a ballroom-type of dance, to counterbalance the previous one.

I saw Esther walking back to her table, her body moving beneath her dress, lovely and desirable, as I had often known her to be. And suddenly I wanted to dance with her. Just to dance. But at least to *dance*. I intersected her path.

"Hey Esther, want to dance this one?" I asked, strangely embarrassed, smiling.

She looked at me. Was I kidding her? Did I have some ulterior motive or a surprise up my sleeve? Was I pulling her leg? Me, *dance*? She quickly evaluated my offer and saw that I wasn't hiding anything; she understood I was being honest and open. I stood there, suspended, awaiting her response.

"Sure, Sol," she said, smiling an old, friendly smile. And, self-consciously, I put one arm around her waist and took her hand with the other, and for a few pleasant moments we shuffled our way around the floor.

After a while, the dancing was over, the meal was over, and soon the whole wedding was about to be over. Heligman and Diann were still making their rounds from table to table, shaking hands, giving kisses, finding something to say to everybody. Then Heligman came over to me and asked if I would do the third blessing of the *sheva brachot* right after *birkat hamazon*, the grace after meals that would end the celebration. Would I? Certainly. It would be an honor. I was more than glad.

"It's going to be in just a minute or two," he said.

"No problem," I answered.

I picked up a little velvet-covered bencher imprinted with their names in gold lettering and I searched through it for the *sheva brachot* in order to practice before having to recite in public. I located the page and began reading the Hebrew, to familiarize myself with the words. I didn't want to stumble over them and show everyone that I was an uneducated jerk, so I read them once, twice, three times, until I felt sufficiently acquainted with them so as not to make any mistakes.

And then I realized I had not paid much attention to their meaning. "Hey," I thought, "what is it they want me to say, anyhow, in front of two hundred people?" Slowly this time, I read the blessing for its meaning.

"Blessed are you, our God, King of the world, who created man in his image, in the image of his own construction, and who fashioned from it an everlasting structure. Blessed are you, who creates man."

"What do you know," I thought, "that's just a euphemism! They gave me an X-rated *brachah!*"

Then I read it again, each word slowly, gathering their deeper intention. No, it wasn't just a euphemism – it was unspecific, referring to a whole range of forces including the sexual, the reproductive, and to forces that had no name but were lumped all together into one single life force. No, it didn't merely put a veil over the sexuality of humankind, but rather stated that somehow, out of all this coming and going, out of the attraction and the doubts, out of the needs that bring people together and then keep them attached, that along with the joys, the pains, the disappointments, the arguments, the peaceful times, that all the things that transpire in the relationship between two people, even past the technology of contraception, life inevitably finds a way to keep on going, to seek regeneration and assert the indomitability of its own presence, assuring a full and mysterious future from only the meager realities of the present.

It was simple and powerful. Powerful indeed, that something had set all this into motion, this inescapable structure, an inevitable, eternal process, of which we, collectively, the human race, were both the objects and the executors. An integral body that existed across time. I marveled at it; I knit my brows in a perplexed consideration of it all.

And as I marveled, still stoned enough to ponder it and amplify its meaning, Max came over and snapped me out of my thoughts.

"Hey Solomon," he said, a bit apologetically, "would you mind if we switched *brachahs*? Heligman asked me to do the seventh, and then said maybe I should do the third and you should do the seventh. Is that all right with you?"

I understood. There was no need to explain. The third was so much longer, while the seventh was short, and Max had a lovely voice, a rich tenor, whereas my flat monotone was almost legendary. There was no need to subject all those people to any more than was necessary.

"Sure, sure," I said. "I'll do the seventh."

I looked at the seventh. Which one was that? *"Boray p'ri hagafen"* – "Who creates the fruit of the vine."

I grinned a resigned grin. Ah, I was hopeless.

Finally, *birkat hamazon* was over, the seven blessings were over, the wine had been poured from two glasses into one goblet and tasted by both the bride and the groom, the wedding party was over, and the guests were leaving. Everyone said their goodbyes and good lucks, reenacting that long parting that terminates every wedding, the women in their long dresses bending over toward each other and kissing faces and cheeks, the men shaking hands, occasionally giving a hug, maybe a peck on the cheek, and I had already gone off to the men's room to change out of my suit, to take off my tie and get back into my jeans.

Everyone was tired and I knew the ride back would be a quiet, thoughtful one, quite unlike the ride down. I looked around for the people who had ridden in the car with me.

"Hey Chief, are you coming with me?" I asked.

"Well, actually, no," he answered. "Leah and I decided to take a ride to New York with these friends of Diann's so that we can go visit a few people we know there. Is that okay with you?"

"Oh, sure," I said. "Well, see you in a few days."

I went to see Myra. "Hey Myra, are you coming back to Boston with me?"

"Is it okay if I go with Linda instead?" she asked. "We haven't had a chance to talk for a while, and this would be a good opportunity. We've been trying for weeks to find some time to talk, but something always got in the way. I hope it's not inconvenient for you."

"No, no," I said, just a little perturbed. "It's just that now I'll be driving back alone."

"Oh," she said. "Well, look, if you want me to come with you, I will."

"No, don't bother. It's all right. I don't mind driving alone. I just didn't expect it. But really, I don't mind."

"Are you sure?"

"Yeah. Don't worry. I don't mind long drives by myself. I do them all the time."

"Okay. Thanks anyway for the offer. I'll see you back in Edomville."

"See you."

I went outside to my car, which was waiting silently, almost patiently, in the dark parking lot. Several cars from around it had already pulled away. Where had they gone already, so fast? Who knew? Each one to its own destination. The knot was unravelling into separate strands, the pieces coming apart and falling their own separate ways.

I opened the car door and hung my suit on the little hook above the window behind the driver's seat. The sign of the man on the go. I got inside and shut the door. I put the key in the ignition and started the engine, and then I just sat there for a moment, letting the motor warm up before setting out in the cold. While I was waiting, my foot lightly on the accelerator, a strange impulse made me look inside my own glove compartment, just to check it out and see what I had in there.

I leaned over, pressed the button, and the little door fell open. I rummaged inside. There was a flashlight, a tire gauge, a pencil and a little pad of blank paper, a yarmulke, auto repair bills, and several maps, lots of maps, some worn, tattered and crumpled, some almost new, all folded this way and that.

It struck me what a sparse and boring glove compartment I had, as far as glove compartments went.

But then the engine was warm, so I slammed the little door shut, shifted the car into drive, stepped on the gas, and drove out of the parking lot, into the night.

HOUSE SEARCH

Tradition and change are sort of – but only sort of – the yin and yang of Jewish culture. Over the years I saw the Havurah change and yet stay the same, lose its energy as the hectic years subsided, and yet mellow and grow stronger, too. I saw people leave and new ones arrive, and then I saw them leave as well, yet all the while the Havurah remained the Havurah, precariously and yet miraculously still afloat. Eventually it became dated and entrenched, like any institution, which was exactly what we had rebelled against. With each year, the average age of the group jumped up another notch.

In the old days, Leah and I used to argue all the time, although each of us, with the years, grew more tolerant of one another's positions. Finally, after a long process, we would stand together in the corner, two old-timers, and commiserate about the way the group was simply not the same, how the spark was gone, and how its strong sense of community was steadily dissipating. We would shake our heads and say how things just weren't like they used to be.

No, they weren't – as I said, in the old days Leah and I used to argue all the time. Mostly, we argued about tradition. Leah, after all, was a proper girl, raised with respect for the tradition and a strong acceptance of it. Exactly how she found her way into the Havurah had always seemed a mystery to me. The dope upset her, as did the ease with which we allowed ourselves to chop up the standard prayer book or jettison ancient observances. Of course, that would only goad me on, and I became unable to restrain myself from being only more outrageous, shooting at her sacred cows and digging at the cornerstones of her belief. She saw me as a perverse imp, stoned and guffawing in the midst of her sacred ceremonies.

It wasn't that I didn't like Leah, or that I was trying to be mean, but she was so easily and deliciously upset by the simplest of unorthodoxies that I allowed myself the full reign of my religious anarchy.

It may have been a cheap way to make my little points, whatever points they may have been, by taking my iconoclasms out on Leah. But at the time they seemed to me to be no small matter at all. These were major issues, as I saw them, and I was fighting for my beliefs, lobbying in the political arena of our tiny Havurah world.

One evening, not during the old days, but towards the later days, we were sitting in the dining room, eating communal meal. Communal meal had changed over the years, from being a weekly gathering, when the house was a blaze of lights and activity, with everybody running this way and that, bearing big dishes of food, excited to see everyone together, and had now become an occasional occurrence, perhaps once a month, irregularly carried over from a previous practice. Newer members had been reluctant to devote so much time to the group, and older members slowly gave up their earlier idealistic visions of what community should be. No one seemed to have time for communal meals during the weekdays anymore, and now it was a vestigial organ, acting up every once in a while, like the human appendix, merely to remind us that it was still with us. And yet, by the very fact that it occasionally flared up, it was perhaps signaling that the time had come to extirpate it, both officially and completely.

On this particular evening, we were sitting around the table, a small group of nine or ten instead of the full contingent of twenty or more, and an unusual feeling of age was sitting upon us. It was a winter's night, the lights were, for some reason, not turned on too brightly, and the house had an old rattly feeling about it. It was as if we were huddled together for warmth and support, survivors and hangers-on, quite familiar with each other by now and used to each other's gestures and movements.

Each of us was there because this was where we wanted to be. It was our home, and a settled inertia had brought us together for the evening. Although there were one or two newer members at the table, most of the participants were the older ones, come to reenact the ritual of the communal meal of earlier days.

It is interesting how, sometimes, people become so identified with their positions over the years that they insist upon them even after they no longer yield anything new. They become our own personal landmarks to which we return, more from a sense of self-identification than one of continuing philosophical or emotional commitment. We were like old socialists still trying to teach Esperanto, or veterans still fighting an enemy who had disappeared into the ideological flux of modern politics.

And so, this evening, as the meal was ending and we were sitting around over tea and dessert, Leah and I recommenced our old debate, not because it awakened a real bone of contention between us, but just because we were settling back into the comfortable territories that we knew.

I don't even remember how our disagreement began. I think it started when Leah mentioned that she thought it might be interesting for the group to study a little Rambam.

"Rambam!" I sneered under my breath.

"Yeah, Rambam," she said, hurt. "What's wrong with Rambam?"

She was on the defensive now, and since I figured that I had her on the run, I pushed it further.

"Hmph," I sneered again. "Rambam!"

Now, I knew very well that Rambam was no moron, to put it mildly. In fact, I thought that studying Rambam might be very interesting indeed, providing that I had sufficient learning and intelligence to understand him. But it wasn't Rambam I was attacking, and Leah knew very well what I was doing. Since Rambam was the advocate of reason and rational moral behavior, I was setting him up as my fall guy, Mr. Straight and Narrow, and then dismissing him as too uptight an authority to learn anything from but inhibitions.

"We don't always have to study *mysticism*, you know," she said pointedly.

I shrugged . . . Ah, no, it wasn't the Rambam conversation that we were having that night. On this particular evening it was something else, far less weighty and more immediate, that started us going. But what exactly was our argument about? Oh, yes, I think I remember. Leah had mentioned – just mentioned, merely in passing – that she had been less than thrilled at my use of tape-recorded music during the *Amidah*. She said she didn't like to use electricity during Shabbos services, and that the *Amidah* was supposed to be a silent prayer. But I'm sure it was the music itself that upset her – it was a tape of pygmy hunting chants, which she undoubtedly didn't find spiritually appropriate, even if presented in the name of experiment and creativity. Anyway, I thought it was fairly successful, if you ask me. But that wasn't what she based her objections on.

"Okay," she said, "I'm not saying you *have to* have complete silence during the Amidah, and that you *mustn't* turn on the electricity, even if it goes against *halachah*. But you have to see *halachah* in terms of tradition, and not just in terms of whether or not you believe in the idea of *averah*, or "sin," for lack of a better word. After we've done something that way for hundreds of years, there's something special about it. If you can't accept that God commands you to do it, at least you can accept that it's been sanctified by years of repetition."

She was acquiescing, no doubt, to the trendy philosophical demands of the day. She might be willing to pay lip service to the possibility that God wasn't carefully watching over our lives with an eagle eye, but she was only trying to appease some of the people in the room. She herself would have none of it – in her heart of hearts, she believed in divine providence and its carefully tallied scorecard of merits and demerits.

For my part, I was prepared to accept her belief with respect, with amazement in fact, but I had the sneaking suspicion that the real reason she believed in God was that she was terrified not to – not of the alternative, of living in a world without God, but rather, she was terrified of the punishment awaiting her if she permitted herself to entertain such a naughty conjecture. And so, of course, I had no choice but to chip away at her vaulted arches, puncturing her security like a mischievous child running around with a pin and no sense of the pain he was inflicting upon others or that he might bring down upon himself in retribution.

"We don't have to do that," I said, quickly jumping into the fray. "We can do whatever we please – we can daven with no clothes on or keep the Torah in the refrigerator." The thought of davening naked in the winter in that cold, drafty house somehow had very little appeal, but its shock value was sufficient to warm my argumentative disposition to a semblance of former life.

"The tradition is only what we make of it," I insisted. "It doesn't have any inherent holiness in itself. It's just a box we can choose to decorate, but there isn't anybody standing over us making sure we use the same wrapping paper that they did."

That was a stupid analogy, I thought, but I let it pass.

Leah looked at me with an edge of anger and frustration. Why were we arguing again? she undoubtedly wondered. She didn't realize – or did she? – that by now I was only acting out of habit, no personal vendetta intended, nor did I have any great intellectual vehemence in my position.

At that moment, the front door opened, a head hesitantly appeared and looked around, and then the person attached to it emerged through the door and entered the hallway, a little uncertain, still tentative in his advance.

"Hello?" we said, all turning to the stranger.

The man who walked in had short hair, wore wire rim glasses and a heavy down parka to keep out the cold. He seemed to be in his early thirties, a few years older than the average age of the people at the table.

"Hi," he said, walking slowly towards us, into the dining room. "My name's Steve Ferst."

Steve Ferst. The name sounded familiar, but I couldn't place where I had heard it before. Perhaps I had read it somewhere. But where?

After a pause, he continued. "I used to be in the Havurah, in the old days, when it was just being started. I happened to be in the neighborhood, so I thought I'd drop by and see what's become of the place."

An old member! This was a rare occurrence indeed. For some reason, old members almost invariably never returned, even for a visit. Something intransgressable, like an invisible hand, kept them away. Was it the pain of leaving, or the disillusionment that made them leave in the first place, or the uncomfortable feeling of no longer belonging where you had once been at home? Or all of these? At any rate, former members almost never reappeared once they had left the Havurah and been lost back into the world.

"Come in, come in," we urged, suddenly excited. Max pulled up another chair and Rebecca went to the kitchen to bring another teacup.

"Take off your coat. Sit down. Stay a while."

"I really wasn't planning to stay very long," he said, hesitantly.

"Oh, relax. Make yourself comfortable," Esther said, soothing him, seducing him to stay.

"Well . . ." He gave in. He pulled off his coat and sat down at the table as Rebecca set the cup before him and poured out some tea. We all looked at him, anxiously, waiting for him to speak.

His eyes wandered around the room, lingering here and there, taking in all the details, registering the simultaneous shock of recognition and strangeness that everything evoked in him.

"The place looks pretty much the same," he said at last. "It hasn't changed much. I see you've painted, and changed some posters, but it doesn't look very different."

He was slowly relaxing, beginning to open up. "That poster's the same," he said, smiling, pointing to the woman with music coming out of her head. "And some of the furniture's the same, too." He looked at the chairs, the lights, the tables we were sitting at. "That rug is new, I see," he remarked.

New? I thought. I hardly would have called it new.

At that moment, Krishna wandered in from the kitchen to see what all the excitement was about.

"Hey – Krishna!" Steve said, in sudden surprise.

Krishna wandered over to Steve, stopped a little bit away from him, and sat down on his haunches, staring.

"Same old Krishna," Steve said. "Amazing."

Krishna began to lick his paws. It didn't seem to him that anything that exciting was going on after all.

"Yes, same old Krishna," he said.

Steve took a sip of tea and began to smile, an inward, personal smile. It seemed that memories were beginning to flood back into him, and for a moment he was savoring them before sharing them with the strangers around him.

"It's funny," he said, thinking out loud. "I remember how much time and energy I poured into this place while I was here. Then, suddenly, it seemed as if it didn't even exist anymore as soon as I left. But look –" he said, with a sweep of his hand, "— it's still here. Whoever realized in the old days that it would still be going on, years later, without any of us?"

Leah leaned forward and asked, "Tell us some things about the old days, the really early days. I'd love to hear."

Haven't we heard enough about the "old days"? I thought. So many stories have been passed along. And yet, as I gave it further reflection, I felt that perhaps there were indeed stories we hadn't heard and that we'd enjoy. Or a new perspective on old events. More than that, I simply wanted to hear about the old days, too, to feel the connection between what I was doing at the moment and events that had been alive in the past.

"Yeah," I said, coaxing him on, "tell us about the early days."

Other voices added to ours. "Tell us what you remember," Rebecca said.

Steve took another sip of tea. He had the floor now and seemed to enjoy it. For the moment, he was the sage, the old wise man. He sat back in his chair, as if he still held onto something that no one else had any access to, save through him.

"In the beginning," he began, "probably the most striking thing about the Havurah was its tremendous energy. It was like an explosion of energy, and that, I suppose, was what almost destroyed it at the very outset.

The energy was too chaotic; everyone thought that *his* ideas were necessarily the right ones. There were those who wanted to study a lot, those who wanted to create an intense community, those who wanted to be poets, and those who wanted to drop a lot of acid. Everybody was pushing his ideas against the others.

"And yet, I think one thing did hold it together, at least enough to enable it to continue. And that was the commitment to spiritual search. Everybody's outlook might have been different, but they were all seriously looking for something and wanted to find it in the Havurah."

I thought for a moment. I wondered how serious my own sense of religious search was any more. Hadn't I just grown too comfortable already? Or had my ideas changed? I looked down at my hands and began picking at my fingernail.

"There were a lot of interesting people here in the beginning, that's for sure," he continued.

"Do you still keep in touch with any of them?" someone interjected.

Steve wrinkled his brow with a pensive look and then changed it to a crooked smile. "No, not really. Once in a while I hear about somebody, but I've pretty much dropped out of contact."

Well, I thought, we're different there. We're still good friends, even if our souls don't burn with the same fire as in former times. But then again, am I just trying to justify myself?

Steve continued. He talked about things I had already heard and about things I hadn't. He talked about the endless meetings, the disputes over policy, the retreats. The problems were the same, it seemed, always repeating themselves. The same yet different. That was the nature of the group.

"You know," he said at last, "I'd like to look around the house. Do you mind if I do it a while?"

"Not at all," Linda answered.

"Why don't we come with you?" Chief suggested. " I'd love to hear your recollections."

"All right," he said. "Let's go."

We arose from the table and followed Steve upstairs. First, he went into the library, and we stood around him, waiting to see what he would sniff out from the room. He looked at the books, running his fingers along the spines. At last he smiled and pulled a book off the shelf. It was a book on ethics, not one of the more often-consulted volumes in the library. He flipped through it and a postcard fell out and onto the floor. He bent down and picked it up. Its face had a picture of a Buddha, and it was addressed to Steve Ferst.

"Did you know that was in there?" I asked, amazed.

"Well," he admitted, "I thought it might be. Somehow some things just stick in your mind like that."

"What does it say?" I asked.

He just shrugged and shook his head. "Oh, never mind," he said. He put the postcard in his pocket and put the book back on the shelf.

Next, we went into the classroom, and Steve began to reminisce about some of the classes he had there: one on midrash, one on sex in the Bible, one on modern Christian and Jewish philosophy. He mentioned some of the people in each class, names I knew and names I didn't know.

Then, he went to the closet and opened the door. There, on the inside of the closet, was a little penciled message: "Steve Ferst was here."

"I was going through an identity crisis of sorts," he said, smiling at himself. "It passed," he added.

After that, we followed him to the bathroom, most of us unable to fit in, and stood outside as he looked around. He opened the medicine closet, which was full of old bottles and tubes that we never got around to throw out. He rummaged inside and pulled out a small bottle that obviously had once contained some kind of liquid, but now only a whitish, caked-on chalky substance stuck to the glass. The label on the bottle read: "S. Ferst. Apply locally, when needed. Not for internal use. Dr. Glickman."

"You can toss that out now," he suggested.

We went from room to room, and Steve had some little anecdote to go with each location, or a little reminder that he had been there. Soon, it seemed that the whole house, this house I thought I knew so well and that spoke so strongly to me about my own life, was now full of Steve Ferst! And it was. There was room for everybody there. And everything was jumbled together, the house yielding up some things easily, others revealed yet hidden. I was amazed at the variety that the house enclosed within it, past and present, a myriad of tales and experiences, providing a home to each in its own way.

"And now," Steve said, after he had finished looking through most of the upstairs, "I'd like to go down into the basement. I think I may even still have some stuff down there."

Max switched on the light that led into the basement and we all followed Steve down the rickety stairs and into the cool, damp underground cellar.

As usual, the basement was still full of old junk and furniture, gathered over the years, a rotating collection that found its way into people's apartments and then later back into the basement. Steve looked around. He was looking for something, but he didn't seem to find it.

"No," he said, shrugging, "I suppose it's disappeared."

"What were you looking for?"

"Oh, nothing, nothing. Just some old stuff I had a long time ago. But I realize that down here, everything eventually disappears. I know that."

We stood around, looking at all the furniture and junk, wondering what its eventual fate would be in this dingy cellar. Things here seemed to return to their original organic state, as if disappearing into the very earth itself. The cellar was like the foundation of the world, the primeval matter from which all things sprang and to which all things returned. From dust to dust.

"Hey, do you folks know what's behind this door?" Steve said, brightening, as if with a hidden surprise.

"What door?"

"This one," he said.

He pointed to the wall, on which a giant bedspring was leaning, as it had been for years. Yes, there was a door behind the bedspring, a door that was hardly discernible, set into the wooden wall, but it had no doorknob to open it. Suddenly, I remembered the door from a long time ago, and I remembered not having been able to open it after an initial, half-hearted attempt to see what was behind it.

"I guess nobody goes in there very often," Steve said. "Come on, let's open it. I think you'll get a kick out of what's inside."

Steve and Chief pushed aside the bedspring so that the door was accessible.

"Get a screwdriver or something," Chief said, and Leah, being helpful, went upstairs and quickly reappeared with the toolbox.

We huddled around the door, expectantly wondering what was about to be revealed.

"Go ahead, Leah," Chief said. "Take a screwdriver and stick it in the hole and just pull it downwards and towards you."

Leah hesitated. "I – I don't know," she said.

"Go ahead," Chief urged, "you can do it."

She hesitated again. "I don't want to open it. You do it."

"Aw, come on, Leah," I cajoled her. "You can open it. Don't be afraid. I don't think anything is going to come out and bite you." I paused. Then, just to rub it in a little, I added. "The worst there could be is a lot of spiders and bugs."

She shivered slightly. She handed the tools to Chief. "Here, you do it," she said, and took a few steps backwards.

Chief took the screwdriver and stuck it in the hole where the door-knob should have been. He pulled and pulled, but the door was stuck and difficult to open. Suddenly, with a dusty, wall-shaking creak, the door finally gave way and swung open.

It was dark inside.

Steve went in, pulled a string, and suddenly the little room lit up.

There was a toilet inside.

"A toilet!" we shouted. "Far out! Look – a toilet!"

It was an old porcelain toilet, in good condition despite its age, the old-fashioned kind with a pull-chain from a little box near the ceiling. The room itself was well preserved, the walls covered with an old style of linoleum tile that was rarely seen anymore except perhaps covered over by layers of paint.

But this was all in new and perfect condition. We were thrilled and fascinated with our discovery.

Chief went in and inspected the toilet. He pulled the old wooden seat up so that we could see into the bowl. Then, capriciously and out of curiosity, he reached up, pulled the chain, and a rush of water swirled into the bowl and disappeared.

"Look – it flushes! It flushes!"

I was almost delirious with glee. What a find, and in our own basement!

"Hey Leah," I teased her, "how do you like the toilet?"

Leah was obviously not as excited about it as I was. In fact, she didn't particularly like it at all. She gave me a wan smile and stood with her arms crossed tightly in front of her chest.

I smirked. In my own cockeyed, hopelessly symbolic way, I thought that this *proved* something, and that I could chalk one up for me in our never-ending debate about the ultimate nature of reality.

But Leah, of course, felt differently. I could see that. So I sidled over to her and, gently, just to let her know that I wasn't a fanatic anymore, I nudged a friendly elbow into her side.

WINE TASTING

Well, it looks like time is almost running out. But I still have some stories left to tell you. Some? Actually, I have hundreds, a thousand, a million – I could go on and on, telling one story after another, still hoping that you'll get a *correct* understanding of the Havurah, and not a distorted one. It's *important* that you get a correct understanding – important and yet utterly impossible. How can I convey it all? Well, if you're going to get a distorted idea, I hope you at least get one that's distorted *correctly*.

So, there's one more story I think you've got to hear, one more story before you're totally fed up and ready to dump this bowl of yogurt right on top of my head. Ah, but you wouldn't do that. You're still a guest, and a polite one at that. And throwing food around would be such a terrible thing to do.

I'm sure you've heard that one before.

It was a Sunday morning, sometime late in the morning, and I was still lying in bed, groggy and squinting at the light that was already pouring in through the window. Suddenly I heard a scratching at the door.

"Oh no. It's Krishna. Here he comes."

I turned my head and saw the door gently move, forward a little, back a little, *scratch scratch* all the while, until finally a furry black and white paw stuck its way into the small opening between the door and the doorpost, and pulled the door backwards. I watched, fascinated, hoping he would go away yet prepared to deal with him if he didn't.

"Here he comes."

Slowly, he managed to pull the door ajar enough to slink into the room and amble over towards my bed. He came right up to my head, which was close to the ground because my bed, if you could call it that, was only a mattress on the floor. He drew his head very close to mine.

I looked at him. He was a big fat cat, all black and white, with a funny face and big green eyes. As for brains, he was no prize, to say the least. Nor was he particularly affectionate. Somehow, though, despite his lack of qualities, he was endearing. I loved him, even though he was a pain in the neck. He stared back. What was *he* thinking about *me*?

"Hello, Krishna. Come here," I said, and I extended a hand from under the covers and began scratching his head. But he didn't want to be petted, not now at least, and I knew it. And he knew that I knew it. He wanted to be fed.

"*Mrrraaa,*" he complained, with almost a Brooklyn twang, opening his mouth wide and showing his throat.

"Give me a break, Krishna. I just got up."

"*Mrraaa,*" he insisted. He sat there on his big tush and stared at me. Then he began to look around, with an expectant eye, surveying the landscape as to how best to pounce onto my bed. That was the worst – he loved jumping on my bed, but then he'd get all his little cat hairs stuck in my blanket and I'd itch for a week. So, it was either get up and feed him or have him jump on my bed.

"No! Don't jump!"

"*Mraa*"

"Okay, okay. Hold on."

I pulled myself to a sitting position. Somehow, Krishna never quite understood that he was just a cat, just our cat. As far as he was concerned, we were just his humans, although some cruel and ironic fate had given us the power of the can opener, the key to his happiness. I pulled on a pair of pants as Krishna impatiently began to walk in little circles, banging his head into the furniture, giving me the "hungry" sign. I never understood why he banged his head when he was hungry.

"Krishna, stop banging your head," I said, but he paid me no mind. He kept banging his head and walking in circles, unable to control himself, working up an appetite. I wondered if he had damaged his brains from all that head banging.

"Okay, come on," I said.

As soon as I made a motion towards the door, Krishna gave a little yelp of excitement and took off down the stairs. I watched as he hurried down the stairs, not leaping lithely like a young cat but waddling clumsily, although with great animation, shifting his weight this way and that, his big tush going boom-boom as he hit each successive step.

Boom-boom-boom, and he disappeared behind the bend in the staircase.

Krishna lived to eat. Years ago, when the Havurah first bought the house, Krishna had suddenly emerged one day, apparently quite at home. And so he stayed on, a permanent boarder. He was young and quick then, the biggest stud on the block. Yet as he got a little older, he would come home bloodier and bloodier, fighting with all the other neighborhood cats and getting more and more badly beaten, until finally he was so mutilated that the vet said that if he weren't fixed, he'd get himself killed.

This sparked off quite a debate at the Havurah: Do we do it? Do we *cut 'em off*? Or do we leave him intact, as a man, but maybe to get killed? Reluctantly – although Krishna himself would undoubtedly have been the most reluctant, had he known what was in store for him – the Havurah paid to have him fixed.

For weeks afterwards, he just sat around, dazed, licking his newest wound. Slowly, he grew fat, slothful, and his desire to eat grew and grew while his other desires subsided. Now he was an almost-old man, no longer potent, content to sleep, sit on the porch, and occasionally lie down in a lap or a bed.

But food still excited him. His appetite was his salvation, giving him something to live for, a purpose and a hobby, which he always looked forward to.

By the time I came down to the kitchen, Krishna had worked himself into a frenzy, banging his head into the legs of the table and the chairs, smashing his head into the white kitchen cabinet, his treasure chest, that holy of holies in which was locked his chiefest of delights. He emitted a noise that sounded like something between an intense purr and an excited growl.

"Okay, Krishna, relax," I said, as I went over to the cabinet to find his breakfast.

I opened the metal door, which made a loud click. That click – so familiar to Krishna – drove him even further into ecstasies of anticipation. He banged his head into my legs as I surveyed the situation.

Krishna's shelf was, on this day, particularly well stocked. I had a large selection to choose from. There was "Ocean Fish," "Tuna Delight," "Beef and Kidney Flavor," "Chicken," and "Gourmet Menu," all of it horrible stuff. Why were there all these different flavors? To me, they all seemed an indistinguishable mess of greasy, disgusting garbage, a sickening brown gook with an amazingly pungent stench. I certainly couldn't tell the difference among them, and I wondered if Krishna could. Or did we buy him different flavors only to vary things for ourselves? Whatever. I made my choice.

"Okay, Krishna. Today you're getting 'Gourmet Menu.'"

I began to open the can, the sound of which only heightened his already feverish desire. The tension was growing tremendous, the noise from his throat climbing higher and higher in pitch. His tail arched and quivered. He could barely contain himself.

The can opened. I pulled out Krishna's special cat-food spoon, and, just before dishing out his ambrosia of enchantments, while Krishna stared up at me and walked around, waiting with his last ounce of proper behavior before going completely berserk, I decided to take a sniff of "Gourmet Menu."

"*Uch!*" I almost gagged. It was awful. I blocked my nose and began to dish it out.

Krishna wouldn't even wait for a second spoonful to drop into his bowl. He pounced on it immediately, ravenous and ecstatic.

"Okay. There! *Ess gezinterheit,*" I said, as I doled out the rest of his portion and as Krishna wolfed down his food like an animal.

I put some plastic wrap over the half-empty can and put it into the refrigerator, in its special place.

That, too, had been a matter of no small Havurah debate. "How can we buy Krishna this *traif* cat food and keep it in the house?"

It was a problem. First, we had to decide whether Krishna was Jewish. If he wasn't, he could eat *traif*. We decided that, after all, he was only a *behemah*, a beast, so how could he be Jewish? The idea that Krishna might not be Jewish was a hard thing to swallow. But we accepted it. And since we had to live with him, it seemed all right to keep his food in the house, as long as it had its own place. So, Krishna had his own corner in the refrigerator, as well as his own *traif* spoon.

I sat down at the table and watched him happily gobbling his *traife* glop.

"Krishna, you're just a *behemah*," I said aloud, just to remind him. He didn't even look up.

While I sat there watching Krishna the *behemah* gobble his beastly meal, Chief came in, slamming the front door behind him and bouncing into the room.

"Hey Shloim! How's your ass?" he exclaimed.

"I'm okay," I said, suddenly feeling groggy again, especially when confronted with Chief's energetic entrance.

"Listen, Shloimie! We really have to bottle and cork the wine. We can't wait any longer or it will go sour."

I looked at him. Now? We had to do this *now*? I just got up. "Today?" I asked, not wanting to bother with it.

"Yeah! Today, man. We can't wait any more. Gotta put it into real bottles and cork it."

"I guess so," I said lazily. "If not now, when? Right?"

"Right!"

"Okay. Let me get dressed. I'll be right down. Why don't you go and bring over the wine."

"Okay, see you soon!" He turned and bounded back towards the door. I slowly got to my feet and shuffled my way upstairs.

"Yeah, I guess it's time," I said to myself.

Chief and I had finally made wine this year – after several years of talking about it but never getting around to doing it – from the grapes that grew in the backyard. In the fall, we had picked the grapes and spent several hours squashing them with our hands into a big plastic garbage can.

After adding the proper ingredients and letting it set for a while, we then emptied the contents of the garbage can into gallon bottles with special little fermenting corks on top. These bottles had sat in Chief's apartment, underneath his kitchen table, for months already. Only once in the interim did we even check on it. We had had to decant it and pour it into different bottles in order to get rid of the sediment, and at that time, to our delight, we found that indeed real wine was fermenting from our humble Havurah grapes. Kosher, too.

And yet, each bottle had had a different quality, some of it good, some of it not so good. It was all a very hit-or-miss operation. And there was still a good chance that by now the wine had turned into nothing but vinegar, after all.

By the time I got dressed and went downstairs, Chief was already coming through the door with his private winery: several large gallon-size bottles filled with wine, lots of smaller empty bottles to transfer it into, long plastic tubes and a corker, all thrown into a big plastic laundry basket, cradled in his arms.

"Well, here it is, Shloim." He was excited by the project.

We cleared the table and laid out the bottles. Now, one of us would have to carefully insert the plastic tube into the larger bottles, while the other sucked on the tube to siphon the wine into the smaller bottles. As we had already learned, the one who sucked on the tube inevitably got a mouthful of wine before being able to transfer the tube into its proper bottle.

"You want to go first?" Chief asked.

"Sure. Why not."

We chose one bottle, which we had marked "the good stuff" when we had first done our initial decanting. What had "the good stuff" become in the interim?

"Should I say a *brachah?*" I asked.

"Well, you're not really *drinking* it, you're only *siphoning* it. I don't know if it's really necessary."

"I guess you're right. Well, anyway – *l'chaim!* Here goes."

With that, I bent down in order to lower the level of the siphon and gave a mighty suck on the tube. The reddish liquid rose up in the tube and traveled quickly down towards my mouth.

"Okay!" Chief yelled, and I jammed the tube into a waiting bottle, but not before receiving a mighty spurt of wine into my mouth. I savored what remained.

"Hey! This *is* good stuff!"

"Yeah?" Chief said, raising his eyebrows in hopeful anticipation.

"Try some!" I poured out a little wine for Chief to try. He closed his eyes and tested it like an expert. Chief was an expert on subtle sensations. He moved his tongue around inside his mouth. Then he smiled, a great satisfied smile.

"It *is* good! It's real wine. A full-bodied, honest to goodness wine. Not fancy, but solid. A strong taste, a nice smell. Like a good French table wine."

"Right," I said. "A bit French. A strong, solid character. A real main-line wine. So, what should we call it?"

"Call it?"

"Yeah. Let's give it a name. For this wine, let's see . . ." I thought for a moment. "How about 'Chateau Rashi'?!"

"Of course! That's perfect. Chateau Rashi – it fits exactly."

At that moment, Krishna, who had been watching all these strange goings-on in the kitchen, demanded to be noticed. He was jealous. He was jealous whenever anybody was ingesting anything in his presence; he wanted some too, whatever it was. He jumped onto a chair and sniffed at the bottles.

"*Mrraaa.*"

"Okay, Krishna. You want to try some? I don't think you'll like it." I dabbed my finger with a few drops of Chateau Rashi and held it to his nose. He sniffed it suspiciously. But after all, since we had drunk it, he would try it, too. He stuck out his rough little tongue and licked my finger.

In an instant, his head jerked backwards. His whole body shuddered and he quickly shook his head, trying to shake off the awful taste that stung his taste buds.

"Didn't like it, did you?" I said to him.

He only sat back down in the chair, no longer curious about tasting any more.

"You just don't appreciate it, Krish," Chief said. "You don't understand the good things in life."

Krishna didn't respond but continued to watch with detached interest as we filled our bottles. Taking turns on the siphon, we filled up four bottles with Chateau Rashi, corked them, and put them aside.

But a couple of pulls on the siphon was no small amount. For some reason, the wine was very strong and immediately we began to feel tipsy.

"Chateau Rashi," Chief said, cocking his head to one side and pointing a finger into the air, making circles, "is an excellent wine. But now, we must advance to the other wines."

"Indeed," I replied, feeling a little silly, "how about this one?" I picked up a bottle that was marked "pretty good," which contained a deep purple wine with a heavy opaque color. "My turn on the siphon," I said.

Chief stuck the siphon into the bottle, and I took another great suck on the plastic tube. The dark wine quickly shot into my mouth.

"*Oooh*, that one's bitter," I exclaimed, and I puckered my lips as I jammed the siphon into the next empty bottle.

"Let me try some." Chief took a mouthful and made a face. "*Woo-o.* That one's harsh. It's not too bitter to drink, but it *is* harsh. Not easy on the palate. Quite a bite to that one."

"Well, it's still kosher," I said.

"Sure, it's kosher. It's fine for kiddush. It's a strong wine, too. A strong, dark, harsh wine. Got to take it in smaller doses. Can't chug-a-lug that one."

"So, what do we call it?" I asked, as the shock of that mouthful's alcohol suddenly hit me, making me blink.

"That one? Hmm . . ." Chief thought for a moment. Then, as if making a great pronouncement, emphasizing his words with his pointed finger, he said solemnly, "Chateau Shammai."

"Chateau Shammai it is!" I said, still blinking. "Now it's your turn."

Chief took the plastic tube and gave a pull. The wine hit him with a jolt, and he stuffed the end of the tube into the next bottle as quickly as he could. By the time we filled up a few bottles with Chateau Shammai, there were wine spills all over the table and little puddles of it on the floor. There was even wine on my pants.

"Well, that's it for Chateau Shammai," I said. "Hey, I'm getting really drunk."

"Me too," Chief answered, with a crooked smile. "This is strong wine we have here."

"Time for the next!" I said, with an overdramatic flourish. "Bring on the next." I hit the table with my fist.

"Here it is," Chief said, picking up a small bottle with not too much wine in it. "This one was "the special stuff," remember? This one was the best of all." Chief picked it up and banged it back onto the table. "This one was different, remember?"

"Right! That one was really good, but there had only been a little of it!" I looked at the bottle, which contained a very light, pinkish wine, clearer than all the others, limpid and translucent.

"This one had been delicious," I recalled. As I said this, I noticed that my knees were beginning to feel rubbery. I sat down.

"I'll do this one," Chief offered. He took the tube, ducked down, and sucked on it. He took a little extra before routing it into the bottle.

"How is it?" I asked eagerly.

A worried look passed over his face, a sort of pensive frown. "Not so good," he said with disappointment. "It turned."

"Whatta you mean?" I asked, crushed.

"It lost its flavor. It only has a weak little taste. It tastes nice enough, but it's not sweet or rich or anything. It's clean and simple. I don't know – it lost something."

I took a taste, and Chief was right! A lovely light wine, but nothing robust, nothing subtle, nothing rich. It lost something in the fermentation.

"It's still good," I ventured, not wishing to downgrade it.

"It's still good," he answered, "but this was the stuff we thought would be great. And it's not."

It was true. In my increasingly inebriated state, it seemed sad. The poor little wine that lost its flavor. And there was only enough for one bottle.

"So, what do we call it?" I asked.

We both thought for a while. We considered the taste, the color, the smell, the texture, and that slightly sad sense of loss that accompanied it. Chateau Who was this?

"Chateau Spinoza," Chief said, throwing his arms out. "That's Chateau Spinoza."

"You're right. Chateau Spinoza."

We corked the bottle and put it slightly off, by itself, for it had no companions.

There was one more gallon to go. Chief hoisted it up onto the table and looked at its label. "This is the raunchy stuff," he declared.

The raunchy stuff. This bottle contained all the leavings, the left-over wine, the dregs, the stuff we almost threw away but couldn't quite bear to part with, so we had tossed it all together into one big bottle and left it, to do whatever it would. I looked at it through my increasing mental fog and I was afraid to taste it.

"You do this one," I said.

"No, man, you start it," Chief said.

"All right. Give me the tube."

Chief had a hard time finding the opening to the bottle. He missed it on the first try. Then he managed to stick the tube in one end, and he handed me the other. He sat down. The three of us – Chief, Krishna and I – just stared at the bottle for a second, waiting.

"Okay, here goes," I said, and I ducked down and took a big pull.

The liquid jumped towards my face and I received another full mouthful before desperately seeking to find a place for the tube. But this wine was really different. Amazingly, it was *good!* It was even delicious. It was a little sweet, and had a clear, fruity flavor. There was no bitterness in it at all.

"Hey, this stuff's good!"

"Yeah?" Chief said, excited. "But this is the raunchy stuff."

"God knows what happened, but it turned out great!"

Chief grabbed the bottle and took a swig. "Incredible! It's really good."

"Gimme another taste." I had some more. It was excellent, no doubt about it.

"*M'kimi me-afar dal!*" I said. "A miracle!"

"A miracle! A mystical miracle!" Chief shouted, and he laughed and smacked the table. "So, what do we call it?"

This one. What *do* we call this one? This one was our pride, our best, the fine vintage from the lowliest of our crop. But my mind was no longer functioning rapidly, and I couldn't think of a name.

Then, a big smile spread over Chief's face. "Chateau Besht. This is Chateau Besht."

"*Aw-mayn,*" I said. "Chateau Besht."

Chief took the tube, to drain out the next quart from Chateau Besht. "My turn," he said. He took a big suck inward, and also got a mouthful.

"Hey, this is different!"

"Whatta you mean different?"

"I don't know, but it's not the same."

"Whatta you mean not the same?"

"It's not as good as the stuff on top of it. I guess the further down you go, the closer to the dregs, the worse it gets."

"Let me taste." And it was true. This wine, although from the same batch, was not as clear and sweet as the liquid above it. It had a decidedly bitter undertaste. The sweetness and the bitterness played off against each other.

"Darn," I said. "It gets bitter."

And this, without a doubt, was Chateau Nachman. For some reason, it seemed funny and sad at the same time. Chief started to giggle along with me. And amid our giggles and sloppy decanting, the next quart that came out proved to be even bitterer still. And yet, it still bore the same taste as Chateau Besht above it, but the harsher strain had come out, and the clear sweet taste had gotten muddied by it. It was as if you had to remember the sweet taste from Chateau Besht to sense it in this newest one.

"This is Chateau Kotsk!"

"Chateau Kotsk!" Chief repeated, and for some strange reason, in our drunken stupor, it seemed uproariously funny. We laughed and laughed, until I fell off my chair. Now, I was lying on the floor, in pools of spilled wine, laughing out loud.

And there was one more quart. The dregs. The bottom stuff. What was this going to be? Chief sucked out a siphon-full and filled the bottle. I just watched as he savored it and couldn't seem to make up his mind. I grabbed the bottle and took a big pull myself.

This was the weirdest stuff of all. It was bitter and sweet and had a strange, fruity flavor that came out of the dregs. It wasn't really bad at all, but it tasted very bizarre. It was a crazy combination of everything in the bottle.

"Chateau Havurah!" I exclaimed.

"Chateau Havurah! L'chaim!" Chief called out, and as he stood up, as if to make a toast, he tripped and fell down, onto me, and we both fell onto the floor, and together we rolled around in a peal of laughter, in the puddle of wine, giggling and snorting in chaotic giddiness.

Krishna, still sitting at the table, didn't have the slightest idea what was going on, and he just looked at us, totally uncomprehending, as if we were out of our minds.

A VISIT TO THE EDOMVILLE SHUL

There's a footnote to that last story. Do you know what we did with the wine when we finished bottling it? We had to store it, of course. We needed a cool, dark place where it would be left alone and undisturbed, where we could shut it away and let it age. You guessed it – we put it in the little toilet room in the basement. There wasn't a better and more convenient place anywhere in the house.

But now it's time to go and make *havdalah*. Let's go out to the porch and look up at the sky. If there are three stars, then Shabbos is over and we can end it here.

Come on out. Look. Look up.

There's one, and there, there's two. Do you see three? I can't see three from here. Maybe if we get off the porch and stand in the street, we can see three. There must already be a third star out there somewhere.

But you know what? – why bother. What good is there in hurrying the end of Shabbos? It's better to prolong it for as long as we possibly can. To seek the end of Shabbos is a silly thing to do. What good will it do us? When the end comes, it comes, but to hurry it along like that, it seems almost an offense.

Do we have so many better things to do, anyway? So, come back inside and have one last cup of tea. There's still another story I want to tell you. Besides, I haven't completely come down yet. Almost, but not completely.

There, make yourself comfortable again. Bear with me for one last story.

By now you've probably realized that we're a mixture of everything – old things, new things, nonsensical things, and things that have their own logic, whatever that logic may be. Sometimes you have to look for it, but it's there.

It poses problems, though, and seeing that we're not as great as the *rabbanim* used to be, we can't always make it all fit together. They couldn't either, actually, no matter how hard they tried. But we don't even try that hard. We make sure not to. But I told you about that yesterday. Anyway, once in a while we get stuck on something.

One question that always gets us stuck is how long we should observe certain holidays. Seven days or eight? One day or two? On the modern side, we reason, why should we bother with the extra day of the holiday? That was only instituted for the people in exile long ago who couldn't be sure on which day the holiday fell, so they celebrated two days to make sure they at least hit it right on one of them. But then that extra day became a tradition. Even though today we can call up the Chief Rabbi in Jerusalem who can tell us over the phone exactly the moment the holiday is to begin (a far cry from fires on the hillside, this electrical wonder), there still is a rationale in keeping two days. Exile. Tradition. And why cheat yourself out of an extra day of holiday?

As a result, there arose a split of opinions in the Havurah – the eight-dayers versus the seven-dayers. How was it resolved? We decided in favor of seven days – that *that* was all the Havurah would officially celebrate. But if anyone wanted to celebrate an extra day, that was fine. Only we wouldn't hold services at the Havurah. We probably wouldn't be able to get a minyan anyway.

So, one Passover, the problem came up again. After seven days, most of us were ready to call it quits. Enough of eating matzah – we were hungry for *humetz*. But a few people just couldn't end it there. They needed that extra day.

Max, Rebecca and Linda decided to go find someplace for services.

To go to services somewhere else may sound like an easy thing to do. But not for someone from the Havurah. It meant giving up control and submitting, if just temporarily, to someone else's trip. It meant being faceless again, if just for a while, in a place where we weren't at home. And it also once again made you ask yourself that fundamental question: Why the heck am I doing this?

Given these discomforts, it was easier to turn a visit to another synagogue into some sort of adventure – a sociological inquiry or a sightseeing tour. To check out how they do it in that place over there. It's always interesting to find out what the other Jews are up to, as long as they don't insist on pulling you in.

And so Max, Rebecca and Linda decided to visit the old Edomville shul.

No one knew exactly where the old Edomville shul was located. We all had some vague sense that it was on the other side of town, not too far, but beyond our own neighborhood. We had never bothered to establish any contact with them and had no idea whether they even knew of our existence. What would we say to them, anyway, and what would they expect from us?

We had left it at that, always feeling, with a slightly guilty uneasiness about our silence, that we really should get in touch with them – after all, we were the only two shuls in Edomville – although we probably never would.

But now a few of us would be making an appearance. I was glad that I wasn't going along. I cringed when I imagined the impossible task of explaining who we were.

Max took out the phone book to find the shul's address. "It's on Oak Street," he said, locating the listing. "Where's Oak Street?"

"I'm not sure," I answered. "I think it's somewhere on the other end of Summer Street. You go up the hill and Oak Street is off to the left somewhere."

"I don't know that part of town," Max said.

"Neither do I," I answered, unable to be of any help.

That afternoon, when they returned, we were curious to find out what happened. What were the people like, how many were there, and what was the shul like?

"They were old," Rebecca told us. "They were a little weird but very friendly." They had been very glad to receive their unexpected guests.

"They gave Max an *aliyah* and made a big fuss over kiddush – all they had was a little wine because they hadn't expected any guests, and so they kept apologizing for not offering us anything else."

"You'll see them all in two weeks, though," Max said, smiling mischievously.

"Whatta you mean?" Chief asked suspiciously.

"We told them the whole Havurah would come for Shabbos in two weeks."

"You *what?* No!"

"Yeah," Linda said, part of the conspiracy. "We did. Now they're expecting us."

They were expecting us!

Oh, no! But it seemed there would be no getting out of it. They had committed us, so we now had no choice but to show up as promised. Not to do so would be worse than rude; it would be a terrible blow to their spirits, no doubt.

"Do we have to get dressed up?" I asked, not relishing the prospect.

"Not too much," Rebecca said. "A little, that's all."

"Do I have to wear a dress?" Myra asked.

"I think so," Rebecca answered.

Oh well, what the hell. We might as well do it to the hilt. Show up, smile, be polite, let them play surrogate bubbie and zeydie for a while. Show them how well we davened. Let them feed us and worry over us. Visit the old age home and get some brownie points.

"Don't worry, you'll like them," Max said. "They're a little eccentric, but that's okay. You'll see."

The Shabbos we were due at the Edomville shul turned out to be a beautiful spring day. The sky was sunny and bright. Soft pink blossoms grew on the trees and the air held a sweet aroma of new growth. It was one of those delicate days that appear only a few times during the year and then are gone so soon.

The Havurah walked along in a long, loosely connected progression. We strolled unhurriedly in little groups of two or three, with large spaces between each group, and yet nevertheless we constituted one long procession, a single body moving through the streets towards a common goal. Up Summer Street we went, up the hill, left onto Oak Street, until we reached the Edomville shul.

I had never seen the Edomville shul before. It was a big, stone, turn-of-the-century synagogue that almost resembled a fort or an armory, sitting on top of the hill. It was surrounded by trees on a quiet street on which

the old houses were still well maintained. The building was not overly aus-
tere, for it had ornamental brick-work and large carved lettering on the
outside, but neither was it frivolous, and it tried to impress the observer
with a solemn gravity.

It represented a strange phenomenon for American Jews. Its size and
appearance told of pride and security, the pride and security of immigrants
who had made it out of poverty and into the comforts of more affluent
surroundings. And yet, that very emphasis on pride and security belied
the tenuousness of that security, which needed such an armored exterior
to protect and enclose it. Large wooden doors were set into the face of the
building, strong portals that had to be swung heavily in order to be opened
or shut.

But we did not go up the broad stone steps and through the large
wooden doors. There was no need for that. Evidently, crowds no longer
came and went, and so instead we walked around the building, stepping
carefully along a path of slate tiles laid in the grass which was almost covered over with heavy growth, and we came to a tiny side entrance nearly
hidden by shrubbery.

We opened the door that led downstairs, down a dark stairway into
the basement of the synagogue. Going in, I immediately recognized a sensation long since lost in my consciousness, the feeling of being in an old
shul. It had that old-shul air about it, an unmistakable quality, something
other than house, school, store, office building, restaurant, gas station, or
any of the many other buildings I was used to. Down the hallway, coming
from a little room, came the sound of a cantor's voice, somewhere already
well along in the *shacharit* service.

At the entrance to the room, an elderly woman, neatly dressed,
greeted us enthusiastically. Not wishing to disturb the service, she said very

little, but was obviously glad to see us. It seemed she had been waiting for us, in anticipation, at the door.

We filed into the small room in our little groups of two's and three's. The room was a drab little square whose ochre-colored walls were peeling and cracked. Pipes ran along the ceiling. Other than the fact that an *aron kodesh* had been brought down and stood in the front of the room, it could have been a storage room or a janitor's office.

We tried to take our seats as quietly as possible. As usual, we were late, and in order not to disturb, we attempted to sit down anywhere and open a *siddur* as quickly as possible.

At first, the cantor tried to ignore our entrance and continue uninterrupted with the service. Although he stood only a few feet in front of the three or four rows of folding chairs that comprised all the seating that the little room could accommodate, he attempted to preserve the dignity and inviolability that he felt the service demanded. The rabbi, an older man, but not as elderly as the majority of his dozen or so congregants, watched with a sharp yet undecided eye as we came in and took our seats.

I flipped through the siddur to find the right page, but instead of starting in to daven, I looked around. Most of congregants were well in their seventies or more. The men wore shapeless old suits with ancient ties knotted asymmetrically at their throats or whose knots were lost, askew, beneath the collars of their yellowed white shirts. They all had the colorless, milky white skin of old age which looked like a transparent membrane pulled over blue veins, and their wisps of white hair, combed carefully across their heads, were topped by large black or white silk yarmulkes. They wore little silk tallises, the diminutive counterparts of the larger woolen wrappings we preferred, which hung around their necks like limp scarves.

As more and more Havurah members straggled in, the cantor grew increasingly disturbed at the minor commotion unfolding in front of him, even as he continued, by heart, with his recitation. He looked over at the rabbi who, still waiting to see what would finally happen, made no sign. The cantor continued.

Soon, a few more Havurah members entered. At this, the cantor stopped, allowing everyone to get settled before he began again. A very professional pause. Let them calm down and then he would proceed. When he felt that the room had sufficiently settled, he began again. But before half a minute had gone by, still more Havurah members came in. Now he stopped completely. There was no continuing anymore. The spell had been entirely broken.

He looked over at the rabbi, who watched as the Havurah members tried to settle into their seats. There were so few seats available that not everyone was able to find a place, and a few Havurah members were already standing in the doorway, unsure what to do. It wasn't that there were so many of us, but even barely an additional twenty was more than the seating could accommodate. It was clear that the service had to be interrupted, because now we had become the center of attention.

"Are there any more of you coming?" the rabbi asked.

"A few. Maybe five or six."

The cantor looked over at the rabbi. "Five or six? We can fit them. Bring out a few more chairs. Maybe some of them will have to stand in the back."

"Okay, come in, come in," the rabbi said, motioning the remainder into the room. "We'll bring some more chairs."

The Havurah members standing by the doorway came into the room, while one of the congregation's "younger" men lumbered off to get a few more folding chairs. But just as he came in with two more chairs, and as the cantor was set to begin again, the last few Havurah members came down the hallway and into the room. The interruption was total, and the room was evidently much too crowded.

"Come in, come in," the rabbi said again, continuing his plan to squeeze us all into the room. Then from somewhere, although I couldn't distinguish whether it was from the rabbi himself, or from the cantor, or from one of the old men in the room, suddenly came the suggestion: "Maybe we should go upstairs?"

"Upstairs?"

"Yes, let's go upstairs," someone seconded.

"Go upstairs?" the rabbi wondered aloud, facing the cantor. "Do you think we should go upstairs?"

The cantor shrugged.

"Yes, let's go upstairs," someone else said.

"No – we have room here," countered someone else.

"Do you want to go upstairs?" the rabbi asked us.

"Whatever you like," we said.

By now, everyone was making the issue into a major debate. The old men were turning to one another and telling each other that either we should go upstairs or that we didn't have to go upstairs. The rabbi looked questioningly at the cantor, and the cantor looked back at him in the same way. The old men told the rabbi what to do, and the rabbi asked himself again. It began to get noisy and we, caught in the middle, just sat there, looking around, in the midst of this suddenly out-of-scale commotion that we had precipitated but which we now took no part in, awaiting its outcome.

The little room was filled with debate and noisy indecision. Upstairs. Not upstairs. Should we? Shouldn't we? Finally, the rabbi banged on his lectern for silence. Everybody quieted down to look at him. And then the rabbi spoke. "All right," he said. "We're going upstairs."

"Upstairs!" cried out the woman at the doorway joyfully. "We're going upstairs!" She was ready to jump from happiness.

"But quickly and quietly," the rabbi called out over everyone's head. "Let's proceed as quickly as possible. Remember, we are in the middle of the service."

He had begun to take charge again, rousing himself from his prior indecision and into a position of authority, even though at the moment his instructions were not entirely necessary.

With an upward sweep of his hands, everyone stood up, took their books, and then followed the rabbi out of the room. We threaded our way through the semi-lit basement corridor, where the pipes, coated with a thick layer of dusty grime, ran along walls that had gone unpainted and grown dingy over the years.

The woman, barely able to contain herself from happiness, whispered to us as we walked. "Oh, it's so beautiful upstairs! I'm so glad we're going upstairs! We so rarely go there anymore."

We walked up a flight of polished wooden stairs that creaked underfoot, and into a large, open, well-kept vestibule whose walls were covered with brass memorial tablets arranged in long rows reaching up to the ceiling. The tablets were everywhere; there was no more space available on the walls. All the many people who had been there, lived there, and died.

At the end of the vestibule, breaking an opening in the rows of tablets, were a series of doors that led, presumably, into the main synagogue. The rabbi carefully approached one of the doors and then, in a decisive gesture, strode through and we followed him into the sanctuary.

Inside, the sanctuary was large and airy. There were row after row of long wooden pews, interrupted only by two long aisles, on the left and on the right, which led down to a high wooden *bimah* on which a large wooden ark, with tall, carved columns on either side, dominated the view.

The walls were white and meticulously clean, which added to the limpid clarity of the interior. High up near the ceiling were several windows with a Star of David inlaid in each, surrounded by a rectangle of yellow glass. It was a simple, minimalist form of stained glass, having nothing of the opulence of medieval windows, but rather the simple dignity of New England design. The entire interior was a seamless blend of traditional New England simplicity and Jewish symbol, and the abundance of wood – wooden pews, wooden doors, wooden floors, all highly polished and carefully maintained – gave a rich yet unpretentious elegance to the large rectangular room. It was the synagogue of people who had come to New England, adopted its flavor, and who then, through death and urban flight, left behind only a few aging congregants, lost and rattling around inside.

We walked down the aisles, passing all the empty rows, row after row, the wooden floorboards giving slightly beneath our tread, until we reached the first few rows right in front of the *bimah*. We took seats, spreading out sparsely, barely thirty people taking up the room for well over a hundred or more. The rabbi and the cantor took their places up on the bimah, the rabbi at one end and the cantor at the other. Then, the services resumed where they had left off.

Although the services recommenced where we had interrupted them, they took on a new, almost surrealistic air. The cantor sang loudly enough so that people could have heard him in the very last row, although it was obvious that no one would walk in late and quietly take a seat in the back. Only the one old woman sat further off, two or three rows behind us, as if observing an invisible *mechitzah*.

All the while, one of the old men, slipping comfortably into senility, sitting there in his hat, leaned over towards Linda and talked incessantly, loudly enough so that we all could make out what he was saying. He asked her about her job, where she lived, her age, and told her over and over bits of information about his children, his grandchildren, and what he ate for breakfast. Even the reprimanding looks of the rabbi could not quiet him, and he continued to provide a running undertone to the cantor's slightly exaggerated recitation.

Dutifully, we stood up when standing up was called for, and again we sat down, the rabbi ceremoniously raising and lowering his arms at the proper moment, as if conducting the tones of a chorus, giving us cues we neither needed nor paid much attention to.

When *shacharit* was over, the Torah reading began. We were called up for all the honors and after each one it was necessary to shake hands with everybody. First with the cantor and the *gabbai*, who stood around the Torah, then with the rabbi who sat in his high-backed wooden chair, and then with the other men as we descended the *bimah*.

Each one had a word to offer; with the exception of the rabbi, each had something to tell us rather than to ask. The rabbi asked where we were from and what we studied, for he assumed that we all were students. The *gabbai* congratulated us on our davening skills. One man, still sharp and perceptive, sitting by the front of the *bimah*, said to each of us as we passed and shook his hand: "I have three sons. Two are doctors. One is a rabbi." He stated it with a sense of urgency, something which we had to understand. It was not as if he wanted us to congratulate him, nor to ask for further details, nor even to act impressed or pleased. Rather, he sensed the oppressiveness of the emptiness of the room and, like a Russian Jew who meets you on the streets of Moscow or Leningrad, whispers "shalom" and then runs away, he wanted to say that these bleak appearances were not everything, that there was hope, that somewhere something was still alive, in secret or merely hidden from our eyes, and that this dead end was not the only end. And the man leaning over Linda shook our hands and told us that he had come from Odessa in 1916 and then, enthusiastically, that he had brought schnapps for the kiddush.

After the Torah reading and a quick haftarah came the rabbi's sermon, the likes of which we had not heard for a very long time. It was simple and homiletic; it pulled passages from the week's reading and used them to show how man should be good to his fellow man, how to be moral, honest and kind. It was a striking contrast to our own mixture of academic biblical criticism, Freudian analysis, myth interpretation, hippie jargon, personal stories, and political and intellectual posturing. The rabbi grew animated on his subject of how to behave in society and in business dealings, and then, delving deeper into his topic, he attempted a few cross references. But then he stopped. He knew approximately what he wanted to say but had forgotten exactly where the references came from. They escaped him.

"You know," he confided in us, smiling a bit to himself, growing ever more personal, "I used to know this a lot better. But I haven't used it for a long time, so I forget." Slightly deflated, he returned to his topic, and soon his sermon was over.

Jerry, who was big and stood over six feet tall, was called to lift the Torah, and the old men marveled at his strength. Then the Torah was rolled up, wrapped, walked around the bimah, kissed, put into the ark, and then, ceremoniously, closed away.

The rest of the service went quickly. The cantor repeated the *amidah* with a rapid-fire display, and even the *kedushah* quickly rolled off his tongue. Then the services ended with their usual string of closing songs and wrapping-up prayers, each bringing us closer to the finish line. And then it was over, and the rabbi invited us to stay for *kiddush.*

The rabbi and cantor came down from the bimah, shook hands all around, and walked back up the aisle, out into the corridor. We exchanged handshakes and greetings with everyone else and then, following the rabbi out into the hallway, were led to a reception room where kiddush was already waiting.

In the reception room we were called on to make kiddush and to share in a l'chaim. Over an abundance of egg kichel and bakery cookies, we began to make the acquaintance of the cast of characters with whom we had just spent a rather strange two hours.

They had been waiting for us patiently, but waiting nevertheless, and now was their chance. They were so happy to have us there that they didn't know what to do: Some were shy and reticent, others talked about anything that came into their heads. The man with the three sons said very little and merely shook our hands. The man who had jabbered away at Linda continued to talk to anyone who would listen, about where he lived, which bus he took, how often he got to see his grandchildren. Some told of their earlier years, about which trade they had worked in, and about the different local merchants and how their businesses fared.

It was strange to hear these people talk about the same city we had been living in for years now, about Daley Square, about Patriot Circle, about the drugstore on our corner, all these shared landmarks, and yet with such a different perspective. That we were not the only Jews whose realities included Daley Square and the Gulley Hill bus line seemed almost inconceivable to us.

And then there were attempts at creating binding ties as well. The rabbi reminded us that this shouldn't be only an isolated visit, but that we should come again, often, and bring others with us. One man, who said he was the head of the ritual committee, although undoubtedly he was also all the members of the committee as well, tried to get us to volunteer to read Torah for them occasionally, or to come over and join their minyan. Politely, we had to remind them that we had our own place to run, and that we had our own services to keep going.

One of the younger men broke in and told us, "Listen, I used to live here, but years ago I moved to Medbury. I still come here on Shabbos because I hate to see the minyan fall apart. They need me here, so I come. But I keep telling them that they have to accept a change, that they should give the place over to the young people already. 'Give it over to the young people,' I tell them. 'What do you want – to wait until there's nobody left except the building? Get the young people in here,' I tell them."

We could only smile, agree with him, agree with the rabbi, agree with everybody who told us anything. But truthfully, were *we* the young people they were thinking about? We already had our own place, our own community, and our own troubles just to keep that afloat. We seemed so strong to them, but to ourselves we knew the precariousness of our existence. We knew how much trouble it was just making sure our own place persevered from week to week.

Anyway, what would we do with an enormous old synagogue in which we ourselves would rattle around like a bunch of loose ball bearings? What would we do with it – tear out the pews and put down five hundred cushions? Knock down the *bimah* and sit in a circle in the middle of a big empty room? Run up and down the long aisles just to find where our heads were? What could we do with it? How would it help us? I had sad visions of the wrecking ball coming some day and smashing into that proud, lovely building, splintering its beautiful, polished wood, shattering the windows into tiny shards of glass. It seemed terribly sad, but there was nothing that I or any of us could really do to stop it. We couldn't take it over, and no Jews were putting down roots in that neighborhood anymore.

But of all the people there, the old woman was the most excited to see us. There was no sadness in her. She couldn't contain herself for happiness. It was she who bought all the cookies, it was she – as head of the Sisterhood and of the Welcoming Committee – who had organized and set up the kiddush.

She talked all about her excitement. "This morning, I wasn't feeling well, I was going to stay home, and then I remembered: Today the young people are coming! I got out of bed, I got dressed, I hurried over. Oh, it's so good to see young people again. Here, there are only a few old people now; we're crabby, we're sick. But *the young people!* I said to myself.

"It's so good to see new faces here. Do you know, I remember when this place would be full. On Rosh Hashanah and Yom Kippur there were no empty seats and people would have to stand in the back. It was so crowded, there were hundreds of people here. Yes! Would you believe it? It was full here, and there were children and families."

She was beaming, allowing herself to revisit memories that, because of our presence, had become something other, more vital, than just the bitter melancholy of painful loss.

She reached out and took my hand with her left hand, and took Linda's with her right. We allowed her the intimacy, glad to provide it, and yet we were self-conscious, too, as she stood there, thinking back. We stood there with her, not knowing what to do. It was as if she were in some way pulling us back with her, into her world of memories, and she stood that way for a long moment, while a rush of sensations filled her, no doubt for the first time in such a long time, with satisfaction and joy.

"I was a bride here," she said finally. "Fifty years ago, I was a bride here."

Well, that was our visit to the Edomville shul. How did it end? It just ended, that's all. It was a nice spring day and we all walked back home, in a long irregular line. No, there's no great message to it, no final twist of fate or dramatic little event that made it all clear, all neat, or summed it up. It happened, it was a morning in our lives, then it was over. It left us with some things to think about, but we made no promises and probably won't go back again.

It was just an experience we had, we did it, and it passed.

But look – now the stars are out in force. You don't even have to go out to the porch. Just look through the window here and see how many stars have already come out. The sky is glittering with them, a million stars are lit up there in the heavens. So it's finally time to say *havdalah*, because Shabbos has definitely ended. Besides, I'm down now, down completely. My head is still ringing a little, but I'm down now, that's for sure.

Okay, now if you don't know how to make *havdalah*, this is how. Are you listening? Don't fade in and out, okay? Okay.

Here, we light this candle and hold it up. You hold it – all right? – while I say the blessing.

Henay el yeshuati evtach v'lo efchad . . . It's all about believing that God will take care of us, that we should put our faith in him. Oh sure, I have trouble with it too. But you can't always worry about that. At least not at the moment.

Baruch ata Adonai, eloheynu melech haolam, boray p'ri hagafen.

Baruch ata Adonai, eloheynu melech haolam, boray minay b'samim.

Here, take these spices and take a good whiff. Smells nice, doesn't it? What's in it? Oh, everything – some cloves, nutmeg, cinnamon, some orange blossoms, incense, some herbal tea, even a pinch of dope, just for the fun of it.

Baruch ata Adonai, eloheynu melech haolam, boray me-oray ha-esh.

Now put your hand up to the candle. Not in the flame, just near it. Cup your hand and look into your palm. Can you see the difference between light and shadow? That means that Shabbos is over and that evening has fallen. It's over for good now. That's right.

And now, drink some of the wine. Sure, as much as you like, just like that, but leave a little over. Like it? That's right – this is Chateau Havurah. I brought up a special bottle, just for the occasion. I thought you might like a taste.

And now, take the candle and dunk the flame into the wine that's remaining. Yeah, dunk it, go ahead, dunk it until it goes out completely.

That's it, just like that.

Now it's dark. Shabbos is over. It's dark and it's all over.

Well, have a good week. May our prosperity and our future generations increase like the sands and the stars in the night. And may Elijah come soon, in our own time, and bring the Messiah with him. Wouldn't that be nice?

Yeah.

Well, put on the light now, just hit that little switch by the wall.

Ah, Thomas Edison's wonderful invention. Where would we be without it?

So here we are. Oh look – it's late. It's time for you to go, I guess.

Anyway, I'm glad you came. It was a real pleasure having you. I hope I didn't talk your ear off too much. No? Good, good. Then maybe you'll come back again soon? It's not that often that we have guests anymore. Somehow, people don't come by too frequently these days. Nobody's interested anymore. The counterculture isn't what it used to be. The world's all different now.

But I'm glad you came. Here's the door. Yup, just turn that little handle there and you're out. Well, take care. Don't forget where we are. You'll remember?

Oh, it was nothing, nothing. We're always glad to be hospitable.

No, you don't have to kiss it. As long as it's there, that's all that matters.

Okay, take care now. Bye-bye. Bye.

So long.

That was a nice guest.

Well, I'm going to shut off the lights down here now, shut off the lights and walk upstairs.

Up the stairs, up to my room. My old book-lined room, with my dead plants and the magical turret. My room in an empty house.

No, it's not like it used to be, not only because nobody new comes by anymore, but even more so because all the people who used to be here have already left. They're gone. Scattered into the wind.

Esther, she's gone. She went down to New Haven to be with her boyfriend, found a job teaching second grade, and she hasn't been back since. Word has it they might be moving out to the suburbs, buying a house and settling down.

And Max and Rebecca are gone too. Max got a job teaching in a little college out in the Midwest and so they packed up and followed where that star led them. Rebecca writes occasional letters to keep in touch, nostalgic letters about how she misses everything back here. It was hard for her to leave the group. But the letters have already grown farther apart. Soon they'll stop, I'm sure.

And Heligman and Diann have disappeared too. Caleb died when he chewed up some rat poison that he found in a garbage can, and that made them close themselves off and turn inward. They're working now, and rumor has it they're thinking of having a baby. Well, Caleb's demise might have had something to do with that.

And Elisha, he's gone too. His story has the strangest twist of all. The shul in Fall River where his father worked finally asked him to be their rabbi. Elisha! He thought and thought and thought about it, and finally he said yes. And so he's slowly gotten *frum* again, believe it or not. No, it's not too hard to believe, really, when you think about it. He's not *frum* like he used to be; there's a healthy tolerance in him now, and a deeper understanding of both sides of the coin. But he's a rabbi again, or after all. It's strange the road life takes you on.

And Linda? Linda's gone too. She left her *shaygetz* boyfriend and she left the Havurah soon after that. She said she got tired of being pulled between too many extremes. She said she didn't have the energy for it anymore. So now she's living downtown, in a little one-bedroom apartment. I call her up at work sometimes and she likes to talk, but it makes her kind of nervous, too. It makes her feel like she shirked her responsibilities somewhere along the line when she left the Havurah. I *try* not to make her feel that way, but I guess I don't succeed. She doesn't go to shul anymore, either. She says she watches a lot of TV on Friday nights.

Chief still comes by once in a while – just to light the *ner tamid*. And then he goes off and spends all day at work. Weekends too, sometimes. He works a lot these days. He says he doesn't seem to find the time to come around much any longer. He avoids Leah, and she avoids him. Neither shows up very often.

And Zack – he finally finished his dissertation and then he couldn't find a job. Nobody was interested in that kind of stuff anymore. So, Zack took off to travel around the world, going from place to place, just trying to figure it all out and see where to go next.

Yes, the heyday of the Havurah is over. The sixties – and the seventies in their wake, trailing behind like a broken cart – they're gone. That's all over now. And it seems that everybody has gone with them.

Our experiment with community happened and now ended. We've turned back into normal American Jews.

In *Pirkei Avot* it says, "Do not separate yourself from the community." But the community has separated itself from itself. I have tried to keep it together in the core of my heart, but my heart is exploded and tossed all over the land.

Oh America, you scatter us. We've had it easy here, I suppose; there's been no real threat to crush us here, to accuse us or drive us away. Nobody here has succeeded to tread on our neck. We've had a haven here. And someday in the future we may look back and say what a golden age we've had here: a golden age, a gilded age, a gaudy gold-plated age. But you scatter us, America. You have taken our resolve and turned it into confusion.

Who are we in you, America?

And who am I in you? An aging Jewish hippie in an echoing Jewish house. And yet, what a fine house it has been. Never had I been more at home than here, with my own chaotic, eccentric, ironic, poetic, and touchy religious bent.

So, what should I do with it now? Should I go dress up in my Sunday best, tie a tie around my neck, looking like I'm off to something that's a cross between a meeting of the board and an East Side singles' bar, and go sit with my hands in my lap while some white-bread rabbi stands up there and lectures me about the gloriousness of holiness, the solemnities of the sacred? Or should I beat my way through the underbrush, out to the back country, where the last few freaks are holding out on country farms, and there I could do my seasonal rain dances and howl nightly at the moon?

No, no – neither is right. Neither seems very satisfying. Better I should stay here, holed up in my Havurah room, surrounded by piles of old books from our library, myself still full of stories, stuck away like an old book in a genizah, left with all the other books from other times and other places.

I'm not bitter, not at all. That's just how it is, I suppose. Every community down through the ages has offered up its own sweet savor and strange fire upon the chopping block of history, before the sacrificial knife comes down and cuts it off, joining it with those that came before.

This one just was quick, that's all.

But what does that matter, indeed, in the greater scope of things? And so what if my stories are only memories now? So what if they are forgotten altogether, and even if I, who guards them so carefully, what if I, like pages of old books which stories get written on, wither away and turn to dust? For there is still one story, a long, rambling, ancient story, scratched in black in an angular hand, all rolled up on parchment and put away in an ebony, satiny, velvet, mahogany, silken, silver, or cardboard box, and as long as we keep telling each other that one story, over and over, from start to finish and then starting again, we will always be assured of having others to accompany it, a jumping, dancing, howling, singing host of stories, a jostling throng, like a million attendants accompanying a bride, endless vibrations dazzling around a constant, solid, unchanging core, a multitude of stories being spawned out into the universe, as the scroll of our own peculiar history unrolls itself inevitably, beneath a black and starry firmament, towards a patient and inscrutable endless end of days.

And some might conclude thus:

> *Hashivenu Adonai elecha v'nashuva*
> *Chadesh yamenu ke-kedem*

> Turn us back to you, God, and we will return,
> Renew our days as of old.

And then again, for whatever their reasons, some might not.

Shmuel and Rav were discussing when one should say the blessing over studying Torah.

"Do you say the blessing when you study from the Torah?"

"Of course," said Rav.

"And what about when you study the rest of the Bible?"

"Then, too," Rav replied.

"Do you say it when you are studying Mishnah?"

"Yes, you say it over Mishnah, too."

"Do you say it when you talk about the discussions of the later rabbis?"

"You say it then as well."

"And what about when the two of us are talking between ourselves – do you say it then, too?"

"Who do you think we are," Rav answered, "just cane cutters in a bog?"

--from the Babylonian Talmud

AFTERWORD: AUTHOR'S NOTE

In Jewish lore, forty years is, proverbially speaking, a long time. It is time enough for one generation to fade away and for another to take its place. It is even long enough to assuage the wrath of God.

It therefore seemed particularly apt that forty years fortuitously elapsed between the time I first wrote *Tales of the Havurah* and when I was ready to pick it up again and revisit it. I had written the book when still a young man, full of ambition and excitement, my career still ahead of me. Now, recently retired, I have returned to it in order to save something that I hope will prove worth preserving, however modest an achievement it might be.

When I originally completed *Tales of the Havurah* in 1978, before the age of the Internet, social media, emails, digital content, self-publishing, and the ready availability of personal computers and word-processing software, I made a reasonable effort to find a publisher in order to enable the work to see the light of day. I sent around fat boxes with photocopied copies of my typed manuscript and shared the text with the relatively small circle of literarily connected individuals I encountered who I felt might open doors.

As a result of these efforts, some portions of the book did manage to appear in small publications, and I am grateful for these acceptances.

The stories "Of Turbot and a Turret" and "Visit to the Edomville Shul" appeared in *Phoenix Rising: Contemporary Jewish Voices;* "Elisha" appeared in the weekly English-language supplement of the *Jewish Daily Forward,* in the days when *The Forward* was still primarily a Yiddish newspaper; a long excerpt from "Tisha b'Av at Fenway Park" appeared in *The Temple of Baseball;* and a short piece excerpted from "Wedding March" was printed in *Menorah: Sparks of Jewish Renewal,* a newsletter targeted to the world of counterculture Jewish communities.

But the complete manuscript was never published. Soon, the exigencies of making a living, and then also of married life and raising a family, caught up with me, and my handful of remaining copies were placed in storage, along with various other accoutrements of my earlier life which I still could not completely part with.

At one point, about ten years ago, I scanned a copy of the typed manuscript in order to convert it into a PDF, a digital copy, just to have it in a more preservable format in case the storage locker ever caught fire or met with some similar, unlikely disaster. At that time, I attempted to read the manuscript, for the first time in so many years, but I could only manage to read a few pages. All I could see were the many infelicities in the text – redundancies, awkward word choices, occasional grammatical errors or punctuational difficulties, and typos. That, combined with the pain of revisiting a work that I had commenced with such enthusiasm but eventually shelved with a feeling of publishing failure, caused me to put the book away again and I didn't look at it for almost another ten years.

But life has a funny way of doubling back on itself, and I have learned – time and again – that any good deed or honest effort is never wholly lost.

As the fiftieth anniversary of the founding of Havurat Shalom – the granddaddy of the Havurah movement, which ultimately did have a profound effect on American Jewish religious life – approached, there arose a small flurry of activity around this milestone. A reunion was organized, academic events were hosted, Brandeis University opened an archive for materials written on the subject, and various scholars and journalists planned retrospective articles.

Among these efforts, Dovid Roskies, a professor of Yiddish literature and Jewish culture at the Jewish Theological Seminary and himself an early Havurah member, decided to do some research into works that were written about Havurat Shalom from that earlier time period. He sought out newspaper articles, monographs, memoirs, whatever. He mentioned this to Bonny Fetterman, an editor and publishing consultant whom I had met many, many years prior and with whom I had shared my manuscript, but whom I had not seen in a very long time – decades, perhaps. She asked Dovid if he had ever seen my manuscript. I am grateful that she even remembered it after such a long period.

Dovid was surprised. Although Dovid and I have known each other for nigh on forty years, since the time I first moved back to New York from Boston, he was unaware that I had ever written anything on the subject. He contacted me and asked if he could see a copy.

I explained that I would be happy – flattered, even – to provide him with a copy, but I had to admit that I felt the work was in serious need of some careful editing. I was embarrassed at all the infelicities I mentioned earlier, which now were all I could see. Whereas forty years earlier I was unable to see any faults in my opus whatsoever, now these flaws were all I could notice. Still, I gave him a copy in PDF format, copied to a small flash drive that I furtively handed him one day in synagogue, slipped quickly into his hand as if completing a drug deal.

Dovid took the flash drive with him on sabbatical and returned many months later to say that he read a different story from the work every Shabbat, and encouraged me to take the time to revisit the work and edit it.

He said there was much he enjoyed, and he felt the book worth preserving and sharing. I resolved to revisit it and edit it, as now I felt I could see it more objectively, especially after half a lifetime of writing (albeit for a very different audience).

Re-reading it for the first time in such a long time, I enjoyed it, too. Not only did I feel good about it, but I also marveled a bit at the person who had poured his energies into writing it, a young man whom I had met in the mirror a long time ago but had parted ways with over the years, as time took its inevitable toll.

Upon re-reading the manuscript, one thing I found particularly striking was the ways in which the world has since changed, in some ways unexpectedly. Whereas, for example, the egalitarianism that was pioneered at Havurat Shalom, where women played an equal role in religious and liturgical matters, became increasingly mainstream in the non-orthodox Jewish world at a steady and ever-gathering pace, who would ever have predicted that today in Boston one can enter a legal and licensed storefront and openly purchase recreational marijuana? Wow.

Finally, I must point out that whereas we have recently celebrated the fiftieth anniversary of Havurat Shalom, *Tales of the Havurah* is about Havurat Chaim Community, a totally fictitious entity. Although I admittedly drew upon experiences at Havurat Shalom, the people depicted in *Tales of the Havurah* are entirely fictional. My and their experiences have been changed, refashioned, fictionalized, and in part wholly invented for the sake of the stories, and anyone who believes that he or she recognizes him/herself is undoubtedly mistaken. Any resemblance to actual persons is an act of pure coincidence, as well as the luck of an author of fiction in achieving a verisimilitude that could induce people into believing that a written text has somehow captured a truth about their own lives.

Still, I want to thank all the many people at Havurat Shalom whose lives intersected with mine, however that may have come about. (And a special acknowledgement to Hillel Goelman, who deserves equal blame in co-writing the Purim spiel parodies.) I hold you all deeply and dearly in my heart. *Rock-a my soul in de bosom o' Abraham, O rock-a my soul.*

DK

New York City, Autumn 2019

GLOSSARY

Acharonim – literally, "the last ones." The leading rabbis from the period of the 15th century to the present, following the period of the "rishonim" (literally, "the first ones").

Akedah – the binding of Isaac, the story told in Genesis 22:1 – 19

Aliyah – "going up," whose main meanings are 1) the honor of going up to the bimah and saying the blessings over reading the Torah, and 2) going to live in Israel.

Apikores – a heretic or free-thinker.

Apikorsus – heretical behavior.

Aron kodesh – the holy Ark, which contains the Torah scroll.

Amidah – the 18 blessings, a central prayer during daily, sabbath and holiday services.

Averah – a sin or transgression.

Ba'al tshuvah – one who returns or makes a commitment to orthodox religious life. Literally, "one who makes repentance."

Balagan – chaos.

Baruch ata Adonai, eloheynu melech haolam, boray p'ri hagafen. – Blessed are You, our God and ruler of the world, who creates the fruit of the vine.

Baruch ata Adonai . . . boray minay b'samim.—Blessed are You . . . who creates varieties of spices.

Baruch ata Adonai . . . boray me'oray ha-esh. – Blessed are You . . . who creates the illumination of fire.

Bencher – a book of blessings, usually of Grace after Meals, often given out and kept as a souvenir at a wedding feast.

Besht – the Ba'al Shem Tov, Rabbi Israel ben Eliezer (c. 1698 – 1760), founder of Hasidism. Literally, "The Master of the Good Name."

Bimah – the stage or raised platform in the synagogue from which the Torah is read or the leader leads services.

Birkat ha-mazon – grace after meals.

Blondiniot – blondes (female).

Boruch ha-Shem – "Blessed be the Holy One," an expression that all is well.

Brachah – a blessing.

Bubbie – Grandma (Yiddish).

Chumash (pl. chumashim) – Volume containing the Five Books of Moses, the first five books of the Bible.

Chuppah – the wedding canopy, under which the wedding ceremony takes place.

Davening – praying, specifically Jewish style.

Dodi li va-ani lo – "My beloved is mine and I am his," a verse taken from The Song of Songs.

Drash – a commentary on sacred text.

Dreck – Yiddish for fecal matter (impolite, but not obscene).

Ess gezinterheit – Yiddish, "eat in good health."

Fleischik – meat.

Frummy – an orthodox person, from the Yiddish word "frum" or observant. Sometimes used as a term of mild condescension.

Gabbai – one who is tasked with keeping track of proper order during services or Torah reading, or who oversees the fulfillment of liturgical roles.

Galut – exile.

Gatkes – Yiddish for "underwear."

Gemara – the part of the Talmud that is comprised of commentary on the Mishnah.

Genizah – a crypt where sacred books or fragments of text are buried or stored when they are too worn for continued use. (Texts containing the name of God are not to be burned or discarded; they must be carefully taken out of use and stored away or buried.)

Halachah – regulations based upon the Torah's commandments.

Halachah k'veit Havurah – "The halachah is decided according to the Havurah's practice;" a reference to rabbinical decisions determining which school of practice to follow.

Hamantaschen – a triangular pastry popular on Purim, usually filled with prune jam, poppy seeds, or other preserves. Often home baked.

Haray aht m'kudeshet li . . . etc. – "Behold you are consecrated to me, according to the laws of Moses and Israel." This is the formal Jewish wedding vow.

Hashgachah pratit – divine providence; literally, "personal" or "private" supervision.

Hasidic – pertaining to Hasidism.

Hasidim – those who practice Hasidism; also, those who follow a particular religious personality or authority.

Hasidism –a religious movement founded by the Ba'al Shem Tov in the 18th century, focusing on good deeds, deep religious intention and mystical ideas. It was a reaction against the then-prevailing order focused on the intensive study of text (mainly Talmud).

Havurah – a group or fellowship.

Havdalah – the brief service marking the ending of the Sabbath and the passage from the holy to the secular.

Hazan – cantor

Hegdish – a mess, a jumble.

Humetz – leavening or something that contains leavening, which is forbidden on Passover.

Kabbala – Jewish mysticism. The kabbalistic tradition describes the ten divine spheres or emanations: Keter (Crown), Chochmah (Wisdom), Binah (Understanding), Chesed (Loving-kindness), Netzach (Eternity or Perpetuity), Din (Judgment), Hod (Splendor), Tiferet (Glory), Yesod (Foundation), and Malkhut (Kingship). Beyond all the divine emanations is Ayn Sof (Endlessness), the indescribable and eternal mystical nature of God.

Kabbalat Shabbat – the Friday evening service that inaugurates, or welcomes in, the Sabbath.

Kaddish – prayer recited in memory of the dead.

Kashrut – observance of the dietary laws.

Kedushah – the central section of the Amidah, with key parts said aloud and in unison by the congregation. (Not recited during private prayer.)

Keren Kayemet – the Jewish National Fund, established in 1901, which purchased land from the Ottoman Empire and then from the British Mandate for Jewish settlement in Palestine, and which continues to support the development of land in Israel.

Kichel – a type of simple, light pastry.

Kiddish – blessing over wine.

Kotsk – a leading center of Hasidic life, established by Rabbi Menachem Mendel of Kotsk (1787–1859), known as the first Kotsker Rebbe, who was a deep spiritual thinker also known for his seclusion and asceticism in the later years of his life.

K'shoshanah beyn ha-chochim – k'nesset Yisroel – "As a lily among thorns – such is the house of Israel," a quotation from the Zohar, commenting upon a verse from the Song of Songs.

L'chaim – a toast, like "cheers" or "to your health," before drinking. (Literally, "to life!").

Ma'ariv – the evening service; also, the name of one of Israel's main daily newspapers.

Machloket – a rabbinical dispute or disagreement over a point of law or interpretation.

Mechitzah – the separation barrier between men and women in orthodox synagogues.

Megillah – a scroll, often denoting the scroll of the Book of Esther, which is read on Purim.

Mi adir al hakol, mi baruch al hakol – opening of the wedding ceremony: "Who is greater than all, who is blessed above all."

Midrash – a legend, usually as a commentary on the Torah or a sacred text.

Mikimi me-afar dal – "Who raises me up from the lowly dust," a citation from Psalm 113, also found in the Hallel service.

Mikvah, mikveh – a ritual bath, during which one enters naked and completely immerses oneself.

Milchik – dairy.

Minyan – a quorum of ten Jewish adults (in orthodox Judaism, ten men) needed for a public prayer service.

Mishegass – craziness (Yiddish).

Mishnah – the compendium of rabbinic oral law comprising the first part of the Talmud, upon which the Gemara further expounded.

Misnagdim – literally, "those who oppose," which became the moniker of those who opposed Hasidism and practiced a more cerebral and formal school of Judaism.

Mitzvah – a commandment or good deed.

Motzi – grace before meals, from the words of the prayer ending in "ha-motzi lechem min ha-aretz" or "who brings forth bread from the earth."

Motzei Shabbos – the ending of the Sabbath; also, the period immediately after the Sabbath, i.e., Saturday evening.

Musaf – the additional prayer service appended to the morning service on Sabbath and holidays.

Mussar – the study of ethical behavior. A *mussar spiel* is a lecture on ethical behavior.

Nachman – Rabbi Nachman of Bratslav (1772 – 1810), a leading Hasidic rabbi and master, who experienced great religious fervor and insight, as well as deep depression.

Nebach – a Yiddish expression indicating something's pitiful nature.

Ner Tamid – the eternal light, a light in the synagogue, usually located above the Ark, that is kept continuously lit.

Niggun (pl. niggunim) – a liturgical melody, often sung without words and sometimes incorporated into the prayer service.

Noodge – a bother, a poke (Yiddish).

Parashah – a weekly section of the Torah.

Pirkei Avot – The Ethics of the Fathers, a compendium of pithy rabbinical sayings and insights from the Mishnaic period.

Rabbanim – the rabbis, also refers to the rabbis of the Talmud.

Rishonim – the leading rabbis of the era from the 11ᵗʰ to the 15ᵗʰ centuries. Literally, "the first ones."

Sefer – literally "a book," but in religious parlance, a holy book.

Seudah – a festive meal, a feast. Seudah Rishonah: the first meal. Seudah Shniah: the second meal. Seudah Shlishit: the third meal at the end of the Sabbath (see Shalesh Shudes).

Shabbat (Hebrew), Shabbos (Yiddish) – the Sabbath. The terms are interchangeable.

Shabbos ha-Malkah – The Sabbath Queen, embodying the spirit of the Sabbath.

Shacharit – the morning service.

Shalach mones – the giving of gifts on Purim, usually food, to friends and neighbors.

Shalosh regalim – the three major pilgrimage holidays, i.e., Passover, Shavuot and Succot.

Shalesh shudes – the third meal of the Sabbath (Yiddish, from the Hebrew, *shalosh seudot*, i.e., three festive meals).

Shaygetz (pl. shkotzim) – a gentile (masculine, sometimes mildly derogatory).

Shehecheyanu – the blessing for reaching a milestone. "Blessed are You who kept us alive, sustained us and brought us to this occasion."

Shekhinah – in mysticism, a feminine aspect of God that dwells close to the material world and accompanies the people of Israel.

Sheva brachot – the seven blessings, recited during a wedding ceremony and at the end of a wedding feast. Also, a week-long series of meals honoring the bride and groom following their wedding.

Shiksa, shikse (pl. shikses) – a gentile woman or girl (sometimes mildly derogatory).

Shiviti – a mystical amulet composed of holy names and other sacred writings.

Shkoyach – vernacular form of *Yosher Koach*, meaning "well done" (see below).

Shmateh – a rag (Yiddish).

Shmutz, shmutzik – dirt, dirty (Yiddish).

Shomer mitzvos – one who observes the commandments.

Shteibl – a small synagogue, often in a house.

Shtender – a bookstand, whose particular form was useful for holding and storing books during study or prayer.

Shuckle – To sway back and forth during prayer.

Shul – synagogue (Yiddish).

Shulchan Aruch – the compilation and codification of the laws found in the Talmud.

Siddur – a prayer book.

Smicha – rabbinic ordination.

Sukkah – a small, impermanent hut, as built to celebrate Sukkot (The Feast of Tabernacles).

Tallis, tallit – a prayer shawl.

Takeh – a expression of emphasis, like "really" or "you know" (Yiddish).

Tefillin – phylacteries (whatever *that* means!). Leather boxes with straps attached, containing the *Sh'ma* ("Hear, O Israel") prayer as well as additional texts, comprised of one for the head and one for the arm, worn during the daily morning service.

T'files ha-derech – "prayer for the road," said upon undertaking a long journey, which asks for divine guardianship against evil and mishaps.

Tikkun – a late-night or midnight study session, especially observed on Shavuot.

Tisha b'Av – the ninth of Av, a day of mourning that marks the destruction of both Temples, and the date upon which other major Jewish tragedies are said to have occurred.

Toomah – ritual uncleanliness or impurity.

Traif, traife – not kosher.

Traifoos – unkosherness.

Tuchas – behind, backside (Yiddish), from which was derived the English slang word "tush" used for the same meaning.

Tzedakah – charity.

Va-y'hi binsoah ha-aron – opening words of the prayer recited upon opening the Ark, from the biblical verse, "And so it was when the Ark was lifted up, and Moses spoke."

[in der] Velt arein – [into] the outer worlds (Yiddish); just for laughs.

Yahrzeit – anniversary marking the passing of a loved one or important person.

Yahrzeit candle – a candle lit to mark a *yahrzeit*. Usually a large candle in a glass holder, big enough to burn for 24 hours.

Yekeh – a German Jew. German Jews were often known for their formality. (The word "yekeh" itself means "jacket," referencing the fact that German Jews dressed more formally than other eastern European Jews.)

Yeshivah – Torah academy. Also, a religious day school.

Yeshivah shel ma'alah – the "upper yeshiva," i.e., the heavenly court.

Yeshiveshe velt – the world of the yeshiva.

Yidiot – short for Yidiot Acharanot, one of Israel's daily newspapers.

Yom Ha-Atzmaut – Israel's Independence Day.

Yomim Noraim – the High Holidays (literally, the Days of Awe).

Yosher koach – "May your strength increase," said as a congratulatory remark or a word of praise for a job well done, often said to someone who has performed a ritual role in public.

Yudkay vovkay – a permissibly pronounceable form of "yud hay vov hay," or the Tetragammaton, the four letters that comprise the ineffable name of God.

Zaydie – Grandpa (Yiddish).

ABOUT THE AUTHOR

DAVID KRONFELD was born in Brooklyn and grew up in Flushing, NY. He moved to the Boston area for college and graduate school, during which time he was also a member of Havurat Shalom for several years. After completing his graduate studies, he spent a year in Paris and Jerusalem, where he wrote *Tales of the Havurah*. He then moved back to New York City but soon afterwards left academics and transitioned into the business world. For over 35 years, he pursued a successful career in corporate communications and financial public relations.

He lives in Manhattan with his wife, Sarah Jacobs, an artist who makes Jewish ritual objects in fabric. They have three grown children. Looking back, he considers helping to raise his family to be his most important achievement.